Expulsion and the Nineteenth-Century Novel

For Johan

Expulsion and the Nineteenth-Century Novel

The Scapegoat in English Realist Fiction

MICHIEL HEYNS

CLARENDON PRESS · OXFORD

Oxford University Press, Great Clarendon Street, Oxford OX2 6DP

Oxford New York
Athens Auckland Bangkok Bogota Bombay
Buenos Aires Calcutta Cape Town Dar es Salaam
Delhi Florence Hong Kong Istanbul Karachi
Kuala Lumpur Madras Madrid Melbourne
Mexico City Nairobi Paris Singapore
Taipei Tokyo Toronto
and associated companies in
Berlin Ibadan

Oxford is a trade mark of Oxford University Press

Published in the United States
by Oxford University Press Inc., New York

British Library Cataloguing in Publication Data
Data available

Library of Congress Cataloging in Publication Data
Heyns, Michiel.
Expulsion and the Nineteenth-century novel: the scapegoat in
English realist fiction / Michiel Heyns.
m.
Includes bibliographical references.
1. English fiction—19th century—History and criticism.
2. Scapegoat in literature. 3. Literature and society—
Great Britain—History—19th century.
4. Realism in literature. I. Title.
PR868.S32H49 1994 823.809353—dc20 94-12798
ISBN 0-19-818270-8

3 5 7 9 10 8 6 4 2

Printed in Great Britain
on acid-free paper by
Ipswich Book Co.Ltd,
Ipswich, Suffolk

Acknowledgements

The debts incurred in writing this book were many and varied, direct and indirect. My most constant and patient reader and adviser has been Adrian Poole, under whose supervision I undertook this piece of work, and who has been most generous with his criticism and encouragement in the unforeseen number of years it has taken to complete. Though he has trimmed the book of many of its excesses, indiscretions, and misjudgements, he is of course not to be held responsible for those that remain.

More indirectly, any number of teachers, colleagues, and friends have helped shape the attitudes that have now assumed this form. To John Harvey and Mary Paterson of the University of Stellenbosch I owe the respect for literature that still seems to me a precondition of criticism; to John Thompson a belief in the critic's accountability to the text; and to Wilbur Sanders the exhilaration of testing the limits of that respect and that accountability. To Lars Engle I owe many years of friendship and many evenings of talk about books; and, I hope, a due sense of what books can and cannot do.

My thanks, too, to the anonymous readers of Oxford University Press, who provided at a crucial time detailed, forthright, and useful criticism. To the editors who saw this book through the press my gratitude for the meticulous and yet flexible way in which they regularized an unruly text.

I am grateful to the University of Stellenbosch for granting me the leave which made it possible to undertake the writing of this book; also to the Master and Fellows of Trinity College, Cambridge, for providing invaluable facilities during that period of leave, and to the Institute for Research Development for financial assistance. None of these institutions should of course be held responsible for any of the views expressed in this book.

An early version of Chapter 1 appeared under the title 'Shock and Horror: The Moral Vocabulary of *Mansfield Park*', in *English Studies in Africa*, 29 (1986), 1–18.

To Johan Kriel, to whom this book is dedicated, a constant debt is due for creating the conditions that made it possible.

M.H.

University of Stellenbosch

Contents

List of Abbreviations and Conventions   ix

Introduction: Complicity, Community, and Critical Method   1

Chapter

1. A Divided Community: Fanny Price and the Readers of
   Mansfield Park   50

2. 'Oh, 'tis love, 'tis love . . .': Privileged Partnership in
   Dickens   90

3. A Peculiar Compassion: George Eliot and Gwendolen
   Harleth   136

4. The Solidarity of the Craft and the Fellowship of
   Illusion: *Lord Jim*   183

5. A Community of Interest: *The Golden Bowl*   227

Conclusion: To Be Continued . . .   269

Bibliography   275

Index   285

List of Abbreviations and Conventions

After the first citation in each chapter, references to the works discussed are given in the text as page numbers, supported by the following abbreviations:

Jane Austen

E	*Emma* (1816); ed. David Lodge (Oxford, 1980).
MP	*Mansfield Park* (1814); ed. James Kinsley (Oxford, 1990).
NA	*Northanger Abbey* (1818); ed. John Davie (Oxford, 1980).
PP	*Pride and Prejudice* (1813); ed. James Kinsley (Oxford, 1980).

Joseph Conrad

'Amy'	'Amy Foster' (1901); in *Typhoon and Other Tales*, ed. Cedric Watts (Oxford, 1986).
HD	'Heart of Darkness' in *Youth, Heart of Darkness, The End of the Tether* (1902); ed. Robert Kimbrough (Oxford, 1984).
LJ	*Lord Jim* (1900); ed. John Batchelor (Oxford, 1983).
PR	*A Personal Record* (1912); ed. Zdzisław Najder (Oxford, 1988).
SA	*The Secret Agent* (1907); ed. Roger Tennant (Oxford, 1984).
Y	'Youth' in *Youth, Heart of Darkness, The End of the Tether* (1902); ed. Robert Kimbrough (Oxford, 1984).

Charles Dickens

BH	*Bleak House* (1852–3); ed. Norman Page (Harmondsworth, 1971).
DC	*David Copperfield* (1849–50); ed. Nina Burgis (Oxford, 1983).
DS	*Dombey and Son* (1846–8); ed. Alan Horsman (Oxford, 1982).
GE	*Great Expectations* (1860–1); ed. Angus Calder (Oxford, 1953).
LD	*Little Dorrit* (1855–7); ed. Harvey Peter Sucksmith (Oxford, 1982).
MC	*Martin Chuzzlewit* (1843–4); ed. Margaret Cardwell (Oxford, 1984).
OMF	*Our Mutual Friend* (1864–5); ed. Michael Cotsell (Oxford, 1989).

George Eliot

AB	*Adam Bede* (1858); introd. Robert Speaight (London, 1960).
DD	*Daniel Deronda* (1876); ed. Graham Handley (Oxford, 1988).
FH	*Felix Holt, the Radical* (1866); ed. Fred C. Thomson (Oxford, 1988).
M	*Middlemarch* (1871–2); ed. David Carroll (Oxford, 1988).
MF	*The Mill on the Floss* (1860); ed. Gordon S. Haight (Oxford, 1981).
R	*Romola* (1863); ed. Andrew Sanders (Harmondsworth, 1980).
SCL	*Scenes of Clerical Life* (1858); ed. David Lodge (Harmondsworth, 1973).

Henry James

GB	*The Golden Bowl* (1905); ed. Virginia Llewellyn Smith (Oxford, 1983).
WD	*The Wings of the Dove* (1902); ed. Peter Brooks (Oxford, 1984).

Other abbreviations

ELH	*English Literary History*
PMLA	*Publications of the Modern Language Association of America*

Where repeated references to a secondary work occur in close proximity, only the first reference is footnoted, subsequent references being given in parentheses in the text.

Introduction: Complicity, Community, and Critical Method

'The subject Mr Casaubon has chosen is as changing as chemistry: new discoveries are constantly making new points of view. Who wants a system on the basis of the four elements, or a book to refute Paracelsus?'[1]

I

Ladislaw's uncharitable readiness to discredit Casaubon in Dorothea's eyes does not invalidate his point; and Casaubon, in so many ways a cautionary figure for scholars, is in this respect more relevant than ever to professional literary critics. We are no longer 'talking about' literature or even just 'reading' it: we are practising a highly self-conscious craft that has to account for itself with every new venture into the open, or risk the jeers of the Ladislaws—and even stronger strictures, to judge by the vaguely menacing reference in the Preface to a recent series of essays, to the 'obligation of teachers and students of literature to declare their political, axiological and aesthetic positions in order to make those positions conscious and available for examination'.[2] Whether or not from a sense of some such obligation, many modern critics do seem anxious to declare their critical allegiance, the shibboleths thudding as authoritatively as rubber stamps at a border post. But a critical position may be arrived at as much as proceeded from, and the making possible of 'new points of view' could be a substantial if incidental benefit of undertaking an extensive critical study. This introduction, then, is intended not so much to 'declare' a critical

---

[1] Will Ladislaw, in George Eliot, *Middlemarch* (1871–2); ed. David Caroll (Oxford, 1988), 182.

[2] General Preface to the series, The Bucknell Lectures in Literary Theory, ed. Michael Payne and Harold Schweizer. This quotation is from Terry Eagleton, *The Significance of Theory* (Oxford, 1990), p. vi.

allegiance as to place the argument of the book in relation to, in conversation with, those influences which have helped to shape it. Arguments being shaped more often by disagreement than by unanimity, the conversation is largely an apparently ungrateful disagreement with other writers—perhaps, after all, an acknowledgement of indebtedness less compromising to the creditors than a blanket expression of gratitude.

The nineteenth-century realist novel has become a politically suspect form. Belief in its political correctness, which is to say its subversive potential,[3] 'what one might call (doing violence to wide differences of approach, but not to the orthodoxy in which they have come to cohere) the "subversion hypothesis" of recent literary studies', has yielded ground to a critical investigation intent on proving that '[w]henever the novel censures policing power, it has already reinvented it, in *the very practice of novelistic representation*'.[4] However, as demonstrations of 'the way in which the novel enforces a certain legality in its very forms and techniques of representation'[5] have lost the impact of unfamiliarity, the method has had to get by on old-fashioned critical acumen—and certainly, as witness both the remarkably observant studies quoted above, nothing sharpens the perceptions like a touch of paranoia. The very suspiciousness of the method uncovers insights unsuspected by a more ingenuous criticism. The danger is that the metaphoric process giving the force of an *equation* to an ingeniously discerned *similarity* may come to marginalize, even nullify, some very real differences. It may be true at some metaphorical level that, as Miller claims, 'Zola wants to register the Parisian *fille* no less than the police' (21); but the analogy has to ignore some painful social realities that the Parisian *fille* would have known more about than

---

[3] See, for instance, George Levine, *The Realistic Imagination: English Fiction from Frankenstein to Lady Chatterley* (Chicago, 1981), for a strong argument of the position that 'Nineteenth-century realism, far from apologizing for what is, deliberately subverts judgments based on dogma, convention, or limited perception and imagination' (20). More recently, Joseph Allen Boone, though repeating the argument that 'novelistic structures . . . undertake a mission analogous to that of society's dominant ideological structures', has contended that this tendency is countered in certain novels by 'those alternative textual voices that have tapped the genre's originally radical impulse to subvert what (and while) it conserves' (*Tradition Counter Tradition: Love and the Form of Fiction* (Chicago, 1987), 8, 2–3).

[4] D. A. Miller, *The Novel and the Police* (Berkeley, Calif., 1988), pp. xi, 20 (Miller's emphasis).

[5] Mark Seltzer, *Henry James and the Art of Power* (Ithaca, NY, 1984), 17-18.

the literary critic, if only through the relative inconvenience of the two methods of registration. There may well be, as Igor Webb has argued, a similarity between the technique of the novel and the method of surveillance proposed by Bentham in his figure of the Panopticon; but to proceed from this perception to the assertion that Brontë, Gaskell, and Dickens 'proceed precisely as Bentham does: the disorder of the mass, its unknowableness, is broken down by means of various kinds of partitioning',[6] is to commute, in the single word *precisely*, a metaphorical resemblance to a literal similarity. Bentham was proposing a system of physical incarceration for purposes of effective control; these novelists were isolating individual subjects (to the extent that they *were* isolating them) in order to make their situation present to a largely middle-class body of readers, usually with a view to changing that situation. Wary as we have become of invoking the concept of intention, there is surely some point in insisting on the different intentions of artistic representation and penal or social surveillance. To argue that a system of representation is in any significant way similar to policing power is perilously close to acting as if policing power were no more sinister than novelistic representation. Nadine Gordimer's 'registering' of the South African black is significantly and decisively different from that of the South African police.[7] To ignore the difference is not so much to brutalize literature as, more insidiously, to normalize by our academic systems an inhuman system of surveillance and control, and perhaps, as Jonathan Culler has warned, to reassure ourselves that our critical practice is in itself a politically efficacious act. [8]

---

[6] Igor Webb, *From Custom to Capital: The English Novel and the Industrial Revolution* (Ithaca, NY, 1981), 192.

[7] Robert Caserio has made a similar point more fully in a different context in his tightly argued 'Supreme Court Discourse vs. Homosexual Fiction' (*The South Atlantic Quarterly*, 88 (1989), 268–99). Caserio compares certain Supreme Court decisions pertaining to homosexual relations as instances of 'general ideology in nonfictional, non-narrative or (at least) anti-narrative discourse, of both a judicial and a policing kind' (272) with the treatment of homosexual relations in homosexual fiction, to demonstrate his belief in the potential of fiction 'to provide an alternative to the ideologies and politics that prevail in the world in which the novel is produced and read' (267).

[8] Jonathan Culler, *Framing the Sign: Criticism and its Institutions* (Oxford, 1988), 68. Culler offers a sympathetic but sceptical account of what he calls 'the strange use of Foucault as model for a politically engaged criticism' (67).

The present study, however, is not intended to clear the novel of all charges of collaboration: it aims rather to examine five central realist works, in relation to one another and other works, hoping to demonstrate both the connectedness and the dissimilarity of the dynamics of novelistic representation and the mechanics of social control. My election of the scapegoat to the subtitle of this study is itself an act of metaphoric appropriation that needs elucidation. Scapegoating is, as René Girard has shown, a mob effect, the mobilization of the prejudices of a society in times of crisis.[9] Clearly, then, to talk of the scapegoat in the novel is to posit some form of transference of societal attitudes to the narrative dynamic, and to take some liberties with the scale on which these attitudes manifest themselves. If we define the scapegoat as that figure that has to bear the burden of guilt of a particular community, usually by being sacrificed or expelled, then, in my model, the narrative itself constitutes a community, generating pressures that eventually expel those characters that disturb the equilibrium which it is the aim of narrative closure to restore. A distinction central to my purpose has been drawn by Girard:

Before invoking the scapegoat in connection with a text we must first ask whether we are dealing with a scapegoat *of* the text (the hidden structural principle) or a scapegoat *in* the text (the clearly visible theme). Only in the first case can the text be defined as one of persecution, entirely subjected to the representation of persecution from the standpoint of the persecutor. This text is controlled by the effect of a scapegoat it does not acknowledge. In the second case, on the contrary, the text acknowledges the scapegoat effect which does not control it. Not only is this text no longer a persecution text, but it even reveals the truth of the persecution. (119)

Thus the process of scapegoating became, in this study, not a constant, a stereotype, that could be identified in a relatively straightforward way as a narrative principle. Rather, it transpired that any particular narrative, in achieving its resolution, renegotiates the equilibrium between the principles animating it. The nineteenth-century novel, the classic realist text, proved less uniform than its convenient generic titles imply. A fair number of

[9] See René Girard, *The Scapegoat* (1982), trans. Yvonne Freccero (London, 1986), esp. ch. 2, 'Stereotypes of Persecution', 12–23.

novelists, simply, seemed to be at least as conscious as I could be of the constraints imposed by their form, even of the ideological implications of that form, although they would not have chosen that term to describe the tension between the energies propelling their narrative and the need to contain those energies. The five chapters that follow, then, attempt to gauge the pressures generated by narrative to void it of those elements impeding the resolution, but also to record the countervailing resistance of realist representation to the coercion of closure.

The novelists discussed, if not the individual novels, are by and large those elected to the Great Tradition of the English novel by F. R. Leavis in 1948 (Dickens had to wait till 1969 for inclusion).[10] Although Leavis's selection was not the basis of my own, the congruence is convenient, in that the contention that realism by its methods is inclined to support the status quo will attach itself more readily to 'canonical' works, works suspect not merely because of their methods but because of their reception in and by an academic environment judged to be reactionary. These novels have become established as in their different ways 'representative' cultural objects; to put it differently, these are the texts most under suspicion of collaboration. Furthermore, with the partial exception of Lord Jim they are all the productions of novelists confident enough of their powers (three of them are last novels) to attempt to extend their own scope—and even Lord Jim, perhaps because of Conrad's agonizing over its creation, emerges as a work searching for new forms of expression. These are, in short, novels aware of themselves as experimenting with their own possibilities, from authors consciously writing for an established audience. More practically, the texts are readily available and familiar: my aim is not so much the exploration of unknown territory as the examination of what we think we know, to introduce ideas into an arena rather than little-known works to the world.[11] These works recur constantly in discussion of the realist novel; if I return to them once again, it is in the belief that they are multifarious enough to survive yet another onslaught. For, finally, I chose these novels because I believed that I could return to them with pleasure

[10] The Dickens chapter, though wider-ranging than the rest, deals in most detail with Our Mutual Friend.

[11] For the same reason, I have wherever possible cited the readily available World's Classics editions of the novels discussed.

even for the number of times and with the minuteness of attention
that this kind of study requires; and that belief has justified itself.

II

Jane Austen is a convenient point of departure, because she would
seem to exemplify so clearly the conservative stance sometimes
ascribed to the genre as a whole. Writing from a secure if not
prosperous social position, within a set of apparently stable literary
conventions, and yet remarkably reticent about the material
conditions underlying that position and those conventions, she
seems a textbook example of that Theory of Literary Production
that holds that 'the work is articulated in relation to the reality from
the ground of which it emerges: not a "natural" empirical reality,
but that intricate reality in which men—both writers and
readers—live, that reality which is *their ideology*. The work is
made on the ground of this ideology, that tacit and original
language: not to speak, reveal, translate or make explicit this
language, but to make possible that absence of words without
which there would be nothing to say.'[12] *Mansfield Park* in
particular is often taken to be an uncompromising embodiment of
the ideological pressures shaping Austen's art: usually seen and
sometimes resented as the least congenial work of a conservative,
even reactionary novelist, it presents an instructive example of that
relationship between ideology and individual talent which the
nineteenth-century novel was to negotiate with some anxiety.

Mansfield Park introduces a question central to the study as a
whole: the constitution of that narrative community, as opposed to
the fictional community, in relation to which the scapegoat has its
being, *against* which, in other words, the scapegoat is defined. If the
scapegoat *in* the text is expelled from the community depicted in the
novel, the scapegoat *of* the text is expelled from that area, that
centre of value, inhabited by implied author, enlightened protagonist, and ideal reader. The relation between the two communities is
thus of some import to this study: the relation, one might say,
between Wuthering Heights and *Wuthering Heights*, between

---

[12] Pierre Macherey, *A Theory of Literary Production* (1966), trans. Geoffrey Wall
(London, 1978), 155. Macherey's italics.

Mansfield Park and *Mansfield Park*. Jane Austen's novels, though they are often taken to subscribe, with whatever minor impatiences, to the values of her depicted communities, typically distinguish between the neighbourhood of values surrounding the heroine, sometimes stiflingly, and that small area in which the value formation of the novel takes place. Mansfield Park itself is seen in many critical accounts as representing, by the end of the novel at least, the repository of the values that the novel has sought to establish. If this is so, why do so many readers feel so uncomfortable within its confines? Why should we resent Fanny Price's timid accession to Mansfield Parsonage?

This mild but unaccommodating heroine raises an uncomfortable question: are we debarred by our modern assumptions from membership of a community that Jane Austen would have shared with her original readers? Studies based on a detailed consideration of the cultural and historical context of the novel have argued that we have to earn our place in the narrative community by an effort of scholarship and humility. Opposed to this are the readers who are content to place the work in no very specific historical period, thus leaving Fanny Price unprotected and unredeemed by her context. The division between the two camps can be made broadly according to the sense attributed to the first four words of the novel: 'About thirty years ago . . . '.[13] Now I suspect that most readers simply gloss that as 'Once upon a time', translated into the conventions of the realist novel. That strategy of the common reader, when adopted, with whatever sophistications, by the professional critic, yields what has been called the 'anachronistic' approach to the novel.[14] The other, or 'historical' approach, implicitly, and at times explicitly, takes Jane Austen's opening phrase—for all that its first word hardly suggests precision—as applying to a precise historical moment: 1781 or 1784, depending on whether the reference point is assumed to be the start of the composition or

---

[13] Jane Austen, *Mansfield Park* (1814); ed. James Kinsley (Oxford, 1990), 1.

[14] The term, though of course readily available, is associated with E. D. Hirsch, Jr., who says of his use of *anachronistic meaning* that it 'is a shorthand, not a pejorative term which comprises all non-authorial meaning, whether or not such meaning was possible within "the linguistic domain common to the author and his original public"' (*The Aims of Interpretation* (Chicago, 1976), 163 n.).

the publication date of the novel.[15] Upon this calculation has been constructed a formidable array of interpretations demonstrating Jane Austen's familiarity with the Peninsular War, the state of the economy, crop failures in Antigua, the abolition of slavery, the Evangelical labours on behalf of the slaves, the intricacies of ordination, the evils of pluralism, the late events in France and Burke's Reflections on them, landscape gardening, the jacobin implications of the plays of the time, Platonic misgivings about acting, Hannah More's Strictures, aristocratic Whiggery, Mary Wollstonecraft's feminism, the political significance of family—and so on, culminating, if that is the word, in the suggestion that Jane Austen was mainly interested in writing a best-seller for the 'new middle classes'.[16]

The sheer fertility of the historical method need not, of course, argue for promiscuity on the part of the begetters or taint any one of its offspring with a suspicion of illegitimacy. One of the strengths of the method is its capacity to re-create a horizon of expectation against which a work's first appearance would have taken place; this in turn can rule out distracting anachronistic responses and create the conditions for a much more objectively verifiable reading. Or so the theory goes, and in some cases also the practice. If the confidence inspired by such a procedure has a disadvantage, it is in its tendency to produce relatively inflexible readings. According to Alistair Duckworth, himself the author of a much-quoted historical study of Austen, historical critics, 'even as they concede the possible

---

[15] See R. W. Chapman in his edition of *Mansfield Park* (London, 1923; 3rd edn., 1934), 553 n.: 'It is natural to suppose that she used the almanacs of 1808 and 1809'. He adds, though, that 'We do not suppose that Miss Austen used an almanac for any purpose except that of convenience, or that she conceived the events of the story as necessarily belonging to an actual year'. Avrom Fleishman has also reconstructed a calendar of events, 'subject to the limitations of any literalist approach to a fictional world' (*A Reading of 'Mansfield Park': An Essay in Critical Synthesis* (Minneapolis, 1967), 91 n.). The 'limitations' of this approach do not prevent him from basing an elaborate reading on his dating of the action.

[16] I cite the sources of most of these allusions in the discussion which follows. The best-seller hypothesis is from David E. Musselwhite's *Partings Welded Together: Politics and Desire in the Nineteenth-Century English Novel* (London, 1987), 30. Musselwhite's contention that 'The whole motivation behind the production of *Mansfield Park* is not the defence of a threatened gentry but the aggressive search for a market' is based on remarks in Austen's letters such as 'I am very greedy' and 'I am trying to harden myself' which Musselwhite interprets, with a literal-mindedness surprising in a reader of Jane Austen, as evidence of 'ruthlessness and exploitative zeal' (22).

significance of "anachronistic" criticism, . . . are likely to claim priority for the *meaning* that is disciplined by a recognition of intellectual and generic contexts and by an attempt to recover the author's intentions, conceived of in other than superficial ways'.[17] In its attempt to limit the field of error, by testing subjective readings against the rigours of the historically possible, the method often seems committed to producing the meaning that closes off all other meaning. But as Duckworth comments, 'there are frictions among various historical approaches, . . . and the problem of multiple *historical* contexts for interpretation remains a real one' (41). A historical context, it would seem, is to some significant extent also the personal construct of the historian, operating not on a body of material objectively 'there', but selected in accordance with criteria to some degree idiosyncratic. Marilyn Butler's clear statement of her own critical procedure may stand as representative of the central assumption underlying historical criticism: 'Jane Austen values a hidden, inexpressive side of Fanny, *one which we have largely to read into her character through our intellectual understanding of the author's intention.'*[18]

In practice, though, such an 'intellectual understanding of the author's intention' may be hardly less arbitrary than the apparently more subjective 'anachronistic' interpretation. We may 'read into' the presentation of Fanny Price any number of 'intentions' depending on how our 'intellectual understanding' is led by our own particular enthusiasm; and indeed, Fanny Price has been found to be the repository of any number of unexpressed attitudes. As Nina Auerbach puts it: 'Failing to charm, Fanny is allowed in compensation to embody worlds.'[19]

This concession, however, is made at Fanny's expense: we can tolerate her because she does not matter very much, in the sense

[17] Alistair Duckworth, 'Jane Austen and the Conflict of Interpretations', in Janet Todd (ed.), *Jane Austen: New Perspectives* (New York, 1983), 40.
[18] Marilyn Butler, *Jane Austen and the War of Ideas* (Oxford, 1975; 2nd edn., Oxford, 1987), 248. My emphasis. For a different reading of 'the hidden, inexpressive side of Fanny', also 'read into' Fanny's very quietness, see Paula Marantz Cohen, 'Stabilizing the Family System at Mansfield Park', *ELH* 54 (1987), 669–93: 'Other Austen heroines spring into relief against the background of their families, but Fanny Price recedes. She shrinks, clings, and hides herself' (669).
[19] Nina Auerbach, 'Jane Austen's Dangerous Charm: Feeling as One Ought about Fanny Price', *Romantic Imprisonment: Women and Other Glorified Outcasts* (New York, 1986), 23.

that, say, Emma matters to *Emma*. Again Marilyn Butler spells out most clearly the critical consequences:

Given the ideological theme, Fanny's experience on a subjective level cannot be the matter at issue. The theme of *Mansfield Park* is the contrast of man-centred or selfish habits of mind, with a temper that is sceptical of self and that refers beyond self to objective values. Since Fanny is the representative of this orthodoxy, the individuality of her consciousness must to a large extent be denied.[20]

But the 'ideological theme' is not 'given': it is assumed by the critic. In this instance that assumption must deny as an irrelevancy 'the individuality of [Fanny's] consciousness'—a sizeable sacrifice in a novel that, as I shall argue, angles its interpretation of events through its heroine's consciousness, quite as deliberately as any other Austen novel, not excluding *Emma*.[21] The price of Marilyn Butler's emphasis, or she might say the price of Austen's allegiance, is the conclusion that 'Fanny is a failure' (248). Now this is not inconceivable; but readers who nevertheless enjoy Fanny Price are likely to resist a critical method that aims to show that their pleasure is based on an intellectual misunderstanding.

But apart from the impoverishment attendant upon the denial of the heroine's consciousness, the dethroning of Fanny in the interests of an 'ideological theme' leaves the centre of the novel open to the claims of other pretenders. Sir Thomas has been, in many accounts, elected as the thematic standard-bearer, representing the ethos of the class which Jane Austen valued, the 'legally constituted authority' at the Park and thus the representative of the principle of social order, as observed by the landed gentry.[22] But this centre of value proves to be

[20] Butler, *War of Ideas*, 246-7. Somewhat similarly, Igor Webb, setting out to show that *Mansfield Park*, like 'any novel written between roughly 1780 and the 1850s is necessarily an expression of and a response to the events we have come to call, somewhat narrowly, the Industrial Revolution', is led by this conviction to find that 'this is a dogmatic novel, in which ideology *must* dominate character and action' (*From Custom to Capital*, 9, 61).

[21] For this reason I disagree with David Lodge's statement that 'There is, to my knowledge, no precedent for such a novel before *Emma*—that is, a novel in which the authorial narrator mediates virtually all the action through the consciousness of an unreliable focalizing character' ('Composition, Distribution, Arrangement: Form and Structure in Jane Austen's Novels', *After Bakhtin: Essays on Fiction and Criticism* (London, 1990), 128).

[22] Tony Tanner, *Jane Austen* (Basingstoke, 1986), 167.

no more immune to challenge than Fanny's own status, and cannot serve as the stable object of Fanny's allegiance to an order that is to be vindicated by the novel. If, as Webb argues, 'Having failed in his duty, Sir Thomas yet remains the patriarchal figure' (62) we may have to consider the grounds and significance of his failure as possible ironic challenges to the moral authority of a 'patriarchal figure'. Thus Avrom Fleishman, drawing on 'public knowledge so widespread at the time that it need not be set out in the novel to have its effect in explaining the action', invokes Evangelical strictures against multiple incumbencies in support of the 'moral criticism' of Edmund and his father for the son's taking up of the living at Mansfield *and* Thornton Lacey. This, Fleishman believes, shows that '*Mansfield Park* is designed to criticize the weaknesses of the gentry'.[23] A more recent study, on the other hand, though conceding that 'What is fruitfully unclear throughout the novel is the nature of the Bertrams' family identity, and hence the problem of how we are to interpret the threats to undermine it', nevertheless concludes that 'It is even the function of Fanny's quiet personal story to render the institution of the family powerfully articulate, to site the domestic in history'.[24] Thus what 'need not be set out in the novel' is all too often a matter of critical conjecture: liberated from the text, constrained only by what it would have been possible to know in 1811–14, interpretation can and does run riot. It is difficult, in short, to centre a reading of the novel on Sir Thomas's threatened social position, when such threat as there is, is left so very vague in the novel. Nor is the case for historical reconstruction much advanced by the categorical statement from a social historian that 'It needs . . . to be said again that the world of the rural elite was neither going bankrupt in the early nineteenth century nor disintegrating spiritually and socially'.[25]

The divergence of emphasis and conclusion compatible with even the most scrupulous historical study does not invalidate the method, any more than the variety of anachronistic readings invalidates that

[23] Fleishman, *A Reading*, 21, 22. Fleishman assumes that Edmund retains the Thornton Lacey living 'in the absence of a textual statement to the contrary' (21). On the same evidence, or absence of it, most Austen heroines remained childless; the implications of this in the light of contemporary views on birth control have yet to be established.
[24] Kathryn Sutherland, '*Jane Eyre's* Literary History: The Case for *Mansfield Park*', *ELH* 59 (1992), 415.
[25] David Spring, 'Interpreters of Jane Austen's Social World: Literary Critics and Historians,' in Todd (ed.), *Jane Austen: New Perspectives*, 67.

method; but at its worst, the reliance on what 'need not be set out in the novel' can fly in the face of probabilities with a confidence denied to mere anachronism. In the hands of a truly ingenious scholar Jane Austen's little bit of ivory seems capable of reconstituting itself as the most pachydermatous of rogue elephants. Sir Thomas's voyage to Antigua, for instance, has produced several off-stage odysseys, assuming a body of contemporary readers not only highly erudite but also preternaturally skilled in ordering their knowledge into coherent narratives:

He goes to Antigua as a planter, presumably opposed to abolition; he occupies himself, for economic reasons, with improving the slaves' condition; he acquires some of the humanitarian or religious message of the Evangelical and other missionaries laboring in the same vineyard; and he returns critical of his own moral realm, with a warmer feeling for his young dependent, a sterner rejection of aristocratic entertainment (especially that with a marked revolutionary content), and a strong defense of his son's dedication to resident pastoral duty.[26]

Yet another reconstruction of Sir Thomas's voyage leads Tony Tanner to the conclusion that it 'indicates a dangerous split in his loyalties: he believes in the values associated with landed property in England; but also in the financial profits to be made from a trade involved in slavery' (149). Is Sir Thomas a hardened slave-owner or a newly converted abolitionist? Do his interests in Antigua divide his loyalties or renew his appreciation of Fanny and set him against *Lover's Vows*? The argument could drift either way, because it is not anchored to anything in the text; and whichever way it went, it could only compete with Jane Austen's implication, which is that Sir Thomas, who 'was grown thinner and had the burnt, fagged, worn look of fatigue and a hot climate' (*MP* 160), is in that state of body and mind in which Mrs Norris and Mr Yates must seem particularly abrasive and Fanny correspondingly assuasive.

---

[26] Fleishman, *A Reading*, 39. I am citing this extract as self-evidently far-fetched. For a more considered critique, see Webb, *From Custom to Capital*, 107–12, who sensibly objects that 'We have no evidence whatever that Sir Thomas ran into any missionaries, or that they impressed him' (109). Unfortunately Webb rejects Fleishman's reading only to advance his own equally unfounded speculation: 'Rather than having to go to Antigua to make major planting decisions, as Fleishman suggests, Sir Thomas was far more likely to have had to return because of the unreliability of his plantation attorneys' (109).

A more recent and more circumspect attempt to ground a reading of the novel on its colonial context is that of Edward Said, whose statement of critical belief is attractively direct: 'Obviously no reading should try to generalize so much as to efface the identity of a particular text, author, or movement. By the same token it should allow that what was, or appeared to be, certain for a given work or author may have become subject to disputation.'[27] In practice, though, this appealing credo produces results hardly distinguishable from those based on more cavalier procedures. The *terminus ad quem* of the argument is still the complicity of narrative structures with the power relations they mirror; in this instance 'the far from accidental convergence between the patterns of narrative authority constitutive of the novel on the one hand, and, on the other, a complex ideological configuration underlying the tendency to imperialism' (82). But Said's reasonable conviction that 'one must connect the structures of a narrative to the ideas, concepts, experiences from which it draws support' (79) yet does not tell us how to go about establishing that connection; and Said's method is disappointingly mechanical. In spite of the evident concern to give due attention to the novel itself, the hermeneutic coercions of his particular emphasis ('reading a text with an understanding of what is involved when an author shows, for instance, that a colonial sugar plantation is seen as important to the process of maintaining a particular style of life in England' (78)) all but destroy the careful discriminations so central to the novel's method:

In *Mansfield Park*, which within Jane Austen's work carefully defines the moral and social values informing her other novels, references to Sir Thomas Bertram's overseas possessions are threaded through; they give him his wealth, occasion his absences, fix his social status at home and abroad, and make possible his values, to which Fanny Price (and Austen herself) finally subscribes. If this is a novel about 'ordination', as Austen says, the right to colonial possessions helps directly to establish social order and moral priorities at home. (73)

This passage offers an instructive instance of the assumed relevance of historical information: proceeding from the incontestable presence of Sir Thomas's overseas possessions in the novel, then

---

[27] Edward Said, *Culture and Imperialism* (London, 1993), 79.

slipping from his 'wealth' through his 'status' to his 'values', Said arrives at colonial possessions as *determinants* of the dominant values in the novel. But if Sir Thomas's possessions do indeed 'make possible' his values, the extent to which 'Fanny Price (and Austen herself) finally subscribes' to those values remains a critical question needing a closer scrutiny than Said's assumption allows.[28] As much of my chapter on the novel is dedicated to showing, Sir Thomas, Fanny, and 'Jane Austen' are the vehicles of three very precisely discriminated idiolects with correspondingly nuanced values, negotiated with great precision *within* the common arena circumscribed by the novel's imperial setting. The 'moral priorities' of the novel are 'finally' constituted at the expense, for instance, of those 'ambitious and mercenary connections' (*MP* 430) which Sir Thomas has to learn to subordinate to the quiet comforts of Fanny's presence. As Mikhail Bakhtin maintains, apropos of *Evgenij Onegin*: 'The language of the novel is a *system* of languages that mutually and ideologically interanimate each other. It is impossible to describe and analyze it as a single unitary language'.[29] Whatever the problems of applying Bakhtin's model to the English realist novel, his definition of the novel as a '*system* of languages' is peculiarly appropriate to the linguistic awareness and self-awareness of a Jane Austen novel. The 'laughter and polyglossia' (82) that Bakhtin ascribes to older parodic forms remains, in Austen, a force which resists authoritarian discourse, even if in certain instances (such as, exactly, *Mansfield Park*), it has to contend with the counter-pressure of the closural movement.

[28] At times Said, in spite of his scrupulous scholarship, seems almost carelessly to assume certain received ideas about the novel. A minor instance is his 'if this is a novel about "ordination", as Austen says': *Mansfield Park* is not a novel about ordination, and Jane Austen does not say it is. See Butler, *War of Ideas*, 236 n.

[29] Mikhail Bakhtin, 'From the Prehistory of Novelistic Discourse', *The Dialogic Imagination: Four Essays*, ed. Michael Holquist, trans. Caryl Emerson and Michael Holquist (Austin, Tex., 1981), 47. Of course Bakhtin raises more questions than can be dealt with in passing; in particular, his statements about 'the novel' and 'novelization' posit a genre that *by definition* escapes the unitary language of older forms. His characterization of the novel thus applies only to an *aspect* of the novel as we know it, referring to a particular capacity ('novelization') of which the realist novel avails itself in varying degrees; as Michael Holquist argues, '"novel" is the name Bakhtin gives to whatever force is at work within a given literary system to reveal the limits, the artificial constraints of that system' (Introduction to *The Dialogic Imagination*, p. xxxi).

Said's injunction that 'one must connect the structures of a narrative to the ideas, concepts, experiences from which it draws support' has been well served by studies of Jane Austen's work in relation to the literary conventions available to her. Reading her, for instance, as 'a latecomer to an established, highly-stylized fictional genre', as Marilyn Butler does, may indeed help us 'to re-learn the code her first readers already knew'—mainly, that is, the conventions of the anti-jacobin novel and the novel of education (p. xxxi). But this method, when taken to demarcate the limits of legitimate meaning, can yield some disappointingly meagre insights. The method may be so intent on establishing the work's intertextuality that it becomes deaf to local reverberations, the use to which an allusion is put, the particular timbre produced by the individual intellect in response to, even in collision with, its environment and its inherited tradition. In short, it may fail to notice that *Mansfield Park* is a comedy. Thus Butler concludes her immensely well-documented research into Jane Austen's intellectual milieu with the firm statement that 'Jane Austen is conservative in a sense no longer current. Her morality is preconceived and inflexible' (298). However valuable this courageously joyless conclusion may be as a counter to irresponsible anachronism, it is not criticism that, in the language of the book-jacket blurb, will send the reader back to the novels with renewed interest and sharpened expectation. May 'Fanny's experience on a subjective level', though ideologically out of bounds, not render her status as 'representative of this orthodoxy' much more ambiguous—and much more interesting—than Butler allows? Granting, on Butler's persuasive evidence, that Austen was writing within the constraints of a conservative genre—may the received tradition in the hands of a highly skilled practitioner not itself be subverted? May 'the incongruity of the old absolutes to the novel, a form which historically is individualistic and morally relative' (248) not produce something more vital than a pale embodiment of orthodoxy?

My own answer to this is, in the case of *Mansfield Park*, a qualified yes. I think the outline of the plot, by which I mean the conventional shaping in terms of the novel of education, demands a particular kind of resolution, to which Jane Austen submits. But the rather prim ethical proposition of the novel of education and the suspicious nature of the anti-jacobin novel were bound to cause trouble in the hands of an author who had from her earliest juvenilia shown a thoroughly irreverent bent. Jane Austen may have intended, in so far as we can speculate about unrealized intentions, a thoroughly conventional heroine; but her own art required, in fleshing out that outline, something more challenging than the stock heroine of the anti-jacobin novel, and produced a wonderfully observed study of a comically deluded heroine. Now marrying off a deluded heroine in her unregenerate state is not a consummation provided for in the convention[30]—hence the real problems with Mary Crawford, who has to be sacrificed to the demands of closure and the belated protests of ideology. My discussion of *Mansfield Park* is an extended attempt to demonstrate both the pleasures of Fanny Price and the price of her vindication.

Feminist criticism has given a new impetus to Austen studies, as to literary criticism in general. Even if not all feminist critics subscribe to Margaret Kirkham's view of Jane Austen as 'an impish, rational feminist',[31] they are in practice more receptive to that strain in the novels which speaks, not of Austen's allegiance to the values of her class, but of her troubled and perhaps even rebellious situation within those values.[32] In the case of *Mansfield Park*, the feminist interest has usefully redirected attention to Fanny as not only a rather self-righteous upholder of the status quo, but also a victim of that system to which she seems to subscribe so uncritically. In such accounts, ideology is less likely to be seen as a monolithic body of doctrine, rather as a complex of expectations affecting both the shape of the novel and the destiny and possibilities of its protagonist. Mary Poovey offers a fine statement of the tenets directing her own study of Wollstonecraft, Mary Shelley, and

[30] Compare Nina Auerbach, *Communities of Women: An Idea in Fiction* (Cambridge, Mass., 1978), 35: 'Jane Austen's *Pride and Prejudice* (1813) is the English novel's paradigmatic courtship romance, memorable in that it . . . allows us, as a successful courtship romance must do, to believe in marriage as an emblem of adulthood achieved.'

[31] Margaret Kirkham, 'Feminist Irony and the Priceless Heroine of *Mansfield Park*', in Todd (ed.), *Jane Austen: New Perspectives* 246. Kirkham argues, on rather slender grounds, 'that either Austen had read Wollstonecraft or that she was familiar with her works through the filtering through of their arguments and examples to other, less controversial writers' (236).

[32] See, for instance, Sandra M. Gilbert and Susan Gubar, *The Madwoman in the Attic: The Woman Writer and the Nineteenth-Century Literary Imagination* (New Haven, Conn., 1979): 'Far from modelling herself on conservative conduct writers like Hannah More or Dr. Gregory or Mrs. Chapone, Austen repeatedly demonstrates her alienation from the aggressively patriarchal tradition that constitutes her Augustan inheritance' (116).

Austen: 'As a social act—and, inevitably, as a political act—the literary work spoke to and now speaks of its moment in social history; it does not simply articulate its producer's unique and inimitable style.'[33]

Here the novel itself is afforded the status of witness rather than exhibit, requiring attention to its way of 'speaking' to and of its social-historical situation. The narrower focus of feminist criticism allows Poovey to control her perspective admirably, and to attend to the way in which 'Austen negotiates a complex contract with her readers in which she makes [an imaginative] participation necessary in order for the reader to understand and evaluate the action *and* the narrator's comments' (44). If my own reading of the novel differs substantially from hers, it is not because I disagree with this vision of Austen's 'complex contract', rather because I believe that in practice Poovey still simplifies that contract to a matter of Fanny's privileged 'point of view': 'The episodes in which our correct judgment is most critical are all narrated from Fanny's point of view because, even before she has learned to trust her moral intuitions, hers are the standards by which we are asked to judge' (222). The assumption that events are 'narrated from Fanny's point of view' posits too passive a relationship between event and registering consciousness, and disregards the extent to which Fanny's impressions are not a 'narration' of events as much as an intensely personal response to those events. My emphasis on 'narrative community' is an attempt to locate the 'contract' in a constantly renegotiated relation between reader, protagonist, and narrator which requires a rather more sceptical distance from Fanny's standards, and indeed from her point of view.

All this should not blind us to the one fact which all contemporary readers would have taken for granted: *Mansfield Park* is a love story, and much of the narrative energy is directed at getting Fanny married to the man she loves; or, in modern parlance, at casting her desire in an ideologically acceptable form. To say that Fanny Price is 'in love with' Edmund may seem like an almost meaninglessly obvious statement, until we reflect that it is the one thing nobody in the novel knows about her. Indeed, that is one measure of the distance between the narrative community and the

[33] Mary Poovey, *The Proper Lady and the Woman Writer: Ideology as Style in the Works of Mary Wollstonecraft, Mary Shelley, and Jane Austen* (Chicago, 1984), 244.

inhabitants of Mansfield Park: we are privy to Fanny's secret as they
are not. How such a surreptitious love makes space for itself in the
rigid class structures of Mansfield Park becomes, then, an indicator
of the social and moral dynamics of a conservative community. Jane
Austen's love plots may well testify to and serve a politically
conservative view of life; but they were conceived *as* love plots, and
amongst other things but by no means marginally, they are
reflections on what makes love necessary, possible, and valuable
in a society such as hers.

III

Jane Austen's peculiarly satisfying acerbity may well have been the
ironic edge of a consciousness schooled in concealment, the
sharpened vision of the consciously and perhaps even willingly
marginalized observer. Whatever her political and moral views, her
angle on her world was ever oblique, resistant to the hearty cheer of
acquiescence and the roar of conviviality. Her narrative community
is a select little group, typically the 'small band of true friends' with
which she rewards Emma's enlightenment,[34] to which the privileged
reader is granted access by Austen's ironical method. By the
contrast that is the point of this preamble, Charles Dickens
postulates a narrative community coextensive with the whole of
his immense readership. His novels are overtly on the side of
popular sentiment: for the most pragmatic of reasons, and perhaps
also for psychological reasons connected with his childhood,
Dickens was a crowd-pleaser. If the complicity ascribed to Jane
Austen is, then, a fairly straightforward matter of her necessary
participation in the opinions and values of her class, time, and
literary milieu, Dickens's is a rather more interesting case of
surreptitious collaboration: the great populist and democrat is
suspected of participation in the systems of control perpetuating
privilege and inequality.

The point has often been made that Dickens's major novels
operate like detective novels, in which the ordering principle
remains hidden, to be revealed in a solution that is also a resolution
of the apparently unresolvable tensions generated by the immensely
varied, disparate materials accumulated in the course of the

[34] Jane Austen, *Emma* (1816); ed. David Lodge (Oxford, 1980), 440.

narrative. To the modern critic schooled, say, in Foucault, such a radical simplification of the data in the interests of apparent intelligibility is a form of mind control; as D. A. Miller puts it: 'In relation to an organization so complex that it often tempts its subjects to misunderstand it as chaos, the detective story realizes the possibility of an easily comprehensible version of order.'[35] The hidden structural principle, then, which ostensibly serves as a suspense-inducing strategy may surreptitiously function as a strategy of containment. Miller extends his analogy by arguing, on the basis of *Bleak House* and the role of Inspector Bucket, that Dickens privileges specifically the detection practised by the *police*, as against various individual interpretative efforts, such as those of Mrs Snagsby and Mr Tulkinghorn, which are shown to be inadequate exactly in being individual. The efficiency of Bucket, placed against both the bungling obfuscation of Chancery and the misdirected individual attempts at detection, establishes the police as the legitimate agency of detection, a kind of master-metaphor of fictional technique: 'For the very closure that secures a formal narrative difference between the novel and bureaucracy implicates the novel in a formal narrative resemblance to the institution that has played a sort of rival to the bureaucracy, the police' (93).

Miller's sophisticated argument is, on the evidence of *Bleak House* alone, very convincing. If I nevertheless advance a reading sceptical of such complicity, it is partly because this model seems to me to be derived too exclusively from a single novel to support the kind of generalizing weight Miller wants to give it. In *Little Dorrit*, for instance, the demystification *is* achieved through the single-minded and solitary efforts of Pancks; here individual, unauthorized detection is the measure of the incompetence of the Circumlocution Office. Similarly, in *Our Mutual Friend*, John Harmon reconstructs his own death with little help from the Night-Inspector; and Bradley Headstone's murderous assault upon Eugene Wrayburn is deliberately, by the orders of the latter, kept from the police.[36]

Furthermore, granted that Dickens's enthusiasm for the New Police renders him to that extent suspect to our century, in which policing has all too often been a sinister instrument of state control, we still

---

[35] Miller, *The Novel and the Police*, 69.
[36] See Charles Dickens, *Our Mutual Friend* (1864–5); ed. Michael Cotsell (Oxford, 1989), 738.

need to examine critically the seductive tidiness of the analogy between control and closure. Closing a case has certain obvious resemblances to closing a narrative; but, as Miller also recognizes, the novelist, in creating the mystery that the policeman 'solves', concerns himself exactly with that which escapes the policeman's docket.[37] Hortense murdered Tulkinghorn: that is the 'solution' of *Bleak House* for the official purposes of Inspector Bucket, and it leaves out almost everything that we feel the novel to be about. A resemblance surely constitutes a significant similarity only where the points of correspondence touch upon the essence of the objects compared; and here the *dissimilarity* between the laws the policeman is called upon to administer and the moral discriminations enacted by the novel seems to me to strike at the root of the analogy.

The role of the police, indeed, is defined sardonically enough through Skimpole, whose own complicity with Bucket, significantly in the apprehension of Jo, is registered against him in his self-exculpation: 'Now, Skimpole wishes to think well of Bucket; Skimpole deems it essential, in its little place, to the general cohesion of things, that he *should* think well of Bucket. The State expressly asks him to trust to Bucket. And he does. And that's all he does!'[38] Bucket's dedication to 'the general cohesion of things' is, in other words, coterminous with his function in the detective plot. In neither case is there any moral content to the project: Bucket is merely doing his job, and thereby serving a system intent upon preserving itself.[39] His bribing of Skimpole, like Skimpole's acceptance of the bribe, 'seemed to involve a disregard of several moral obligations' (*BH* 884): moral obligations are not the province of Inspector Bucket, or really of the detective plot, which is generally dependent on having a victim unpleasant enough to have

---

[37] 'However skillfully prosecuted, the work of detection appears capable only of attaining a shell from which the vital principle has departed' (Miller, *The Novel and the Police*, 96).

[38] Charles Dickens, *Bleak House* (1852–3); ed. Norman Page (Harmondsworth, 1971), 886. This passage and the others I quote here seem to me to contradict Kate Flint's assertion, on the evidence of Mr Bucket's ubiquitous efficacy, that 'The authority of the detective and the social structure which it supports hence occupy a position which the text never openly questions' (*Dickens* (Brighton, 1986), 36).

[39] The essentially conservative bias of co-operation with the police is made clear enough through Sir Leicester Dedlock's high-minded assent to Bucket's investigation: 'And it does not become us, who assist in making the laws, to impede or interfere with those who carry them into execution' (*BH* 775).

been murderable by any number of more or less amiable people. But moral obligations are very much the concern of *Bleak House*, which thereby subordinates Bucket's inquiry to its own far more indeterminate investigation. The more urgent mystery of *Bleak House* is who killed Jo; and it is not a mystery, Dickens suggests, that it is in the interests of 'the general cohesion of things' to solve or even inquire into.[40] The novelist devises, as it were, an alternative inquiry generated in part by the interrelations of the novel itself.

In *Our Mutual Friend*, indeed, Dickens seems to invoke the mystery of the Man from Nowhere only in order to subordinate it to a mystery of a different order. The narrative dynamics are directed not so much at revelation as at redemption, a redemption signalled by Wrayburn's request to Lightwood *not* to reveal the name of his assailant: the issue here is not the bringing to justice of the criminal, but the newly awakened concern for Lizzie that prompts Wrayburn's request. Again Eugene Wrayburn places the emphasis explicitly, in reply to Mortimer Lightwood's 'I would that you answered my three questions! What is to come of it? What are you doing? Where are you going?':

'And, my dear Mortimer,' returned Eugene, lightly fanning away the smoke with his hand for the better exposition of his frankness of face and manner, 'believe me, I would answer them instantly if I could. But to enable me to do so, I must first have found out the troublesome conundrum long abandoned. Here it is. Eugene Wrayburn.' Tapping his forehead and breast. (*OMF* 295)

Conundrum rather than mystery, redemption rather than justice: it is this distinction, presumably, that Dickens had in mind when, in his postscript to the first book publication of *Our Mutual Friend*, he denied having had any interest in concealing the identity of John Rokesmith, intending rather 'To keep for a long time unsuspected, yet always working itself out, another purpose originating in that leading incident, and turning it to a pleasant and useful account at last' (821).

---

[40] This is the basis of my disagreement with Catherine Belsey's implicit equation of 'detective story' and novel in terms of what she sees as their common movement towards a closure that clears up all mysteries. This leads her also to find *Bleak House* 'smoothing over the contradictions it has so powerfully dramatized in the interests of a single, unified, coherent "truth" ' (*Critical Practice* (London, 1980), 81).

But redemption as *telos* creates its own expectations of closure. Robert Caserio has spelt out the implications of this for the Dickens plot:

The end, considered not as finale but as *telos*, organizes all that precedes, explains all suspenseful mysteries and indeterminacies, marshalls every earlier detail and contingency, every event and character, into a structure revealed—at the last—as purposeful. And the final disclosure fully discriminates the value as well as the meaning of what comes before.[41]

This is an admirably clear statement of the overt structure of a Dickens novel, the organizing principle which connects his mystery plots with the redemptive plot. I think, however, that it too readily takes the manifest intention for the execution; in practice, as I shall try to show, some of Dickens's most troubling implications are generated by that which escapes the final ordering of purposeful plot, the solution to the spiritual conundrum as much as the answer to the detective mystery. I argue that the 'pursuit of meaning and value', though undeniably present, has to contend with a contrary pull towards dissolution and despair. The drive towards socialization and inclusion is countered by a powerful impulse towards rejection and expulsion; the domestic virtues so insistently celebrated in most of the novels are a refuge from terrifying possibilities of disintegration.[42]

As in my discussion of *Mansfield Park*, I treat the novel itself as a form of community with its own implicit rules and regulations, its conditions of membership, often opposed to those of the society depicted in the novel. The actual fictional community created in *Our Mutual Friend*, of course, is very different from Jane Austen's community: whereas Jane Austen typically sets her individuals against a relatively homogeneous community, Dickens creates communities that cohere, if at all, only very uneasily. This is one

---

[41] Robert Caserio, *Plot, Story, and the Novel* (Princeton, NJ, 1979), 169.

[42] Thus Edward Said seems to me to take the snugness of Dickens's domestic scenes too much at face value in arguing that 'In the main . . . the nineteenth-century European novel is a cultural form consolidating but also refining and articulating the authority of the status quo. However much Dickens, for example, stirs up his readers against the legal system, provincial schools, or the bureaucracy, his novels finally enact what one critic has called a "fiction of resolution". The most frequent figure for this is the reunification of the family, which in Dickens's case always serves as a microcosm of society' (*Culture and Imperialism*, 91).

way of repeating the familiar point that Dickens's characters are essentially city people who, as Raymond Williams has said, 'do not so much relate as pass each other and then sometimes collide'.[43] But for all their isolation, or perhaps because of it, these people are almost obsessively intent upon forming relations, and generally succeed in drawing at least one other person into their ambit. For Dickens, the basic unit of social interaction is neither the individual nor the undifferentiated mass, but the couple: Dickens's characters tend to do things in pairs. I discuss this structural principle, which seems to me to be central to Dickens's vision, as a matter of partnership—it being of the nature of partnerships to be formed for a particular purpose. The implicit narrative community, which his plots oppose to the fragmented fictional community, typically constitutes itself in terms of ideal partnerships, founded on love and trust. But where Jane Austen's closural partnerships stand highlighted against a comparatively uniform backdrop, Dickens's privileged partners are variants on a pattern replicated and refracted behind them, of obsessive and exploitative associations. The scapegoat of this pattern is the character who embodies all the loneliness and exclusion that impel the other characters into their various alliances. The obsessive formation of partnerships derives its impetus from the scapegoat's solitary banishment, validating by his or her exclusion the celebrations of partnership and community.

This emphasis differs from the more traditional stress on Dickens's rendering of the vast complexity of a city culture, as described, for instance, by Barbara Hardy: 'Dickens is primarily concerned with the nature of society, and his individual characters are pretty plainly illustrations, created by needs and roles, seen as agents and victims, within a critical analysis of contemporary England.'[44] I should not want to underrate the importance, the breadth, or the comprehensiveness of Dickens's social vision, and of course these are the terms in which Dickens himself would have wanted to be read. But an exclusively mimetic concern with 'the nature of society' may lose sight of the nature of fiction and of its own peculiar dealings with its subjects. Dickens's characters have their representational aspect, of course, which is closely linked to the reformist intentions of his

---

[43] Raymond Williams, *The English Novel from Dickens to Lawrence* (1970; rpt. St Albans, 1974), 29.
[44] Barbara Hardy, *The Moral Art of Dickens* (London, 1970), 4.

novels. Claiming, in the 1867 Preface to *Martin Chuzzlewit* that 'In
all my writings, I hope I have taken every available opportunity of
showing the want of sanitary improvements in the neglected
dwellings of the poor', he continues: 'Mrs. Sarah Gamp was, four-
and-twenty years ago, a fair representation of the hired attendants
on the poor in sickness.' But Mrs Gamp's fictional presence is not
dependent on that representational aspect, as Dickens well knows in
resubmitting her to delighted public disapprobation long after 'that
class of persons' had been 'greatly improved through the agency of
good women'.[45] And when we are told, as in a recent study we are,
that Mrs Gamp was a 'gross caricature' of Victorian nurses,[46] we
may revise our opinion of Victorian nurses, but not of Mrs Gamp.
Most Dickens characters, in short, are robust enough not to be
exhausted by their representative function. A figure like Slackbridge
is clearly, given the schematic nature of *Hard Times*, intended as no
more than a judgement on the type he represents, and is thus
vulnerable to more balanced historical assessments of union
organizers. To challenge Slackbridge's representative accuracy is to
question his reason for existence; but Mrs Gamp, we feel, would
have survived even Florence Nightingale.

Dickens's superb handling of his multistranded narratives in the
interests of a central design is clearly an aspect of his genius which no
account of the novels can afford to ignore. But there is the danger
that a concentration on the brilliance of Dickens's organization, its
'organic unity', the coherence of his novels around a single theme,
may reinforce the view that his anarchic vision is contained by a
structure which ultimately endorses the society that it sets out to
criticize: Tom-all-Alone's, Chancery, all are forgotten in the
comfortable sense that Mr Jarndyce is in the Growlery and all's
right with the world. By the same token, elements that cannot be
made to cohere with the central design are at times criticized as
extraneous to the 'proper' business of the novel. H. M. Daleski, for
instance, complains that 'Woven into the brilliant imaginative design
[of *Bleak House*], there is the palpably melodramatic and

---

[45] Charles Dickens, *Martin Chuzzlewit* (1843–4); ed. Margaret Cardwell (Oxford,
1984), 720.
[46] Anne Summers, 'The Mysterious Demise of Sarah Gamp: The Domiciliary
Nurse and her Detractors, c.1830-1860', *Victorian Studies*, 32 (1989), 365.
Summers, a medical historian, objects to the stereotype of the domiciliary nurse
fostered in part by Mrs Gamp's notoriety.

distractingly irrelevant figure of an Hortense'.[47] But the 'irrelevance' may point to something other than mere clumsiness of plotting on Dickens's part: it may reveal the point at which Dickens is driven, even if only by the exigencies of plotting, to admit elements hostile to his ethical design—only to expel them again in the interests of resolution. The scapegoat in Dickens's narratives, I shall argue, is always to some extent 'distractingly irrelevant', in not having an unambiguous place in the moral design. It may well be in the development of irrelevance into a major thematic interest that Dickens at last permitted himself to look fully at the discontents left seething under the surface of his resolutions.

But to talk of irrelevance is to posit some centre from which relevance is measured. That centre is occupied by the heroes and heroines, the repositories of the moral positives implicit, or more often made all too explicit, in the novels. The emphasis on organic form tends to render that centre very still indeed, perhaps even static, the heroes and heroines emerging as symbols of abstract Qualities rather than as imaginative realities or dynamic agents. 'To examine the heroes and heroines of Dickens', says Angus Wilson, 'is to dwell on his weaknesses and failures.'[48] Now I have little to say about or for heroes like Walter Gay, Allan Woodcourt, and John Harmon; Mario Praz's characterization of these men as 'sepulchral monuments . . . angels with mild, stupid faces', though unkind, is not unjust.[49] But the heroines seem to me another matter. To see them, as Praz does, as representatives of 'the Victorian sentiment that idealized woman as a weak, angelic creature' (135–6) does justice only to the sanctifying rhetoric so stiflingly surrounding them; as agents of the plot they have a curious potency. Terry Eagleton complains of the women in Hard Times, in terms which he later extends to all Dickens's women, that 'Most of them are defined in relation to men, having little or no autonomous life of their own; and almost all of them display a meek, self-sacrificial conformity to the male power which oppresses them'.[50] This is true enough if we

[47] H. M. Daleski, Dickens and the Art of Analogy (London, 1970), 159.
[48] Angus Wilson, 'The Heroes and Heroines of Dickens', in John Gross and Gabriel Pearson (eds.), Dickens and the Twentieth Century (London, 1962), 3.
[49] Mario Praz, The Hero in Eclipse in Victorian Fiction, trans. Angus Davidson (London, 1956), 136.
[50] Terry Eagleton, 'Critical Commentary', in Charles Dickens, Hard Times (London, 1987), 308.

consider only the social manner, as it were, of the women in *Hard Times*: Louisa, Sissy, even Mrs Sparsit, all submit with various degrees of mildness to male authority; but they all survive to triumph, with various degrees of complacency, over their male oppressors, adversaries, or relations. And so with all Dickens's heroines: for all their damp subservience, they are remarkably tough. Their strength, if that is the word for this plot-derived predominance, clearly does not lie in any great vividness or complexity of characterization. And yet they are intrinsic to the design, and have their beings both as protégées and as essential functions of the moralized plot; for all their angelic mildness, they are quite indomitable. My discussion attempts to account for that invincibility as an aspect of the need to contain the novel's intractable energies in the idealizing vision of redemption through domestic happiness.

I have for the most part, in my chapter on Dickens and elsewhere, consciously refrained from 'explaining' fictional matter in terms of unresolved tensions in the author's life. It seems perfectly plausible that the ambivalence in the treatment of Bradley Headstone and Wrayburn may owe something to Dickens's own reticence about his childhood, the famous period in the blacking-factory, just as his sentimentality about a certain type of woman may be traced back to his feelings for Mary Hogarth, and the Estella-type be taken back to his youthful infatuation with Maria Beadnell (or his involvement with Ellen Ternan at the time of writing *Great Expectations*); more generally and probably crucially, the pervasive domesticity of his novels must be coloured for us by that knowledge of Dickens's own marriage which we have the debatable advantage over his contemporaries of possessing. These connections seem to me legitimate extensions of the 'meaning' of the work; but I must confess myself uncomfortable with accounts intent on reducing fictional creation to what is usually perceived as the prolonged adolescence of the author, and offering the author's pathetic or faintly ludicrous insecurities as an explanation of the novels. Thus Terry Eagleton's confident exposition of 'part of the meaning' of Bounderby in *Hard Times* makes everything of imputed origins and almost nothing of artistic product. With all the aplomb, though little of the terseness, of Mr Hubble pronouncing Pip 'Naterally wicious', Eagleton anatomizes Dickens's case:

Bounderby is despised as a tradesman and social climber at the very moment that he is being ridiculed for not really being an outsider at all; and part of the meaning of this is that Dickens is trying in the figure of Bounderby to cope with his own petty-bourgeois aggression towards the upper class by denying, in effect, that it has any justifiable biographical roots. . . . Dickens is afraid of his own sympathies with the dispossessed, partly because they threaten his own laboriously achieved social identity, but also because they touch in him a bitter personal resentment which is ideologically dangerous.[51]

'Everybody', poor Pip reports, 'then murmured "True!" and looked at me in a particularly unpleasant and personal manner.'[52] Perhaps authors must endure the unpleasant and personal manner as part of the price of their fame; but the appropriateness of that manner to the matter remains a question for the critic. If Eagleton's diagnosis may well yield 'part of' the meaning of Bounderby, much of the rest of that meaning must inhere in the less sophisticated response of those readers of *Hard Times* who find Bounderby simply enormously funny.[53] The fact that Dickens can turn his 'bitter personal resentment' into comedy of this order is surely admissible, even essential, evidence in any consideration of his art.

By this I do not mean to imply that Dickens was an unrelievedly cheery writer who sublimated all his darker suspicions in comic villains and dreams of Christmas cheer, and that the novels yield nothing but confirmation of 'the carefully maintained domestic image' which the 'Dickens machinery for public relations' so

[51] Ibid. 305. Eagleton's treatment of Dickens is consistent with his earlier contention that criticism's 'task is to show the text as it cannot know itself, to manifest those conditions of its making (inscribed in its very letter) about which it is necessarily silent' (*Criticism and Ideology* (1976; rpt. London, 1978), 43). It is, however, at odds with the 'redemptive hermeneutic' which Eagleton professes in a later work, as part of a 'shift of climate in left criticism, possibly datable from the early eighties onwards, where, having done that necessary work [of "a kind of demystificatory criticism"], it then became important to see what [of the canon] one could salvage, reconstruct, re-evaluate, recycle' ('Criticism, Ideology and Fiction' in *The Significance of Theory*, 73).

[52] Charles Dickens, *Great Expectations* (1860–1); ed. Angus Calder (Oxford, 1953), 23.

[53] George Bernard Shaw, for instance, who was by no means blind to the failures of Dickens's 'middle-class imagination', but who was not thereby incapacitated in the face of Dickens's humour, could gauge the implications of that humour precisely in terms of its being 'so unexpectedly and excruciatingly funny that it is almost impossible to feel duly angry with the odious Bounderby afterwards' (*Introduction to Hard Times* (1912; rpt. in the Norton Critical Edition (New York, 1966), 336).

sedulously maintained.[54] Dickens is, on the contrary, a compelling
chronicler of waste, neglect, rejection, and self-disgust. He is much
more than this, of course, as I hope my account also demonstrates.
But to counteract what I regard as too exclusive an emphasis on the
conventionalizing aspect of Dickens, my reading of the novels
attempts to show how certain figures, those that I identify as the
scapegoats of Dickens's narratives, embody the qualities that his
novels cannot afford to sanction, and that are yet central to their
conception. As the truculent uninvited guest may try the precarious
equilibrium of the 'correctly' constituted social occasion, so the
scapegoat tests the strength of the fictional fabric, the stability of the
reconstituted community. Thus I argue that Headstone is the
culmination of a strong narrative pressure exerted by the realist plot
against the romance plot and its mythical resolution. If, as Edgar
Johnson maintains, 'Bradley Headstone [is] latent in the youthful
Charles Dickens so caught . . . between his hurt pride and his
anguished passion'[55] then my analysis can be taken to show how
Bradley Headstone is latent also in any number of earlier creations;
that is, that a covert theme of Dickens's novels has always been
exclusion, despair, obsession.

My argument centres, then, on the conception of Bradley
Headstone as the embodiment of a loneliness that is also a threat.
Lurking on the staircase outside Eugene Wrayburn's door, he
presents a terrible image of solitude, but also a chilling figure of
menace.[56] He incarnates that exclusion which makes the cosy
inclusiveness of Dickens's family groups meaningful and thereby
necessary, as we make real to ourselves the pleasures of the fireside
by reflecting piously on the unfortunate travellers out in such
weather, or prudently on the strange creatures that make it their
element. Bradley Headstone is what is shut out from the hearth, and

[54] Claire Tomalin, *The Invisible Woman: The Story of Nelly Ternan and Charles
Dickens* (1990; rpt. Harmondsworth, 1991), 4.
[55] Edgar Johnson, *Charles Dickens: His Tragedy and Triumph* (Boston, Mass.,
1952), 82.
[56] At this point my argument intersects with George Levine's postulation, in *The
Realistic Imagination*, of Frankenstein's monster as a recurring presence in the realist
novel. This leads him to find that monster in domesticated form in even the tamest
conclusions. He traces, thus, a movement of inclusion, whereby the realist novel
contains within its closural energy those energies that have threatened to erupt in the
course of the fiction. My own emphasis on exclusion stresses the complementary
movement whereby the threat is not so much contained in the privileged characters as
expelled through the peripheral characters.

perhaps what keeps us from wandering around on the heath at night. He is the outcast who never makes it, the orphan who finds no fairy godfather, the industrious apprentice who does not prosper, the patron rejected by his protégé, the love-stricken young man who finds no consolation for his rejection. Deracinated, rejected, humiliated, he is the truly solitary, asocial being, against which all Dickens's sentimentalities are shored up. He is, then, in Girard's term, the hidden structural principle of Dickens's plots.

IV

George Eliot would seem on a superficial consideration to be in every respect less conventional than Dickens: as intelligent woman, she was bound to resent the self-sacrificing simpering which so often constituted his idea of femininity; as victim of the Victorian veneration of wedlock, she must have had reservations about his idealization of the state; as atheist, or even just as sceptic, she could not have been edified by his frequently maudlin exploitation of religious sentiment; as realist, she would have found his romance plots implausible and even pernicious; as literary and social critic, she objected to 'his frequently false psychology, his preternaturally virtuous poor children and artisans, his melodramatic boatmen and courtezans' as potentially 'noxious . . . in encouraging the miserable fallacy that high morality and refined sentiment can grow out of harsh social relations, ignorance and want'.[57] In short, any consideration of her life and fiction would seem to posit an author iconoclastic as Dickens could not afford to be, even if he had been temperamentally so inclined.[58]

And yet Eliot is generally regarded as a conservative in a sense not applied to Dickens, that sense for which the most usual label is 'Puritan': a matter less of the abstract opinions ascribed to her than of the manner in which those opinions are perceived to be held. Leslie Stephen's strictures seem still representative of the kind of

---

[57] George Eliot, 'The Natural History of German Life', *Westminster Review*, 66 (1850), rpt. in *Essays of George Eliot*, ed. Thomas Pinney (London, 1968), 271-2.

[58] I am not disregarding the to us inescapable fact of Dickens's desertion of his wife and ten children; as Claire Tomalin argues: 'Amazing as it now seems, the break-up of his family left [the Dickens legend] unaffected; Dickens preserved his renown as the jovial keeper of hearth, home, children and dogs at Gad's Hill even as he was ridding himself of wife and children' (*The Invisible Woman*, 4).

distrust, even dislike, Eliot's novels can inspire in readers of a certain temperament: in a by and large appreciative assessment after her death, he deplored 'the presence of something jarring and depressing in the later work', and by the same token 'the loss of that early charm'.[59] Later critics have not always agreed on the precise identity of that 'something jarring and depressing', or on the nature and location of the 'charm', but there has been a general feeling that reading George Eliot is not an exhilarating experience. Robert Liddell, though finding George Eliot's beliefs 'far less narrow . . . than those of Puritanism', maintains that 'its influence on her cannot be denied', and ascribes to that influence, amongst other undesirable effects, 'her feeling that there are some subjects on which jests may not be made—a very unEnglish feeling'.[60] Less chauvinistically but not much more appreciatively, Walter Allen claims that 'she lacks tact, as she lacks wit, except a ponderous irony'.[61] Charm, wit, tact—with the possible exception of tact, these are Gwendolen Harleth's qualities, which is to say that Eliot does not so much lack them as aim to subdue them. Thomas Hardy, say, who truly did lack all three, could for that reason not treat of them as issues in his novels; Eliot devoted whole novels to their eradication (*Romola* seems almost single-mindedly dedicated to a demonstration of the fatal effects of charm).

My own reading of Eliot's novels in general and *Daniel Deronda* in particular attempts, then, not to place them in terms of particular opinions or qualities which they may have or lack, but to trace the characteristic punitive movement of the Eliot plot. This method is, perhaps, at odds with a critical climate that has become more hospitable to George Eliot. With the ascent of a new criticism, serious, intellectual, often feminist, and not overly concerned with tact, wit, and charm, Eliot's fortunes have also risen, her moral seriousness treated historically as a necessary strategy for a woman in her time and position. In a study representative of this vein, Dorothea Barrett usefully outlines the history of Eliot criticism, arguing that the 'sibyl image' was in the first place created by Eliot as 'the means by which an embattled woman, whose character and circumstances threatened the dominant ideology, gained peace,

[59] Leslie Stephen, 'George Eliot', *Cornhill Magazine*, 43 (1881), rpt. in Gordon S. Haight (ed.), *A Century of George Eliot Criticism* (London, 1966), 148, 147.
[60] Robert Liddell, *The Novels of George Eliot* (London, 1977), 15, 18.
[61] Walter Allen, *George Eliot* (New York, 1964), 83.

power, and acceptance in Victorian England', and was then perpetuated through Eliot scholarship by a few influential contemporary (male) accounts, notably F. W. H. Myers's oft-quoted apocalyptic account of George Eliot in the Trinity Fellows' Garden.[62] Barrett's own account posits a much more independent, iconoclastic writer than the tradition allows for, on good biographical evidence. Whether the novels themselves support her advocacy of them as 'not a series of elaborate moral fables but rather a protean vision of the dialectical engagement of human realities and possibilities' (13) is another matter, which I discuss at some length in my chapter on Eliot. At this point one example of Barrett's critical method will serve to demonstrate the critical issue involved. Barrett chooses the history of Hetty Sorrel to illustrate the Eliot 'dialectic': noting that Hetty is 'at odds with her community, disliked by her narrator, and ultimately evicted from the novel of which she threatened to become the unquestionable centre', Barrett advances 'her strength and stature' as 'a victory of what can be seen as the subconscious subversive in George Eliot, whereas Dinah is a product of the conscious conservative moralist in her author' (44). The distinction between the subconscious subversive and the conscious conservative moralist founds Eliot's subversiveness on our dissatisfaction with her conservatism: since she created, in a sense, the dissatisfaction, she is also subversive. By this logic, however, we may wonder what text, then, is *not* subversive. If Hetty had indeed emerged as a character of 'strength and stature' we might have seen her as Eliot's tribute to human resilience in the face of disaster; but as I try to show in my discussion of *Adam Bede*, Hetty is reduced to a pathetic victim of Eliot's moral purpose as much as of Arthur Donnithorne's irresponsibility. In as radically tolerant a reading as Barrett's, 'George Eliot' as author with a moral intention independent of our own ideological programme ceases to exist.

The contested matter of Eliot's feminism manifests in slightly different form the larger critical question of how we read today moral strictures that we find antipathetic to our own sense of justice—a sense which may itself be historically determined by whatever discourse we ourselves have absorbed. Eliot's feminist

[62] Dorothea Barrett, *Vocation and Desire: George Eliot's Heroines* (London, 1989), 5.

standing may well tell us as much about the current state of the
feminist debate as about Eliot's novels.[63] Thus Eliot's concern with
the exceptional woman has been seen as indifference to the fate of
ordinary women;[64] ironically, she came to be distrusted upon the
very grounds that Henry James selected, after her death, for his
tribute to her contribution to the feminist cause:

To her own sex her memory, her example, will remain of the highest value;
those of them for whom the 'development' of woman is the hope of the
future ought to erect a monument to George Eliot. She helped on the cause
more than any one, in proving how few limitations are of necessity implied
in the feminine organism. She went so far that such a distance seems
enough, and in her effort she sacrificed no tenderness, no grace. There is
much talk to-day about things being 'open to women'; but George Eliot
showed that there is nothing that is closed.[65]

In other words, she showed that feminists don't have a case: if she
succeeded, so can other women. James's well-meaning commendation brands Eliot as the Samuel Smiles of feminism. As Elaine
Showalter says, in discussing the reluctance of some of Eliot's
women contemporaries to worship at the shrine: 'Eliot's unquestioned ascendancy as a fictional realist and moralist defined the
boundaries of aspiration for the women forced into secondary
status in relation to her.'[66]

[63] For an overview of Eliot's standing in feminist criticism, see, in chronological
order, Elaine Showalter, 'The Greening of Sister George', Nineteenth-Century Fiction,
35 (1980), 292–311; Gillian Beer, George Eliot (Brighton, 1986), 1–29; Dorothea
Barrett, Vocation and Desire, 175–88. All three of these critics argue for some sort of
accommodation of George Eliot within a feminist criticism, even though they all
acknowledge the attendant problems.
[64] See Elaine Showalter, A Literature of their Own: British Women Novelists from
Brontë to Lessing (1977; rev. London, 1982), esp. 100–32, for a consideration of
Eliot's attitude to other women. The issue is taken up and expanded by Pauline
Nestor in Female Friendships and Communities: Charlotte Brontë, George Eliot,
Elizabeth Gaskell (Oxford, 1985). In her sixth chapter Nestor discusses biographical
evidence for Eliot's 'personal reserve, amounting at times to a general antipathy,
towards other women' (146); the following chapter concentrates on the fiction and
'its tendencies to define female characters in relation to men rather than to each other
and to create male mentors as the crucial figures in the heroines' lives' (167).
Although Nestor is inclined to equate Eliot's views with those of her characters,
ascribing to the author, say, Gwendolen Harleth's indifference to other women, her
chapter does convincingly demonstrate her point that 'those relationships between
women remain fundamentally secondary to their relationships with men' (181).
[65] Henry James, 'The Life of George Eliot', Atlantic Monthly (1885); rpt. in
Partial Portraits (Ann Arbor, Mich., 1970), 62.
[66] Showalter, 'The Greening of Sister George', 293.

To women not labouring in her shadow, Eliot's achievement
might have seemed less oppressive, even positively encouraging; but
even here her novels lend little support to a feminism that defines
itself, say, as a manifest belief in the injustice of woman's fate as
conditioned by her disadvantaged position in a patriarchal society.
Such a feminist position would have cast Hetty more purely as a
victim, and interpreted Gwendolen's behaviour as an intelligible
response to disenfranchisement (as Dorothea Barrett in fact does).
Now Eliot does open up these perspectives, but invariably to adjust
them to her own doctrine of individual responsibility: she is, it
seems to me, too much of a moralist to be a feminist in this sense.
Whether she is a feminist in any other sense is a matter of
classification; and, say, Gillian Beer's anxiety to define a feminism
which does accommodate Eliot is perhaps more a matter of
constructive special pleading to clear the name of a respected author
than strictly consistent taxonomy:

We do not need to convert her into a radical feminist: it would be pointless to
pretend to do so. What is demonstrable is that she was intimately familiar
with the current writing and actions of the women's movement and that in
Middlemarch particularly, she brooded on the curtailment of women's lives
in terms drawn from that movement and in sympathy with it. (180)

Somewhat similarly differentiating between the views historically
held by George Eliot and the attitudes implicit in her novels,
Dorothea Barrett maintains that although 'Marian Lewes was not a
feminist . . . [i]t is nevertheless true that George Eliot is feminist'
(175). With *feminist* shifting from substantive force to adjectival
qualification, the overt opinions and actions of Marian Lewes are
set against the present implications of the fiction, and the latter is
read to support broad feminist tenets.[67] As Pauline Nestor sums it

---

[67] An alternative strategy, employed by Eve Kosofsky Sedgwick, is to distinguish
between the (non-feminist) *valuations* of Eliot's fiction and its (feminist) *analysis*: '[In
Adam Bede] the normative female role must change from Mrs. Poyser's to one like
Mrs. Bede's. . . . Of course, the degree to which the novel is not a feminist one in its
valuations is clear from the lengths to which it goes to make this change seem
palatable; but the full measure of the lengths which, as it also clearly shows, there are
to go for that purpose, demonstrates the thoroughness of its feminist *analysis*'
(*Between Men: English Literature and Male Homosocial Desire* (New York, 1985),

up: 'In the face of Eliot's ambivalence toward the women's movement and her tendency to dissociate herself from the common lot of
women, apologists frequently focus not so much on Eliot's attitudes
as on her achievements' (165).

My own account of Eliot is not concerned with the precise placing
of her fiction on a spectrum of feminist allegiance, but I do consider
the extent to which Eliot tends to scapegoat the *woman*. Certainly
Hetty's expulsion and her femaleness are closely linked: she is a
scapegoat in a sense that no man could have been, and yet her
femaleness is not available in mitigation of the judgement passed on
her. Gwendolen, too, has specifically a woman's destiny to confront,
and her own sense that her opportunities are limited by her gender is
supported by her plight in the novel, without being countenanced by
its rhetoric. My reading of Eliot as a conservative novelist, then,
would argue against the current rehabilitation of Eliot as feminist; as
I understand feminism, its interest in the social construction of
identity is alien to Eliot's insistence on individual morality.[68] In Eliot,
a gazing male does not automatically generate a male gaze, in the
sense in which that term is now used. The novel, unlike gender-
oriented analysis, attends also to the reciprocal nature of the event,
the woman's participation in the male gaze. Gwendolen's awareness
of being gazed *at* is at least as important an element of the novel's
opening as Deronda's attempts to categorize her. Politically, this may
not deflect the thrust of a feminist analysis—the woman's consent to
her own objectification does not release her from that objectification—but for Eliot the difference was crucial. If, as Catherine Belsey
has commented, 'the text . . . presents . . . an account of the social
production of femininity'[69] it also presents an account of the
woman's complicity in that process. Belsey asks for a critical
approach that will 'instead of looking to *Daniel Deronda* for a
confirmation of a banal morality' (as she implies Leavis does), reveal

---

[68] Patricia Spacks, talking of the 'most remarkable nineteenth-century woman
writers who rebelled in print against the injustices of women's lot', by which she
means Eliot, Charlotte Brontë, and Kate Chopin, says: 'Impatient as they may be
with social injustice, they concern themselves more with the primacy of personal
moral effort. And they dramatize a point of view now highly unfashionable: that the
limitations imposed upon women, like the different limitations imposed upon men,
may provide opportunities rather than impediments in the struggle for moral and
emotional fulfillment' (*The Female Imagination* (New York, 1976), 45).

[69] Catherine Belsey, 'Re-reading the Great Tradition', in Peter Widdowson (ed.),
Re-Reading English (London, 1982), 132.

the novel's relevance in 'challenging the sexual power relations of its society in ways which have an identifiable bearing on our own' (130). But it is not merely banal and irrelevant, indeed it is quite pertinent to power relations in our own time, to note that if femininity is so produced, different women respond differently to that process. Eliot might have agreed that Gwendolen is a victim of her society's discourse, but she would have wanted to know what could be done about it—by Gwendolen.[70] The third chapter of this book is an extended consideration of this question, hinging as it does on the matter of Gwendolen Harleth's 'conversion' and the woman's negotiation of her own status in an environment intent upon objectifying her—that environment then including also the novel in which she happens to find herself.

An instructive instance of the divergent aims of criticism is provided by the debate over that notoriously absent subject, Daniel Deronda's foreskin. Since Steven Marcus claimed in 1975 for his student, Mr Davis, the distinction of first having noticed the discrepancy between Deronda's Jewishness and his apparent unawareness of his own circumcision,[71] several articles have addressed this *aporia*. Cynthia Chase's deconstructive reading of the novel, though by no means wholly based upon this evidence, finds in it support for her contention that 'far from representing the truth of the human situation, the subject's origin and destiny in a history, narrative represents with authority nothing more than its own structural operations'.[72] Less ambitiously but more soberly,

[70] E. Ann Kaplan, in 'Is the Gaze Male?', in Anne Snitow, Christine Stansell, Sharon Thompson (eds.), *Powers of Desire: The Politics of Sexuality* (New York, 1983), approaches the general question through a Lacanian analysis of the presentation of women in film. The essay, though not purporting to say anything about fiction, usefully demonstrates the feminist-psychoanalytical denial of individual responsibility, in analysing the woman's response purely as a function of her 'positioning'. For a crustily commonsensical rejoinder to the charge that cinematic representation mimicking the male gaze is by that token sexist, see Seymour Chatman, 'What Novels Can Do That Films Can't (and Vice Versa)', in W. J. T. Mitchell (ed.), *On Narrative* (Chicago, 1981), 135–6 n. For a lively and undoctrinaire discussion of the issue in a variety of artistic contexts, see Wendy Lesser, *His Other Half: Men Looking at Women through Art* (Cambridge, Mass., 1991). Lesser's book is based on her belief that 'The rich world of men's artistic vision of women cannot be summarized with a mere reference to the artist's sex' (4).

[71] Steven Marcus, *Representations: Essays on Literature and Society* (New York, 1975), 212 n.

[72] Cynthia Chase, 'The Decomposition of the Elephants: Double-Reading *Daniel Deronda*', PMLA 93 (1978), 220.

K. M. Newton pointed out in 1981 that it would have been perfectly plausible for Deronda to have been circumcised, known it, and yet not to have assumed that he was Jewish.[73] Furthermore, Newton shows that Eliot was about as explicit on the subject as she could well have been in a Victorian novel, that 'Deronda's circumcision is realistically present in the novel though not mentioned in so many words' (315). Now I find Newton's argument and evidence entirely convincing, and so, probably, would Chase; but I imagine that she would not be moved by this to alter her article in any significant respect. Newton's unabashedly referential account is concerned with recovering the 'real' events behind the represented fiction; Chase is intent upon emptying the novel of such reference exactly through analysis of the 'realistic' surface against its own rhetorical implications, and is probably not much interested in the medical–historical evidence, in a sense is not really interested in *Daniel Deronda* except as the occasion of her analysis. Chase offers a brilliant application of a theory to a text which happens to lend itself to that approach; whether it tells us anything about *Daniel Deronda* itself is secondary. As Jonathan Culler has commented, apropos of Chase's essay: 'One could argue that every narrative operates according to this double logic, presenting its plot as a sequence of events which is prior to and independent of the given perspective on these events, and, at the same time, suggesting by its implicit claims to significance that these events are justified by their appropriateness to a thematic structure.'[74] Chase's essay is best seen, then, as a comment on narrative in general, drawing attention to that aspect of fiction which is of necessity fictive, that is, preconstructed, teleologically aware. Whether it follows that 'far from representing the truth of the human situation . . . narrative represents with authority nothing more than its own structural operations' is another matter, which is by implication, and at times explicitly, addressed in the rest of this book.

The tendency of modern criticism to feed on itself is well illustrated by a recent essay prompted by Chase's virtuoso analysis. Recruiting both Lacan and Cixous in her assault upon phallocentric theory, Mary Wilson Carpenter offers an elaborate and fascinating

[73] K. M. Newton, '*Daniel Deronda* and Circumcision', *Essays in Criticism*, 31 (1981), 313–27.
[74] Jonathan Culler, *The Pursuit of Signs: Semiotics, Literature, Deconstruction* (London, 1981), 178.

deconstruction of the Protestant hermeneutics of circumcision, intent upon showing that 'the "crossing-over" of Daniel's and Gwendolen's stories marked by the sign of Circumcision . . . writes a maternal thematics that phallocentric theory can only partially explain'.[75] She argues that Daniel's advice to Gwendolen to 'turn her fear into a safeguard', occurring on 1 January, the Feast of the Circumcision, echoes Keble's poem for the day, in its insistence both on pain 'blood for sin must flow') and on fear ('If thou wouldst reap in love, First sow in holy fear') (14). The correspondence is certainly striking, and supports a general point, which I develop in the main body of this work, about the Victorian didactics of pain—so conveniently so that it seems pedantic to point out that the conversation does not in fact take place on 1 January.[76] Since Carpenter's argument leans quite heavily on this coincidence of dates, is it invalidated by a mere point of fact? If, as Chase maintains, 'narrative represents with authority nothing more than its own structural operations', is a matter like a date part of those operations, or does it resort under that 'truth of the human situation' which it is not the business of fiction to render? What is forfeited is of course the suggestion that the interpretation is following the intention of the author—to the extent that such a suggestion may be inferred from, say, Carpenter's reference to 'George Eliot's location of circumcision in the center of her narrative', as opposed to the more cautious implications elsewhere on the same page that 'the text', 'the narrative', 'the discourse', or just 'Daniel Deronda', 'constructs a maternal thematics' (15). A correspondence which was improbable in the first place, but which might have seemed deliberate in its completeness, now lacks that coherence, reviving the issue of the status of accidental 'meaning'. Carpenter seems less intent upon making claims for Eliot than upon refuting Lacan's 'phallocentric theory'; but as a discussible statement appealing to common hermeneutic standards, her essay tells us little about Daniel Deronda, and leaves Eliot's status as feminist pretty much where it found it.

---

[75] Mary Wilson Carpenter, '"A Bit of Her Flesh": Circumcision and "The Signification of the Phallus" in Daniel Deronda', Genders, 1 (1988), 15.

[76] An inconclusive discussion takes place at the ball on New Year's Eve; 'The next day . . . she determined . . . to talk . . . with Deronda; but no opportunities occurred.' On New Year's Day, then, Gwendolen does not talk to Deronda; 'But the last morning came' and it is on this 'last morning' that the conversation takes place (Daniel Deronda (1876); ed. Graham Handley (Oxford, 1988), 384–5).

Suzanne Graver has defined the implied reader of Eliot's fiction as belonging to a 'community of readers', which 'presupposes an author whose avowed purpose is the nurturing of "those vital elements which bind men together"; a text that fosters a collaboration between author and reader; and a readership that brings to bear on the everyday world the demands made upon it by a fictional one'.[77] That collaboration has proved congenial to the kind of criticism that uses the 'everyday world' as a yardstick. Robert Liddell's impatient dismissal of Gwendolen Harleth as 'an unpleasant young woman'[78] is characteristic of this approach, which in its brusque pragmatism would now probably be seen as unscientific. 'Mordecai is as intolerable as Daniel, and his story and Mirah's is further weighted down by the presence of an insufferable family of Aryan bores, the Meyricks' (164): this is, except for the reference to 'story', the kind of thing that we might say in uncharitable moments about our acquaintances. It follows, then, that this mode of criticism should use as touchstone our probable responses 'in life' to particular characters. Walter Allen, for instance, would give Adam Bede the cold shoulder: 'he is a sententious, loquacious prig of a kind that in life one would walk a long way to avoid.'[79] This approach implicitly endorses Lawrence's famous definition of literary criticism as 'no more than a reasoned account of the feeling produced upon the critic by the book he is criticizing'.[80] The danger of such an affective approach, well exemplified by Liddell, is that criticism may degenerate into sheer opinionatedness ('autodidacticism will not take the place of instilled or inherited culture'—161) and broad impressionism ('For though a most imperfect artist, she is a great novelist, and though we deny her our affection, she commands our admiration—and that largely for reasons that defy definition'—188). The critic, trusting so entirely to his own 'sincere and vital emotion', seems to feel no need to elaborate the 'reasoned account' over-much, and if the work is nevertheless worth reading, as Liddell's is, that is largely because a strongly individual opinion vigorously expressed has an appeal irrespective of its justice.

[77] Suzanne Graver, *George Eliot and Community: A Study in Social Theory and Fictional Form* (Berkeley, Calif., 1984), 11.
[78] Liddell, *The Novels of George Eliot*, 69.
[79] Allen, *George Eliot*, 103.
[80] D. H. Lawrence, 'John Galsworthy' (1928); rpt. in *Phoenix* (London, 1961), 539.

Such intensely personal criticism is not fashionable, but it represents a component, whether acknowledged or not, of all but the most aridly academic criticism, however 'scientifically' pursued. Thus, to take an extreme example, Cynthia Chase's apparently totally detached deconstruction of *Daniel Deronda*, proving through a brilliant analysis of Hans Meyrick's letter that his 'deconstructive gesture reconceives the significant action of human subjects as the purposeless play of signifiers'(219), can nevertheless not rid itself of a (subjective) response to human subjects exercising their subjectivity. Chase, in spite of the novel's 'ironic mode of a sort that subverts rather than serves the establishment of meaning and value' (216), resorts to statements like 'From the reader's point of view, one of the erring heroine's more admirable and interesting qualities is her satirical spirit, her critical eye' (215–16). To admire and be interested in an erring heroine and to imbue a purposeless play of signifiers with a satirical spirit is a reassuringly traditional way of reading a novel, meaning and value and all, and I hope my own emphasis has managed to retain something of this personal engagement with the text, while yet avoiding the impatient ostracisms of guest-list criticism.

V

It is fitting that George Eliot should occupy the central position in this study, because, as I try to demonstrate in my discussion of her fiction in general and *Daniel Deronda* in particular, she exemplifies so engrossingly its central argument: the techniques and forms of realist representation, adapted to an ethical intention, both necessitate and militate against scapegoating. If in Eliot the pressure towards scapegoating is stronger than the counterpressure, that is because she does not succeed in resolving the inherent contradiction between the realist claim to be rendering an external reality, and its concern with an ethical dispensation of the universe. In my chapters on Conrad and James I try to show how the self-awareness often associated with modernism, that concern with fiction *as* fiction, can serve to break the realist deadlock. The argument rests on a demonstration that the scapegoating effect of narrative is inhibited by being recognized as such, by becoming a subject of rather than a function of the narrative. In Joseph Conrad's *Lord Jim* the artificiality of closure becomes itself a major theme: partly, perhaps, because of the difficulty Conrad experienced in completing the novel, *Lord Jim* is itself a record of narrative anxiety, the conflict between the need to write *Finis* and the cost of doing so, even between the faith in writing and the distrust of the written word.

My discussion of this novel addresses, though largely implicitly, Fredric Jameson's claim that 'the literary work or cultural object, as though for the first time, brings into being that very situation to which it is also, at one and the same time, a reaction'.[81] Jameson's study of narrative in general and, for my purposes, his discussion of *Lord Jim* in particular, represent a formidable challenge to the assumption of liberal-humanist criticism that fiction can oppose itself to a dominant ideology. To him, following Lévi-Strauss, 'all cultural artifacts are to be read as symbolic resolutions of real political and social contradictions' (80)—whether that artefact be Conrad's novel or, to take the example he culls from Lévi-Strauss, the face-painting of the Caduveo Indians.

In Jameson's bracketing of 'the literary work' with 'the cultural object' he aligns himself with, and goes beyond, that strain of criticism which, by tracing in novels the archetypal structures of the folk-tale, stresses the survival of the tradition in even the most sophisticated narratives.[82] Now clearly a novel *is* a cultural artefact, and as such open to structural analysis; but when such analysis is offered as interpretation it is obliged to disregard everything distinctive about fiction in the interests of developing its analogies with other forms of cultural expression. At a particular level of abstraction, *Lord Jim* may well operate like a face decoration, as

[81] Fredric Jameson, *The Political Unconscious: Narrative as a Socially Symbolic Act* (London, 1981), 82. An extended critique of Jameson's work on Conrad and of his narratalogical analysis is to be found in Jacques Berthoud's 'Narrative and Ideology: A Critique of Fredric Jameson's *The Political Unconscious*', in Jeremy Hawthorn (ed.), *Narrative: From Mallory to Motion Pictures* (London, 1985), 101–15. Jameson's use of Deleuze and Guatarri is stringently criticized in App. II of David E. Musselwhite's *Partings Welded Together*, 240–51. A much more appreciative, indeed wholly admiring, account is that of W. C. Dowling in *Jameson, Althusser, Marx* (London, 1984). Dowling does not discuss Jameson's analysis of individual works, but does find 'a thousand illuminations' in his discussion of Conrad (20).

[82] For a critique of this procedure, see Susanne Kappeler, *Writing and Reading in Henry James* (London, 1980), especially ch. 1, 'The relevance of folkloristics to the analysis of modern narrative' (3–13). Kappeler cogently defends her contention that 'to assume that modern narratives are structural derivatives of the folktale is to confuse structural with historical ancestry' (3).

Jameson demonstrates; but whereas nobody, not even the Caduveo Indians, can tell Lévi-Strauss that he is 'wrong' in his interpretation, novels tend to talk back at their interpreters. They are both more determinate and more indeterminate than face-painting: more determinate in being couched in the same verbal medium as that which purports to interpret them, and thus less docile to that medium; and more indeterminate in not consisting in the first place of horizontal and vertical lines. The lines have to be drawn by the interpreter, a process which in itself involves not only a radical simplification of intricate verbal structures, but a good deal of aleatory and reductive attribution of axes. As J. Hillis Miller says, though perhaps without the polemical intent to which I am here appropriating his words: 'No literary text has a manifest pattern, like the pattern of a rug, which the eye of the critic can survey from the outside and describe as a spatial form. . . . The critic must enter into the text, follow its threads as they weave in and out, appearing and disappearing, crossing with other threads'.[83]

Jameson, following Lévi-Strauss, does describe *Lord Jim* as a spatial form, albeit not a 'manifest pattern': he constructs the 'unconscious' pattern as a semantic rectangle derived from Greimas, for 'the staging of the fundamental problems of the narrative text—the antinomies or ideological closure it is called upon to imagine away—and in the evaluation of the narrative solution, or sequence of provisional solutions, invoked for this purpose' (256). As constructed upon *Lord Jim*, the rectangle produces the four terms *activity* and *value, not-activity* and *not-value*, assumed as symptoms of 'the restless life of the system'. These terms then produce 'characterological types, that can embody and manifest such contradictions' (254)—for instance, 'it does not seem particularly farfetched to suggest that the synthesis of value and not-activity can be embodied only by the pilgrims, who are a breathing and living presence which does not exteriorize itself in any particular activity, in acts, struggles, "goal-oriented behavior" ' (254–5). But to accept that this synthesis 'can be embodied only by the pilgrims' we have first to be persuaded that 'eight hundred men

---

[83] J. Hillis Miller, 'The Interpretation of *Lord Jim*,' in Morton W. Bloomfield (ed.), *The Interpretation of Narrative: Theory and Practice*, (Cambridge, Mass., 1970), 211. This belief leads Miller to an interestingly indeterminate reading of *Lord Jim*, concluding 'that the process of interpreting [Jim's] story is a ceaseless movement toward a light which always remains hidden' (228).

and women . . . treading the jungle paths, descending the rivers, coasting in praus along the shallows, crossing in small canoes from island to island, passing through suffering, meeting strange sights, beset by strange fears, upheld by one desire'[84] present a plausible example of not-activity and the absence of 'goal-oriented behavior'. Jameson sees the pilgrimage as 'simply the emanation of their being' (255); but in so far as that vaporous phrase means anything, it is equally available to 'explain' the actions of 'active' characters like Gentleman Brown. In short, the characterological types are produced by the rectangle and Jameson's selection of terms, not generated by the text. A rectangle is only as strong as the prior act of interpretation which has gone into its construction.

But if this proves only that the bed of Procrustes is not the more accommodating for being rectangular, Jameson's reading of Jim himself as 'the ideal synthesis of the two major terms of the contradiction and thus the latter's unimaginable and impossible resolution and *Aufhebung*; the union of activity and value' produces, on whatever grounds, an interesting typification of the Patusan section of the novel as 'the wish-fulfilling romance, which is marked as a degraded narrative precisely by its claim to have "resolved" the contradiction and generated the impossible hero' (255). Jim's heroic status and by extension the status of the romance which potentializes that heroism are perennial critical conundrums, and Jameson's formulation is useful in suggesting an approach to the question by way of the tension between narrative form and ideology, rather than in terms of the more usual 'ethical' preoccupations of its readers. Such an approach, though, if it is to be responsive to the complex angling of narrative in *Lord Jim*, will need to measure the 'degraded narrative' *in situ*, as it were—that is, as part of Marlow's narration, which in turn opens up into other narrations. My own contention, which I develop in detail later, is that the highly self-conscious narration in Conrad's novel is itself too aware of contradictions to proffer the romance as anything but that, or Jim's heroism as anything but a self-validating fiction of his romantic imagination.

---

[84] Joseph Conrad, *Lord Jim* (1900); ed. John Batchelor (Oxford, 1983), 14.

VI

But self-consciousness has its perils, as critics of Henry James have long pointed out. Henry James, or at any rate the Henry James of the late novels, has come to be, in the critical heritage, something like the Chief Accountant in Conrad's 'Heart of Darkness', cherishing the apple-pie order of his books and ignoring with gentle annoyance the distractions of the horror out there. The misplaced devotion to transmuting a chaotic reality into the serene order of books, the fastidious turning away from the distractions of living and dying, the withdrawal: these accusations have with various degrees of hostility been levelled against James for as long as his novels have received critical attention. In essence this was the ground of E. M. Forster's and F. R. Leavis's early strictures against the Master;[85] but more recent criticism still postulates, although not necessarily disapprovingly, a James serenely detached from life outside the cavernous chambers of his mind, his novels absorbed in the processes of their own production, his characters caught up in the labyrinths of their own consciousnesses. Not surprisingly, the tone has become less critical the further the critic in question moves in time from the stern imperatives of Leavis. Thus John Holloway can still express misgivings about the 'many-dimensional kaleidoscope of surfaces' in late James, and Raymond Williams can note to James's detriment, though in a critical vocabulary more sympathetic to James's effects, 'a transfer of process from the signified to the signifier; from the material to the work on material; from the life to the art'. John Goode notes fairly blandly that 'I don't think necessarily that James made moral judgments on the world he was depicting, unless it was to endorse its structure by seeing in it the potential of aesthetic contemplation', and Michael Bell is more intent on describing the 'infinitely self-qualifying plasticity of the language' than in passing judgement on it, though he does find an 'aesthetic stance' emerging from it, which he compares to its disadvantage with the 'organicist assumption' of realism.[86]

---

[85] E. M. Forster, *Aspects of the Novel* (1927; rpt. Harmondsworth, 1962); F. R. Leavis, *The Great Tradition* (1948; rpt. Harmondsworth, 1962).

[86] John Holloway, 'The Literary Scene', in Boris Ford (ed.), *The Modern Age* (Harmondsworth, 1963), 56; Raymond Williams, *The English Novel*, 109; John Goode, 'The Pervasive Mystery of Style', in John Goode (ed.), *The Air of Reality: New Essays on Henry James* (London, 1972), 297; Michael Bell, 'Introduction: Modern Movements in Literature', in Michael Bell (ed.), *The Context of English Literature: 1900–1930* (London, 1980), 65.

At its best, this emphasis on the enclosed and self-referential aspects of James's fiction, the sense of the novels as dramatizing an elaborate game, of the characters speaking a language of their own, has opened up illuminating passages between James's practice and modern critical theory, and made it possible to assess the fiction by criteria more appropriate to its modernist elements than those somewhat narrowly derived from its Victorian predecessors. Where Leavis found in James's 'technical elaboration' a loss of that 'full sense of life' that he hails as the informing spirit of the Great Tradition, modern criticism has enabled us to see in James's 'specialized interest' an important contribution to the development of the novel (178). More recent approaches to the novel, with their greater receptivity to the very idea of openness, not committed to the idea of a single meaning, or at any rate a coherent central moral position, may better be able to cope with a novel as intensely self-conscious as *The Golden Bowl* about its own hermeneutic processes. We may feel, without claiming any greater critical acumen for ourselves, that we are now in a better position simply to *understand* late James than Leavis was in 1948.

And yet our complacency may be troubled by a suspicion that we are leaving out an important aspect of fiction; that is, unless we attribute the omission to James, as Williams does in his reading of the James world as 'cutting off' the characters from 'where the lives are made in direct relationship' (109). Much of modern criticism, though, seems not to notice any such omission, or notice it only for slightly aloof dismissal, the disdain of the tightrope-walker for the earth below. Mark Seltzer has very cogently argued that in James criticism 'problems of social reference have characteristically been converted into problems of textual self-reference'.[87] Thus even as illuminating an account as Ruth Yeazell's produces, by implication at least, a body of fiction almost entirely self-reflecting, relatively indifferent to any social reality 'out there'.[88] It is possible that this

---

[87] Seltzer, *Henry James and the Art of Power*, (Ithaca, NY, 1984), 14. Kenneth Graham, in *The Drama of Fulfilment* (Oxford, 1975), expresses somewhat similar misgivings about 'the most hermetic of formalist approaches to James. . . . the one which suggests that the novels are really *about* the methods of their own creation' (pp. xii-xiii). For a vigorous attack on the anti-realism of post-modernist criticism, see Raymond Tallis, *Not Saussure: A Critique of Post-Saussurean Literary Theory* (Basingstoke, 1988) and, by the same author, *In Defence of Realism* (London, 1988).

[88] Ruth Yeazell, *Language and Knowledge in the Late Novels of Henry James* (Chicago, 1976).

emphasis in James criticism has derived from Laurence Holland's influential *The Expense of Vision*, which maintains, in keeping with Holland's reading of the whole *œuvre* as a reflection on James's complicity with his fiction, that 'The novel sustains an unbroken analogy between itself as fictive creation and the action it projects or the life it images'.[89] I find the evidence proffered in support of this 'unbroken analogy' less than convincing, resting as it does largely on an analogy between the golden bowl and *The Golden Bowl*, derived rather factitiously from the image of a pawn-shop that James uses in his Preface to *The Portrait*. The James world, in this version of it, seems almost entirely self-referential, the house of fiction a windowless labyrinth.

This is not to deny the apparently self-reflective nature of a novel like *The Golden Bowl*. Rather, it is to suggest that the kaleidoscopic fragmentation of 'treatment' is not to be separated from a social dimension, that referential refraction may be an adjustment of the mimetic mode to a social reality that itself strives to adapt or bend its meanings to its purposes. My own reading of *The Golden Bowl* is an attempt at a synthesis of the older mimesis-oriented readings, which concentrated on the novel's representational aspect at the expense of its self-referential qualities, and the modern readings which tend to divorce the novel from any reference outside itself.

Amongst the 'mimetic' critics the Ververs have proved as divisive as Fanny Price, the division taking place along much the same lines, that is between readers who admire the Ververs, others who abhor them but believe that James admired them, and yet others who abhor them and who believe that James did likewise.[90] Of those who do not much admire the Ververs but who believe that they are protected by their symbolic function, an influential but now waning school has found a religious-allegorical justification embedded in

---

[89] Laurence Bedwell Holland, *The Expense of Vision: Essays on the Craft of Henry James* (Princeton, NJ, 1964), 337–8.

[90] If Joseph Firebaugh had prevailed, the debate surrounding the Ververs would have been terminated in 1954 by his total demolition in 'The Ververs', *Essays in Criticism*, 4 (1954), 400–10. But this was not to be, and the debate rages on unabated. For a summary of the state of play, see Greg Zacharias, 'The Language of Light and Dark and James's Moral Argument in *The Golden Bowl*', *Papers on Language and Literature*, 26 (1990), 249–70. Zacharias concentrates on critical estimates of Adam Verver, and distinguishes between those 'who do not endorse Verver's role as a model of living well', those 'on the other side of the debate', and a 'middle position': he counts 9, 8, 7 (249–50 n.).

the text, with Adam Verver, in his inscrutability and power, 'likened to God Himself'.[91] This strain of criticism, directed at rescuing James from accusations of an insensitivity 'nothing short of obscene'[92] in condoning the behaviour of the Ververs, tends, following Quentin Anderson's Swedenborgian reading,[93] to take the action out of the sphere of human judgement altogether. Thus Adam Verver came to be equated with an allegorical representation of 'divine wisdom'[94] or as an agent of 'quasi-divine justice',[95] a reading that has the disadvantage of ascribing to 'divine love' behaviour that we would regard as 'obscene' in a human being: the parable becomes a flat contradiction of the surface of the narrative. Furthermore, and more damagingly, the Christianizing of the text, an example of what Jonathan Culler calls 'the complicity of literary study with religion',[96] turns James's sardonic satire on the paternalistic discourse of Christianity into itself an example of such discourse.

I argue for a more 'realistic' reading of Adam Verver, one that takes into account his resemblance to the great American financiers and industrialists of the time: in other words, while accepting the self-enclosed nature of the novel's system of signification, I yet find here a mimetic method and a finite meaning. For if we have all taken the post-modernist point that all readings are misreadings, we all nevertheless believe that our misreadings are sounder than other people's. Surprisingly for a novel that has proved to be so

[91] Frederick C. Crews, *The Tragedy of Manners: Moral Drama in the Later Novels of Henry James* (1957; rpt. Hamden, Conn., 1971), 107. Crews's interpretation is more circumspect than this extract suggests, leaving open the possibility of an ironic use of religious terminology. More literal-mindedly, Dorothea Krook believes that Adam is 'so to speak, a figure of the Just God of Judaism and Christianity as Maggie is a figure of the Loving God' (*The Ordeal of Consciousness in Henry James* (Cambridge, 1962), 288).

[92] F. O. Matthiessen, *Henry James: The Major Phase* (1944; rpt. London, 1946), 100.

[93] In Anderson, *The American Henry James* (London, 1958).

[94] Francis Fergusson, '*The Golden Bowl* Revisited', *Sewanee Review*, 64 (1955), 26. In Fergusson's scheme, derived from Anderson, Charlotte comes to allegorize 'the evil-idolised human self', Maggie is 'divine love', and the Prince is 'natural man', with even the Principino having a role, as 'the humanity to come, divine-natural man' (26–7).

[95] Krook, *Ordeal of Consciousness*, 286. Krook seems herself uncomfortable with this allegory, as witness her willingness only to grant Adam quasi-divine status, and her 'as the religious would say' parentheses elsewhere.

[96] Culler, *Framing the Sign*, 78.

intractable to finite meaning, *The Golden Bowl* would seem almost overtly to invite interpretation and judgement, if only because the characters themselves spend so much of their time submitting their own and other people's experiences to analysis. But that analysis, which forms so much of the substance of the novel, has the effect of 'floating' the novel's moral terminology—in one sense an extremely orthodox terminology, reducible at times to terms as apparently rudimentary as 'right' and 'wrong', 'good' and 'evil', in another sense an entirely bewildering board game in which the counters keep changing their values according to who handles them and which square they're manipulated into. If, as I argue in my discussion of *Mansfield Park*, narrative community, that conspiracy with the implied author from which we as readers take our bearings, is dependent upon a common language, then it follows that if no such common language can be found, no community of meaning can be formed.[97] Sallie Sears has argued that the late novels of James differ from traditional novels in that writer and reader cease to be 'secret bedfellows to the exclusion of the actors': these novels 'do not presuppose a "correct" response (i.e. some final, objective truth). . . . All that is required for intelligibility in such works is the coherence of each separate view or "fiction".'[98] Now the notion of *The Golden Bowl* as dramatizing the various 'fictions' fabricated by its characters, with Maggie usually seen as the creator of the dominant fiction, has achieved wide currency. In practice, however, the critics who demonstrate the coherence of the various fictions nevertheless produce a super-fiction that supersedes those of the characters. Sears, for instance, produces one of the more absolute of recent readings of the novel, concluding that

[97] As Meili Steele has argued: 'The narrator of *The Golden Bowl* proposes no authoritarian language that embraces all events. Actions, appearances, and words take on their meanings from the system, the speech-community into which they are inserted. There is no englobing community that unites character, narrator, and reader. The characters battle for a common language, a struggle that the narrator refuses to pre-empt by telling the reader what is "really" happening' ('The Drama of Reference in James's *The Golden Bowl*', *Novel*, 21 (1987), 83).

[98] Sallie Sears, *The Negative Imagination: Form and Perspective in the Novels of Henry James* (Ithaca, NY, 1968), 176. Like many commentators who favour this view, Sears privileges Maggie Verver's 'fiction': 'What Maggie as "author" does to herself and the three people closest to her is analogous to what James "does" to the same characters: he brought them into conjunction, determined their conditions, and then ravaged them, wielding the artist's prerogative over life and death of his fictional universe' (179).

'Maggie is a false saint' (220). *The Golden Bowl*, in short, seems to attract claims to 'objective truth' even in critics intent on avoiding it.

To this my own interpretation is no exception. I take issue with the many interpretations which maintain that *The Golden Bowl*, though perfectly aware of the lies on which its society is based, ultimately condones that lie in the interests of the civilization that it tries to preserve and protect;[99] on the contrary, I maintain, the novel exposes the coercive and manipulative potential of 'morality' itself, that is, of the moral structures a society erects for its own protection and the exclusion of threats to its power. Maggie is the perpetrator of a fiction that achieves closure in the terms most advantageous and flattering to the 'power of the rich peoples', the 'rare power of purchase' sponsoring the fiction. Maggie, indeed, is in the position ascribed to the realist novelist by those theorists who maintain that the novel is committed, by its methods of representation, to the perpetuation of the social structures it analyzes.

I argue, then, that it is in its own self-consciousness and in its reliance on the self-consciousness of the reader that the novel becomes something other than a method of surveillance. In the case of *The Golden Bowl*, I argue, language, that creator of community and complicity, exploits also its capacity to turn its surveillance upon itself. The doctrine of the 'political unconscious', with its emphasis on the helpless complicity of the author in the discursive practices of his culture, depends for its demonstration on a more naïve appropriation of the dominant discourse than James permits himself, and does not allow for a novelistic practice that anticipates the procedures of criticism exactly in the critical intelligence of its analysis. Thus the argument that *The Golden Bowl* 'reveals . . . the culturally idealized patriarchal and bourgeois familial relations of late nineteenth-century England—at the same time that it necessarily distorts and conceals their fundamental socioeconomic basis'[100] finds distortion and concealment in the 'silences' of James's text by no other 'necessity' than the critical edicts of Jameson and

---

[99] Leon Edel, for instance, argues that the novel upholds 'the lies by which civilization can be held together' and that James 'places himself on the side of the "illusions" by which man lives' (*Henry James: The Master 1901–1916* (London, 1972), 221).

[100] Mimi Kairschner, 'The Traces of Capitalistic Patriarchy in the Silences of *The Golden Bowl*', *The Henry James Review*, 5 (1984), 187.

Macherey. As the article in question goes some way towards proving, and as I try to demonstrate in my discussion of the novel, *The Golden Bowl* itself provides us with remarkably specific data to fill in the 'lacunae' in the text. James is indeed depicting a culture that cannot afford to examine its own meanings—but the depiction itself constitutes that examination that is so carefully avoided by the characters in the novel. As Michael Sprinker asks, responding to, amongst others, the paper quoted above: 'By what right and with what means do contemporary readers of James claim to see through the mystifications of the Jamesian imaginary in ways that, *ex hypothesi*, James's texts and James himself were not capable of realizing?'[101] Now a reader may be capable of an analysis *of* an author that the author would have been blind to; but if we posit a latent content that is itself so coherent and so sophisticated, the coherence may well be a matter of choice and design rather than accident. As the whole of this book will try to demonstrate, it is possible and necessary to distinguish between levels of coherence and self-consciousness; no theory of literary production can account for all literary productions, and such theories must remain open to verification against the material they purport to illuminate—or become depressing instances of what Bakhtin called 'The utter inadequacy of literary theory . . . when it is forced to deal with the novel'.[102]

This book is offered, if not as a verification of any particular theory, then as a sustained enquiry into both the subversive and collaborative potential of literary form; initiated in a spirit of sceptical enquiry, it has come to argue that the realist novel, though formally and structurally predisposed to the ideological accommodation of closure, possesses in its own mode of representation the resources to escape appropriation to the status quo. How convincingly that belief is based upon the evidence I have assembled, the rest of this work must show.

---

[101] Michael Sprinker, 'Historicizing Henry James', *The Henry James Review*, 5 (1984), 204.
[102] Mikhail Bakhtin, 'Epic and Novel: Toward a Methodology for the Study of the Novel', *The Dialogic Imagination*, 8.

Chapter 1

A Divided Community: Fanny Price and the Readers of *Mansfield Park*

'And I hope—I hope Miss Morland, *you* will not be sorry to see me.'

'Oh! dear, not at all. There are very few people I am sorry to see. Company is always cheerful.'

'That is just my way of thinking. Give me but a little cheerful company, let me only have the company of the people I love, let me only be where I like and with whom I like, and the devil take the rest, say I.—And I am heartily glad to hear you say the same. But I have a notion, Miss Morland, you and I think pretty much alike upon most matters.'[1]

I

That two people so completely mistaken about each other's sentiments can terminate a conversation believing themselves to have reached some kind of accord is not very wonderful, given that the two people concerned are Catherine Morland and John Thorpe. But how, if not through Catherine, do we measure John Thorpe's pompous self-delusion? And how, if not through John Thorpe, do we register Catherine's naïve goodwill? We read partly against an outline of expectation which we have by this stage built up: we are unlikely to discern a deliberate slight, for instance, in Catherine's so very undistinguishing readiness to receive John Thorpe, nor to read his discovery of common ground as the enchanted illusion of a man in love. We assume that we share with Jane Austen a standard of judgement which enables us to place the characters just where they should be. We feel, in other words, contained within a narrative community that defines itself, if not in opposition to the actual community of the novel, then as privileged over it in being able to

---

[1] Jane Austen, *Northanger Abbey* (1818); ed. John Davie (Oxford, 1980), 98. rpt. Oxford, 98.

claim the author, rather than Catherine Morland or John Thorpe, as its patron.

But of course that narrative community does not really define *itself*: it is defined, not in the abstract and not in advance, but through our participation in it, which is to say that we partly define it ourselves—and not always as confidently as when dealing with the inexperience of Catherine Morland or the bumptiousness of John Thorpe. Here, for instance, is another conversation apparently ending in unanimity:

'She made me almost laugh; but I cannot rate so very highly the love or good nature of a brother, who will not give himself the trouble of writing any thing worth reading, to his sisters, when they are separated. I am sure William would never have used *me* so, under any circumstances. And what right had she to suppose, that *you* would not write long letters when you were absent?'

'The right of a lively mind, Fanny, seizing whatever may contribute to its own amusement or that of others; perfectly allowable, when untinctured by ill humour or roughness; and there is not a shadow of either in the countenance or manner of Miss Crawford, nothing sharp, or loud, or coarse. She is perfectly feminine, except in the instances we have been speaking of. *There* she cannot be justified. I am glad you saw it all as I did.'[2]

The unanimity here is hardly less tenuous than Catherine's and John Thorpe's, and the grounds of the misunderstanding not much less obvious: we know that Fanny is very young, very fond of her brother, tentatively in love with Edmund, and potentially jealous of Mary Crawford; we know that Edmund takes a schoolmasterish pleasure in instructing Fanny and a young man's delight in her admiration, and that he is in a fair way towards falling in love with Mary Crawford. Their agreement, if such it be, is, like Catherine's and John Thorpe's, the accidental common issue of their very different sentiments. Once again we feel we are privileged listeners to a miscommunication which only we are receiving correctly; but this time we are less sure of our ground. Fanny's 'She made me almost laugh': a grudging concession to a rival, or the inhibited response of somebody who never seems to laugh if she can help it? Edmund's 'perfectly allowable, when untinctured by ill humour or roughness': the humane allowance of an upright young man to

---

[2] Jane Austen, *Mansfield Park* (1814); ed. James Kinsley (Oxford, 1990), 57–8.

natures more spontaneous than his own, or the prematurely pompous didacticism of the clergyman whose charity obliges him to suffer frivolity gladly? We are uncertain, because Fanny and Edmund do not place themselves as readily as Catherine and John Thorpe against the exact discriminations of Jane Austen's comedy.

This is partly because Mary Crawford, important at this stage mainly as the occasion that reveals the disjunction between Fanny's incipient jealousy and Edmund's nascent infatuation, nevertheless establishes claims of her own to the reader's judgement. Although the exact degree of Mary Crawford's deviation from the norm of delicacy matters less than the subtle comedy of cross purposes which enables Edmund to assume that Fanny 'saw it all as I did', a sort of spurious interest in her moral nature has been established and will survive, ultimately to form the basis of Mary's expulsion. As Edmund and Fanny's 'agreement' here rests on their both interpreting their emotions in a moral light, so their eventual union will require a moral sanction. Fanny's judgement of the Crawfords thus comes to be enthroned as the official version; as she gradually usurps the moral vocabulary of the novel, the unerring perspicacity which is the natural medium of Jane Austen's comedy yields to the artless judgements of Fanny Price. Surprisingly, in a heroine with so little physical presence and such meagre dialogue, Fanny assumes control of her novel and bends it to her ends.

II

Mary Crawford's expulsion, thus described, constitutes a simplified model of scapegoating, whereby the narrative requirement of closure demands the exclusion of such characters as threaten the desired equilibrium of the narrative community. The present chapter seeks to chart the scapegoating process in terms of that narrative community that comes into being between reader and Jane Austen's narrative, as distinct from and privileged above the more or less complacent little societies in which their heroines live. The 'organic, hierarchical, small community' for which, according to Marilyn Butler, Jane Austen's novels 'speak',[3] is nevertheless all too often a community of fools, which it is the trick of her novels to

[3] Marilyn Butler, *Jane Austen and the War of Ideas* (Oxford, 1975; 2nd edn., 1987), 3.

expose as such without seeming to subvert it: the novels speak *to* a different community, party to all the essential discriminations implied or enacted in the novel.

Observing, for instance, the misunderstanding between the two cousins, we are seeing them as they cannot see themselves; we share with the narrator a perspective of which they are incapable. Fanny's earnest criticism does not in the first place establish a perspective on Mary: it reveals her own youthful methods of judgement solemnly missing the point of Mary's 'lively mind'—just as Edmund's appreciation of that lively mind may be more indulgent and less sage than he believes. If, as Andrew Wright says, 'always the novel has been a conspiracy, sometimes a much disguised conspiracy, between writer and reader',[4] then in Jane Austen it is most frequently a conspiracy of humour; and in this instance it unites us with the author against, or at any rate as distinguished from, her two romantic leads. For the time being, they are outside the circle of irony.

The reader, then, is privileged in having access both to the fictional community—Fanny and Edmund at Mansfield—and to the narrative community. But if for us, Jane Austen's narrative community and fictional community seldom coincide, for her heroines they nevertheless have to coexist: hence the frequent sense of potential rupture held in check, the heroine's accommodation to the demands, so often so unreasonable, of the fictional community in which she must live her life, while owing allegiance also to that other community of values. Of course, some heroines are themselves in a process of transition between the two communities: Emma, in solemnly explaining to Harriet why 'the world' takes an uncharitable view of Miss Bates, shows herself to be at least as uncharitable as that world ('And the distinction is not quite so much against the candour and common sense of the world as appears at first; for a very narrow income has a tendency to contract the mind, and sour the temper');[5] even Elizabeth Bennet is for a while uncharacteristically united with her mother in a common estimate of Darcy. But for the most part the heroines are defined *against* the ruling standards of their communities, even

---

[4] Andrew Wright, 'The Novel as a Conspiracy', in Robert Speaight (ed.), *Essays by Divers Hands, being the Transactions of the Royal Society of Literature*, 37 (London, 1972), 124.

[5] Jane Austen, *Emma* (1816); ed. David Lodge (Oxford, 1980), 77.

while having to recognize the claims of that community. Mrs Elton must, it is true, be tolerated at a picnic, if only not to give pain to Mrs Weston, whose inconveniently sociable husband has extended the invitation; and Miss Bates must be more than tolerated, because though not a prominent member of the narrative community, she has earned honorary citizenship in it. But there is a limit to the accommodation that is compatible with integrity. Hence the appeal of Marianne Dashwood—and hence, perhaps, the famous 'regulated hatred': a symptom of the strain attendant upon the effort of reconciling the two communities, reflecting, according to D. W. Harding, Austen's own desperate attempt at 'finding some mode of existence for her critical attitudes'.[6] The narrative community of *Emma* can contain, 'manage' Miss Bates; indeed, Emma has to learn to regulate her own impatience with Miss Bates before she is judged worthy of her privileged place in the narrative as in the actual community. But in extreme cases the imperfections of others cease to be regulated by the narrative; or rather, the only form of regulation deemed adequate is expulsion.

Even expulsion, however, has its gradations. Mrs Elton cannot be physically removed from Highbury, but the novel can render her harmless by pointedly excluding her from the 'small band of true friends' (*E* 440) rejoicing in Emma's marriage; Lady Catherine, having been routed by the lovers, nevertheless 'condescended to wait on them at Pemberley'[7] (though once again the novel uses its last sentence to exclude her from the select circle around the heroine); even Mrs Ferrars cannot be entirely banished, and has to be placated in order to be prevented from being a nuisance. But there are other characters whose very presence would interfere with the equilibrium of the comic ending, and who are driven from narrative and fictional communities alike. Wickham and Lydia are allowed one token visit to Longbourn before being 'banished to the North' (*PP* 277), into obscurity and genteel poverty; Willoughby is permitted one late-evening call before he is dispatched to wealth, ease, and regret; Isabella Thorpe disappears into an uncertain future; with a severity unusual in Jane Austen towards such near relations, Sir Walter and Elizabeth Elliot are written off in Anne's

[6] D. W. Harding, 'Regulated Hatred: An Aspect of the Work of Jane Austen', *Scrutiny*, 8 (1940), 351.

[7] Jane Austen, *Pride and Prejudice* (1813); ed. James Kinsley (Oxford, 1980), 345.

'consciousness of having no relations to bestow on [her husband] which a man of sense could value'.[8] And the Crawfords are expelled from *Mansfield Park* as from the Park, to nurse their remorse at a safe distance from the happy if ruthlessly depleted community.

III

And it is at this point, towards which this excursus has been leading, that the community divides. Conditioned by our reading of Jane Austen's other novels, we assume here a similar moral patterning, whereby the reconstituted fictional community coincides with the narrative community, and 'we are all hastening together to perfect felicity' (*NA* 203). Perfect felicity—with *Fanny Price*? That 'poor sort of heroine' whom 'nobody . . . has ever found it possible to like'? That 'failure'? That 'monster of complacency and pride'? That 'static, solitary predator'?[9] Couldn't we rather have Mary Crawford? The dissatisfaction many readers feel with *Mansfield Park* may be a kind of jealous fascination (what can Jane Austen *possibly* see in her?), a matter of feeling our normal pleasant fellowship of judgement disrupted by the pale discontented presence of Fanny Price, felt rather than seen, perpetually lying just out of sight on a sofa with a headache for which we were probably responsible. Nina Auerbach's rather startling contention that 'Like Frankenstein and his monster, those spirits of solitude, Fanny is a killjoy, a blighter of ceremonies and divider of families',[10] is really only an extreme statement of the effect Fanny has on the spirits of many readers. Having earned, we complacently believe, our place in

---

[8] Jane Austen, *Persuasion* (1818); ed. John Davie (Oxford, 1980), 236.

[9] The insults are levelled, with varying degrees of animosity, by, in order, Tony Tanner, *Jane Austen* (Basingstoke, 1986), 167; Lionel Trilling, *The Opposing Self* (London, 1955), 212; Butler, *War of Ideas*, 248; Kingsley Amis, 'What Became of Jane Austen?', *The Spectator*, 4 Oct. 1957, rpt. in Ian Watt (ed.), *Jane Austen: A Collection of Critical Essays* (Englewood Cliffs, NJ, 1963), 140; Nina Auerbach, 'Jane Austen's Dangerous Charm: Feeling as One Ought About Fanny Price', *Romantic Imprisonment: Women and Other Glorified Outcasts* (New York, 1986), 35.

[10] Ibid. 25. Auerbach talks of Jane Austen's 'apparent withdrawal from the reader's fellowship'—a formulation less misleading than her later, less tentative, reference to 'Jane Austen's withdrawal from a commonality of delight' (23). As my discussion is intended to demonstrate, even if the reader and Jane Austen part company on the question of Fanny's accession to Mansfield, for much of the novel the 'commonality of delight' is as vital as ever, sustained by Austen's wryly realistic rendering of her immature heroine.

the narrative community, we suddenly find ourselves having to share the privileged circle with a heroine whose very presence there seems to put into question our own. This may lead us to resent the novel itself, to find, like Joseph Duffy, that '*Mansfield Park* at its worst is dry, academic, unrelaxed, and querulous'.[11]

But if Fanny's installation is a defeat for the good humour we have come to expect from Jane Austen's comic resolutions, it is, I believe, a more enjoyable process than is allowed for in the assumption that she is simply the personification of a conservative ideology. If indeed Fanny is a 'failure', it is in being more interesting than the type, the standard heroine of the anti-jacobin novel, or the novel of education, allowed for—perhaps not, as we say, interesting as a *person* ('Would you have this woman to dinner?' being the implied poser behind this view of literary character),[12] but as a literary creation. Fanny Price, in short, is funny. After *Pride and Prejudice*, no doubt, most readers find the humour of *Mansfield Park* less than exuberant: thus a study concentrating on the actual dialogue in the novel can refer to the 'pervasively somber tone of the novel'.[13] The comedy of *Mansfield Park* does not sparkle on the surface of its dialogue: it resides rather in a particular relationship between narrator and reader, a matter of catching the narrator's eye behind the unsuspecting backs of her characters. Though Fanny is incapable of a witticism or an aphorism, and even a smile seems to strain her constitution, her prim and colourless presence is irradiated by a cool glow of affectionate irony—often at her expense.

In being subject to an irony which unites ironist and audience, Fanny is distinguished from those privileged characters in Austen's novels who are admitted to this commonality, to share our and the narrator's sense of the aberrancy of the ironized. Some characters hold this position from the outset, or hold it with only brief interruptions of their tenure: Anne Elliot, Mr Knightley, Henry Tilney, Elinor Dashwood. Often, though, the character has to earn

---

[11] Joseph M. Duffy, Jr., 'Moral Integrity and Moral Anarchy in *Mansfield Park*', *ELH* 23 (1956), 72.

[12] As Nina Auerbach says: 'The question is important because, for [some] theorists ..., the more bravely realism departs from the commonality of fellowship, the more radically it tilts towards a monstrosity that undermines the realistic community itself' ('Jane Austen's Dangerous Charm', 23–4).

[13] Howard S. Babb, *Jane Austen's Novels: The Fabric of Dialogue* (Columbus, Ohio, 1962), 147.

his, or more often her, rights of residence; indeed, the moral education of the character may be seen as a progress towards inclusion in the narrative community established by the irony. This is what happens, clearly enough, to Elizabeth Bennet, to Emma Woodhouse, and to Catherine Morland, as each moves from her excluded state to stand next to the narrator and reader and smile with them at her previous delusions. If Elizabeth Bennet's enlightenment is the most heartfelt recognition of former error in Jane Austen's novels ('"How despicably have I acted!" she cried.—"I, who have prided myself on my discernment!—I, who have valued myself on my abilities! . . . Till this moment, I never knew myself."'—*PP* 185), Emma's is perhaps the most engaging:

It is remarkable, that Emma, in the many, very many, points of view in which she was now beginning to consider Donwell Abbey, was never struck with any sense of injury to her nephew Henry, whose rights as heir expectant had formerly been so tenaciously regarded. Think she must of the possible difference to the poor little boy; and yet she only gave herself a saucy conscious smile about it, and found amusement in detecting the real cause of that violent dislike of Mr Knightley's marrying Jane Fairfax, or any body else, which at the time she had wholly imputed to the amiable solicitude of the sister and the aunt. (*E* 408)

Emma's 'saucy conscious smile' signals her accession to the ironic community: *alazon* becomes *eiron* as she winks at herself in the mirror; the ironist, if need be, can be her own audience, even where as here, she is also the ironized. In entering the ironic community, she leaves behind her Mrs Elton, to whose company she has been hitherto condemned not only by the rigours of small-town sociability, but by the narrative laws placing her in the same unconscious circle of the ironized. The conclusion of *Emma*, then, finds narrator, reader, and heroine sharing not only a vantage point but a vocabulary, a way of judging experience. It may be the narrator who finds Emma's change of heart 'remarkable'; but by the time we get to the 'poor little boy', narrator and Emma are sharing the latter's saucy smile, and we cannot determine whose joke it is: it is, as it were, a communal joke.

This commonality of humour Fanny never achieves. At first, when she comes to Mansfield as an over-awed child, the humour serves to protect her—not from the neglect of the inmates of the Park, but from our indifference; invited to share the narrator's wry glance at the Miss Bertrams ('They could not but hold her cheap on finding that she had but two sashes, and had never learnt French'—*MP* 11), we also adopt its corollary concern for Fanny. The Miss Bertrams are placed for us, as it turns out irrevocably, by their own standards of judgement; but, less obviously, the assessment is made in some area that excludes Fanny as effectively as the Miss Bertrams, though of course not for the same reasons. They are excluded because they are the butt of the irony; she because she is incapable both of forming the judgement and of expressing it in these terms. The Bertram daughters are clearly demonstrating, amongst other failings more personal to themselves, the deficiencies of contemporary female education.[14] But it does not follow that Fanny is a moral exemplar in the tradition of the novel of education, set up against her cousins, 'entirely deficient' as they are 'in the less common acquirements of self-knowledge, generosity, and humility' (16). Fanny is at this stage as unaware of the judgements being passed over her head as the young Catherine Morland is of being the occasion of Jane Austen's satire on Gothic heroines; and as she is too young to share in the relatively sophisticated technique of judgement employed by the narrative, so she is too insubstantial to stand as the exemplar of these lofty qualities. In short, as protégée of the humour Fanny cannot also serve as its sponsor. We have to follow her into the age of judgement to assess the relation of her perceptions to the novel's own value system.

IV

Fanny's first lesson, and one that is basic to her whole education, is in the excellences of Edmund: 'She regarded her cousin as an example of every thing good and great, as possessing worth, which no one but herself could ever appreciate, and as entitled to such gratitude from her, as no feelings could be strong enough to pay' (32–3). If Fanny's feelings, prompted by Edmund's gift of a horse,

---

[14] See Butler, *War of Ideas*, 219–20, for a discussion of *Mansfield Park* as a variant of the novel of education. See also Kenneth L. Moler, *Jane Austen's Art of Allusion* (1968; rpt. Lincoln, Nebr., 1977), 120: 'Their indirect description of their schooling tallies almost exactly with the accounts of poor educational programs found in the works of Hannah More and others.' D. D. Devlin, in *Jane Austen and Education* (London, 1975) argues for the influence of John Locke's *Some Thoughts Concerning Education* in Austen's work in general; in *Mansfield Park*, however, Devlin argues, 'it is not the heroine who has to learn to see clearly but Edmund and his father' (5).

are 'beyond all her words to express', her narrator nevertheless gives us a shrewd enough idea of them, in the hyperbolic bent of Fanny's appreciation ('every thing . . . no one . . . ever . . . no feelings'), and in the tendency of her gratitude to appropriate its own object, the slight possessiveness of her conviction that 'no one but herself could ever appreciate' his worth. The stage is set for the entrance of Mary Crawford, and for Fanny's assumption of the burden of judgement. As she becomes aware of her own emotional needs, so she develops a sense of the shortcomings of those who threaten those needs; or rather, debarred by her position of inferiority and her natural timidity from any expression of her needs, she redirects her desire into the safer channel of moral disapprobation.[15] The customary constraints upon the expression of female desire are in Fanny's case reinforced by her situation as a poor relation, carefully brought up to a sense of her own inferiority, in keeping with Sir Thomas's scheme, 'without depressing her spirits too far, to make her remember that she is not a *Miss Bertram*' (8). Largely through the offices of Mrs Norris, Fanny is in no danger of forgetting this, though the depression of her spirits has not been as precisely adjusted as Sir Thomas could have wished. Nevertheless, desire does not accommodate itself to convention as readily as conduct, and Fanny's unacknowledged and largely unconscious tendency is to cast her love in a form commensurate with her position. The most readily available outlet for her suppressed feeling is in the moral judgement trained by Edmund and thus sanctioned by both heart and mind. And as Fanny moves into judgement, develops a voice, so the narrator unobtrusively withdraws her protection from Fanny, and like all the other characters in the novel Fanny is allowed to define herself through her language.

Fanny being Fanny, this definition does not take place through confident pronouncement, as in Emma's wonderfully self-revealing speeches or even in Catherine Morland's rejection of 'the whole city of Bath, as unworthy to make part of a landscape' (*NA* 87); for the most

---

[15] In this respect, Fanny conforms to the pattern of suppressed desire Mary Poovey has traced in the novels of Fanny Burney: 'Forbidden by convention to declare their desires, the heroines must struggle, often ineffectually, to communicate by indirection or even deceit, and the interest of the plot lies in the nuances of frustration and achievement that mark their efforts' (*The Proper Lady and the Woman Writer: Ideology as Style in the Works of Mary Wollstonecraft, Mary Shelley, and Jane Austen* (Chicago, 1984), 43).

part, Fanny is given to us through her interior monologue, rendered in free indirect style. Jane Austen's use of this mode has been frequently studied, but without showing, I think, how central it is to this novel's mediation between protagonist and reader.[16] Its capacity, in that division of it which has been called free indirect thought, 'to slip from narrative statement to interior portrayal without the reader noticing what has occurred',[17] accounts for most of our knowledge of Fanny, and also for most of the critical misunderstanding of her. The merging of narrator and character may lead the reader to attribute Fanny's reflections to the narrator, in a way that no alert reader would, for instance, confuse Mrs Norris and the narrator in the brilliant deadpan of the following:

Sir Thomas's sending away his son, seemed to her so like a parent's care, under the influence of a foreboding of evil to himself, that she could not help feeling dreadful presentiments; and as the long evenings of autumn came on, was so terribly haunted by these ideas, in the sad solitariness of her cottage, as to be obliged to take daily refuge in the dining room of the park. (33)

Our general distrust of Mrs Norris and our knowledge of her parsimony easily decode her involuntary self-revelations, whereas the heroine convention inclines us to take Fanny at her own interpretation when exactly the same technique is applied to her. The reader who misjudges the provenance of the judgements proffered through Fanny may be led to believe, like Howard Babb, that 'we have almost no sense of being dramatically implicated in a partial, perhaps unreliable, view of what is going on, and certainly no sense that the meaning of *Mansfield Park* hinges in any significant way on the limits of Fanny's perceptions as an individual' (145). Our sense of these things is of course our own; but the novelist has at her disposal the means to direct our sense, and if we attend to her meticulous characterization of Fanny, it should be impossible to conclude, as has been concluded, that Fanny is 'never, ever, wrong'.[18]

[16] Kenneth Moler draws attention to Fanny's manifest immaturity, her '"schoolroom" mentality', revealed, according to him, by 'two distinctive conversational styles [that] run through her speeches' ('The Two Voices of Fanny Price', in John Halperin (ed.), *Jane Austen: Bicentenary Essays* (Cambridge, 1975), 173). Moler, however, restricts himself largely to instances of Fanny's direct speech.

[17] Geoffrey N. Leech and Michael A. Short, *Style in Fiction: A Linguistic Introduction to English Fictional Prose* (London, 1981), 340.

[18] This sweeping exculpation is Tony Tanner's (*Jane Austen*, 142), but it may serve as trenchant summary of those readings which seek to rescue the novel by making its

This is to say that the reassuring complicity between narrator and reader gradually comes to test the reader's agility. The convention of the omniscient narrator, combined with our inclination to identify with a central consciousness, predisposes us towards finding a transparent presentation of Fanny where there is in fact the amused mimicking of the prim meditations of a morally and emotionally immature girl. Thus Marilyn Butler's likening of 'Fanny's acutely sensitive consciousness [to] an unexposed film on which all that is said and done, and one person's responses to another, become sharply imprinted'[19] ignores the crucial fact that Fanny's consciousness has been pre-exposed, as it were, to Edmund's influence, and that all her perceptions thereafter are tinged by her love for him. Butler, in claiming that 'Fanny Price's voice comes to speak for everything at Mansfield; the reader, deprived of any version of events but hers, grows less and less qualified to resist her' (p. xvii) is identifying the problem correctly, but drawing, I feel, the wrong conclusion from it. The question of finding authority for reading against the narrative voice is a tricky one, but simply accepting that voice at its own valuation leaves us helpless against the beguilements of subjective narration and deafens us to the contending strains of the total implication of the work. Thus this chapter will look in some detail at the tonal fluctuations of a voice that emerges by the end of the novel to pronounce upon Mary Crawford—confidently, finally, and inaccurately.

A characteristic passage, and one of the first in which we are allowed access to Fanny's mental and moral processes, dramatizes Fanny's response to Mary Crawford's use of the horse that Edmund has considerately placed at her disposal—and then as considerately and perhaps with more enthusiasm placed at Mary's. The loan of the horse, we remember, was what occasioned Fanny's renewed sense of Edmund's inestimable worth. Now poor Fanny, ready for her daily exercise, is left to wait for the use of the horse, while observing from a distance the prowess of Mary Crawford:

heroine seem insufferable. See, for another instance, Alistair M. Duckworth, *The Improvement of the Estate: A Study of Jane Austen's Novels* (Baltimore, 1971), 75: 'To see a complex irony subverting Fanny's moral character is, I believe, as misguided as to consider her occasional enthusiasms—bookish and poetically mediated as these usually are—subject to ironical undercutting.'

[19] Butler, Introduction, *Mansfield Park*, p. xviii.

A happy party it appeared to her—all interested in one object—cheerful beyond a doubt, for the sound of merriment ascended even to her. It was a sound which did not make *her* cheerful; she wondered that Edmund should forget her, and felt a pang. She could not turn her eyes from the meadow, she could not help watching all that passed. At first Miss Crawford and her companion made the circuit of the field, which was not small, at a foot's pace; then, at *her* apparent suggestion, they rose into a canter; and to Fanny's timid nature it was most astonishing to see how well she sat. After a few minutes, they stopt entirely, Edmund was close to her, he was speaking to her, he was evidently directing her management of the bridle, he had hold of her hand; she saw it, or the imagination supplied what the eye could not reach. She must not wonder at all this; what could be more natural than that Edmund should be making himself useful, and proving his good-nature by any one? She could not but think indeed that Mr. Crawford might as well have saved him the trouble; that it would have been particularly proper and becoming in a brother to have done it himself; but Mr. Crawford, with all his boasted good-nature, and all his coachmanship, probably knew nothing of the matter, and had no active kindness in comparison of Edmund. She began to think it rather hard upon the mare to have such double duty; if she were forgotten the poor mare should be remembered. (60–1)

The scene typifies Fanny's position in much of the novel. Standing alone, at a remove from events, while 'the sound of merriment ascended even to her' and 'she could not help watching all that passed', Fanny would seem to be placed with a view to judgement.[20] But as Fanny judges, so she is in turn judged, though *judgement* is perhaps too severe a term for the humane comic measure that is brought to bear on her: the narrative surreptitiously withdraws its support from Fanny, absorbed in her critical survey of the others, and turns its scrutiny on her, dissociating itself from her perceptions by such phrases as 'it appeared to her', 'she could not help', 'she could not but think'—recalling, incidentally, the Miss Bertrams who 'could not but hold [Fanny] cheap' and Mrs Norris who 'could not help feeling'. But since up to this point Fanny's thoughts have mainly been reported from the outside, albeit sympathetically, it is possible on a hasty reading not to notice how much of this comes straight from her feelings of exclusion and jealousy.

---

[20] As is argued, for instance, by Devlin in citing this passage as evidence that 'Fanny in the first part of the book is insistently presented as the detached observer' (*Jane Austen and Education*, 88).

The passage combines narratorial comment with Fanny's perceptions, imaginings, and judgements in a subtle comedy of self-deception. 'She wondered that' may seem to be a mere report of Fanny's surprise at Edmund's neglect, but clearly the 'wonder' conceals, and not very effectively, a reproach, although the euphemistic formulation renders also Fanny's reluctance to articulate that reproach. Similarly, the construction of 'She could not turn her eyes . . . she could not help watching . . .', though on one level an 'objective' description, on another level re-creates through *anaphora* the urgent fascination of a young girl staring at what she dreads to see. The same device is used in conjunction with free indirect thought to mimic the breathlessness with which Fanny observes that 'Edmund was close to her, he was speaking to her, he was evidently directing her management of the bridle, he had hold of her hand'—climaxing in the almost accusatory 'she saw it', which then immediately slips into the slight withdrawal of 'or the imagination supplied what the eye could not reach', as the narrator intercedes with a qualification beyond the reach of Fanny. But she returns us immediately to Fanny's own perceptions and imaginings, in her rebuke to herself ('She must not wonder'); this turns out, however, not to be the expected confrontation of an unwelcome truth ('She must not wonder at Edmund's admiration of Miss Crawford', for instance), but an attempt to argue away that truth by ascribing Edmund's action to his universal good nature. Fanny's generosity can accommodate Edmund's usefulness and good nature—to 'any one'—quite comfortably; it is Mary Crawford's attraction it cannot afford to acknowledge.

Fanny's general irritation with all Crawfords, combined with her desire to exculpate Edmund on grounds of gallantry and universal goodwill, issues in an entirely unmerited attack on the unsuspecting Henry Crawford—guilty, presumably, of not interposing himself between Edmund and his sister. The prim 'she could not but think indeed that Mr. Crawford might as well have saved him the trouble' beautifully combines the self-consolatory, in the forlorn assumption that Edmund finds it trouble to hold Mary Crawford's hand, with the accusatory, in the rather tart 'she could not but think indeed'—an asperity which the form of indirect thought ('she thought that') could not have rendered. Fanny, in short, is feeling resentful, and cannot afford to refer that resentment to its true source—Edmund's neglect of her in his fascination with Mary Crawford. Thus the unconscious drift of her thoughts is to exculpate Edmund at Henry's expense: Crawford is not only responsible for Edmund's holding Mary's hand, he 'knew nothing of the matter' and is generally disagreeable to boot.

Now we know, if we consider it worth noting, that Crawford, whatever his other shortcomings, is unfailingly fond of his sister. Fanny is, in short, wrong about Edmund, wrong about Henry, and wrong about her own feelings—though it would be a severe moralist who could hold this against her. Fanny's fumbling for a moral handle to her indignation, culminating wonderfully in an attempt to interpret her own sense of neglect as concern for the over-exercised mare (which does not prevent her from getting on to the 'poor mare's' back the moment Mary Crawford vacates it), is not really the occasion for hard-hearted reflections on her slightly self-righteous self-deception; but unless we can see that Fanny characteristically shies away from the real ground of her judgement, that, clear-sighted as she is in many respects, there are several crucial occasions on which 'the imagination supplied what the eye could not reach', we are likely to misinterpret more important scenes than this one. Fanny's first essay in 'self-knowledge, generosity, and humility' does not bode well for the future.

V

Fanny's rapidly forming judgements are called upon to manifest themselves publicly in the notorious matter of her resistance to the home theatricals. The incident has attracted considerable scholarly elucidation, generally intended to establish the political grounds of Fanny's disapprobation more clearly than Jane Austen is felt to have done, and to settle Fanny's behaviour in the matter as the norm: 'Unless the modern reader feels, like Fanny, the anarchic connotation of the whole play—rather than, like Edmund and Mary, the daring of individual speeches—he is in no position to understand its significance in relation to Mansfield Park and its owner, Sir Thomas.'[21] It seems strange though, given the pressure on Fanny, that she does not produce this cogent argument against

[21] Butler, *War of Ideas*, 234. Butler is in the first place distinguishing between Fanny's reading of the *whole* play as against the others' (presumed) partial reading, but she also endows Fanny with an understanding of the political implications of the play.

her participation. Nor is it clear why two such educated people as Edmund and Mary should miss the subversive significance of Kotzebue when 'in the minds of Jane Austen and most of her readers' his name 'was synonymous with everything most sinister in German literature of the period'.[22] Sir Thomas on the other hand, by another reading, has only to walk into the billiard room to grasp in all its ramifications the onslaught on his own position represented by the play, the significance of its importation from Ecclesford, 'the seat of an effete class and its self-destructive tastes' and its manifestation of 'the Whig aristocracy's flirtation with the culture of the French revolution'.[23]

Since Jane Austen named *Lover's Vows* as the play decided upon, it seems likely that the nature of the play itself does form part of its function in the novel. Moreover, Fanny's reluctance to act reveals a characteristic inability to assume a character other than her own, just as Henry Crawford's facility in acting displays a significant fluidity of personality. But to ascribe our own political understanding of the play, or our own view of the relation of acting to personality, to Fanny herself and to her shrinking from the publicity of acting, is to cast her against type as a strong-principled political theorist and moralist. Fanny's 'heroism of principle' is part shyness, part a defence of Edmund's objections.[24] The moral element to her resistance is derived from Edmund's strictures (113–15), renewed by her reading of the play with its improper sexual groupings, and, once Edmund has abandoned her to her disapprobation, reinforced by her jealousy:

[22] Ibid. Kotzebue's name is, of course, not mentioned in the novel, since it is Mrs Inchbald's version of the play that is acted; and whatever Kotzebue's name may have been synonymous with, it is clear from a detail cited by Gordon Rattray Taylor that Mrs Inchbald, at least, was anxious to preserve the proprieties of the age: '[I]n 1798, Mary Wollstonecraft was instantly "dropped" by Mrs. Siddons and Mrs. Inchbald, as soon as it became clear that she had previously been living in sin with Imlay' (*The Angel Makers: A Study in the Psychological Origins of Historical Change 1750–1850* (London, 1958), 42–3).

[23] Avrom Fleishman, *A Reading of 'Mansfield Park': An Essay in Critical Synthesis* (Minneapolis, 1967), 29.

[24] The phrase 'heroism of principle' is sometimes seized upon as if it were an entirely uncritical commendation of Fanny. Tony Tanner, for instance, talks of 'the strain she incurs through her "heroism of principle"' (*Jane Austen*, 156) and says that Jane Austen 'wanted to show how much there was to be said for the "heroism of principle"' (173). Mary Poovey equally carelessly states that 'For Jane Austen, the "heroism of principle" is the most important lesson of *Mansfield Park*' (*The Proper*

To be acting! After all his objections—objections so just and so public!
After all that she had heard him say, and seen him look, and known him to
be feeling. Could it be possible? Edmund so inconsistent. Was he not
deceiving himself? Was he not wrong? Alas! It was all Miss Crawford's
doing. (141)

As so often with Fanny's free indirect thought, we need to
discriminate between the abstract judgement and the emotion
informing that judgement. Accepting from Fanny the 'justness' of
Edmund's objections to acting, we judge, like Fanny, Edmund to be
'inconsistent'; but the anxiety with which is ventured the dread
possibility that he could be 'deceiving himself', or even downright
'wrong', is Fanny's, as is the deft cartwheel pivoting on that
ambiguous 'alas' (sorrow at Edmund's inconsistency or concern at
Miss Crawford's influence?) to alight on the far more comfortable
conclusion that 'it was all Miss Crawford's doing'—whereas Mary
has in fact refrained from any 'doing' at all in the matter.

Fanny's resistance to the theatricals is thus a more mixed affair
than the 'heroic' readings allow for. If her 'heart and her judgement
were equally against Edmund's decision', then the fact that '[s]he
was full of jealousy and agitation' suggests that heart is about to
take control. Certainly her interpretation of Mary Crawford's
'looks of gaiety' as an 'insult' are hardly based on rational
opposition to the play in itself.[25] Whatever the symbolic
significance of acting, whatever the jacobin implications of the
play, whatever the sanctity of Mansfield Park and the importance of
its preservation against the incursions of Ecclesford and
London—in short, whatever perfectly rational grounds we may
advance against home theatricals at this time and in this house, they
are not Fanny's grounds. She feels, rather more naturally given her
age and lovelorn state, left out of other people's pleasure, and is
disappointed that instead of uniting her with Edmund, her

Lady, 219). In context, however, the phrase is much less laudatory: 'She had all the
heroism of principle, and was determined to do her duty; but having also many of the
feelings of youth and nature, let her not be much wondered at if, after making all
these good resolutions on the side of self-government, she seized the scrap of paper'
(*MP* 240). In other words, 'heroism of principle' refers to a *theoretical* heroism that
Fanny is incapable of sustaining in practice. The irony is very tolerant, but it does
prevent us from taking the phrase as evidence of Fanny's strength of mind or as the
novel's moral centre.

[25] All these details occur in an unusually explicit paragraph in *MP* 143.

disapproval has separated her from him. Thus it is not surprising that her scruples do not prevent her from playing her part in the theatricals, as long as that part does not involve a public performance; and as she finds that her services are after all needed, so she becomes happier: 'she was as far from finding herself without employment or utility amongst them, as without a companion in uneasiness; quite as far from having no demand on her leisure as on her compassion. The gloom of her first anticipations was proved to have been unfounded' (149).

'Compassion' may not be the most appropriate word for Fanny's very human tendency to take comfort in another person's uneasiness. More to the point, though, is the readiness with which she enters into the preparations for a 'scheme which, considering only her uncle, she must condemn altogether' (143). Instead of avoiding complicity, she familiarizes herself with the subversive text itself, and serves as prompter to the actors in the improper drama. But Fanny, of course, is not 'considering only her uncle', nor would we expect her to. Though she is here very often in the position of observer, and can note acutely the petty vanities and jealousies agitating almost every other participant, she is to a much larger degree than she recognizes a party to the confusion of motives and emotions that besets the theatricals. She is lonely, shy, and jealous; and if this inclines one to pity rather than to censure, it by the same token prevents one from taking too heroic a view of her qualified participation in an ill-judged scheme. Furthermore, as we shall see in her response to Crawford's proposal, her resistance to pressure is not informed by any political validation: if her refusal to take part in the theatricals places her, as it were, on Sir Thomas's side of an ideological divide, her refusal of Crawford places her on the other side. The constant in the two cases is her love of Edmund, not the political bearing of her stance.

VI

Fanny's dismay at Edmund's imminent proposal to Mary is an intensified form of her disapproval of the theatricals: once again she must find a moral basis for her jealousy—and the fact that such a basis is available makes it all the more difficult for Fanny (and the reader) to see how much of her judgement is directed by her heart. She *is* aware of the danger of allowing her love and jealousy to distort her judgement: 'She would endeavour to be rational, and to deserve the right of judging of Miss Crawford's character and the privilege of true solicitude for him by a sound intellect and an honest heart' (239–40). But these admirable aspirations are as usual less generous than they seem to Fanny's earnest self-regard. What she hopes to achieve by rationality is the 'right' to an *objectively* unfavourable judgement of Mary, a favourable judgement being hardly allowed for in the 'solicitude' which she foresees as the reward of her objectivity. Fanny never does achieve this objectivity—which does not prevent her from exercising both the 'right of judging' and the 'privilege of true solicitude'. Thus she reflects gloomily that Edmund and Mary are likely soon to reach an understanding, since 'the scruples of his integrity' and 'the doubts and hesitations of her ambition were equally got over': 'His good and her bad feelings yielded to love, and such love must unite them' (333). Of course, if Mary's 'bad feelings' really did yield to love, neither Edmund's 'good feelings' nor his 'integrity' would be unduly compromised by the marriage; thus the suspicion that Mary may just redeem herself has to be resisted with all Fanny's moral earnestness: 'In their very last conversation, Miss Crawford, in spite of some amiable sensations, and much personal kindness, had still been Miss Crawford, still shewn a mind led astray and bewildered, and without any suspicion of being so; darkened, yet fancying itself light' (333–4).

The Crawfords are flawed, and convincingly dramatized as such; but this does not mean that Fanny is right about them. Jane Austen creates, in Mary Crawford especially but to a certain extent even in Henry, a kind of unsoundness that Fanny's powers of judgement can deal with only in rudimentary outlines. Mary's defects have been convincingly demonstrated in several excellent critical accounts,[26] but it can be said of all of them that Fanny would not really have understood them: they have a subtlety beyond her youthful categories and her emotional investment in her own judgements. Mary is a woman taken unawares by feelings she has carefully refrained from having; and to seize upon her deliberately

[26] Lionel Trilling's account of Mary Crawford in *The Opposing Self* is justly famous. Susan Morgan, in *In the Meantime* (Chicago, 1980), 138–48, offers a long and persuasive analysis of Mary as 'Austen's vision of waste' (139); and Kenneth Moler demonstrates Mary's unsoundness by showing that her dialogue frequently 'rings flat' (*Art of Allusion*, 136).

light-minded comments as if they were proof of what Fanny would call her 'real character' is to miss how much of Mary's real character is unknown even to Mary. Her upbringing, as Fanny is so quick to see, has been worldly to a degree, and she has learned her lesson well; it issues, though, not in the unthinking, unselfconscious superficiality of the Miss Bertrams, but in a wry ironic play which depends on her perception of the possible other case. Her attribution to herself of 'the true London maxim, that every thing is to be got with money' (52) does something more interesting than 'betray . . . her materialism' or place her in 'a world governed only by considerations of money', as has been suggested:[27] it reveals a double awareness both of her participation in a particular value system and of the deficiencies of the system. D. A. Miller has brilliantly demonstrated, in an extended analysis, his belief that 'Mary's language lays claim both to her blindness and to her ironical purchase on her blindness'.[28] The ruminations he discusses are part of Mary's interior monologue on Tom's superior claims as a potential husband, culminating in the free indirect rendering of 'She had felt an early presentiment that she *should* like the eldest best. She knew it was her way' (42). Miller neglects, though, to point out that apart from anything else Mary proves to be wrong about herself: for all her disarmingly arch self-criticism, she turns out to prefer, contrary to her 'way' and her worldly advantage, the younger brother.

What makes Mary interesting is that she is so nearly a good woman; Fanny can see her only as a bad woman who nearly marries Edmund. Fanny's much-praised percipience in seeing through Mary's vices is largely a matter of being blind to her virtues, of subordinating, morally as syntactically, 'some amiable sensations, and much personal kindness' to 'a mind led astray'. In the conversation which leads Fanny to this judgement, we are

---

[27] Butler, *War of Ideas* 224; Tanner, *Jane Austen*, 150. Igor Webb also talks of this as 'an ingenious damning passage' in which Mary 'without any sense of self-exposure' gives a 'damning account of herself' (*From Custom to Capital: The English Novel and the Industrial Revolution* (Ithaca, NY, 1981), 59). But Mary is cleverer than this: as in her disarming confession to selfishness in depriving Fanny of the use of the horse, she pre-empts criticism exactly by overt and perfectly conscious self-exposure.

[28] D. A. Miller, *Narrative and its Discontents: Problems of Closure in the Traditional Novel* (Princeton, NJ, 1981), 31. The full analysis extends from p. 27 to p. 33.

certainly given a sobering display of the values of the London marriage market; not so much a matter, though, of a mind 'darkened, yet fancying itself light' as of a darkened mind puzzled by a light it does not as yet see very clearly. We are given, not a heroine confronting a villain, but two women who do not understand each other—and even here Mary has the advantage: it is one of the more striking ironies of the novel that she is more just to Fanny than Fanny is to her. Of course, she can afford to be: not recognizing Fanny as a rival, she has nothing to fear from her; but generosity does not necessarily require that the donor give a gift beyond her means. As for Fanny, she gives Mary not the benefit of a single doubt.

In her refusal of Henry Crawford, Fanny is of course on much firmer ground than in her disapproval of Mary: she simply does not love him, and she has witnessed enough truly reprehensible behaviour on his part to justify her disdain. Furthermore, in warding off his persistent onslaughts, she shows considerable courage, also in resisting the pressure of people she is accustomed to obey. Her timid opposition to Sir Thomas, in particular, goes some way towards establishing an independent moral standard, at odds with the worldly standards of Mansfield Park. Sir Thomas's behaviour in this section does little to vindicate the critical reputation he has gained as the moral centre of Mansfield Park, the symbolic upholder of those values of the gentry Jane Austen is said to have treasured.[29] In fact Fanny's most determined stand is *against* many of the values of Mansfield: marriage for money and connections, patriarchal coercion, the denial of her right to choose whom she wants to marry, the concept of a 'good' marriage as a *duty*—all the values, in short, Sir Thomas appeals to in his ponderous reprimand to a terrified Fanny:

I had thought you peculiarly free from wilfulness of temper, self-conceit, and every tendency to that independence of spirit, which prevails so much in modern days, even in young women, and which in young women is

---

[29] This seems to me an important weakness in Edward Said's post-colonial reading of the novel, which unites Sir Thomas and Fanny in a common colonial ethos, dependent upon the existence and support of overseas possessions. Said's reading leads him to see Sir Thomas as 'her mentor, the man whose estate she inherits', whereas, strictly speaking, he is neither (*Culture and Imperialism* (London, 1993), 106).

offensive and disgusting beyond all common offence. But you have now shewn me that you can be wilful and perverse, that you can and will decide for yourself, without any consideration or deference for those who have surely some right to guide you—without even asking their advice. You have shewn yourself very, very different from any thing that I had imagined. The advantage or disadvantage of your family—of your parents—your brothers and sisters—never seems to have had a moment's share in your thoughts on this occasion. . . . You think only of yourself. (287–8)

If we were to read *Mansfield Park* in the anti-jacobin tradition, we would be obliged to take Sir Thomas's 'opinion' as speaking for that subordination of the self to duty that the anti-jacobin novel celebrated.[30] For Sir Thomas here appeals to the stern imperatives of a conservatism based upon duty to family, authority, and property, and which abhors 'that independence of spirit, which prevails so much in modern days';[31] he is, in short, here most explicitly that guardian of traditional values that the anti-jacobin versions of the novel would have him be.[32] As such, he stands opposed to Fanny, who is here the victim of the values to whose protection she has been entrusted. There is something comical in the trembling and sobbing Fanny's being cast as the type of the 'offensive and disgusting' independence of women; but, more seriously, the satire on Sir Thomas's patriarchal certainties reveals also the expectations ruling the selection of a marriage partner: Fanny is

[30] See in particular Marilyn Butler's discussion of the anti-jacobin novel's attitude to marriage (*War of Ideas*, 108–10). She quotes from Charles Lloyd's *Edmund Oliver* (1798) the sage advice of Edmund's virtuous clergyman friend: 'If you marry, marry from serious and well-grounded esteem, and not from love' (109).

[31] Sir Thomas, in fact, comes close to echoing Hannah More's *Strictures* here: 'Who can forbear observing and regretting in a variety of instances, that not only sons, but daughters, have adopted something of that spirit of independence and disdain of control, which characterises the times? The rights of man have been discussed, till we are somewhat wearied with the discussion. To these have been opposed . . . the rights of women. It follows that the world will next have—grave descants on the rights of youth—the rights of children—the rights of babies!' (quoted by Gordon Rattray Taylor, *The Angel Makers*, 110–11).

[32] Alistair Duckworth, whose influential study argues for Jane Austen's 'faith in the substantial existence of certain pre-existing structures of morality and religion', concedes that Sir Thomas 'shows his values to have a mercenary tinge' (*Improvement of the Estate*, 57, 71). I would say that the mercenary tinge of his values here blends quite convincingly with a pre-existing structure of morality and religion. For the argument that 'There is no excuse for identifying Jane Austen's values with those of Sir Thomas. It is Sir Thomas who is her chief target', see Devlin, *Jane Austen and Education*, 99.

expected to seek 'advice' on the subject, to meet the expectations of her guardian, to improve the condition of her parents, brothers and sisters—in not wanting to marry to please others she is 'Self-willed, obstinate, selfish, and ungrateful' (289). Joseph Duffy, in arguing that 'Sir Thomas is a human personification of the Park and nearly always speaks, not *as* a man, a husband, or a father, but as a governing body or institution',[33] draws a distinction that all but destroys the point of this scene: it is exactly as man, husband, and father that Sir Thomas has his being as governing institution. His exertion of control is presented not as an abstract and unthinking power, but as a function of a quite recognizable, even humorously observed calculation—in his relenting, for instance, on the matter of Fanny's giving Henry Crawford her own answer: 'when he looked at his niece, and saw the state of feature and complexion which her crying had brought her into, he thought there might be as much lost as gained by an immediate interview' (290). The most insidious part of Sir Thomas's onslaught is not his overt attack, but the strategy of kindness which prompts him 'to abstain from all farther importunity with his niece': 'Upon her disposition he believed kindness might be the best way of working' (298). In Sir Thomas's 'working' we see the appropriation of even the most admirable qualities of Mansfield—that 'attention towards every body' that Fanny idealizingly attributes to 'her uncle's house' once she is in Portsmouth (348)—to the systematic undermining of individual resistance. It is no doubt common decency that prompts him to have a fire lit in her room, which moves her to resolve not to be 'ungrateful' (292); but it seems unlikely that he should not have counted on his consideration to have just this effect. Fanny is caught in a conspiracy of kindness—in which Sir Thomas is abetted, though of course unwittingly, by Edmund's gentle persuasion.

We may thus be inclined to see Fanny's martyrdom and her heroism as constituted here, in her defiance of the pressures brought to bear upon her. The point is, though, that her resistance here, as in the case of the theatricals, has little bearing on abstract principles, either moral or (least of all) political.[34] Crawford's unattractive behaviour to the Miss Bertrams gives Fanny the moral justification

---

[33] Duffy, 'Moral Integrity', 75.

[34] Duckworth argues that 'in thematic terms, her resistance upholds the traditional character of the "house." Were she to accept Crawford, then Edmund would marry Mary, Tom eventually accede to the Park, and theatricality and radical

she needs to reinforce her resistance; but the real source of her strength is her love for Edmund. Untrained, however, in an ethos that would set up individual desire against the pressure of authority, Fanny's love does not present itself, even to her, as a permissible basis of resistance. Thus, as Crawford threatens to reform his wicked ways, Fanny must preserve a belief in his wickedness to sanction, on safely impersonal grounds, her indifference to him. Consequently, his procurement of William's commission obliges her to be grateful to Crawford without surrendering her right to disapproval. The modern distrust of nepotism probably finds Crawford's activity on William's behalf at least as distasteful as his flirting; Fanny's tolerance of the practice may indicate either that Jane Austen herself did not have the modern eye for these things, or that she wanted to suggest a blind spot in Fanny's adoration of William.[35] Be that as it may, instead of deciding that his act did indeed show a true desire to please her, but nevertheless does not oblige her to marry him, Fanny has to conclude that he is quite as bad as ever:

Here was again a want of delicacy and regard for others which had formerly so struck and disgusted her. Here was again a something of the same Mr. Crawford whom she had so reprobated before. How evidently was there a gross want of feeling and humanity where his own pleasure was concerned—And, alas! how always no known principle to supply as a duty what the heart was deficient in. Had her own affections been as free—as perhaps they ought to have been—he never could have engaged them. (297)

---

improvements destroy the estate' (76). This ignores the fact that Tom *does* inherit the estate; 'house'-centred readings of the novel tend by implication to elevate Fanny to mistress of Mansfield Park, and to forget that the house is saved from perpetual theatricals and Mr Yateses not by her, but by the chastening effects of Tom's illness.

[35] Park Honan, in his *Jane Austen: Her Life* (London, 1987), is not helpful. Citing instances of what would seem to us (and clearly seem to him) very dubious intercessions by Jane Austen's father on behalf of his sons, Honan comments: 'Jane herself wanted her brothers to succeed. . . . but she mocked the system of patronage . . . she was to take up patronage explicitly in *Mansfield Park*, where the morally corrupt Henry Crawford schemes with his degenerate uncle (Admiral Crawford) to promote Fanny Price's naval brother William' (69). Honan forbears to mention that Fanny herself is very grateful to Crawford for his 'scheming', and seems to see it, if anything, as an alleviation of his moral corruption. Our problem remains to fix Jane Austen's own attitude to this.

The moral fervour of this is surely inappropriate to the occasion. What so renews Fanny's disgust and reprobation, Crawford's 'gross want of feeling and humanity', is simply his assurance that he does not intend to stop loving her, which in any other man even Fanny would have seen as constancy, however inconvenient to herself. The irrational basis of her resistance, however well reinforced by her considered moral judgement, reveals itself in every gasp of her excited rhetoric. The triumphant repetition of 'Here was again', the clumsy handling of the two exclamations ('How evidently . . . how always . . .'), leading to a collapse of syntax as Fanny tries to combine a self-conscious and totally insincere 'alas' with the reminder that she had 'always known' about these defects: the inept rhetoric of the passage is a register of the emotions implicated in the judgement,[36] and increases the distance between Fanny's agitated judgement and the habitual restraint of her narrator. The latter in fact withdraws slightly after Fanny's declaration that she never could love Crawford, to comment, surely with a smile, 'So thought Fanny in good truth and sober sadness'; and she later contradicts Fanny's conviction by telling us that 'there would have been every probability of success and felicity for him' if Edmund had married Mary and he had 'persevered, and uprightly' (426).

Fanny's reluctance to render Crawford even such justice as he deserves is concisely rendered by one terse sentence tellingly placed at the end of a chapter. Relieved at being spared 'so horrible an evil' as having Crawford witness the Price family's table manners (which are apparently of such a nature as to put Fanny off her food), Fanny concludes that '*She* was nice only from natural delicacy, but *he* had been brought up in a school of luxury and epicurism' (371). In the light of Crawford's considerate conduct during the Portsmouth visit, we are surely meant to note Fanny's double standard, the unconsciously self-righteous assumption that even her fastidiousness is purer than that of the likes of Crawford.[37] It is a trivial

[36] Chapman has 'how always known' in his edition of *Mansfield Park* (Oxford, 1934), which he designates a 'certainly corrupt place' (548 n.). As my argument above implies, and as Tanner also suggests in his edition ((Harmondsworth, 1966), 463 n.), the syntax may be confused because Fanny is angry, not because the text is corrupt. The emendation in the present edition does not, in any case, improve the syntax.

[37] *Pace* John Lucas, who maintains, in his Introduction to the 1980 World's Classics edition of *Mansfield Park*, that 'No amount of talk about points of view can disguise the fact that Jane Austen is identified with her heroine at this point' (p. xvii).

incident, but it relates closely to the issue of the use of 'value' words in the novel. Norman Page cites this sentence as one of the occurrences of the word *delicacy* which lead him to conclude that 'The successive appearances of such a word have the effect both of furnishing the reader with a moral yardstick, and of refining the word itself as a precision instrument'.[38] The effect seems to me to be just the opposite: that of devaluing such words by their application to trivial occasions, and of showing that Fanny has no very precise sense of their meaning.

Fanny's 'delicacy' in dealing with her Portsmouth family is as problematic as everything else about this inconvenient heroine. If we presume a unified ideological purpose here, and argue with John Lucas that the depiction of Portsmouth 'springs from a deeply conservative element in Jane Austen's thought, for it celebrates the virtues of the settled order of the gentry' (p. xviii), we find ourselves having to ascribe some strange lapses to Jane Austen—having to accept as privileged judgement, for instance, passages such as the following:

As for any society in Portsmouth, that could at all make amends for deficiencies at home, there were none within the circle of her father's and mother's acquaintance to afford her the smallest satisfaction; she saw nobody in whose favour she could wish to overcome her own shyness and reserve. The men appeared to her all coarse, the women all pert, every body under-bred; and she gave as little contentment as she received from introductions either to old or new acquaintance. (359–60)

Igor Webb argues that 'There is no hint of irony or discordance in this passage; Fanny and Jane Austen mean what it says; we are not intended to raise our eyebrows and smile at Fanny's special pleading for Mansfield'.[39] But to talk of 'Fanny and Jane Austen' in one breath in this instance is tantamount to referring to Emma and Jane Austen's assessment of Mr Robert Martin: the 'special pleading' which Webb notices is itself surely the 'hint of irony or discordance' which he denies. It is hardly thinkable that Jane Austen, however blinded by ideology, could unironically allow Fanny to recollect 'her uncle's house' with its 'attention towards every body' (348) as a place where 'every body had their due importance; every body's

[38] Norman Page, *The Language of Jane Austen* (Oxford, 1972), 76.
[39] Webb, *From Custom to Capital*, 66–7.

feelings were consulted', a haven of gentle considerateness only minimally disrupted by 'the little irritations, sometimes introduced by Aunt Norris' (357). The technique in the Portsmouth section, I would suggest, is consistent with that employed throughout the novel: Fanny is being allowed to form her judgements and take the consequences. Portsmouth clearly *is* noisy and disorderly; Fanny just as clearly is less able to sustain noise and disorder than most other people. The possession of 'a frame and temper, delicate and nervous, like Fanny's' (357) is not reprehensible, but nor is it, as has been suggested, the mark of a rich 'inner life': under the circumstances, it is merely a disadvantage, noted as that, which leads her to idealize the 'elegance, propriety, regularity, harmony—and perhaps, above all, the peace and tranquillity of Mansfield' (357). This is surely not a 'fundamental conflict between Fanny's own Christian values and what she now perceives as a many-sided, anarchic, irreligious modernity':[40] it is the discomfort of her physical and mental constitution in a noisy and uncouth environment.[41]

The Prices are not barbarians, but they are not very refined; Fanny is not a democrat, but she does try to fit in. When Sam is shipped off 'with more than half his linen ready' with Fanny's help, we can share her 'great pleasure in feeling her usefulness' without wondering with her 'how they would have managed without her' (356). The Prices would have managed as they always have, and Sam would have managed with a quarter of his linen. Fanny's earnest attempts, in helping Susan, to convert her own disapprobation into something more constructive, are not invalidated through being the redirection of a 'flattering scheme of being of consequence' to her mother (354); but nor is Fanny's ache to be useful separable from her sense of neglect, familiar to us from the Park but apparently forgotten by Fanny.

The rendering of Fanny's parental home in all its quotidian detail of grimy walls and scarred furniture has led David Musselwhite to argue that 'What Portsmouth shows is that there remained a whole

---

[40] Butler, *War of Ideas*, 243–4. Butler, who sees Portsmouth as significant in being 'destructive of the inner life' (242), argues that we must make 'the connection Fanny makes, the subtle association between Portsmouth and London' (243).

[41] For a balanced discussion of the Portsmouth sequence, see Michael Irwin, *Picturing: Description and Illusion in the Nineteenth-Century Novel* (London, 1979), 127–32.

social strata [*sic*] that lay beyond the pale of Mansfield and where
its ideological writ did not run and with which its "system of
narration" could not cope'.[42] But this is to underestimate the
flexibility of Jane Austen's realism, and to conflate the novel's
'system of narration' with Fanny Price's constitution. The
Portsmouth of butter melting in the sun and clouds of moving
dust (400) is, it is true, an alien setting to Fanny; but the quality of
Jane Austen's attention here is not essentially different to, say, the
references to 'the remaining cold pork bones and mustard in
William's plate' and 'the broken egg-shells in Mr. Crawford's' (255)
which anchor Fanny's grief at William's departure from Mansfield.
Portsmouth does not have a monopoly on the prosaic details of
existence. The superbly unjudgemental, undoctrinaire poise of the
Portsmouth sequence, as of much of the novel, is epitomized in a
passage like the following, as a horrified Fanny finds herself having
to introduce her father ('whose appearance was not the better from
its being Saturday') to Henry Crawford:

She could not have a doubt of the manner in which Mr. Crawford must be
struck. He must be ashamed and disgusted altogether. He must soon give
her up, and cease to have the smallest inclination for the match; and yet,
though she had been so much wanting his affection to be cured, this was a
sort of cure that would be almost as bad as the complaint; and I believe,
there is scarcely a young lady in the united kingdoms, who would not
rather put up with the misfortune of being sought by a clever, agreeable
man, than have him driven away by the vulgarity of her nearest relations.
(366–7)

---

[42] David E. Musselwhite *Partings Welded Together: Politics and Desire in the
Nineteenth-Century English Novel* (London, 1987), 40. Musselwhite argues that
'"Portsmouth" . . . is that area of threat and "otherness" that the ideological
framework elaborated by *Mansfield Park* is designed specifically to exclude, silence,
marginalize' (11). But Portsmouth is not so easily silenced: for all that it does not
provide the refuge Fanny seeks, it shows a robust indifference to those standards that
would 'marginalize' it. And in the novel Portsmouth presents no threat to Mansfield
Park, a fact which seems to me to undermine also Kathryn Sutherland's contention
that 'we sense the potential for revolutionary upheaval, reflected in the chaos,
squalor, and familial disrespect of the Price household' ('*Jane Eyre's* Literary History:
The Case for *Mansfield Park*', *ELH* 59 (1992), 418). See also Webb, *From Custom to
Capital*, 69: 'one objects to the hostility expressed toward Portsmouth and the
animosity against it which the novel, and the novelist, indulge the better to raise
Mansfield.' Fanny's discomfort, I submit, does not constitute animosity on the part of
the novel or the novelist.

The shift from Fanny's free indirect thought to the direct address of the narrator re-enacts a process that has animated the whole novel: Fanny's certainties ('she could not have a doubt . . . must . . . must . . . must') are gently undercut by a shrewd but tolerant scrutiny, noting the heroine's youthful agitation for our amusement. Austen's 'system of narration' copes effortlessly with the barbarities of Mr Price, the urbanity of Henry Crawford, the not-very-generous anxieties of Fanny Price: her comic measure deals as easily with the High Street of Portsmouth as with the drawing-room at Mansfield.

VII

This is the context into which the news of Crawford and Maria's elopement is flung. It seems worth stressing that it is a comic context, and that not the least comic thing about it is that it is a substantial defeat for that 'good sense and good breeding' (357) that Fanny has so indiscriminately ascribed to all at Mansfield Park. Of course, in terms of the official ethos of *Mansfield Park* and all Jane Austen's novels, there can be no two opinions about the open immorality of Crawford and Maria Bertram;[43] but there are different ways of holding a 'correct' opinion, as we remember from Mr Collins's 'Christian' counsel to Mr Bennet on a similar occasion. Adultery here, as in Jane Austen's other novels, is partly a convenient plotting device, partly an occasion for revealing moral responses under pressure. In dramatizing Fanny's own response, Jane Austen is not holding up the horrors of adultery: she is rendering the attempts of a 'mind like Fanny's' (in its way as 'delicate and nervous' as 'a frame and temper . . . like Fanny's') to grasp a previously unimaginable horror: 'every moment was quickening her perception of the horrible evil' (402). But Fanny's quickened perception does nothing for her vocabulary: her characterization of the elopement as a 'horrible evil' comically recalls her apprehension at the prospect of Mr Crawford's 'taking his mutton' with the Prices (371).

[43] Jane Austen herself was rather less horrified than her heroines by adultery; see, for instance, Honan, *Her Life*, 174: 'her quiet independence allowed her to enjoy the company of an interesting man whose adultery was his concern, not hers . . . : he was far worthier than silly Miss Twistleton.' Miss Twistleton, 'the Adultress', was Jane Austen's relative, whom she reported to look 'rather quietly contented and silly than anything else' (173).

David Lodge argues that in this novel Jane Austen, in her use of 'value-words', 'insists on the most careful discrimination between, for instance, social and moral lapses'.[44] This may well be so, but then only in the sense that she meticulously presents her heroine's failure to articulate this distinction. A writer as sensitive to language as Jane Austen does not inadvertently repeat as excessive a phrase as 'horrible evil' on two such dissimilar occasions; she is not, as Lodge maintains, 'schooling her readers in a vocabulary of discrimination which embraces the finest shades of social and moral value' (99): she is demonstrating Fanny's incapacity for such shades of discrimination. This is not to say that Fanny cannot distinguish between a social embarrassment and an act of open immorality; but the failure of her vocabulary so to distinguish suggests an untrained moral sensibility which can surely not serve as the standard of judgement in the novel. Indeed, Fanny's quite literally feverish response to the news of the elopement seems to set her apart from both the rigours and the relentings of that standard:

Fanny seemed to herself never to have been shocked before. There was no possibility of rest. The evening passed, without a pause of misery, the night was totally sleepless. She passed only from feelings of sickness to shudderings of horror; and from hot fits of fever to cold. The event was so shocking, that there were moments even when her heart revolted from it as impossible—when she thought it could not be. . . . it was too horrible a confusion of guilt, too gross a complication of evil, for human nature, not in a state of utter barbarism, to be capable of! (402)

This is not a considered evaluation of conduct as much as a record of a very particular response to that conduct: 'shocked',' horror', 'shocking', 'horrible', 'evil', all in the space of a few lines. Fanny's shock is the perfectly natural convulsion of a very young person's moralized sexuality forced into confrontation with adult sexuality uncontained by social and conventional forms. Her parents' blunted response to the event represents the opposite extreme of experienced unshockability, serving to measure Fanny's response as much as to place itself. Jane Austen deftly adjusts the comic register of her dramatic scene: having put the cat amongst the pigeons, she gives us only one agitated pigeon:

[44] David Lodge, *Language of Fiction: Essays in Criticism and Verbal Analysis of the English Novel* (London, 1966), 101.

Mr. Price cared too little about the report, to make her much answer. 'It might be all a lie,' he acknowledged, 'but so many fine ladies were going to the devil now-a-days that way, that there was no answering for anybody.'

'Indeed, I hope it is not true,' said Mrs. Price plaintively, 'it would be so very shocking!—If I have spoke once to Rebecca about that carpet, I am sure I have spoke at least a dozen times; have not I, Betsey?—And it would not be ten minutes work.' (401)

This, of course, is not given to us as an example of the right way of thinking about these things; but the comedy of it prevents us from entering too undistractedly into Fanny's state of mind. Mr Price's cynical shrug at the 'fine ladies . . . going to the devil now-a-days' contrasts flatly, as an assessment of the morals of sophisticated society, with Fanny's delightful assumption that adultery is the province of 'utter barbarism'. Neither Mr Price nor Fanny, in short, is allowed the last word on 'human nature'. Jane Austen is not interested in such ultimate pronouncements: she is smiling on the edge of the comic abyss that has opened up between Fanny's youthful horror and her father's complacent cynicism. And if carpets matter more than adultery to Mrs Price, that also is a priority that comedy allows for. Her disengaged echo of Fanny's stock term ('shocking') is no more than the preoccupied flick of a moral duster at a universe whose disarray she has come to accept as a natural state; but it alerts us to the imprecision of the term itself, and suggests that all that Fanny has available is the language of conventional judgement. She is perfectly sincere in her delirium of shock and horror, but we recognize a characteristic redirection of moral energy in the alacrity with which she turns on Mary Crawford: 'if there was a woman of character in existence, who could treat as a trifle this sin of the first magnitude, who could try to gloss it over, and desire to have it unpunished, she could believe Miss Crawford to be the woman!' (402).

Fanny's placid mother, presumably, does not qualify as a 'woman of character'; but more to the point, for us as for Fanny, is her extension of Henry and Maria's guilt to Mary. We need not distance ourselves from Fanny's estimate of 'this sin of the first magnitude' to follow the instinctive bent of her judgement: again, as with Edmund's capitulation on the question of the theatricals, Mary is found to be the sinner of somebody else's sin. To be sure, her sin in this instance consists in not taking a punitive enough view of the sin

of others, upon which laxity Fanny undertakes to improve—
though, having no precise moral vocabulary in which to couch and
thus order her response, the best she can do is a lurid prevision of
madness and death for poor Sir Thomas and Edmund:

Sir Thomas's parental solicitude, and high sense of honour and decorum,
Edmund's upright principles, unsuspicious temper, and genuine strength of
feeling, made her think it scarcely possible for them to support life and
reason under such disgrace; and it appeared to her, that as far as this world
alone was concerned, the greatest blessing to every one of kindred with
Mrs. Rushworth would be instant annihilation. (403)

Deeply upset as both Sir Thomas and Edmund no doubt are, it
seems unlikely that they would thank Fanny for wishing upon them
the 'blessing' of 'instant annihilation', the less so that she is not
prepared to guarantee its efficacy beyond 'this world alone'. What is
being examined here, in short, is not the significance *sub specie
aeternitatis* of Mrs Rushworth's conduct, but the nature of Fanny's
response to it.[45]

It is appropriate, given the cool realism which has consistently
contained Fanny's moral hysteria, that she should, through a
combination of Edmund's preoccupied but victualled haste ('He had
already ate'—406) and the usual Price dilatoriness, leave
Portsmouth without her breakfast. A hungry heroine is not
rendered less trustworthy by her condition than one who
transcends earthly appetites, but she *is* subjected to a different
kind of scrutiny by her author. Jane Austen, in short, is amusing
herself and her reader, at least partly at the expense of her heroine's
agitation. Mary Lascelles identifies an aspect of the problem raised

---

[45] Fanny's horror at Maria's elopement and then at what she regards as Mary's
inadequate disapproval is reminiscent of what Eric Trudgill calls 'the virtuous
woman's violent moral censure' of the fallen woman, for which he holds responsible
the protectedness of Victorian women (and he dates the Victorian era in his sense
from the middle of the eighteenth century): 'Many women . . . were brought up as
virtual moral idiots, insulation from a sullying knowledge of the world making them
ignorant, timid, and conventional, especially in sexual matters: so it was that
ignorant distortions of the fallen woman's nature, timid fear of the impulse she
personified, apprehension of losing caste by any laxity in censure, all combined to
make her predisposed to censure. Above all, and these factors would apply too to the
more intelligent angel woman, there were her jealous fears of the immoral woman's
special and dangerous attractions' (*Madonnas and Magdalens: The Origins and
Development of Victorian Sexual Attitudes* (London, 1976), 106).

by this, in arguing that 'the violent act which precipitates the catastrophe (though carefully kept below the level of tragedy) is not essentially comic; nor can it be made to appear so, without breach of the author's moral purpose'.[46] But it seems to me that the aftermath of the 'violent act', if not the act itself, does present itself to Jane Austen as essentially comic, and does cause a breach of her moral purpose; or rather, her moral and comic purpose, which has been indivisible up to this point, now divides. The effect is something as if Catherine Morland were to discover that General Tilney had murdered his wife after all.

Jane Austen's return to the realities of sober moral judgement is effected, though not without severe strain, by the repudiation of Mary Crawford for not taking a serious enough view of the act: 'To hear the woman whom—no harsher name than folly given!—so voluntarily, so freely, so coolly to canvass it!—No reluctance, no horror, no feminine—shall I say? no modest loathings!' (415). It may be an over-simplification to say, as Norman Page does, that 'inflated language . . . in Jane Austen is an invariable sign of foolishness or worse'[47], but certainly Edmund's broken sentences do not make up in substance what they lack in style. As Robert Garis says: 'This isn't the vocabulary of serious moral drama'; but it could be the vocabulary of serious moral comedy, and where he discerns 'Jane Austen's deliberate blunting of her *own* sense of language',[48] I would locate her habitual sensitivity employed in revealing the inadequacies of Edmund's judgement. He is deeply hurt, of course, at what he takes to be the crudity of the woman he loved and probably still loves; but his speech then becomes a measure of his disappointment rather than of Mary Crawford's conduct. The man who expects 'horror' and 'modest loathings' from the girl he loves, deserves Fanny Price, and it is humorously appropriate that they should be united in their rather prim outrage. But simultaneously Jane Austen needs to establish a basis for the expulsion of Mary: it is partly a technical problem, but it signals the intervention of that ideological form that requires a resolution in terms of easily assimilable values.

---

[46] Mary Lascelles, *Jane Austen and her Art* (Oxford, 1939), 76.

[47] Page, *The Language of Jane Austen*, 143.

[48] Robert Garis, 'Learning Experience and Change' in B. C. Southam (ed.), *Critical Essays on Jane Austen*, (London, 1968), 69.

The effect is curiously double-edged. Whereas it manages, in terms of plot, to relegate Mary Crawford to the outer darkness where Fanny has wanted her all along, it also produces a Fanny who has matured not into self-knowledge, humility, and generosity, but into self-righteous opportunism. The comedy of Fanny's repressed passion acquires a disconcerting edge as her jealousy of Mary is at last given the power and the moral sanction to express itself freely; '"Cruel!" said Fanny—"quite cruel! . . . Absolute cruelty"' (416). As even Edmund can see and point out, Fanny's modest loathings are here directed at the wrong object; but what he does not see are the limitations of Fanny's own tenderness for him. Her concern does not prevent her, 'now at liberty to speak openly', from 'adding to his knowledge of [Mary's] real character, by some hint of what share his brother's state of health might be supposed to have in her wish for a complete reconciliation' (419). Since the 'hint' presumably amounts to the implication that the woman he loved wanted him for a title and an estate, it seems rather crueller than Mary's unthinking shallowness. Furthermore, in 'adding' to Edmund's 'knowledge of her real character' (as defined by whom?), Fanny is not adding truth to truth, but falsehood to conjecture. Much as Tom's illness 'might be supposed' to have enhanced Edmund's attractions in Mary's eyes, she had, as Fanny well knew, fallen in love with him long before that: Fanny herself, we remember, thought 'her acceptance . . . as certain as his offer'. 'Seldom, very seldom, does complete truth belong to any human disclosure' Austen says in *Emma* (391), in humane indulgence of diplomatic suppressions; but Fanny's conduct here constitutes a conscious deception at the expense of an absent third party, which is another matter altogether.

For this to be presented to us, albeit through Sir Thomas, as an example of 'the sterling good of principle and temper' (430) is to ignore all that we have been shown of Fanny's lapses from the kind of self-knowledge held up as a supreme principle in the novel. If, as Marilyn Butler argues, 'The heroine who is fallible and learns, and the heroine who is Christian and exemplary, are the standard heroine-types of reactionary novels of the 1790s',[49] and if these types were indeed Jane Austen's models, then it would seem that in Fanny Price she produced a paradoxical hybrid: for much of the

[49] Butler, *War of Ideas*, 294.

novel Fanny is comically fallible; but, without learning very much, by the end of the novel she is set up as exemplary. If Jane Austen had been content merely to copy the models available to her, she could have kept Fanny within the limits set by her moral scheme and by her readers' horizon of expectations: she could have created a perfectly admirable, perfectly dull heroine, as Fanny is indeed often taken to be. Instead she created a believable, amusing, but ultimately self-deceived and not very likeable heroine. Fanny's immaturity is hardly more culpable than Catherine Morland's;[50] but the exigencies of moral patterning, the vestiges of the moralistic form Austen is adapting to her ends, require that the novel withdraw from the implications of this immaturity, and proffer it as a standard whereby to judge the events of the novel.

In life, no doubt, most people never reach insight into the nature of their failings, without thereby noticeably offending against the order of the universe, and it is tempting to assume that in this respect too Jane Austen shows herself to be more humane than the conventions at her disposal. It has in fact been argued that the ending remains open to a more sceptical reading, more consistent with the novel's refusal elsewhere to take Edmund and Fanny at their own assessment: 'We are not asked to regard Fanny and Edmund as the ideal couple but only as the possessors of rewards appropriate to their merits—each other.'[51] This admittedly more attractive reading can point, perhaps, to something like the following, as marking the dissonances unresolved in the closing chords:

[50] Muriel Bradbrook has made much the same point in arguing that Fanny is 'very often comically mistaken'. She adds that Fanny 'is to be surveyed through the eyes of an aunt looking indulgently but not uncritically at a favourite niece' ('A Note on Fanny Price', *Essays in Criticism*, 5 (1955), 289). I agree that this is how Jane Austen seems to regard Fanny, but unlike Bradbrook, I feel that Fanny's mistakes differ significantly from Catherine Morland's in ultimately being held up for our admiration.

[51] Fleishman, *A Reading*, 55–6. See also Michael Williams, *Jane Austen: Six Novels and their Methods* (London, 1986), for a strongly argued case that all Austen's novels have an unresolved residue, that complete closure is never achieved. Ellen Serlen Uffen's interesting conclusion that 'The novel contains neither the promise of comedy nor the weight of tragedy, rather, simply and profoundly, the sadness of loss' is, unfortunately, based on a rather strained art–nature dichotomy, with 'the realm of nature' implausibly represented by the Crawfords ('The Art of *Mansfield Park*', in Janet Todd (ed.), *Be Good, Sweet Maid: An Anthology of Women and Literature*, (New York, 1981), 29, 21).

In *her* [Susan's] usefulness, in Fanny's excellence, in William's continued good conduct, and rising fame, and in the general well-doing and success of the other members of the family, all assisting to advance each other, and doing credit to his countenance and aid, Sir Thomas saw repeated, and for ever repeated reason to rejoice in what he had done for them all, and acknowledge the advantages of early hardship and discipline, and the consciousness of being born to struggle and endure. (431–2)

This unusually inept sentence must presumably be taken to render Sir Thomas's self-congratulation as filtered through his own mental processes: Jane Austen's habitual syntactic balance yields to the uncontrolled momentum of the final chorus of a comic opera, with a piling-up of verbs and participles that all but collapse in a breathless heap of exhausted syntax. Furthermore, the reflections contain quite a few false notes: are we to rejoice in Sir Thomas's joy in the 'credit' accruing to him from his lucky investment; and are we to take seriously, as coming from Sir Thomas, the 'advantages [for others, presumably] of early hardship and discipline'? And what are we to make of the 'consciousness of being born to struggle and endure', except as a syntactically dangling tail imperfectly pinned to a deformed body of doctrine? In short, this is muddled and pompous rhetoric, and as such quite appropriate to Sir Thomas as he has come to define himself in the novel. The difficulty is to find support for our own resistance to this browbeating: Jane Austen allows it to stand unchallenged in the privileged spotlight of the closing curtain—indeed, in adding 'true merit and true love' to the list of blessings attending the cousins, she seems intent on endorsing Sir Thomas's comfortable view of the resolution. She is indulging a convention to which in as early a work as *Northanger Abbey* she gave no more than perfunctory if good-humoured assent: 'Henry and Catherine were married, the bells rang and every body smiled' (*NA* 205). But in a novel that has gone so much further than *Northanger Abbey* in testing the connection between feeling and morality, such perfunctoriness is less likely to charm us into acquiescence; we feel that Jane Austen is reneging on a contract which most of the novel has enforced. That ground which we shared with the narrator at the beginning of the novel seems to have shifted—or perhaps it is just that she herself seems to have deserted it and joined the woefully depleted community of Mansfield Park.

VIII

As so often with the investiture of a new order, a purge has to take place: Mansfield Park has to be cleared of uncomfortable reminders of past misjudgements. Maria, of course, has placed herself beyond the pale, and in Mrs Norris's 'resolving to quit Mansfield, and devote herself to her unfortunate Maria' (424) two potential causes of embarrassment are disposed of—'in an establishment being formed for them in another country—remote and private, where, shut up together with little society, on one side no affection, on the other, no judgment, it may be reasonably supposed that their tempers became their mutual punishment' (424). This is the closest Jane Austen ever gets to committing anybody to hell, and it is a sobering performance. Sir Thomas's emotional needs are directing events, rather than that comic dispensation whereby, in other novels, the monsters are somehow accommodated on the periphery, as minor inconveniences not likely to disturb the happiness of those united by their love and good sense. The novel is quite explicit on Sir Thomas's reasons: 'He had felt [Mrs Norris] as an hourly evil, which was so much the worse, as there seemed no chance of its ceasing but with life; she seemed a part of himself, that must be borne for ever' (424).

This formulation gives some weight to Leo Bersani's view that 'Mrs. Norris's departure at the end of the story purifies the place of its most seriously discordant element; Fanny and Edmund will now have a community adequate to their moral worth'.[52] But from Fanny's point of view, which is now the privileged one, the 'most seriously discordant element' has for some time been Mary Crawford rather than Mrs Norris. If Mrs Norris had been only slightly less awful, she could have been relegated to the middle distance, like Lady Catherine, instead of being sent quite away; but if Mary Crawford had been only slightly better, she could have married Edmund. That danger is averted by her shouldering the

---

[52] Leo Bersani, *A Future for Astyanax: Character and Desire in Literature* (New York, 1984), 80. David Musselwhite also identifies Mrs Norris as the scapegoat of the novel, but in the sense that she takes upon herself *Jane Austen's* guilt, in having calculatedly produced a novel intended to be a best-seller: 'With the creation of Mrs Norris what Jane Austen allowed herself was the luxury of a scapegoat upon which she could discharge all the rage provoked by the sense of meanness and betrayal with which she herself had become complicit in the course of writing the book' (*Partings Welded Together*, 42).

burden of guilt and being sent into the desert.[53] The vilification of Mary is the price of Fanny's vindication—though to her Jane Austen is more merciful than to Maria and Mrs Norris, endowing her with 'the true kindness of her sister's heart, and the rational tranquillity of her ways' (428). At a safe distance from Mansfield she is allowed the cold comfort of the 'better taste she had acquired at Mansfield' (428), which unfits her for the kind of life she had been used to lead, without offering her the usual recompense of the man she had learnt to value.

Joseph Duffy, in maintaining that 'Jane Austen would not have understood those heroic compromised women of later fiction—Edith Dombey, Gwendolen Harleth, and Kate Croy, for example—but in fashioning Mary Crawford she prepared the way for them',[54] traces a legitimate line for Mary, but does less than justice, surely, to Austen's understanding of her creation. In Mary's chastened enlightenment, in the ambivalent advantages of her dissatisfaction with her former way of life, Jane Austen seems to me to measure quite precisely both the compromise and the heroism of Mary's position. Mary is the heroine *manquée* of *Mansfield Park*, and in the restraint of her expulsion, after the moral convulsion precipitating that expulsion, Jane Austen makes some amends to the values betrayed in Fanny's vindication. In that relenting gesture, Jane Austen acknowledges the power of her own art to disrupt the ideology of form, and prepares the way not only for the heroically compromised women Duffy mentions, but for that sustained battle in the Victorian novel between the need to conform to socially sanctioned values and the urge to defy them; between the generic convention of closure and the barely contained impulse towards disruption. If, as Kathryn Sutherland maintains, 'Fanny Price, Austen's sickly Christian heroine, is clearly the prototypical "good" female for a host of Victorian novelists, among them, disconcertingly, the misogynist Dickens', anticipating 'the mid-century commodification of feminine goodness . . . effective in restoring

---

[53] For the view that it is *Fanny* who is the scapegoat, at any rate in the initial stages of the novel, see Paula Marantz Cohen, 'Stabilizing the Family System at Mansfield Park', *ELH* 54 (1987), 669–93. She traces a pattern whereby '"law," understood as patriarchal law, scapegoats the female, and "sympathy" arises from the internalized guilt that the sternness of patriarchal law engenders in those who wield it' (670). A scapegoat, though, that returns from banishment to rule the fold seems to me to escape the conditions of its own definition.

[54] Duffy, 'Moral Integrity', 91.

the authentic political relations of the family in danger from internal and external corruption',[55] then Mary Crawford anticipates the reaction against such commodification—or perhaps the threat that necessitated the commodification in the first place.

Fanny Price and Mary Crawford, in their uneasy dependence upon each other for definition-by-contrast, thus anticipate those paired Victorian woman characters who time and again act out the contest between the domestic virtues of the fireside and the dangerous allure of illicit desire, the protection and privileging of a 'feminine' and thus unthreatening heroine against a sometimes immoral, frequently dangerous, and always intractable rival. It is the kind of pairing, say, that Thackeray was to attempt in his Becky Sharp and Amelia Sedley, or Trollope in Hetta Carbury and Mrs Hurtle; even Elizabeth Gaskell, not normally nervous of female strength, disposes of the lively Cynthia Kirkpatrick to leave the field clear for the less assertive Molly Gibson. In their different ways, all these novels attempt to vindicate the dutiful heroine against the dangerously attractive anti-heroine. Henry James was to make that procedure part of the subject of his last novel, in tracing the process of Maggie Verver's ambiguous victory over Charlotte Stant—and, as I shall argue in the last chapter of this book, in calculating the cost of that triumph with a perspicacity derived partly from attending closely to his predecessors.

Of those predecessors, Dickens, the subject of the next chapter, perhaps embodies most variously the profound perplexity underlying the apparent certainties of the age. In his novels, virtuous femininity, the object of stock Victorian piety, came to assume its most ambiguous potency, in relation to that threat which the heroine is so often called upon to ward off or domesticate. The retiring, unchallengingly virtuous heroine was to Jane Austen only one variation on a range of female possibilities; to Dickens the Angel in the House was an almost obsessively recurring ideal. But though, as one would expect, gender is a particularly strong scapegoating pressure, Dickens knows also that there are various ways of being marginalized, not all of them gender-related. On the outskirts of Dickens's fictional arena is the discontented presence, male as well as female, calling into question the cosy arrangements

<hr />

[55] Sutherland, 'The Case for *Mansfield Park*', 414.

arrived at by the privileged few; indeed, paradoxically calling into *being* those arrangements. Little Dorrit, we might say, is the creature of Bradley Headstone; and he is, by the same token, expelled by the very redemptive plot that he has set in motion.

Chapter 2

'Oh, 'tis love, 'tis love . . .': Privileged Partnership in Dickens

> When she spoke, Tom held his breath, so eagerly he listened; when she sang, he sat like one entranced. She touched his organ, and from that bright epoch, even it, the old companion of his happiest hours, incapable as he had thought of elevation, began a new and deified existence.[1]

I

Mary Graham, the woman with these restorative powers, is exceptional amongst Dickensian heroines only in the unusual manifestation of her influence. Angelically mild though they all are, they have in common the ability to subjugate the male by a power that dare not breathe its name. Speculation as to the source and nature of that power is kept at bay by the sublimating rhetoric in which these women are swathed—except when, as above, the rhetoric flounders into exactly that area of experience it was designed to camouflage. We are never told that a Dickens heroine is sexually attractive; those women, like Edith Dombey or Lady Dedlock, whose roles depend on the relatively overt exercise of sexual power, are by that token suspect, at best granted a grudging admiration for their spirit or pride, their uprightness in the defeat which is invariably their lot. The heroines, on the other hand, without asserting themselves at all, inspire strong men to deeds of heroism, desperation, folly, and madness, and generally impose their designs upon their novels—unless it would be more accurate to say that the novels annex the heroines to their designs.[2]

---

[1] Charles Dickens, *Martin Chuzzlewit* (1843–4); ed. Margaret Cardwell (Oxford, 1984), 340.

[2] From a different perspective, Elizabeth Langland has argued that Victorian women were more powerful than their apparent subservience to men would seem to suggest: 'the wife, the presiding hearth angel of Victorian social myth, actually

Since the manifest design of a Dickens novel is directed at redemption and restoration, the heroine is most often and most overtly the agent of such rescue; but more surreptitiously, she is almost as often a medium of devastation. A surprising number of Dickens's heroines bring about, albeit indirectly, the downfall or death of some male sharer of their fictional space: Florence Dombey's influence on her stepmother leads to the rejection and death of Carker; Esther Summerson's declining of the services of Hortense mobilizes the murderous resentment of the Frenchwoman against Tulkinghorn; Biddy's rejection of Old Orlick helps to urge him into a life of crime; Agnes Wickfield is similarly implicated in the criminal degeneration of Uriah Heep; Sissy Jupe destroys the career of a promising young political economist; a respectable young teacher and a worthless scoundrel drown each other for Lizzie Hexam's sake; and Rosa Bud, as far as we can tell, provides a choir-master with a motive to murder his beloved nephew. The heroines survive to live happily ever after with the men of their choice. By the logic of moralized plotting, the vindication and enthronement of the heroine necessitates the ritual sacrifice of certain sharers of her fictional arena.

Now all these victims, with the to me crucial exception of Bradley Headstone, may be said richly to deserve their fates; but even quite innocent men suffer, if nothing more, the agonies of unrequited love. Mary Graham's touch, for instance, whose effect upon Tom Pinch is recorded above, is described as 'no common touch, but one that smote, though gently as an angel hand, upon the deepest chord within [him]'; and Tom's enchantment is ominously hailed as 'the dawning of a story, Tom, that it were well for thee had never been begun!' (*MC* 395). Even Little Dorrit leaves in her wake the wrecked hopes of Young John Chivery. But it is Tom Pinch's and Young John's good fortune to inhabit the comic variant of a pattern that elsewhere has graver consequences, subordinating the welfare of lesser characters to the heroine's pursuit of duty and attainment

performed a more significant and extensive economic and political function than is usually perceived' ('Nobody's Angels: Domestic Ideology and Middle-Class Women in the Victorian Novel', *PMLA* 107 (1992), 290–1). This, according to Langland, led to the disappearance of the eighteenth-century plot of the serving girl marrying her social superior—'marriage between a working-class woman and a higher-class man has become nonnarratable' (290). She discusses *Our Mutual Friend* as an exception to this pattern.

of happiness. Dickens's exemplary women have their strongest reality as near-symbolic incarnations of the novel's overt teleology, foci of its legitimate desires and repositories of its official values. More simply put, it is the business of a Dickens novel to arrange the marriage of its heroine, at any price.

II

But that, notoriously, is the business of so many traditional novels: if a Dickens novel resembles in this respect, say, a Jane Austen novel, it differs decisively from her single-minded pursuit of matrimony in also tracing, more deviously, the formation and rupturing of a multitude of other relationships. The heroine's exemplary union is only a privileged permutation of the numerous other pairings taking place around her, in accordance with a simple compulsion or narrative law: any single character, if permitted to interact for a while with the rest of the cast, will tend to attach itself to another character. In most novels, of course, some of the characters are at some stage drawn into partnerships of collaboration or consanguinity, but nowhere with the almost obsessive attraction that Dickens's characters seem to exercise upon each other. The composite figure of Spenlow and Jorkins is merely an extreme form of a process that is at work all the time in these novels: the fusing of individual identities in the interests of, broadly speaking, a common purpose. Flora Casby's flustered attempt at avoiding the personal by merging Arthur Clennam in the supposedly neutral appellation of Doyce and Clennam is a comic equivalent of that process—complicated here by its reversal, again by the linguistically agile Flora, in the startling restoration of separate identities to such a neutral co-operative:

'Pray, madam,' said Mr. Dorrit, referring to the handbill again, 'who is Clennam and Co.? . . . Is it the individual of whom I had formerly—hum—some—ha—slight transitory knowledge, and to whom I believe you have referred? Is it—ha—that person?'

'It's a very different person indeed,' replied Flora, 'with no limbs and wheels instead and the grimmest of women though his mother.'

'Clennam and Co. a—hum—a mother!' exclaimed Mr. Dorrit.

'And an old man besides,' said Flora.

Mr. Dorrit looked as if he must immediately be driven out of his mind by this account.[3]

Through the fissures of Flora's elliptical definition emerges, for the reader better informed than Mr Dorrit, the grim figure of Mrs Clennam and her uneasy dependence on the sinister Flintwich. Clennam and Co. is, indeed, a mother and an old man; just as mothers, daughters, sisters, combine endlessly with one another and with fathers, sons, brothers, to form partnerships that make their individual qualities if not irrelevant, then secondary to the purpose of the association.

Not all these alliances are necessarily as benign as Doyce and Clennam or even as co-operative as Clennam and Co.; on the contrary, the majority of them are at best politic, at worst exploitative. The principle is stated by Carker in *Dombey and Son*, with his usual ruthless clarity: 'But our interest and convenience commonly oblige many of us to make professions that we cannot feel. We have partnerships of interest and convenience, friendships of interest and convenience, dealings of interest and convenience, marriages of interest and convenience, every day.'[4] If the sinister Carker represents only one possible application of the principle of couple-formation, these 'partnerships of interest and convenience' are nevertheless not aberrations from the norm so much as variants of the basic teleology of Dickens's novels. Exactly *why* society should have presented itself to Dickens in this aspect is on one level probably a matter of biographical speculation—and something is no doubt to be made of Dickens's many collaborations, or of his dealings with firms like Chapman and Hall or Bradbury and Evans, in those days still represented by the actual men behind the names. For my purposes, however, the question is one of narrative dynamics: what is there in Dickens's conception of character that produces, on being activated in plot, this impulse towards associations so often detrimental to the participants?

---

[3] Charles Dickens, *Little Dorrit* (1855–7); ed. Harvey Peter Sucksmith (Oxford, 1982), 522.
[4] Charles Dickens, *Dombey and Son* (1846–8); ed. Alan Horsman (Oxford, 1982), 524.

Again Carker may help us to an answer. If he states the principle of partnership in its most reductive form, he also furnishes, though hardly voluntarily, the starkest example of the alternative. Once he has alienated his partnership of interest and convenience with Dombey and has been refused a liaison of interest and convenience by Edith Dombey, he is left alone, a haunted, terrified man, driven to his death by, in effect, solitude. Partnerships are at the centre of Dickens's design, but at its base is that loneliness and exclusion from one's own kind to which almost anything seems preferable. If love and marriage are privileged in Dickens's novels, that may be not so much because, as in Jane Austen, they are made to seem the natural termini of a certain kind of social existence, but because they offer a wish-fulfilling alternative to that vision of human life as loneliness relieved only by alliances of degradation, exploitation, or manipulation. Driving the mechanics of his most complex plots is the notion of the single human being as incomplete, needing to be complemented by other human beings.

In many respects, then, exploitative partnerships are the model, if not the norm; the novels are propelled by an energy that they cannot acknowledge, and that cannot be contained by the idealized partnerships intended to act as its resolution. And yet Dickens privileges, again and again, the archetypal partnership of marriage, reducing his vast social order to a vision of two people happily exempt from the exploitation and greed that he sees everywhere. Given the multifarious relations generated by the compulsive pairings of his characters, Dickens's resolutions are acts of drastic simplification: a single strand of the almost infinitely variable pattern must somehow seem to make the whole design fall into place. The victims of this paring-down are the representatives of that other, more potent vision; they are the unacknowledged energants of the plot, who challenge the novel's resolution without, as it were, being given a hearing. These are the scapegoats of the narrative, the bearers of the hidden and disavowed structural principle, that solitude and exclusion which the narrative labours to defeat: Carker, Uriah Heep, Rosa Dartle, Hortense, Miss Wade, Old Orlick, and Bradley Headstone —moving on the margins of their narratives, they have in common their doomed search for partnership. The heroines, then, derive strength from what they are the alternatives to: their energy is borrowed from that which is suppressed or evaded through them, the fates they escape.[5]

My reading of Dickens, then, will skirt that privileged area inhabited by the heroine and her retinue, though keeping it in sight, for purposes of orientation, as the site of the work's official agenda. By this emphasis, Carker's horrible death is not an aberration as much as a particularly lurid dramatization of a common fate. It is as if in him the teleology of closure is reversed: initially incorporated into a smoothly functioning social configuration and effective partnership, he is gradually driven out of the various structures that define his identity, to die in a 'retired spot, on the borders of a little wood' (DS 649).

III

The 'retired spot', literally or figuratively, is more often the point of departure than the destination of Dickens's characters. An extraordinary proportion of his novels open on scenes of desolation, a vision of alienation which the narrative aims to reshape in the fireside dream of domestic inclusion. D. A. Miller neglects the desolation, and does justice only to that dream in his choice of Bleak House as representative of the narrative and thematic range of the Victorian novel:

A Victorian novel such as Bleak House speaks not merely for the hearth, in its prudent care to avoid materials or levels of explicitness about them unsuitable for family entertainment, but from the hearth as well, implicitly grounding its critical perspective on the world within a domesticity that is more or less protected against mundane contamination.[6]

Miller is right in stressing the prophylactic function of the hearth, the power imputed to it of warding off those dangers too perilous even to be named, forever lurking just beyond the circumference of

[5] Kate Flint develops a somewhat similar argument from the perspective of Dickens's portrayal of female sexuality. Arguing that 'within and outside Dickens' texts, we do discover the presence of those whose deviance is so pronounced that they have the effect of denying this supposed or desired [i.e. gender-determined] norm', she maintains that 'the presence of Miss Wade . . . acts . . . as a strong reminder of the potentially unstable grounds on which Dickens' desired norm is founded' (Dickens (Brighton, 1986), 113, 132–3).

[6] D. A. Miller, The Novel and the Police (Berkeley, Calif., 1988), 82.

the family circle. But the view from the hearth, for all that it resolutely excludes any threats to its own security, cannot altogether banish an uneasy consciousness, a peripheral perception of just that mundane contamination it is the function of the hearth to deny.

In Ruskin's famous encomium on the home, the confident rhetorical leaps, linguistically establishing as the norm what is at best an ideal, imperfectly conceal the panic awareness of contamination as potentially carried by one of the denizens of the hallowed sphere:

The man, in his rough work in open world, must encounter all peril and trial:—to him, therefore, the failure, the offence, the inevitable error: often he must be wounded, or subdued, often misled, and *always* hardened. But he guards the woman from all this; within his house, as ruled by her, unless she herself has sought it, need enter no danger, no temptation, no cause of error or offence. This is the true nature of home—it is the place of Peace; the shelter, not only from all injury, but from all terror, doubt, and division. In so far as it is not this, it is not home; so far as the anxieties of the outer life penetrate into it, and the inconsistently-minded, unknown, unloved, or hostile society of the outer world is allowed by either husband or wife to cross the threshold, it ceases to be home . . .[7]

Thus the concept of home is kept pure by Ruskin's semantic trick of declaring only that to be true which accords with the ideal ('In so far as it is not this, it is not home'): the home can by definition not be defiled, because then 'it ceases to be home'. But even in the confident definition of the 'true' home we hear a suppressed consciousness of that which threatens the idealizing vision, the possibility that the 'hostile society of the outer world is allowed by either husband or wife to cross the threshold'. Ruskin expresses simultaneously the most pious certitudes and the most nagging doubts of his age and class. Is family really a refuge from 'the inconsistently-minded, unknown, unloved, or hostile society of the outer world', or is it merely a disguised form of it? As E. J. Hobsbawm says:

The home was the quintessential bourgeois world, for in it, and only in it, could the problems and contradictions of his society be forgotten or

[7] John Ruskin, 'Of Queens' Gardens' (1864), *Sesame and Lilies* (London, 1907), 59.

artificially eliminated. Here and here alone the bourgeois and even more the petty bourgeois family could maintain the illusion of a harmonious, hierarchic happiness, surrounded by the material artefacts which demonstrated it and made it possible, the dream-life which found its culminating expression in the domestic ritual systematically developed for this purpose, the celebration of Christmas. The Christmas dinner (celebrated by Dickens), the Christmas tree . . . the Christmas song . . . symbolised at one and the same time the cold of the outside world, the warmth of the family circle within, and the contrast between the two.[8]

I shall argue that Dickens, though an influential and prosperous purveyor of exactly this illusion, was also a powerful depicter of the anxiety underlying and necessitating the illusion. If his novels do tend to end on the hearth and to enforce a closing perspective adapted to its values, they open on the heath. The justly celebrated beginnings owe much of their power to their capacity to establish the conflicting fields of force animating their novels. If each beginning implies its own resolution, it also contains the potential for the disruption of that resolution.

Dombey and Son opens on a birth and a death; but there is no easy sense that the death is compensated for or even thematically balanced by the birth. Both death and birth contribute equally to a vision of great loneliness; the hearth is here the focus of mental and spiritual desolation:

Dombey sat in the corner of the darkened room in the great arm-chair by the bedside, and Son lay tucked up warm in a little basket bedstead, carefully disposed on a low settee immediately in front of the fire and close to it, as if his constitution were analogous to that of a muffin, and it was essential to toast him brown while he was very new. (*DS* 1)

The trappings of domestic cosiness, the 'little basket bedstead', the muffin, may momentarily lull us into accepting this for the warm family scene Dickens celebrates elsewhere; but it soon becomes evident that these fire-side elements serve mainly as ironic comments on the prevailing disunity and separation.[9] 'Dombey . . . and Son': the novel whose very title promises a partnership,

---

[8] E. J. Hobsbawm, *The Age of Capital: 1848–1875* (1975; rpt. London, 1988), 270–1.

[9] The pattern, much simplified, is used also in *The Haunted Man*, the Christmas Book which Dickens published in 1847, after *Dombey and Son*. The haunted man,

separates father and son from the start, denying the partnership the father so longingly foresees. This separation is sustained in the staccato sentences which insistently isolate father and son: 'Dombey was about eight-and-forty years of age. Son about eight-and-forty minutes.' Little Paul Dombey is born to be the absent term in a partnership of somebody else's making.

But not only father and son are separated. Dombey can only with the greatest of difficulty bring himself to call his wife 'my dear' ('as being a man but little used to that form of address'—(1)) and is entirely indifferent to Florence, who 'had stolen into the chamber unobserved, [and] was now crouching timidly, in a corner whence she could see her mother's face' (2). The most poignant loss here is Florence's, in the death of her mother; but united with her mother in a last embrace, she is less isolated than Mr Dombey, excluded as he is by both situation and temperament from participation in this loss. Mr Dombey is from the start alienated from all but his doomed ambition:

The last time he had seen his slighted child, there had been that in the sad embrace between her and her dying mother, which was at once a revelation and a reproach to him. Let him be absorbed as he would in the Son on whom he built such high hopes, he could not forget that closing scene. He could not forget that he had had no part in it. That, at the bottom of its clear depths of tenderness and truth, lay those two figures clasped in each other's arms, while he stood on the bank above them, looking down a mere spectator—not a sharer with them—quite shut out. (25)

This embrace in loving unity would have formed merely a contrast to Dombey's exclusion, had it not been the 'sad embrace' between mother and daughter being separated in the moment of the embrace. Furthermore, for all the rhetorical insistence on 'tenderness and truth', the two figures 'clasped in each other's arms' at the bottom of a 'clear depth' inescapably form an image of

Redlaw, is first discovered 'pondering in his chair before the rusted grate and red flame, moving his thin mouth as if in speech, but silent as the dead' (in *Christmas Books* (1852; rpt. London, 1954), 318). Here the ghost of his own past self haunts his hearth, to be vanquished by Milly Swidger, completely adequately described in the List of Characters as 'the embodiment of goodness, gentleness, love, and domesticity'. The consciously sentimentalizing simplification of the plot, like the schematization of the heroine, offers a useful diagram of Dickens's more complex intentions in his novels.

drowning. This profoundly ambiguous embrace anticipates the consistent connection of the sea with death in *Dombey and Son*; but it also generates complex resonances with the many other images of drowning in Dickens's novels. If here it serves as an image of closeness and sharing, elsewhere it is the expression of a mutually destructive hatred, a fatal intimacy—as in that other closing scene, the picture of Rogue Riderhood and Bradley Headstone locked to each other in the waters of the lock.

IV

This is to anticipate my own argument by several steps. The strange ambivalence of Florence's embrace has its relevance to the more general question of Dickens's portrayal of love; but at this point my interest is in the figure of Mr Dombey, 'on the bank above them . . . quite shut out'. That figure is also to recur; indeed, the figure 'quite shut out' is at the centre of this chapter as, by my argument, it is at the centre of Dickens's design. Something of the persistence of this figure may be appreciated by noting how its terms are reversed in a later rewriting, in a completely different register, of this opening. In *Our Mutual Friend*, after the wedding meal of John Harmon and Bella Wilfer, the newly married couple are seeing Bella's father off, soon after she has told him 'Now we are a partnership of three, dear Pa'. Wilfer is leaving by steamboat from Greenwich to London:

Having thus concluded his address, the amiable cherub embraced his daughter, and took his flight to the steamboat which was to convey him to London, and was then lying at the floating pier, doing its best to bump the same to bits. But the happy couple were not going to part with him in that way, and before he had been on board two minutes, there they were, looking down at him from the wharf above.

'Pa, dear!' cried Bella, beckoning him with her parasol to approach the side, and bending gracefully to whisper.[10]

Thus in the idealized partnership that is marriage, 'the happy couple' extends itself to include also the deserving parent, whereby Mr Wilfer's solitary state on the steamboat is alleviated by the words from the bank. The parting between daughter and father is

[10] Charles Dickens, *Our Mutual Friend* (1864–5); ed. Michael Cotsell (Oxford, 1989), 668, 671.

intended to counteract the powerful but repressed scenario of the parent excluded from the joy of the child, a scenario hinted at by Bella in her question to her father: 'And you don't feel solitary or neglected, going away by yourself; do you, Pa?' (OMF 671). Bella Wilfer's 'partnership of three' is an attempted denial of the loneliness and exclusion so often implicit in Dickensian partnerships; the whole marriage meal is an attempt to imagine the parent as a 'mutual friend' of the bride and groom, as the whole sequence is a willed alternative to a much darker vision. Similarly, in Martin Chuzzlewit, the reader is reassured that Tom Pinch will not be left desolate by the marriage of his sister to his friend:

They soon began to talk of Tom again.
'I hope he will be glad to hear of it!' said John, with sparkling eyes.
Ruth drew the little hands a little tighter when he said it, and looked up seriously into his face.
'I am never to leave him, am I, dear? I could never leave Tom. I am sure you know that.'
'Do you think I would ask you?' he returned with a—well! Never mind with what. (MC 700)

The overpowering sweetness of both these scenes is not merely an effect of heavy Victorian confectionery on the fastidious twentieth-century constitution. The falsification is measurable against the terms of the novels in which they occur, as the sentimentalizing revision of a far stronger, darker impulse: these resolutions are at odds not only with our more austere taste in emotional expression, but also with their own origins. They derive such strength as they have from the tragic alternative which they avert, the potential pathos flirted with and yet resisted by the coy rhetoric. As Dickens well knew, the secure inclusiveness of the family circle owes much of its cosiness to its exclusiveness, to the fact that the alternative is not only imaginable but, to the less fortunate, real. That knowledge serves both to glamorize the cosiness and to imbue that which is excluded with a threatening potency.

But Dickens's novels dramatize also another ambivalence: the persistence of division and solitude not only as possible alternative to but also as unacknowledged component of achieved intimacy and inclusion. Again Dombey and Son offers a convenient model of the process. The novel, of course, has its own equivalent to the 'partnership of three' in Dombey's eventually being taken into the home of Florence and Walter. If Dombey and Son never does come into existence, the opening scene contains, as Dickens's openings so often do, its own implicit *telos*, here adumbrated by the dramatic irony of Dombey's indifference to Florence: Dombey and Daughter is the resolution towards which *Dombey and Son* is to work. The reconciliation achieved at the end of the novel, then, takes its origins in, derives its energy from, this image of isolation; indeed, it draws on the same ambiguous embrace as that which parts Florence and her mother. As Florence kneels by her father, 'His head, now grey, was encircled by her arm'; and in their 'remaining clasped in one another's arms' (*DS* 706) he is at last included in that bond from which he was shut out in the beginning. There is, as I hinted above, something not quite comfortable about this resolution which mimics so closely that other, grimmer, ending: whereas its intention may have been to supplant the memory of that sadder embrace, the effect is to imbue this embrace with something of that poignancy, indeed even with a certain macabre resonance. The heroine, implacably excluded from her father's love for so long, now takes possession.[11] Drawn into his daughter's arms, Dombey relinquishes all that is not Florence—indeed, all that has made him the Dombey that the novel was about. Mr Dombey's redemption is a belated and troubled violation of a separateness that the novel has established as an absolute condition.

[11] H. M. Daleski also notes the continuity between the opening of *Dombey and Son*, Florence's rescue of her father, and the theme of drowning in *Our Mutual Friend*, but places the emphasis differently: ' "Clasped" in his daughter's arms, Dombey is at last able to give himself to the embrace of love . . . Incapsulated in the water image and its implicit extension in this passage is the kernel of the complex imaginative vision of *Our Mutual Friend* with its near-drownings that precede spiritual rebirth and its presentation of love as a regenerative force' (*Dickens and the Art of Analogy* (London, 1970), 154–5). Daleski does not mention the actual drownings in *Our Mutual Friend*, which develop the series towards a different resolution. Closer to my own emphasis is that of Julian Moynahan, who unkindly suggests that 'Florence wants to get Dombey's head down on the pillow where she can drown him in dissolving love' ('Dealings with the Firm of Dombey and Son: Firmness vs. Wetness', in John Gross and Gabriel Pearson (eds.), *Dickens and the Twentieth Century* (London, 1962), 126). For a sympathetic and cogent realignment and augmentation of Moynahan's argument, see Nina Auerbach, 'Dickens and Dombey: A Daughter After All', in *Romantic Imprisonment: Women and Other Glorified Outcasts* (New York, 1986), 107–29.

V

This pattern recurs in Dickens's major novels. What I have called the repressed scenario, the Dombey-like isolation from the companionship of others, remains the unacknowledged mainspring propelling the narratives, both to their determinedly cheerful conclusions and to those other more disquieting endings contained within, or straining against containment in, the closing movement. All too often the effect is one of falsification, as of Esther Summerson's doll's house attempting to supplant Tom-All-Alone's in the memory of the reader of *Bleak House*.

The great exception is *Great Expectations*, which I shall be using to gauge the flexibility and profundity of Dickens's method when undistracted by lukewarm pieties, and to illustrate the richness of his ingenious plotting when serving a vision correspondingly complex. The tension between isolation and partnership, which as the novel unfolds is not so much resolved as creatively extended, is established with wonderful conciseness and concreteness in the famous opening. Pip's narration commences upon a recollection of himself in an almost archetypal Dickensian situation: his 'first and most vivid impression' is also a heightened representation of 'the identity of things' in the Dickens world:

At such a time I found out for certain, that this bleak place overgrown with nettles was the churchyard; and that Philip Pirrip, late of this parish, and also Georgiana wife of the above, were dead and buried; and that Alexander, Bartholomew, Abraham, Tobias, and Roger, infant children of the aforesaid, were also dead and buried; and that the dark flat wilderness beyond the churchyard, intersected with dykes and mounds and gates, with scattered cattle feeding on it, was the marshes; and that the low leaden line beyond, was the river; and that the distant savage lair from which the wind was rushing, was the sea; and that the small bundle of shivers growing afraid of it all and beginning to cry, was Pip.[12]

This experience of the 'identity of things' as consisting largely of dead and buried absences haunts the novel as a note of melancholy sounding just below the threshold of narration. This bleak place remains in the memory, not only as the origins of Pip's great expectations, but as the centre of the novel's emotional landscape. If

[12] Charles Dickens, *Great Expectations* (1860–1); ed. Angus Calder (Oxford, 1953), 1.

Pip's chimney-corner provides an alternative focus, in the warm domesticity of the companionable exchanges with Joe, it very early in the novel becomes imbued with the presence of the marshes and their denizens: 'For, the fugitive out on the marshes with the ironed leg, the mysterious young man, the file, the food, and the dreadful pledge I was under to commit a larceny on those sheltering premises, rose before me in the avenging coals' (*GE* 7–8). As Pip and Joe sit by the fire, the booming of the guns signalling the escape of a convict from the Hulks reminds us again how precarious a refuge 'those sheltering premises' are—and how ineffectual against the threat from within, the baleful eye of Mrs Joe. A dreadful parody of the Angel in the House, 'a slave with her apron never off' (19), she turns nurture into grounds of blackmail, the fire in the hearth into avenging coals, domesticity into resentful durance—and Pip's Christmas into a travesty of Dickens's own cosy Christmas gatherings in the *Christmas Books*.

As in *Dombey and Son*, the opening of *Great Expectations* establishes loneliness as the datum upon which the rest of the novel is structured; and as in that novel, the opening is charged with a dramatic irony which is to be defused by the resolution of the novel. Pip's loneliness is not so much relieved as intensified by the sudden appearance of the convict who is in fact destined to take the place of his 'dead and buried' family. The meeting of the terrified Pip with his future 'benefactor' and ultimate redeemer is quite as rich in dramatic irony as Dombey's indifference to Florence, but the resolution of that irony does not strain the terms of its conception. Pip's unforeseen partnership with Magwitch is the mainspring of the plot, but is itself worked into a pattern that grants it only relative validity. Pip's great expectations, initiated by the 'larceny' he commits at Magwitch's behest, are ultimately referable to an older and deadlier partnership, Magwitch's criminal collaboration with Compeyson. It is a partnership not so much terminated by betrayal as transformed into a bond of hatred, as, conversely, Pip's terrified coercion and, later, his snobbish disdain of his unwanted benefactor are transformed into a bond of love. The two partnerships have a common issue: Magwitch's death. And if Pip's loving farewell from the dying Magwitch signals his own redemption, it does not cancel the memory of how Magwitch and Compeyson 'had gone down, fiercely locked in each other's arms' (423). The fatal embrace and the loving parting are both given their due weight in a resolution that does not privilege either, but recognizes their interdependence. In the working-out of Pip's partnership Dickens is for once not drawn into wish-fulfilling fantasy.

VI

The delicate balance of implications sustained by *Great Expectations* is too often, in Dickens's other novels, sacrificed to the simplifications required by resolutions seeking to privilege the domestic partnership over all others. That simplification, though, fails to release all the energies generated by Dickens's dynamic plots; and it is one of the functions of Dickens's scapegoats to discharge that excess of energy. Bradley Headstone is the most fully drawn of these characters; but he is anticipated by more inchoate but no less disturbing figures.

Since the scapegoat is by my definition not acknowledged as such by the community of the novel, the figure is to be distinguished from those victims of conventional morality who are, as it were, ritually purified by the narrative community. In *Dombey and Son*, for instance, Edith Dombey and Alice Marwood, the almost-fallen and the quite-fallen, are transparently victims of the values and hypocrisies of society, and their expulsion from that society, as from the novel, is a function of society's keen desire to preserve appearances, as, at another level, it is an effect of Dickens's reluctance openly to condone sexual irregularity. Both women are brought to make their peace with the community of values they have estranged themselves from. Alice especially is brought to abject repentance: after an initial angry rejection of Harriet Carker's call to repentance ('Why should *I* be penitent, and all the world go free'—*DS* 407), she is finally reduced to penitence and death, to figure as the subject of a narratorial homily: 'Scorn, rage, defiance, recklessness, look here! This is the end' (689). Her fierce indictment of the society that made her what she is, is defeated by the resolute kindness of Harriet Carker, as she confesses herself 'made . . . human by woman's looks and words, and angel's deeds!' (689).

Edith Dombey, too, though saved from the ultimate degradation, is brought low before the angelic power of Florence:

'Florence!' she cried. 'My better angel! Before I am mad again, before my stubbornness comes back and strikes me dumb, believe me, upon my soul I am innocent!'

'Mama!'

'Guilty of much! Guilty of that which sets a waste between us evermore. Guilty of what must separate me, through the whole remainder of my life, from purity and innocence—from you, of all the earth. Guilty of a blind and passionate resentment, of which I do not, cannot, will not, even now, repent; but not guilty with that dead man. Before God!' (725–6)

Purity and innocence must not be corrupted by the force of 'blind and passionate resentment'; 'stubbornness' must acknowledge itself vanquished by the 'better angel'. Clearly a ritual sacrifice is taking place at the altar of respectability. But it is a public sacrifice, enacted in the high street of the narrative. Though expelled from their own communities, Edith and Alice remain within the narrative community by virtue of the scarlet letter they consent to wear.

More desolate, then, than these domesticated scapegoats are those characters doomed to expulsion without benefit of repentance. In *Dombey and Son* the plot is structured towards the redemption of Dombey and the vindication of Florence; this dual purpose is achieved through the destruction of Dombey's pride, partly by financial ruin, partly by the failure of his marriage. But animating much of the intrigue, indeed the common term connecting Edith and Alice, is the figure of Carker, solitary and searching for connection. Both Dombey's financial ruin and the failure of his marriage are brought about by Carker, who becomes an unacknowledged partner in his firm, and a valued associate in his wooing and humiliation of Edith. Carker, from my point of view, is a transitional figure. Conceived in the tradition of the motiveless evil of the stage villain, 'sly of manner, sharp of tooth, soft of foot, watchful of eye, oily of tongue, cruel of heart, nice of habit' (250), he grows into something more interesting and more indeterminate. Useful as a plot mechanism, he also provides a convenient exculpation of everybody else, at least in the version put forward by Edith Dombey's Cousin Feenix, who is 'strongly of opinion that if it hadn't been for the infernal scoundrel Barker—man with white teeth—everything would have gone on pretty smoothly' (729). This facile scapegoating is firmly placed by its provenance—Cousin Feenix not being one of the sages of the novel—but it does mimic that simplifying tendency of the narrative movement itself, whereby discordant elements are reduced to convenient categories before being disposed of. Carker's insight into the nature of partnerships is borne out by most of the novel—only to be defeated by Florence Dombey's selfless pursuit of service to her father. We can believe, with Cousin Feenix, that everything would have gone on pretty smoothly if it had not been for troublesome individuals like Carker, whose expulsion therefore purifies the community. Carker embodies a central ambivalence: the recognition that villainy and dissolution are but the practices of society writ large, contending with the pious belief or hope that sin is a result of individual error and villainy. Carker's death disposes of that ambivalence and clears the way for Dombey's humiliation and regeneration.

If *Dombey and Son* is about pride, *David Copperfield* is about love. The over-simplification is useful, if only to prevent us from assuming that what Dickens offers as the novel's resolution, the love of David and Agnes, is more than merely one manifestation of a theme that has been taken through almost all its possible variations: maternal love (Mrs Copperfield-Murdstone, Mrs Steerforth, and—yes—Mrs Heep), paternal love (Mr Wickfield), filial love (David, Agnes, and—yes—Uriah Heep), disinterested affection (Peggotty, Mr Peggotty); sentimental effusion (Julia Mills); youthful infatuation (David–Dora); marital love in various degrees of happiness (the Micawbers, the Murdstones, Peggotty and Barkis, Doctor and Mrs Strong, Betsey Trotwood and her worthless husband), youthful hero-worship (David–Steerforth), warm friendship (Tommy Traddles–David, Betsey Trotwood–Mr Dick)—and so on. What the scheme makes clear is that there are certain permutations that are not permitted any place in the resolution. Little Emily's unwise infatuation with Steerforth combines, in its intensity, David's beguilement with Dora, and, in its object, his love for Steerforth. She pays, as it were, by proxy for his mistaken affections. Both Dora and Steerforth die, thus liberating David's mature affections to attach themselves to the angelic Agnes; Little Emily is banished to Australia.

In this respect, Little Emily does figure as the scapegoat, bearing the burden of youthful folly to the Antipodes—significantly accompanied by Martha, the exponent of a different kind of forbidden love. *David Copperfield*, like *Dombey and Son*, then, also contains its official scapegoats, its women of fallen virtue who are allowed happiness only at a safe distance from the reconstituted community. For all Dickens's sympathy with fallen women, he dare not suggest that they could possibly survive their fall within the community where they were known and loved.[13] But these transportations are, like their equivalents in *Dombey and Son*, at least provided for in the design of the novel. Whereas we may find the punishment grossly disproportionate to the 'crime', and may even suspect Dickens of bowing to conventional judgement here, these expulsions do take place in the unadventurous spirit of the novel's ruling morality. But there are more interesting variations on the novel's concern with love: the otherwise diametrically opposed figures of Rosa Dartle and Uriah Heep are united in striking at the roots of that morality.

Rosa Dartle is skilfully used, in her attack on Little Emily, to distinguish her vindictive tirade from the novel's own processes of judgement. Clearly Rosa's outrage has little to do with morality and everything with suppressed passion; in an insane version of Mrs Steerforth's uncritical devotion to her son, Rosa turns her suppressed passion upon the only available object, the defenceless Little Emily: 'I would have her branded on the face, drest in rags, and cast out in the streets to starve.'[14] Rosa's moral fervour is clearly an effect of her frustrated love for Steerforth, her hatred of Emily transparently jealousy. But in a sense, as redirected love, Rosa's judgement is more intelligible than the punishment meted out to Emily by the novel: 'I saw the flashing black eyes, and the passion-wasted figure; and I saw the scar, with its white track cutting through her lips, quivering and throbbing as she spoke' (*DC* 585). The passion that has wasted Rosa is love, for all that it is here

[13] George Levine, writing about the Victorian novel in general, but given his choice of examples perhaps thinking particularly of Dickens, locates the form's subversive potential in the fact that 'Even as they articulate the social codes, these novels complicate them, engaging our sympathy with lost women, tyrannical husbands, murderers, revolutionaries, moral weaklings, rebellious girls, spend-thrifts, and dilettantes' (*The Realistic Imagination: English Fiction from Frankenstein to Lady Chatterley* (Chicago, 1981), 20). I agree that these novels do not 'articulate the social codes' in any simple manner, but as my discussion of Emily and company is meant to show, our sympathy is 'engaged' in a very cautious and incomplete way.

[14] Charles Dickens, *David Copperfield* (1849–50); ed. Nina Burgis (Oxford, 1983), 385.

manifested as unrelenting hatred; the quivering and throbbing scar is the still-sensitive mark of Steerforth's callous violation of her. This is to say that Rosa, more strongly than Emily and Martha, represents the darker possibilities of the selfless love that Dickens as a rule celebrates. In her, devotion is a debilitating obsessiveness; she embodies the passion and resentment that Agnes, the official heroine, is not permitted to feel. Agnes, who ultimately confesses to having loved David all her life, has to countenance his marriage to another woman unresentfully, indeed to become that woman's friend and nurse, and to rejoice in being regarded by David as a sister. Her reward is in the death of Dora and the love of David; Rosa is left to fret her life away by Mrs Steerforth's side, quarrelling about who loved Steerforth the better.

But if Rosa is the Other of Agnes, David is also doubled by another exemplary son much by his mother. In producing Uriah Heep at this point I am not suggesting that he is in any way bearable. But he is relevant to my purpose in that he starts life as a simple exemplar of near-motiveless mischief, and modulates into something of a commentator on the community from which he is ultimately expelled. Uriah is almost metaphysically repulsive to the young David: 'But oh, what a clammy hand his was!' (183). But again, as in the case of Carker, the straitjacket of the villain does not altogether fit him. Whereas for much of the time his malignancy is made to seem simply an exhalation of his dreadful person, of a piece with his lashless red-brown eyes, there are suggestions of a more complex maladjustment, of the resentment of the consciously unlikeable person. His claim 'And yet I always liked you, Copper-field!' (507) may simply be part of his impossible umbleness, contradicted as it is by his later declaration that 'Copperfield, I have always hated you. You've always been an upstart, and you've always been against me' (621). And yet, the contradiction does not necessarily signal insincerity. Heep's hatred of David is clearly that perverted form of love and admiration that we call envy. His pursuit of Agnes, as indeed his pursuit of riches in general, seems motivated largely by a hatred that is indistinguishable from emulation; as Traddles explains about Heep's embezzlement of Betsey Trotwood's money: 'A most remarkable circumstance is, that I really don't think he grasped this sum even so much for the gratification of his avarice, which was inordinate, as in the hatred he felt for Copperfield. He said so to me, plainly. He said he would even have spent so much, to baulk or injure Copperfield' (636).[15]

Most readers probably sense in the representation of Uriah Heep something disturbingly different from Dickens's usual comic monsters, say Mrs Gamp or Chadband. There is a raw-skinned vulnerability about him that makes one uncomfortable about disliking him as heartily as he would seem to deserve—unless we dislike him all the more vehemently for the moral discomfort he inspires. Heep's hateful hurtability has been read as a creation of Dickens's identification with what he rejects, his 'self-lacerating rage against the social upstart'.[16] But the attribution of self-lacerating rage to Dickens does not so much explain Heep as use him to postulate an author pathologically unconscious of the meaning of his creation. Granted that literary creation re-enacts psychological structures which it may not 'understand' with the brilliance of post-Freudian analysis, it yet has its own methods of analysis, for instance in the technique of locating in a character called David Copperfield such 'rage' as Heep inspires, so as to make those attitudes themselves available to judgement—as the attitudes, precisely, of an 'upstart', which is what Heep accuses David of being (621). Dickens gives to Heep, indeed, an unanswerable analysis of his own case, which is to say his own umbleness:

[15] By René Girard's theory of triangular desire, Uriah Heep in his envy and resentment of Copperfield could be seen as pursuing the ostensible object of passion (Agnes) in imitation of some other model (or 'mediator'), in this case Copperfield: 'The impulse toward the object is ultimately an impulse toward the mediator; in internal mediation this impulse is checked by the mediator himself since he desires, or perhaps possesses, the object. Fascinated by his model, the disciple inevitably sees, in the mechanical obstacle which he puts in his way, proof of the ill will borne him. . . . The subject is convinced that the model considers himself too superior to accept him as a disciple. The subject is torn between two opposite feelings toward his model—the most submissive reverence and the most intense malice. This is the passion we call *hatred*. Only someone who prevents us from satisfying a desire which he himself has inspired in us is truly an object of hatred' (*Deceit, Desire, and the Novel: Self and Other in Literary Structure*, trans. Yvonne Freccero (Baltimore, Md., 1965), 10–11). Girard is not writing about Dickens here, but his description is strikingly apposite not only to *David Copperfield* but also to *Great Expectations*, *Our Mutual Friend*, and *The Mystery of Edwin Drood*. Dickens's treatment of jealousy corresponds closely to Girard's model: ' true jealousy . . . always contains an element of fascination with the insolent rival' (12).

[16] Terry Eagleton, 'Critical Commentary', in Charles Dickens, *Hard Times* (London, 1987), 306.

'I am not fond of professions of humility,' I returned, 'or professions of anything else.'

'There now!' said Uriah, looking flabby and lead-colored in the moonlight. 'Didn't I know it! But how little you think of the rightful umbleness of a person in my station, Master Copperfield! Father and me was both brought up at a foundation school for boys; and mother, she was likewise brought up at a public, sort of charitable, establishment. They taught us all a deal of umbleness—not much else that I know of, from morning to night. We was to be umble to this person, and umble to that; and to pull off our caps here, and to make bows there; and always to know our place, and abase ourselves before our betters. And we had such a lot of betters! Father got the monitor-medal by being umble. So did I. Father got made a sexton by being umble. He had the character, among the gentlefolks, of being such a well-behaved man, that they were determined to bring him in. "Be umble, Uriah," says father to me, "and you'll get on. It was what was always being dinned into you and me at the school; it's what goes down best. Be umble," says father, "and you'll do!" And really it ain't done bad!' (468-9)

David's self-conscious deprecations of 'professions' seem, in fact, a bit priggish in the face of such unsparing self-analysis. Uriah Heep for once presents his own worm's-eye view of the world, and he emerges as society's own creature, rigorously applying society's own lesson. If his usurpation of the Wickfield home, his insinuation of himself into a partnership with Mr Wickfield, and his designs upon Agnes are on one level unconscionable presumption, on another they are merely the determined grabbing from society what society would never have given him of its own accord.

But again, in the resolution of this strain of the plot, with Mr Micawber's triumphant unmasking of Heep, we have the simplification: 'HEEP, and only HEEP, is the mainspring of that machine. HEEP, and only HEEP, is the Forger and the Cheat' (613). Mr Micawber's account may not be quite as inadequate as Cousin Feenix's blanket exoneration of the whole Dombey clan at the expense of Carker, but the two are similar in reflecting only the actual cause-and-effect of plot: the machine of which Heep is the mainspring is also the plot, which in Micawber's account becomes indistinguishable from Heep's own design. Plot exposition stands in for resolution. Heep's criminal responsibility absolves the novel of all further responsibility for him.

VII

The image of the mainspring of the machine, which reduces a complex mechanical process to its simplest component ('HEEP, and only HEEP'), is a useful figure for the function whereby plot mechanism is driven by a principle that needs to be simplified, that is, 'explained' before being disposed of. Dickens had learnt enough from the mystery plot to avail himself on occasion of its violent simplifications. In *Bleak House* the purely functional device of Hortense remains almost exclusively in the realm of the mystery novel, and Dickens does not expend very much energy on providing her with a fully drawn set of motives. And yet even here the demands of realism endow Hortense with a rudimentary kind of humanity, whereby her malignancy figures as the reaction of neglected affection, establishing its own relevance to the design of the novel. The image of 'the Frenchwoman . . . unnoticed, looking on with her lips very tightly set',[17] as Lady Dedlock receives a shawl from her new favourite, is a figure of pure resentment, acutely conscious of her excluded state—as Lady Dedlock is herself excluded from the affection she yearns for and seeks a substitute for in Rosa, the girl who supplants Hortense. Thus Hortense's murder of Tulkinghorn is woven into the design of *Bleak House*, and rendered intelligible as an act of outrage, the illicit alternative to Esther Summerson's self-abasement.[18] But illicit: that much Dickens insists on, and Hortense's claims are never dwelt on. As the keeper's wife says, 'she's mortal high and passionate—powerful high and passionate' (*BH* 312)—and high passion is too dangerous to be tolerated in the community of Bleak House. Even Esther's tolerance draws back from the threat represented by Hortense, and readily finds an image for the nature of the threat: 'There was a lowering energy in her face . . . which seemed to bring visibly before me some woman from the streets of Paris in the reign of terror' (373). Dickens is clearly availing himself of a readily available stereotype in preparing Hortense for the scaffold. High passion, energy, and Frenchness add up to Terror, to that kind of social dissatisfaction

---

[17] Charles Dickens, *Bleak House* (1852–3); ed. Norman Page (Harmondsworth, 1971), 311.

[18] Robert Caserio makes, from his own perspective of 'rescue', a point that interestingly relates to my treatment of Hortense; see *Plot, Story, and the Novel* (Princeton, NJ, 1979), 119.

that *Bleak House*, for all its stringent social criticism, refuses to countenance. Lady Dedlock's own high passion, of course, comes to a sad end; but as with Edith Dombey and Alice Marwood, her repentance is publicly enacted and accommodated. Hortense feels and shows no repentance, and is as a consequence denied access to the narrative community. Scornfully turning her back on that community, she takes with her, as the scapegoat always does, a suggestion of a tale untold, an alternative narrative of which she might be the protagonist, if not the heroine. (Who has not wondered about Mary Crawford's version of events at Mansfield? Or speculated, like Jean Rhys, about Mrs Rochester's story?)

If Hortense's resentment is peripheral to the thematic complex of *Bleak House*, in *Little Dorrit* resentment is one of the twin engines of the plot. As one possible application of the motto *Do Not Forget*, Mrs Clennam's bitter brooding on the past provides the counterweight to the novel's other impulse of gratitude and forgiveness. Thus if the mystery part of the plot is closely linked to the will which was made in gratitude, an equal proportion hinges on Mrs Clennam's vindictive hounding of the sinful. But Mrs Clennam's sins are visited upon her in the novel, and she is offered the opportunity of expiation: as with the other 'officially' vilified characters I have mentioned, she is drawn into the novel's design and resolution. The character 'quite shut out' here is the woman whose aching resentment, like Rosa Dartle's, is offered no place in the novel's scheme of redemption: Miss Wade. She has indeed not forgotten, and her mind is twisted by her recollection of the wrongs she has suffered. She is what Esther Summerson might have become as a consequence of her illegitimacy, but her plot function is closer to that of Hortense. Adopting a subtler plot strategy than in *Bleak House*, where Hortense was little more than the melodramatic foreign villain, Dickens creates a much more interesting figure: Hortense's resentment at being ousted by Rosa, her possessiveness of Lady Dedlock, which counted for relatively little in *Bleak House*, here become the hunger of the outsider, a torment of exclusion which is doomed to perpetuate itself by its morbid sensitivity. Miss Wade is a Dombey fully aware of her excluded state, but ascribing that state to the machinations of others, as in her interpretation of the nurse's kindness as a plot to alienate the children's affections: 'How could I wonder, when I saw their innocent faces shrinking away, and their arms twining round her neck, instead of mine?' (*LD* 557).

It is perfectly plausible that a sensitive child could become distrustful of all affection, and regard all kindness as patronage; in this respect Dickens's portrayal of Miss Wade is courageous and unsentimental. But in making her so completely responsible for her own suffering ('The history of a self-tormentor'), Dickens discredits her as a critic of that society that, on his own showing, is very vulnerable to her criticism. *Little Dorrit* teems with false patrons, or, as Miss Wade calls it, 'swollen patronage and selfishness, calling themselves kindness, protection, benevolence, and other fine names' (*LD* 561); given the appropriateness of this description to much of the patronage in the novel, from William Dorrit through Mrs Gowan and Jack Gowan to Mr Casby, it is strange that Miss Wade's judgement should be so completely discredited, as a distortion wrought by her morbid sensitivity. By the same token, her desire for acceptance and love must be a destructive possessiveness, as in her interpretation of the outgoing nature of her school-friend:

Her plan was, to make them all fond of her—and so drive me wild with jealousy. To be familiar and endearing with them all—and so make me mad with envying them. When we were left alone in our bedroom at night, I would reproach her with my perfect knowledge of her baseness; and then she would cry and cry and say I was cruel, and then I would hold her in my arms till morning: loving her as much as ever, and often feeling as if, rather than suffer so, I could so hold her in my arms and plunge to the bottom of a river—where I would still hold her, after we were both dead. (555)

The startlingly decadent eroticism of this need not blind us to the real torment dramatized here: if on one level Dickens is going out of his way to neutralize his 'self tormentor' through the sheer excess of her resentment and the unreasonableness of her claims, on another he gives an acrid reality to the hunger for acceptance and love that drives her. Her fantasy of drowning with the girl she loves repeats the combination of love and death imaged in Dombey's vision of his wife and daughter 'at the bottom of its clear depth . . . clasped in each other's arms': Dickens seems to be drawing, in imagining Miss Wade's 'twisted' state of mind, on the same imaginative source as in his depiction of the love that elsewhere he posits as the norm. But here Miss Wade's passion cannot be accommodated: the embrace that is potentially a murder, the wish to be together in death rather than separated in life, are impulses that the novel does not understand—or rather, does not recognize except as abnormalities to be shunned, or warned against by that hardly most acute of analysts, Mr Meagles, as the distortions of 'a woman, who, from whatever cause, has a perverted delight in making a sister-woman as wretched as she is (I am old enough to have heard of such)' (277).

We would not expect from Mr Meagles, or from Dickens even, a twentieth-century sophistication about lesbianism. The homosexual element of Miss Wade's attachment is briefly admitted into the novel, and then shunned as an impermissible alternative to the socially sanctioned partnership within the family. Like so many other Dickensian characters, Miss Wade strives to achieve a partnership, some companionship in her bitter rejection of the world; but love, which elsewhere is seen as a desire to make the loved one happy, is here interpreted as a perverse desire to inflict one's own unhappiness on others. What is disturbing about the denunciation of Miss Wade is not its rejection of her morbid possessiveness, but its merging of the several elements of her complex state of mind into a single, simple, evil to which a single, simple, remedy exists. Tattycoram's repentance is made the occasion for the pointing of the moral and the dismissal of Miss Wade from the novel and our concern alike:

'Oh! I have been so wretched,' cried Tattycoram . . . 'always so unhappy, and so repentant! I was afraid of her, from the first time I ever saw her. I knew she had got a power over me, through understanding what was bad in me, so well. It was a madness in me, and she could raise it whenever she liked . . . I have had Miss Wade before me all this time, as if it was my own self grown ripe—turning everything the wrong way, and twisting all good into evil.' (676)

It is the simplicity of the expulsion that is objectionable here, the blandly formulaic 'explanation'. The question *why* Miss Wade could 'raise' the 'madness' in Tattycoram 'whenever she liked' is not given an airing; it is ascribed unquestioningly to 'what was bad in me'. Elsewhere Dickens takes pains to locate the source of such 'bad': here 'good' and 'evil' become simple, distinct, knowable: 'kindness, protection, benevolence' and the other fine names are vindicated, and 'swollen patronage and selfishness' made to seem the figment of a twisted imagination. Thus whatever may have been justifiable in Tattycoram's rebellion, or comprehensible in Miss

Wade's compulsions, is prosed away in Mr Meagles's improving speech, with Little Dorrit as its exemplar:

'I have heard tell, Tattycoram, that her young life has been one of active resignation, goodness, and noble service. Shall I tell you what I consider those eyes of hers that were here just now, to have always looked at, to get that expression?'

'Yes, if you please, sir.'

'Duty, Tattycoram.' (677)

Dickens recognizes that there is something insensitive about Mr Meagles's patronizing of Daniel Doyce, but apparently asks us to accept the same tone, when applied to Tattycoram, as simple benevolence. As alternative to Miss Wade's bitterness, Little Dorrit's 'active resignation, goodness, and noble service' are made to seem justified in themselves, notwithstanding the fact that they have been expended largely upon the unworthy object of William Dorrit. Duty, if defined as a matter of indulging an indolent snob in his fantasies of grandeur, would hardly have seemed an ideal worth pursuing; but defined negatively, as an antidote to the *ressentiment* of Miss Wade, it may seem, if not more attractive, then at least obscurely necessary as a safeguard against the 'dark spirit' (277) against which Mr Meagles warns Tattycoram. Little Dorrit and what she represents have to steal their redemptive energy from the threat of the unresolved resentment of Miss Wade.

If the scapegoat is produced by the inadequate incorporation of the novel's structural principle into its resolution, we should not expect *Great Expectations*, so clear-sighted about its own processes, to harbour a scapegoat. And yet it does contain the figure of Old Orlick, in many ways a sketch for Bradley Headstone. As Pip's 'rival' for Biddy, and in shadowing Pip in London as Headstone does Wrayburn, he serves a plot function roughly analogous to that of Headstone. A more important parallel, though, is in his obsessive hatred of Pip, his resentment of everything that Pip has and that is denied him: 'You was always in old Orlick's way since ever you was a child' (*GE* 403). Old Orlick, in short, stands in a line of development from Uriah Heep, through Miss Wade to Bradley Headstone. The difference is that he is used to develop the novel's implications rather than to muffle them. To understand his relevance is to find the novel's implications extended and reinforced by it; to understand, say, Heep's relevance is to note a certain obtuseness in David Copperfield himself, an obtuseness to which his novel acquiesces in the comic vilification of Heep. *Great Expectations* embodies its positive values of fidelity and friendship in Joe and Biddy, in whom these values speak for themselves, and Orlick is not called upon to provide the occasion for their vindication. In the flawed world of *Great Expectations*, Old Orlick is intelligible; that is, the novel understands him as *Little Dorrit* does not understand Miss Wade. He is not, like Miss Wade, made the object of a homily on duty: there is no Little Dorrit around who needs to be commended at his expense. Orlick's significance, in other words, is allowed to reside more in himself.

In the first place, Orlick is a reminder of what Pip might have been but for the love of Joe: a friendless, neglected orphan, whose only hope for survival is to be 'taken up', like Magwitch, by various patrons. Orlick, in fact, having lost his job through Pip's intervention, is taken up by Compeyson, Magwitch's perfidious partner, in one of those coincidences that Dickens contrives in order to underline the interconnectedness of his themes. Ultimately Orlick is not treated very much more charitably than Uriah Heep (both, after all, end up in prison); but at least he is not called upon to bear the burden of the novel's guilt. Indeed, if the scapegoat characteristically serves to exculpate its community, Orlick explicitly attempts to inculpate Pip. Adapting the novel's formula of debt and payment to his own distorted perception, Orlick enables us to see Pip's loneliness and feelings of rejection as relative to a much more desolating solitude, that of the consciously unlikeable person; Orlick is to Pip as Uriah Heep is to David Copperfield, and Bradley Headstone to Eugene Wrayburn. In Orlick Dickens seems to be externalizing that plot principle that elsewhere remains concealed, whereby the happiness of the protagonist is purchased at the price of the vilification of others. Dickens does provide Orlick with some legitimate grounds of grievance (Pip cost him his job at Miss Havisham's), but more powerful than this is his strange resentment of Pip's position as favourite: 'You was favoured, and he was bullied and beat. Old Orlick bullied and beat, eh? Now you pays for it. You done it; now you pays for it' (405). Though Pip may not have intended to harm Orlick, his very presence militated against Orlick's interests, and he is brought to account for that. It is as if Florence Dombey were to be arraigned for Carker's death: absurd, and yet a weird recognition of a causal link. As Q. D. Leavis has shown, 'Pip, though, or through, having acted for the best has Orlick on his conscience as though the situation of being "guilty yet innocent" were the human condition, inevitable'. Or, in Julian Moynahan's words: 'The novel dramatises the loss of innocence, and does not glibly present the hope of a redemptory second birth for either its guilty hero or the guilty society which shaped him.'[19]

VIII

In *Our Mutual Friend* the hope of a redemptory second birth, if not for society then for the guilty hero, provides, ostensibly, much of the narrative drive. Indeed, this is perhaps the most redemption-directed of all Dickens's novels; and yet in no other novel is there as strong a contrary pull towards dissolution and damnation. The figure 'quite shut out', though ultimately still subordinated to the inclusive movement of the plot, acquires a prominence that suggests that Dickens was moving towards a recognition of its imaginative potency. As if to counteract that recognition, the contrary redemptive strain is urged all the more strongly, resulting in a starker disjunction between official morality and imaginative energy than in any other novel by Dickens. And yet, in becoming in a sense the acknowledged embodiment of that disjunction, Bradley Headstone opens up Dickens's fiction to a hitherto averted challenge, that of the unsocialized spirit of resentment.

Our Mutual Friend's redemptive theme finds its most potent expression in the trope of rescue: literally a rescue from drowning, figuratively a rescue from spiritual death. It is thus appropriate and yet disquieting that the novel should open on a parodic inversion of the idea of rescue, Gaffer Hexam's fishing for corpses to plunder:

In these times of ours, though concerning the exact year there is no need to be precise, a boat of dirty and disreputable appearance, with two figures in

---

[19] Q. D. Leavis, 'How We Must Read *Great Expectations*', *Dickens the Novelist* (1970; rpt. Harmondsworth, 1972), 404–5; Julian Moynahan, 'The Hero's Guilt: The Case of *Great Expectations*', *Essays in Criticism*, 10 (1960), 60–79, rpt. in Norman Page (ed.), *Hard Times, Great Expectations and Our Mutual Friend: A Casebook* (London, 1979), 103–18. Moynahan's extraordinarily interesting essay contains the most thoroughgoing discussion of Orlick's role that I know.

it, floated on the Thames, between Southwark Bridge which is of iron, and London Bridge which is of stone, as an autumn evening was closing in.

The figures in this boat were those of a strong man with ragged grizzly hair and a sun-browned face, and a dark girl of nineteen or twenty, sufficiently like him to be recognisable as his daughter. The girl rowed, pulling a pair of sculls very easily; the man, with the rudder-lines slack in his hands, and his hands loose in his waistband, kept an eager look-out. . . . there was no clue to what he looked for, but he looked for something, with a most intent and searching gaze. The tide, which had turned an hour before, was running down, and his eyes watched every little race and eddy in its broad sweep, as the boat made slight headway against it, or drove stern foremost before it, according as he directed his daughter by a movement of his head. She watched his face as earnestly as she watched the river. But, in the intensity of her look there was a touch of dread and horror. (*OMF* 1)

Like so many of Dickens's novels, *Our Mutual Friend* opens on something of a compendium of the novel's imaginative sources. In the first place, the mortality rate of the characters we meet in the first chapter is inordinately high (exceeded only by *Great Expectations*, which opens in a churchyard): of the four, one is already dead and two will die, all three by drowning. The participants, moreover, enact in their own way the alienation that is at the heart of the novel. Of these, one is shut out in the most grisly of senses: the dead man being towed behind the boat, who is to be 'revived' as John Harmon, is 'present' in the scene only as a tell-tale ripple in the wake of the boat. The living participants, however, are separated from each other hardly less absolutely. In a grim echo of Dombey and Daughter, Hexam and Lizzie, literally in the same boat, are engaged, with whatever revulsion on her part, in a common task, hunting as a couple. But the near-instinctive communication whereby the father 'directed his daughter by a movement of his head' is rendered ominous by the 'touch of dread and horror' with which she watches his face—a horror that, as we are to find out, is of a piece with her determination to release her brother from this environment and this livelihood, that is, to disperse the family.

The novel starts, then, on a family group that is also a partnership, both destined to be disbanded. In this, it serves to introduce the multiple pairings and ruptures that make up the complicated plot. That principle of partnership which characteristically structures Dickens's social vision is here all-pervasive: human beings are complemented by other human beings, either in antipathy or attraction, common purpose or mutual exploitation, dolls for the dressing or corpses for the plundering. The Veneering gathering becomes, in this respect as in others, a grotesque parody of the values and procedures of society, distinguished from other groupings only by the perplexing promiscuity of Veneering's pairings: 'Twemlow . . . approaches the conclusion that he really is Veneering's oldest friend, when his brain softens again and all is lost, through his eyes encountering Veneering and the large man [Podsnap, who mistook Twemlow for Veneering five minutes earlier] linked together as twin brothers . . . and through his ears informing him in the tones of Mrs. Veneering that the same large man is to be baby's godfather' (9). As in Society, so everywhere: partnerships are constantly being negotiated and renegotiated, if not everywhere with the fickleness of Mr Veneering. The conceit of being 'linked together as twin brothers', for instance, can be taken through a variety of permutations, from the casually mentioned 'two young sisters what tied themselves together with a handkercher' (22) before drowning themselves, through Venus and Wegg 'interlocked like a couple of preposterous gladiators' (486), to that final fatal 'iron ring' connecting Bradley Headstone and Rogue Riderhood, after being 'twinned' through Headstone's disguising himself as Riderhood.

Twin brother, godfather, oldest friend—the novel abounds in the kind of pairings comically adumbrated here. Indeed, to list the partnerships in the novel is tantamount to providing a synopsis of the plot. Gaffer's partnership with Lizzie is doubled by Rogue Riderhood's reliance on *his* daughter Pleasant; Bella Wilfer and her father are united in their resistance to the domestic tyranny of Mrs Wilfer; Lizzie and Charley are constant companions until he leaves to become a pupil teacher with Bradley Headstone; John Harmon becomes Mr Boffin's secretary but also his partner in the deception of Bella and Wegg; Mr Boffin makes of Bella Wilfer an unwilling partner in his humiliation of John Harmon, and of his wife an unwilling partner in the fooling of Bella; Mr Boffin and Silas Wegg co-operate in the Rise and Fall of the Russian Empire; Venus, disappointed in his love for Pleasant Riderhood, becomes Wegg's accomplice in the defrauding of Boffin, only to combine with Boffin in the exposure of his erstwhile partner; Fledgeby uses Riah as an unwilling accomplice in his fleecing of indigent members of society; the Lammles form a pact to prey together upon the world, in the spirit of which they conspire with Fledgeby to marry him to Georgiana Podsnap; Mrs Lammle involves Twemlow in her rescue of Georgiana; Jenny Wren and Lizzie share a house, as do Eugene Wrayburn and Mortimer Lightwood, who are also business associates; Betty Higden and Sloppy share the labour of child-minding; Sloppy becomes Mr Boffin's agent in the mortification of Wegg; Eugene uses Mr Dolls as his instrument; Emma Peecher and Mary Anne are united not only by the pupil–teacher relationship but by their watching for Bradley Headstone and Charley. And Bradley Headstone, rejected by his erstwhile protégé and companion, forms his fatal partnership with Riderhood.

In narrative terms, the principle of partnership is a dynamic one; that is, the plot works towards the dissolution of some of these partnerships, the consolidation of others, and the formation of new partnerships. Thus Mr Boffin and Rokesmith are revealed to have been in league with each other; Sloppy turns out to have been Mr Boffin's agent in the bower, in a comic parody of the shadowing of Wrayburn; Venus and Wegg prove not to be partners at all; Venus instead at last prevails upon Pleasant Riderhood not to regard him 'in that bony light'; Riah can rupture his 'partnership' with Fledgeby; Mr Lammle, on hearing of the true identity of Riah's principal, can terminate his enthralment to Fledgeby, and the Lammles can undertake the rest of their lives together; Bella commits herself to the idyllic pairing with John Harmon; Eugene and Lizzie get married, and it is strongly suggested that Sloppy may be that *He* that Jenny Wren has been anticipating; even Twemlow and Lightwood at the very last form a strange partnership on which to end the novel.

But the single partnership on which the novel opens anticipates other partnerships, not merely in *being* a partnership, but in the nature of the business being transacted. If Hexam and Lizzie on one level prefigure the partnership of Reginald Wilfer and Bella and *their* far more congenial outing on the river, they also foreshadow the predatory partnership of the Lammles, united in the plundering of the corpses of Society: 'And who now so pleasant or so well assorted as Mr. and Mrs. Alfred Lammle, he all sparkle, she all gracious contentment, both at occasional intervals exchanging looks like partners at cards, who played a game against All

England?' (135). The Lammles, in turn, act out a sardonic travesty of the union of the Harmons.[20] This kind of moralized patterning, whereby the normative is implicitly opposed to the aberrant, is of course not new in or to Dickens; but the Wilfer–Lammle modulation on the pattern enacts in relatively simple form that tension between the redemptive and the expulsive movements which generates the major narrative impetus: the expulsive carefully, indeed schematically, balanced by the redemptive, and yet not cancelled by it.

IX

This tension and balance, too, are anticipated in the opening scene. On one level, Lizzie's complicity with her father prefigures her rescue of Eugene Wrayburn. Through extraordinarily skilful plotting Dickens will contrive that the same woman will use the same hated skill to retrieve from the water, not a dead man to be robbed, but the half-dead man she is to redeem. From coerced partnership with the man she loves as her father, Lizzie moves to willing dedication to the man she will love as her husband, and thereby rescue from the moral death to which he is in danger of succumbing. Eugene Wrayburn, first discovered 'buried alive' at a Veneering dinner (11), fastidiously disdainful of the dance of death around him and yet part of it, is roused by the news of the discovery of the corpse of the Man from Nowhere—a discovery in which Lizzie has played her part. The summons from dinner, in other words, initiates his revitalizing estrangement from the world of Society.

And yet, this redemptive potential does not altogether dispel the macabre resonances of the opening. Lizzie Hexam is not, as we have noted, the first Dickens heroine to be intimately acquainted with death; but she *is* the only one to be introduced to us actually towing a corpse. Nor is this association entirely inappropriate to her function in the plot. If her rescue of Wrayburn aesthetically closes the pattern established by Gaffer's robbing of the drowned corpse, it

---

[20] Thus, after the 'mutual agreement' between the Lammles 'to work together in furtherance of our own schemes' (126), 'the happy pair, with this hopeful marriage contract thus signed, sealed, and delivered, repair homeward . . . in the light of the setting sun' (127); the newly-wed Bella and John after the signing and sealing of *their* marriage contract, 'turned homeward by a rosy path which the gracious sun struck out for them in its setting' (671).

also issues in the mutual drowning of Bradley Headstone and Rogue Riderhood. Lizzie's influence, regenerating the morally moribund Wrayburn, in the same narrative movement destroys the respectable Bradley Headstone. The opening, characteristically projected towards its own resolution, draws on imaginative springs that cannot be contained in that resolution.

Indeed, whereas the opening chapter in the first place sets in motion the process of Wrayburn's rescue, it no less crucially introduces a third character and a second relation: that of the excluded partner. Father and daughter are accosted by Gaffer's erstwhile partner, Rogue Riderhood. 'I am no pardner of yours' (4) says Gaffer to Riderhood, in the interest of 'the high moralities' (5)—that is, his distinction between taking money from a corpse and robbing a live sailor. It is extremely difficult, even perverse, to summon up sympathy for Rogue Riderhood, but it is only fair to note that he is the victim of a very tenuous moral distinction. It is a distinction, though, that is ratified by Miss Abbey Potterson, that voice of respectability, in telling him 'the Fellowships don't want you at all' (63). Rejected by his former partner, 'quite shut out' from the Jolly Fellowship-Porters, shunned by all, this victim of respectable morality is driven by his irrational resentment towards the fatal partnership with Bradley Headstone, that other figure of resentment. Their death, clenched together in a fatal embrace, is as much predestined by this opening as is Lizzie's rescue of Eugene Wrayburn, and this murderous impulse counts for at least as much in the dynamics of the novel as the redemptive strain. But Rogue Riderhood is merely the quintessence of a resentment that in Bradley Headstone is contextualized much more fully and much more subversively to the redemptive pattern. The schematically conceived pattern of the novel needs Headstone, the Other whose destruction is to effect the redemption of his favoured opposite. The plot is, as it were, conspiring against him: he is a victim of both the redemptive and the damnatory pattern.

X

I have mentioned, in the introductory chapter, René Girard's distinction between the scapegoat *in* the text and the scapegoat *of* the text, a distinction that may bear repetition at this point. According to Girard, 'The scapegoat that we must disengage from the text for ourselves is the scapegoat *of* the text. He cannot appear in the text though he controls all its themes; he is never mentioned as such. He cannot become the theme of the text that he *shapes*. This is not a theme but a mechanism for giving *structure*.' This usefully sums up the difference between characters such as Magwitch and a figure like Bradley Headstone: the former does become a theme of his novel in being acknowledged as the scapegoat of the judicial process which condemns him; the latter remains unacknowledged as the 'hidden structural principle'[21] that his resentment constitutes. He is the representative of a dark vision of obsession and exclusion inseparable from the dream of love and fellowship. As unacknowledged structural principle, Headstone is in a precise etymological sense the energumen of *Our Mutual Friend*: possessed as he is, he is also the active principle of the plot; having been worked on, he works the plot.

Indeed, Headstone may be seen as the scapegoat not only of his own novel, but of Dickens's fiction in general, in that in him are activated those sources of energy that Dickens's plots most anxiously resist in their ostensible directedness towards union and marriage. Narrative patterns that elsewhere are redemptive pursue him unremittingly to his doom. Working his way, like Oliver Twist, out of a pauper background, he falls into the hands of one of the most unregenerate scoundrels in all of Dickens. Having achieved a decent place in a useful profession, apparently equipped for the 'modest life of usefulness and happiness' awaiting Little Dorrit and Arthur Clennam at the end of their novel (*LD* 688), he is deprived of its rewards by a love that is as obsessive as it is hopeless. Having won the respect of a young man he has patronized, he is contemptuously spurned by his protégé and partner: his interest in Charley, not unlike that of Magwitch in Pip, is repaid with respectable horror at his criminal deed, without the later relenting of a Pip. Loved, like David Copperfield, by a woman intellectually and emotionally suited to his ambitions, Headstone remains untouched by her self-sacrificing devotion. In his loneliness he contracts a partnership of interest and convenience, like any number of Dickens characters, and is killed by his partner. The victim of class snobbery, like Mr Mell, he is goaded by it to his

[21] René Girard, *The Scapegoat*, trans. Yvonne Freccero (1982; London, 1986), 118, 119.

death. In him, the death-directed passion of Miss Wade and Rosa Dartle finally achieves its destination. And of all the partnerships in Dickens, that between Bradley Headstone and Eugene Wrayburn is the most obsessive and the most deadly.[22]

Not the least strange thing about Bradley Headstone is that he should have been elected for this fate in the first place. His qualities of sober industry are those that Dickens elsewhere takes pains to reward, just as, conversely, Wrayburn's indolent cynicism is, in Steerforth, Harthouse, and Jack Gowan, a blight upon the women who love them. It would be naïve to complain that in the interests of the higher morality Eugene Wrayburn should have been punished as Steerforth is punished. In some ways the unwaveringly unsentimental treatment of the outcast and of the favourite is more honest in *Our Mutual Friend* than in the earlier novel: Dickens has come to see that the favourites of fortune simply *are* favoured, whether fairly or not, because their qualities are of a kind to claim concessions that mere virtue could never have earned. David Copperfield recognizes the irrationality of his infatuation with Steerforth even as he yields to it: 'There was an ease in his manner—a gay and light manner it was, but not swaggering—which I still believe to have borne a kind of enchantment with it' (*DC* 83).

It is part, perhaps, of this gay and light manner to feel or affect no concern for those less fortunate than itself. Indeed, there may be something in the favourite which constitutionally hates the outcast, seems to regard his abjectness as an affront; and something in the favourite which fascinates the outcast. The combination produces a bond of surprising intimacy, as when Headstone, consciously at a disadvantage with only the callow Charley as support, confronts Wrayburn on his own hearth:

Composedly smoking, he leaned an elbow on the chimney-piece, at the side of the fire, and looked at the schoolmaster. It was a cruel look, in its cold disdain of him, as a creature of no worth. The schoolmaster looked at him, and that, too, was a cruel look, though of the different kind, that it had a raging jealousy and fiery wrath in it.

Very remarkably, neither Eugene Wrayburn nor Bradley Headstone looked at all at the boy. Through the ensuing dialogue, those two, no

---

[22] With the significant exception of Jasper and Edwin Drood in Dickens's last, unfinished novel. I discuss this below.

matter who spoke, or whom was addressed, looked at each other. There
was some secret, sure perception between them, which set them against one
another in all ways. (*OMF* 288)

The 'ensuing dialogue', in the event, seems to go all Wrayburn's
way. It is easy to see the point of the young Henry James's
complaint that 'The friction of two *men*, of two characters, of two
passions, produces stronger sparks than Wrayburn's boyish
repartees and Headstone's melodramatic commonplaces'.[23] The
interchange is at the level of schoolboy insults; Headstone, as he
himself is painfully aware, is not capable of anything other than
'melodramatic commonplaces', and Wrayburn does not pay him
the compliment of carving him as a dish fit for the gods: the insult
resides exactly in his air of not making an effort. But James is
surely wrong when he continues: 'Such scenes as this are useful in
fixing the limits of Mr. Dickens's insight.' Dickens's insight, it is
true, is not attuned to the refined savagery which James might
later have devised for the occasion, but in the 'secret, sure
perception' between the two men there is a quality of interaction
that James's term 'friction' does little justice to, and that his
reading of the confrontation in terms of 'two *men*, of two
characters, of two passions' subtly distorts. Much of the tension of
the scene inheres in the unstated assumptions underlying it, in the
divisions, pressures, and hostilities that James was perhaps too
civilized or, in 1865, possibly just too American to appreciate. For
whereas Wrayburn and Headstone are strong individuals ('two
men'), they confront each other also as members of two different
classes, near-instinctively and instantly recognizing in the other an
opposite term—not a simple upper–lower dichotomy, but a much
deadlier battle for the middle ground, an area sharply enough
defined, and yet made vulnerable to constant renegotiation by that
moral component which has always complicated the word
gentleman. This component is clumsily invoked by Headstone in
claiming 'a right to be considered a better man than [Wrayburn],
with better reasons for being proud' (293). In class terms,
however, Wrayburn is incontestably the 'better man', and it is
only by restricting the battle to those lines that he can ward off

[23] Henry James, review of *Our Mutual Friend*, *The Nation*, (1865), rpt. as 'The
Limitations of Dickens', in *Views and Reviews* (Boston, Mass., 1908), and in George
H. Ford and Lauriat Lane, Jr. (eds.), *The Dickens Critics* (Ithaca, NY, 1961), 52.

the moral force of Headstone's claim. Conversely, Headstone in trying to shift the battle on to moral ground, helplessly reveals by that very act his vulnerability, a consciousness of 'origin' and 'bringing-up' (293) that has been the driving force behind his whole history. Wrayburn does not need to protest his social status to Headstone: he knows that Headstone's very hatred is a recognition of it.

And as Headstone hates and envies the automatic assumption of superiority which comes with privilege, so Wrayburn hates the avid belligerence of the consciously self-made man—and perhaps, 'so soon bored, so constantly, so fatally' (147), envies the goal-directed single-mindedness driving the schoolmaster. In his insistence on calling Headstone 'Schoolmaster' there is a strange desire to humiliate him for his calling—strange, and yet understandable, as coming from a man who, 'putting his legs up' can say languidly 'I hate my profession' (19). Having allowed himself to be pushed by family pressure into a profession of which he cannot see the point, Wrayburn's discontent at the futility of his existence issues in a resentment of the energy and purpose which he lacks: 'If there is a word in the dictionary under any letter from A to Z that I abominate, it is energy' (20). Wrayburn's contempt for Headstone is of a piece with his abomination of energy—a resentment of his own shortcomings. In an odd sense, Wrayburn does recognize in Headstone the better man, and hates him for it.

The battle is thus more equally waged than appears on the surface, an equality which accounts for the deadly goading which follows. Both Headstone and Wrayburn have an ally, a potentially benign partnership: Lightwood's rudimentary moral sense could be of value to Wrayburn, and Headstone's concern for Charley is a possibly humanizing form of affection. Yet both men momentarily lose all awareness of their allies in their exclusive consciousness of each other: the attraction to the hated other is that much stronger than the affection for the similar. And though the partnerships regroup after the routing of Headstone, a bond has been created between Headstone and Wrayburn which can be severed only by the death of one or the other. Headstone's attempt upon Wrayburn's life is the consummation of that relation; after that, both men are thrown back upon their allies: Wrayburn to be sustained by the devotion of his lifelong friend, Headstone to be rejected by the self-seeking respectability of his protégé.

The description of love at first sight may serve also to characterize the hatred between Wrayburn and Headstone: 'Love at first sight is a trite expression quite sufficiently discussed; enough that in certain smouldering natures like this man's, that passion leaps into a blaze, and makes such head as fire does in a rage of wind, when other passions, but for its mastery, could be held in chains' (341). This perverse partnership is based on a hatred so intense as to constitute a bond of attraction—or alternatively, an attraction so strongly resisted as to manifest itself as hatred. Either way, the mutual awareness rivals, even surpasses in its intensity its ostensible cause, the attraction exerted by Lizzie Hexam on both men. Headstone, we remember, is made aware of Wrayburn almost immediately after meeting Lizzie for the first time; emerging from her house, Headstone and Charley cross the path of Eugene Wrayburn 'holding possession of twice as much pavement as another would have claimed' (229). Headstone's interest is immediate and strong, and thereafter his obsession with Lizzie is inseparable from his resentment of Wrayburn. Wrayburn likewise asks Lizzie about her brother's companion; for all his nonchalance, he has noted Headstone with the same acuteness of instant antagonism. Lizzie gradually becomes not so much the object of their affections as the focus of their enmity. The two men seek each other out, divert their frustrated passion for Lizzie on to each other: 'Then soberly and plainly, Mortimer, I goad the schoolmaster to madness. . . . The amiable occupation has been the solace of my life, since I was baulked in the manner unnecessary to recall' (542).

It's an odd kind of occupation and a strange solace. For all Wrayburn's flippancy on the subject, it is clear that the goading of Headstone has become a matter of deadly seriousness for him. There is no apparent motive for his torment of Headstone: he does not take him seriously as a rival for Lizzie's favour, and claims to disregard him as a human being. And yet, in this partnership founded on temperamental, class, and sexual antipathy there seems to be a mutual need, and Wrayburn's need is to humiliate Headstone. There is something of the air of a tryst about his nocturnal meetings with Headstone: 'I do it thus: I stroll out after dark, stroll a little way, look in at a window and furtively look out for the schoolmaster' (542). If Wrayburn's taunting of Headstone has taken the place of his meetings with Lizzie, to Headstone himself Lizzie has in a sense come to represent Wrayburn, as he confesses to her:

'He is nothing to you, I think,' said Lizzie, with an indignation she could not repress.

'Oh yes, he is. There you mistake. He is much to me. . . . With Mr. Eugene Wrayburn in my mind, I went on. With Mr. Eugene Wrayburn in my mind, I spoke to you just now. With Mr. Eugene Wrayburn in my mind, I have been set aside and I have been cast out.' (399)

This rather curious declaration merely makes explicit what the novel dramatizes: that Headstone is increasingly driven by hatred of Wrayburn as much as by love of Lizzie. Surprisingly, his hatred is reciprocated as his love is not; and his hatred manifests itself in symptoms not unlike those of love. Headstone's presence outside Wrayburn's rooms, for instance, though explicable as the jealous fantasy of Wrayburn's harbouring Lizzie there, becomes, as dramatized, a triangle of quite another kind, with Headstone excluded from the companionship of Wrayburn and Lightwood inside. His eavesdropping on the conversation of the two friends serves merely to satisfy him that she is not there, and it is not an exclusion that he seems to register as such; but the image of Headstone on the dark stairs outside Wrayburn's rooms lingers as that of a jealous lover.[24] The passion of Bradley Headstone thus develops also in this respect the implications of other Dickens novels: if the power of the heroine resides in her ability to arouse male desire, that desire in its turn activates and is activated by other but related desires and lacks.

Lizzie Hexam, as representative of the sanctioned values within the novel, presides, narratively speaking, over the systematic thwarting of Headstone's plot of social and sexual ambition. It is therefore appropriate that Headstone's nemesis should have been prepared for him, as we have seen, by that encounter between Gaffer Hexam and Rogue Riderhood in the first chapter, an encounter at which Lizzie too was present. As her redemptive

[24] Eve Kosofsky Sedgwick has explored this aspect of *Our Mutual Friend*, *Great Expectations*, and *The Mystery of Edwin Drood* in *Between Men: English Literature and Male Homosocial Desire* (New York, 1985). Drawing on Girard's concept of triangular desire, she argues that its effect is to decentre the ostensible object of desire, that is, usually, the woman, and to shift the emphasis to the bond of rivalry between the males, thus perpetuating in fiction the power relations prevailing in a male-dominated society: 'Specifically, each of these novels sites an important plot in triangular, heterosexual romance—in the Romance tradition—and then changes its focus as if by compulsion from the heterosexual bonds of the triangle to the male-homosocial one, here called "erotic rivalry"' (162).

function is launched here, so is Riderhood's course of destruction, to intersect with the departure of Headstone, excluded from the companionship of his kind, from Wrayburn's chambers. The sardonic workings of the plot provide Headstone with the partner he has lacked, in this most unreliable of companions. In selecting Riderhood as potentially useful tool ('Here is an instrument. Can I use it?'—551), Headstone assumes his part in the complex of manipulative relationships underpinning the novel: his action doubles, for instance, that of Wrayburn in his ruthless use of Mr Dolls to find out Lizzie's whereabouts.

More and more, then, Headstone becomes the locus of relational types that in him are taken to their most disastrous consequences. His patronage of Charley, for instance, originates in a benign enough concern for the boy, a concern that elsewhere takes the form, say, of Mrs Boffin's whim to adopt an orphan, or Lizzie's friendship with Jenny Wren. Charley's desertion of Headstone is perhaps the most devastating blow suffered by this most rejected of figures, representing the loss of such human warmth as he has ever experienced: 'he drooped his devoted head when the boy was gone, and shrank together on the floor, and grovelled there, with the palms of his hands tight-clasping his hot temples, in unutterable misery, and unrelieved by a single tear' (713).

Of the various terminations of partnership in this novel, this is the most painful. It repeats, in a different register, the drubbing that Fledgeby is given by Lammle, or the humiliating expulsion of Wegg into a dustcart; but Fledgeby and Wegg are not conceived as capable of this kind of pain, which is why they are dealt a punishment suited to their sensibilities. Headstone is our measure, in human terms, of what such rejection means. He is the bearer, in short, of much of the novel's pain, and it is a not inconsiderable burden: the 'desolate air of utter and complete loneliness [that] fell upon him, like a visible shade' (710) is the terrible fate that only Dickens's most wretched characters suffer.

XI

But it is in his conception and experience of love that Headstone most starkly confronts the novel's wistful sentimentalities. If Dickens can rhapsodize, apropos of Bella's marriage to John Harmon, that 'oh, 'tis love, 'tis love, that makes the world go round'

(671), he can also, through Headstone, explore the grimmer possibilities of love as propulsive force. Headstone's wild declaration of love to Lizzie merges the destructive and the redemptive potential of love in picturing sexual attraction as an immense, almost literal, 'drawing' force. Initially he conceives of Lizzie's influence as liberating, though his terms are characteristically violent: 'If I were shut up in a strong prison, you would draw me out. I should break through the wall to come to you. If I were lying on a sick bed, you would draw me up—to stagger to your feet and fall there' (396). Headstone hypothetically attributes to Lizzie the power Little Dorrit actually exercises upon Clennam, in coming to his sick-bed and leading him from the Marshalsea. But Headstone can spell out, as *Little Dorrit* cannot, the helplessness of the male in being 'drawn' to liberation—'to stagger to your feet and fall there'. And the rest of his declaration develops female power not as a liberating attraction but as a destructive seduction: 'You could draw me to fire, you could draw me to water, you could draw me to the gallows, you could draw me to any death, you could draw me to anything I have most avoided, you could draw me to any exposure and disgrace' (*OMF* 397).

This is clearly meant to be read with the redemptive powers of love, the influence that John Harmon exercises upon Bella, or Lizzie upon Wrayburn, and does not claim to be a definitive statement: 'What other men may mean when they use that expression, I cannot tell', says Headstone (397). But redemptive love is itself dependent for its effect upon the power released by destructive passion. As described by Lizzie Hexam, it is entirely self-sacrificing: 'Her heart—is given him, with all its love and truth. She would joyfully die with him, or, better than that, die for him' (349). Thus this self-effacing love, like Little Dorrit's, conceives of its own extreme as death. In the event, though, Lizzie dies neither for nor with Wrayburn; on the contrary, she rescues him from both physical and spiritual death. It is Bradley who dies for the beloved, enacting the possibility that energizes the depiction of love throughout Dickens's fiction. That association between death and love that so many of his novels hint at is most fully dramatized in Bradley Headstone; in Lizzie it remains a noble willingness. Like most of Dickens's heroines, her strength is constituted on the helplessness of the male. In a gesture that we by now recognize as the heroine's assumption of power, Lizzie sustains her new husband: 'When the ceremony was done, and all the rest departed from the room, she drew her arm under his head, and laid her own head down upon the pillow by his side' (752).

The emphasis is, of course, on the restorative power of this possession. The 'utter helplessness of the wreck of him that lay cast ashore there now' (753) connects Wrayburn's regeneration with the death that in a sense it atones for, the drowning of Steerforth. But the instrumentality of Headstone implicates paradoxically the heroine in the incapacitation of the man she is to redeem. Mary Graham's touch, we remember, 'smote' Tom Pinch; in the violent consequences of Lizzie's effect on Headstone and Wrayburn that blow is literalized: lamenting his own 'cursed carelessness', Wrayburn says to Lizzie: 'You have struck it dead, I think, and I sometimes almost wish you had struck me dead along with it' (692). In the event he is almost granted his almost-wish: he comes close to being struck dead, if not by Lizzie, then by the man who in a sense becomes the instrument of her redemptive-avenging function. Wrayburn's metaphor implicates Lizzie in the violence of the redemptive process; in terms of plot-accountability, Lizzie strikes at Wrayburn through Headstone, and the attack delivers Wrayburn over to her ministrations. Headstone's damnation is the prerequisite for Wrayburn's redemption: his destructive passion activates Lizzie's self-sacrificing devotion. As the bitterest consequence of his deed, Headstone is made to recognize his own instrumentality: 'For then he saw that through his desperate attempt to separate those two for ever, he had been made the means of uniting them. That he had dipped his hands in blood, to mark himself a miserable fool and tool' (791). He has also been the fool and tool of Dickens's narrative purpose: that 'Fate, or Providence, or be the Directing Power what it might' which he curses for 'having put a fraud upon him' (791–2), is also the plot, intent upon uniting the lovers.

If there is any clumsiness in Dickens's handling of his wonderfully convoluted plot, it is in the thematic burden it places upon a relationship that has something almost self-confessedly *ad hoc* about it. Given the novel's examination of exploitation as the basis of relationships, the partnership of Headstone and Riderhood is intelligible enough as an extreme of malignant coupling. But Headstone is destroyed by love, not by lovelessness, and there is something awkward about Riderhood's standing in for a relationship to which he has been so extraneous. The consummation the novel works towards, the true price of Lizzie's virtue, is the mutual drowning of Wrayburn and Headstone. But such a resolution is not allowed for, either in the romance plot or the redemptive fiction; thus Riderhood, anointed for the role by his parodic rescue from death by water, becomes Wrayburn's surrogate, freeing Wrayburn for the restorative powers of Lizzie.

Under the circumstances, this is a skilful enough solution to a plotting problem, and suffers only by comparison with Dickens's handling of a related complex in *Great Expectations*. There the dynamic principle of destructive love, though less fully released than in *Our Mutual Friend*, is not subordinated to the claims of romantic resolution. Estella, brought up to break men's hearts, is the exponent of a power that the other heroines possess but never use so consciously. Pip's infatuation with her is ruefully recognized for what it is, the aspiration of youth and deprivation to the consolations of the fairy-tale. The romance plot is transferred to Pip's self-deluding imagination; the slowly emerging 'real' plot is revealed to have had its origins in Miss Havisham's savage resentment on the one hand, and the jealous murder committed by Estella's mother on the other, leading to Magwitch's incrimination. We might say, with some schematic simplification, that the vindictive plot is here authorized by Miss Havisham, the redemptive plot by Magwitch, and the romance plot by Pip: the resolution then being the rewriting and revision of that romance in the light of Pip's painfully acquired knowledge of his own status as plotted-against protagonist, victim both of Miss Havisham's resentment and Magwitch's gratitude. Pip comes to see the inadequacy of his romantic infatuation in the face of a love like Miss Havisham's that is 'inseparable from jealousy at all times, and from sharp pain' (*GE* 290).

Miss Havisham's definition of love has been formed by her acquaintance with Compeyson, the lover-enemy who broke faith not only with her but also with Magwitch, whose desire for revenge is no less obsessive than hers. The broken engagement and the betrayed partnership thus reinforce each other in driving a plot of which Pip is the victim-beneficiary, the fool and tool. Magwitch achieves what Miss Havisham only symbolically attempts through Estella, the fatal embrace of the enemy-partner, and he dies as much because of his vengeful attack upon Compeyson as because of Compeyson's betrayal of him. This embrace, then, more fully engages with and resolves the energies that have impelled the plot than does the equivalent embrace in *Our Mutual Friend*. Furthermore, in *Great Expectations* the alternative to this murderous love is given its due without any attempt to suggest that it's what makes the world go round. Joe's affection for Pip, and Pip's growing loyalty to Magwitch, self-sacrificing as they both are, need not claim any more for their quiet usefulness than the plot can support.

If *Our Mutual Friend* is nevertheless, for all its implausibilities and sentimentalities, in many ways Dickens's most powerful novel, it owes much of its energy to the presence of Bradley Headstone, in whom Dickens at last fully dramatizes the darkest possibilities of his fiction, the most destructive potential of partnership and of love. Our sense that Carker, Rosa Dartle, Miss Wade, Uriah Heep, Old Orlick, even Hortense, stand for more than they are allowed to express, is here confirmed in a character who personifies all their resentment at rejection and dies for it. Given this development, it is not surprising that in the unfinished *Mystery of Edwin Drood* Dickens seems to have given even greater prominence to the type that elsewhere figures as the scapegoat: John Jasper, as far as we can tell, ceases to be what I have called the unacknowledged mainspring of the plot, and becomes overtly the prime mover. The love interest, which elsewhere provides the ostensible driving force, is here subordinated to Jasper's murderous love. To put it differently, whereas it may be possible to regard *Our Mutual Friend* as being 'about' Lizzie Hexam and Eugene Wrayburn, or John Harmon and Bella Wilfer, here there is little doubt that Rosa Bud and Edwin Drood, even Tartar, are generated by the murder plot and secondary to it. There is no redemptive plot in *Edwin Drood*. Neville Landless will of course exonerate himself, but there is never any doubt as to his general soundness: all the energy seems directed at trapping Jasper and bringing him to justice, which is to say the gallows—or, more probably, death by drowning. The relationship between Jasper and Drood is extraordinarily interesting, in being an overt exploration of an ambivalence that is elsewhere seldom recognized as such, an almost obsessive attachment that can find its fulfilment only in death, the destructive counterpart to the bond between Crisparkle and Tartar:

'My old fag!' said Mr. Crisparkle.
'My old master!' said Mr. Tartar.
'You saved me from drowning!' said Mr. Crisparkle.[25]

The bond between Jasper and Drood is such as to suggest much more clearly than in the case of Wrayburn and Headstone that the woman is merely a commodity in a male transaction, though she does still provide the conventional rationale for the murder. Drood, we might say, is punished for not taking a serious enough interest in Rosa Bud, and in this sense the novel repeats the pattern of the attack on Eugene Wrayburn; but this merges with the Wrayburn-Lightwood relationship, to unite the twin strains of love and hate in a single relationship.

But given the incompleteness of *The Mystery of Edwin Drood*, this remains speculative. Bradley Headstone is the most complete exploration we have in Dickens of the profoundly anti-social impulse at the heart of so many of his novels: directed towards equilibrium and clarification, they are propelled by disequilibrium and ambivalence. Apparently celebrating romantic love, they show that love to be merely one aspect of a need so strong as to be capable of murder. The intimacy of human companionship is a desperate refuge from solitude as well as an opening for relentless exploitation. The closing embrace of Headstone and Riderhood concludes the long series of embraces in Dickens which have so disturbingly combined love and death; ultimately Headstone is a manifestation also of the imaginative energies that launched a tale of redemptive love upon the image of Florence Dombey embracing her dying mother. Mr Dombey 'quite shut out' was redeemed by being 'encircled' in the loving embrace of his daughter; Bradley Headstone, rejected by the heroine and disowned by his protégé, is dragged to the depths of the Lock. His death figures as a consummation that has always hovered under the surface of Dickens's most optimistic conclusions, and has always been latent within his openings. The heroine's function as loved object is coextensive with her potency as avenging angel. The scapegoat validates, exemplifies, and energizes the power of the heroine; in extreme cases, executes that power. Bradley Headstone's bloodied hand is the instrument of Mary Graham's angel touch, and his death is the consummation of her influence.

---

[25] Charles Dickens, *The Mystery of Edwin Drood* (1870); ed. Margaret Cardwell (Oxford, 1982), 185.

As the great popular novelist of his time, Dickens voices, or rather pictures, both the dreams and the nightmares of his society—much of the time simultaneously, as we have seen. To move from him to George Eliot is to leave behind the wistful, haunted world of romance, and to enter the more sober world of the moralized fable, speaking to that earnestness that is so often taken to be the keynote of the Victorian era. Here the scapegoat is not the apparition that imprints itself upon the peripheries of the averted gaze; it is rather the worldly portrait of charm and beauty, meticulously created and yet shunned as a distraction from the exalted inner vision that the novels strive to realize.

Chapter 3

A Peculiar Compassion: George Eliot and Gwendolen Harleth

> She then glanced over the letters and diary, and wherever there was a predominance of Zion, the River of Life, and notes of exclamation, she turned over to the next page; but any passage in which she saw such promising nouns as 'small-pox', 'pony', or 'boots and shoes', at once arrested her.[1]

> She could not reconcile the anxieties of a spiritual life involving eternal consequences, with a keen interest in guimp and artificial protrusions of drapery.[2]

I

In their divergent views on the relative importance of haberdashery and Zion, Mrs Linnet and Dorothea Brooke represent two conflicting impulses in George Eliot's fiction: her commitment, as realist novelist, to a world in which action is more often directed by a keen interest in guimp than by a consciousness of eternal consequences; and her distrust, as moralist, of the material universe as a distraction from the pursuit of spiritual meaning.[3] Eliot's sense of the guimps and grograms, the drapery, upholstery, millinery, and haberdashery of her day—and of earlier days, as *Romola* so exhaustingly proves—is comprehensive enough to furnish, drape,

---

[1] Mrs Linnet, in George Eliot, 'Janet's Repentance', *Scenes of Clerical Life* (1858); ed. David Lodge (Harmondsworth, 1973), 271.

[2] Dorothea Brooke, in George Eliot, *Middlemarch* (1871–2); ed. David Carroll (Oxford, 1988), 30.

[3] U. C. Knoepflmacher makes a somewhat similar point: 'George Eliot's novels are dominated by two conflicting impulses. She wanted to unfold before her readers the temporal actuality she believed in; yet she also wanted to assure them—and herself—that man's inescapable subjection to the flux of time did not invalidate a trust in justice, perfectibility, and order. This double allegiance drew her, over almost twenty years, to seek fictional modes that could accommodate both the actual and the ideal laws that she wanted to portray' (*George Eliot's Early Novels: The Limits of Realism* (Berkeley, Calif., 1968), 1).

and clothe a realist universe. And yet she also fails, like Dorothea though in a different sense, to reconcile the spiritual and the mundane: not through ignorance or indifference, rather through an inability or unwillingness to clothe a religious vision in the mortal dress which the realist novel insists on.[4]

This is a stark simplification of a complex matter, the continually renegotiated relation in George Eliot's novels between the objects of the material world and the human subjectivities partly constituted by their participation in that material world, partly defined by their efforts to transcend it. Her characters are the vessels of a spiritual vision, and yet denizens of a recognizable world, in which, through which, and in spite of which they have to discover and fulfil their destinies. That pressure towards fulfilment of the individual self that we have seen Dickens and Austen in their different ways incorporating into their designs is here not so much absent as deflected towards an ambition beyond the self, yet paradoxically rooted in the self.

Eliot's plight as realist novelist is thus frequently replicated in the dilemmas of her characters: the modern St Theresa lacking a theatre for her actions doubles for the modern novelist seeking an appropriate medium for the chronicling of heroic action. The greatness of *Middlemarch* lies partly in giving full play both to Eliot's relish for the details of mundane existence and to her exasperation with their triviality, enabling, in a sense forcing, her to subject her moral seriousness to the test of realism. But if *Middlemarch* is central to its author's work, it also speaks for its time, in its analysis both minute and extensive of what E. J. Hobsbawm has called the Victorian 'duality of matter and spirit'. He locates the most conspicuous manifestation of this duality in the 'internal accumulations' of the home:

Its objects, like the houses which contained them, were *solid* . . . They were made to last, and they did. At the same time they must express the higher and spiritual aspirations of life through their beauty. . . . Beauty therefore meant decoration, something applied to the surface of objects.

This duality between solidity and beauty thus expressed a sharp division between the material and the ideal, the bodily and the spiritual, highly

---

[4] For an extended discussion of this aspect of the realist novel, its commitment to and reliance on the physical aspect and circumstances of its characters, see Michael Irwin, *Picturing: Description and Illusion in the Nineteenth-Century Novel* (London, 1979).

typical of the bourgeois world; yet spirit and ideal in it depended on matter, and could be expressed only through matter, or at least through the money which could buy it. Nothing was more spiritual than music, but the characteristic form in which it entered the bourgeois home was the piano, an exceedingly large, elaborate and expensive apparatus.[5]

This is to say, though Hobsbawm does not say it, that the characteristic Victorian duality lends itself particularly well to realist representation, dependent as that mode is on the rendering of the spiritual, or at any rate non-material, in material terms. And as Eliot's fiction shows, the novelist's representation is also a mode of analysis: the historian's abstraction, 'the bourgeois world', is plotted on a scale of behaviour that extends from the Dodsons of *The Mill on the Floss* through the Vincys of *Middlemarch* to the Arrowpoints of *Daniel Deronda*. Hobsbawm's example of the cumbersome piano as expensive symbol of the spiritual life enables us to recognize that Rosamond Vincy and Catherine Arrowpoint both came to music as a step in their parents' upwards social mobility, with Mrs Arrowpoint, as 'the heiress of a fortune gained by some moist or dry business in the city',[6] simply capable of more extensive—and expensive—improvements than the Vincys: she can afford a real musician to operate the piano. But if historically Miss Arrowpoint's music is, like Rosamond Vincy's, simply another example of the cultural advantages of bourgeois aspiration, Eliot's interest is also in the real dedication which sets Catherine Arrowpoint apart from Gwendolen Harleth, and in the disinterested love for Klesmer which distinguishes her from Rosamond's designs upon Lydgate. In Eliot, then, there is the constant play of particularized detail against historical generality, enabling her, perhaps supremely amongst English novelists, to render the sense of an age in terms of the trappings of its everyday life. Linguistically, her novels are less poised than Jane Austen's; scenically and tonally, less varied than Dickens's; but her ability to moralize the surfaces of her realist universe is unrivalled. In their different ways her characters unconsciously, even naïvely, simply by interacting with their physical environment, enact a conflict of values which they could no more understand than express: it takes Eliot's sardonic eye

[5] E. J. Hobsbawm, *The Age of Capital: 1848–1875* (1975; rpt. London, 1988), 273, 271–2.

[6] George Eliot, *Daniel Deronda* (1876); ed. Graham Handley (Oxford, 1988), 35.

to note the ironic discrepancy in the fact that, in Renaissance Florence, 'on the gold florins there has always been the image of San Giovanni',[7] the spiritual literally constituting the other side of the material coin.

But that duality which Eliot depicts so observantly, the 'division between the material and the ideal', figures in her fiction not only as part of her subject-matter, but also as an ambivalence affecting her novelistic practice: her novels are constantly, anxiously plotting the status of objects in relation to 'the higher and spiritual aspirations in life'. Committed as these novels are to the concrete manifestation of spiritual values, they retain a certain suspicion of the material—which all too easily figures in the moral lexicon as the superficial or the trivial. If, as Hobsbawm maintains, to the Victorian bourgeoisie 'beauty . . . meant decoration, something applied to the surface of objects', then it was exactly the decorative and superficial aspect of beauty that Eliot distrusted, while yet wistfully entertaining the possibility that beauty might after all signify spiritual value. The greater part of this chapter will be devoted to a consideration of Eliot's last novel and last heroine as a manifestation of that duality. Gwendolen is a participant in a conflict of which she is ultimately the victim: that is, her spiritual struggle is part of a larger debate in Eliot's fiction, and her 'conversion' is the defeat and attempted nullification of those realist values which give her fictional identity. In discovering the smallness of her own world and her own self, Gwendolen is reduced to a 'speck' (DD 689) against the visionary horizon of Mordecai and Daniel, which Eliot attempts to dramatize as a higher reality. The split, the notorious separation into the 'Jewish part' and the 'Gwendolen part', constitutes, then, Eliot's own failure to reconcile 'the anxieties of a spiritual life involving eternal consequences, with a keen interest in guimp', taking guimp to represent all that material aspect of the realist universe to which Eliot is so attentive. Gwendolen can find no place in Eliot's narrative community other than as the wistful outsider, trying to understand the scale of values that has reduced her to insignificance.

[7] George Eliot, Romola (1863); ed. Andrew Sanders (Harmondsworth, 1980), 130.

II

But long before Gwendolen Harleth, Eliot was anxiously pondering the question of the worldly and material in relation to the eternal and spiritual, and trying to fuse the two in a fictional vision. One way of doing so, it seemed, was to idealize the actual, to spiritualize the very ordinariness of things. For the commitment to realism to serve also the cause of spiritual truth, the everyday world had to be imbued with a potential for exaltation, by an artist not distracted by the grandiose aims of a more heroic concept of art. Eliot's famous defence, in *Adam Bede*, of realist art links her own art by implication with that of the Dutch realist painters and their observation of humble domestic subjects:

I turn, without shrinking, from cloud-borne angels, from prophets, sybils, and heroic warriors, to an old woman bending over her flower-pot, or eating her solitary dinner, while the noonday light, softened perhaps by a screen of leaves, falls on her mob-cap, and just touches the rim of her spinning-wheel, and her stone jug, and all those common things which are the precious necessaries of life to her.[8]

This has come to be taken as one of the central statements of literary realism, and its relevance to Eliot's own art is easily demonstrated from any number of loving transfigurations of the quotidian in her fiction. But the implied analogy between painting and fiction is as misleading as it is instructive. The woman and surrounding objects derive their value, or compositional 'values', from the artist's visual ordering; strictly speaking, the woman is herself no more than one object amongst others, although she may be privileged by the composition. In Eliot's fiction, on the other hand, the pictorial element is characteristically subordinated to or co-ordinated with non-pictorial relations. Writing, even an apparently neutrally descriptive passage such as the above, imposes an interpretation and a context upon the subject. Here Eliot's possessive pronouns simplify the relation between woman and surrounding objects into an assumption that flower-pot, mob-cap, spinning-wheel, and dinner *belong* to the old woman. Of course, this is a reasonable enough assumption—it would be perverse to wonder if perhaps the old woman were eating somebody else's

---

[8] George Eliot, *Adam Bede* (1858); introd. Robert Speaight (London, 1960), 173.

dinner—but it is still an assumption, deictically transformed into a factual state of affairs. And such assumptions are rebuttable: the Lydgates, for instance, also assume that they are eating *their* dinner with *their* forks and spoons, until the assumption is proved to be the polite but unstable fiction of a society based on credit. Their 'precious necessaries of life' are supplied by a trader whose own necessaries of life are dependent on the price he expects to be paid for the forks and spoons. In fiction 'those common things' have their meaning in relation to a community of things and meanings, and that relation remains potentially negotiable, even disputable. The 'couple of old termagants . . . tearing each other's caps',[9] glimpsed briefly from the stage-coach which traverses the landscape of *Felix Holt*, may figure as a simplified embodiment of a rule governing the precious necessaries of life: they have often to be wrested from somebody else's grasp, or defended against the acquisitive grasp or spiteful grab of another. The negotiability of objects complicates a 'pure' realist representation.

Caps, as it happens, occur frequently in Eliot's fiction, and usefully illustrate the narrative potential of physical objects. Of course, in life people simply do—or did—wear caps; but in Eliot's fiction caps are more than mere badges of verisimilitude, guarantees of corporeality like Daniel Deronda's coat-collar: they assume a semiotic function, as signs of value. The thoroughly worldly Bess Cranage in *Adam Bede*, 'lost in the puzzling speculation as to what pleasure and satisfaction there could be in life to a young woman who wore a cap like Dinah's' (*AB* 30), is a more representative citizen of the realist novel than Dinah Morris herself, serenely unaware of her own appearance and her own cap. Bess, deaf for the moment to the spiritual content of Dinah's sermon, relates the material object to a rudimentary system of signification of which 'pleasure and satisfaction' are the main constituents: she is, we might say, constructing her own plot around Dinah's cap. Adam Bede's reflections on the same cap serve to place him, too, in relation to Dinah, though he constructs a different kind of plot: 'the cap seemed to fit her face somehow as th'acorn cup fits th'acorn, and I shouldn't like to see her so well without it' (217). And Hetty's donning of Dinah's cap to the amusement of the company offers an

[9] George Eliot, *Felix Holt, the Radical* (1866); ed. Fred C. Thomson (Oxford, 1988), 7.

implicit comment on Adam's relation to the two women: if Adam 'liked Dinah's cap and gown better nor my clothes' (222) what is he doing courting Hetty? Adam's admiration of Dinah distinguishes him from Chad's Bess and from Hetty to provide, after all, a reply to Bess's question: Dinah has the pleasure and satisfaction of gaining Adam's admiration and all that follows from that—and Hetty's light-minded pursuit of pleasure and satisfaction is punished with awesome severity. These mere objects, though trivial in themselves, serve to mediate values more momentous, or narratively more significant, than the material or aesthetic. Mrs Bulstrode, learning of her husband's disgrace, shows some understanding of this principle by 'her way of expressing to all spectators visible or invisible that she had begun a new life in which she embraced humiliation': 'She took off all her ornaments and put on a plain black gown, and instead of wearing her much-adorned cap and large bows of hair, she brushed her hair down and put on a plain bonnet-cap, which made her look suddenly like an early Methodist' (M 615).

III

This chapter is partly an essay on the status of *objects* in George Eliot's fiction. In particular it is concerned with the problem of beauty—and in Eliot beauty *is* a problem—as both symbolic of the spiritual aspirations of her characters, the transfiguration of the material universe, and token of the frivolity of human ambitions in a corrupt world. Dorothea Brooke, in this as in other respects, voices her creator's ambivalence. Looking at the jewels left to the sisters by their mother, her first distaste is countered by a sudden apprehension of the beauty of the gems 'under a new current of feeling': 'They look like fragments of heaven. I think that emerald is more beautiful than any of them' (12); but in a fallen world, even fragments of heaven fetch a price, for the enrichment of people who value these things more pragmatically: 'Yet what miserable men find such things, and work at them, and sell them!' exclaims Dorothea in another revulsion from the spell of beauty (12–13).

In the quotidian subjects of realism Eliot attempts to find a beauty not subject to human avarice, exploitation, or vanity. 'Let us always have men ready to give the loving pains of a life to the faithful representing of commonplace things', she continues her appreciation of realist representation, '—men who see beauty in these commonplace things, and delight in showing how kindly the light of heaven falls on them' (*AB* 174). But if beauty is partly a creation of the observing eye, as it is for those who *see* beauty in 'these commonplace things', then that 'faithful representing' must be faithful not so much to the observed object as to the realist doctrine which declares the ordinary to be beautiful. And *showing* 'how kindly the light of heaven falls on them' may, by the same token, not be a showing of a pre-existent effect but an act of deliberate creation, even falsification.[10] The 'rare, precious quality of truthfulness' Eliot admires in the Dutch pictures may reveal, if it were *really* truthful, an existence utterly dispiriting in its commonplaceness. The 'monotonous, homely existence' in which she finds a source of 'delicious sympathy', may, when actually observed or imagined, stifle every creative impulse and every manifestation of that ardour which Eliot admires so passionately. In short, 'truthfulness' as Eliot describes it here, is not necessarily more true to the ordinary lives of ordinary people than the cloud-borne angels.

This would be mere logic-chopping were it not that the contradictions undermining Eliot's generalizations also underlie her fiction. In her well-known *Westminster Review* article of 1850, 'The Natural History of German Life', Eliot deplored the tendency to sentimentalize the ordinary, especially those classes deemed to be 'picturesque':

The notion that peasants are joyous, that the typical moment to represent a man in a smock-frock is when he is cracking a joke and showing a row of sound teeth, that cottage matrons are usually buxom, and village children necessarily rosy and merry, are prejudices difficult to dislodge from the artistic mind, which looks for its subjects into literature instead of life.[11]

Although at this stage Eliot had not attempted fiction, her statements prepare us for her later emphasis on drawing her

---

[10] As U. C. Knoepflmacher has it: 'Instead of faithfully copying the circumstances of external life, George Eliot arranged reality to make it substantiate her moral values' (*The Limits of Realism*, 1). Later he spells out the consequences of this for her fiction: 'Throughout her career, George Eliot's desire to be faithful to the conditions of actual existence clashed with her efforts to transcend or dignify the meanness of those conditions' (34–5).

[11] Repr. in *Essays of George Eliot*, ed. Thomas Pinney (London, 1968), 269.

subjects from 'life'. But how to accommodate, say, morose peasants
with broken teeth, slatternly wives, and dirty children, in a fiction
intent upon demonstrating 'how kindly the light of heaven falls on
them'? For the most part, Eliot avoids such extremes of poverty as
to locate suffering exclusively in the misery of material deprivation.
But even an existence less pinched by necessity, more comfortable
materially, may be to the ardent spirit an intolerable confinement.
Maggie Tulliver, in this respect the quintessential Eliot heroine, must
struggle to create and sustain value amidst the narrowness of soul
that passes for respectability in St Ogg's: 'She thought it was part of
the hardship of her life that there was laid upon her the burthen of
larger wants than others seemed to feel—that she had to endure this
wide hopeless yearning for that something, whatever it was, that
was greatest and best on this earth.'[12] Thus a long digression in *The
Mill on the Floss* departs significantly from the celebration of the
ordinary in *Adam Bede*. Finding in 'these Rhine castles' a 'sense of
poetry' through their associations with 'the grand historic life of
humanity', Eliot contrasts them to the ruined villages on the Rhone:

But these dead-tinted, hollow-eyed, angular skeletons of villages on the
Rhone oppress me with the feeling that human life—very much of it—is a
narrow, ugly, grovelling existence, which even calamity does not elevate,
but rather tends to exhibit in all its bare vulgarity of conception; and I have
a cruel conviction that the lives these ruins are the traces of, were part of a
gross sum of obscure vitality, that will be swept into the same oblivion with
the generation of ants and beavers.

Perhaps something akin to this oppressive feeling may have weighed
upon you in watching this old-fashioned family life on the banks of the
Floss, which even sorrow hardly suffices to lift above the level of the tragi-
comic. (271–2)

This apparent concession to the tastes of her readers leads George
Eliot to a defence of her own practice in choosing nevertheless to
portray 'these emmet-like Dodsons and Tullivers'. But she does not
proffer the oppressive ordinariness of St Ogg's as the subject of
reverence or even respect: she urges only the need to know it, in
order to understand how it affects the destinies of 'young natures ...
risen above the mental level of the generation before them' (*MF*

---

[12] George Eliot, *The Mill on the Floss* (1860); ed. Gordon S. Haight (Oxford,
1981), 288.

273). Partly through her identification with Maggie, Eliot is brought to the limits of that 'delicious sympathy' she feels in *Adam Bede*, and sees beyond it a weary exasperation with 'obscure vitality'.

Realism, then, while claiming a transcendent value for the workaday world, has to recognize that 'human life—very much of it—is a narrow, ugly, grovelling existence'. How to transfigure or even just dignify such narrowness is the quandary facing George Eliot as much as Maggie Tulliver. The escape from material conditions *through* material conditions is easier for the artisan-heroes, who transform the daily task into duty, felt with religious intensity and devotion: profession and vocation coincide here, with each other and with a sense of beauty, as they cannot for the middle-class heroines. Adam Bede's dedication to his calling satisfies also his religious sense: as his vocabulary testifies, carpentry is for him a religious matter, and religion largely a matter of carpentry. But even Adam, who believes—uncontentiously enough—that 'it's better to see when your perpendicular's true, than to see a ghost' (*AB* 51), concedes 'I know there's a deal in a man's inward life as you can't measure by the square' (177), and is brought to experience that unquantifiable depth of human experience in his suffering over Hetty's fate: 'now there was no margin of dreams for him beyond this daylight reality, no holiday-time in the working-day world' (468).

Even here, where the daily task is unusually fulfilling, the 'daylight reality', the 'working-day world', the site of realist meaning, needs to be lightened by a 'margin of dreams': the recognition is crucial to Eliot's art, a formal as much as a moral requirement. Adam has, we gather, been sustained in his dutiful pursuit of his profession by the romantic escape of his love for Hetty; but that romance has failed, along with Hetty. And Hetty has failed because of indulging her own romance: she too went 'about her work in a sort of dream . . . as if she were living not in this solid world of brick and stone, but in a beautified world, such as the sun lights up for us in the waters' (98). But Hetty's dream is of Arthur, and she is destroyed by it. The daylight reality may exact a terrible price for the sustaining dream.

In the event, Adam recovers some of that 'margin of dreams' in his love for Dinah, and the narrator comments, rather ponderously, 'I am of opinion that love is a great and beautiful thing too' (473). But George Eliot also knows that *love* is too multifarious a phenomenon to be generalized about in this way: as she says in *Daniel Deronda*: 'The word of all work Love will no more express the myriad modes of mutual attraction, than the word Thought can inform you what is passing through your neighbour's mind' (*DD* 256). For Eliot, love in its 'myriad modes', does not provide that unquestioned validation of human endeavour that Dickens wants it to be, and that Austen can make it seem to be. What Dorothea and her kind yearn for is fellowship with 'that fervid piety, that passionate sense of the infinite, that active sympathy, that clear-sighted demand for the subjection of selfish interests to the general good' attributed in *Romola* to 'the greatest of mankind'.[13] Whatever else this complex state of mind entails, it is *restless*. The fervid, passionate, active demand does not leave time or leisure for passive contentment: Eliot's major figures are all in some sense discontented with the world. Her own fiction is as much an exploration of the limits of human endurance of the ordinary as a celebration of that ordinariness.

IV

There is often something assertive in Eliot's commendations of the ordinary, as if in haranguing us she is also reminding herself of her moral duty. Thus Eliot's first published work, *Scenes of Clerical Life*, announces its moral programme with unabashed forth-rightness: 'I wish to stir your sympathy with commonplace troubles—to win your tears for real sorrow: sorrow such as may live next door to you—such as walks neither in rags nor in velvet, but in very ordinary decent apparel.'[14] But even here, in 'Amos Barton', there is a suggestion that our tears are being sought not so much in spite of the story's ordinariness as *for* the ordinariness of 'these commonplace people': 'Nay, is there not a pathos in their very insignificance—in our comparison of their dim and narrow existence with the glorious possibilities of that human nature which they share?' (*SCL* 81).

In the event, 'Amos Barton' makes good its promise to show us the pathos of insignificance—which is something different from the

---

[13] *R* 300. The fact that it is Savonarola to whom these qualities are here ascribed suggests also the possible dangers of such intensity of vision, when combined with his 'need of personal predominance'.

[14] George Eliot, 'The Sad Fortunes of the Rev. Amos Barton', *SCL* 97.

sublimity of the commonplace that Eliot may have intended. The story lacks a plot in the normal sense of the word: ordinary troubles in the nature of things tend not to generate very dynamic plots, and the contrast they make with 'the glorious possibilities of . . . human nature' is a theoretical abstraction not in itself narratively productive. The commonplace surface of the events is not as yet incorporated into the moral concerns of the tale: elements which in Eliot's later fiction are to become decisive determinants of plot are introduced without being exploited. The Countess, for instance, remains a lightly drawn portrait of a selfishness that does not animate the plot as, say, Rosamond's determines events in *Middlemarch*. The Countess is 'a little vain, a little ambitious, a little selfish, a little shallow and frivolous, a little given to white lies' (78–9)—which is to say that, give or take a weakness or two, she is the precursor of a good number of Eliot's most plot-productively flawed characters: Arthur Donnithorne, Hetty, Tito Melema, Rosamond Vincy, Esther Lyon, ultimately Gwendolen Harleth. But here the Countess's 'little' failings remain trivial: in the absence of a moralized plot, the Countess has nowhere to go but away and Milly Barton has nothing to do but die. Plot is, as yet, independent of the characters' relation to their physical world.

It is as if in this early work Eliot had only imperfectly apprehended a principle to shape that sympathy which she sees as the moral justification of her fiction into a narrative of spiritual regeneration. In the second of the *Scenes of Clerical Life*, 'Mr Gilfil's Love-Story'—which in truth has, apart from the framing narrative, more of the silver fork than the cloth about it—Eliot seems to lack a vantage point on her own action: Tina, somewhat petulantly in love with a worthless man, is in part victim, in part the tormentor of Mr Gilfil. So uncertainly placed is the heroine that it's difficult to decide whether she reminds us most of Fanny Price or of Becky Sharp.[15] The moral centre, in so far as the tale has one, is Mr Gilfil's selfless devotion, and even that, given its object, comes to seem so pointless as to be perverse. The most vivid thing in the tale is Mr Gilfil's present of a piece of bacon to Dame Fripp because she is too fond of

---

[15] Sandra M. Gilbert and Susan Gubar, though proposing a more unified reading of Tina as 'a model of female submission', liken her to a variety of dissimilar heroines: 'Like Jane [Eyre] or like Rochester's ward Adèle . . . Like Catherine Earnshaw . . . ' (*The Madwoman in the Attic: The Woman Writer and the Nineteenth-Century Literary Imagination* (New Haven, Conn., 1979), 485, 486).

her pig to kill it; and that, needless to say, has strictly nothing to do with the main plot. If, on the one hand, the sober realism of 'Amos Barton' remains rather static, on the other hand the frantic sensationalism of 'Mr Gilfil's Love-Story' usurps and smothers the interest that is a precondition to that sympathy that became so central to Eliot's conception of her characters.

In 'Janet's Repentance' the centre of the tale lies in its conscientious treatment of Evangelicalism, and, less obtrusively, in the suggestion that the truly redemptive influence is the humanity of Mr Tryan, rather than the strict religion that he practises and preaches. It is an early study, not only for *Daniel Deronda*, but for all George Eliot's tales of conversion. Gwendolen's reflections on Deronda, blending with the narratorial musing on the nature of conversion, hold equally well for Janet Dempster and subsequent converts like Esther Lyon and Romola:

Had he some way of looking at things which might be a new footing for her—an inward safeguard against possible events which she dreaded as stored-up retribution? It is one of the secrets in that change of mental poise which has been fitly named conversion, that to many among us neither heaven nor earth has any revelation till some personality touches theirs with a peculiar influence, subduing them into receptiveness. (*DD* 368)

This late quotation brings out more frankly than the early fiction the coercive nature of this conversion: the 'peculiar influence' is seen as a 'subduing' of the errant partner, the 'personality' thus affecting others being correspondingly forceful. This is clearly enough so in the case of Felix Holt and Savonarola, both of them types of the moral-spiritual bully. But even Dinah Morris in *Adam Bede*, for all her mildness, exercises her influence through an act of coercion rather than gentle persuasion. A scene from the second chapter of this novel, 'The Preaching', contains in simplified and dramatized form many of the elements that are to recur in Eliot's later fiction, and exemplifies Eliot's characteristic double plot, the movement of sympathetic identification doubled by a retributive or punitive principle.

V

Dinah's sermon is delivered in a landscape itself schematically symbolic. We are in 'that rich undulating district of Loamshire to which Hayslope belonged'; but it 'lies close to a grim outskirt of Stonyshire' (*AB* 18). Loamshire and Stonyshire remain as a moral tension in Eliot's fiction, although never again in as simple a topographical division. Dinah, preaching on the Hayslope Green, is not a voice crying in the wilderness as much as a voice from the desert attempting to rouse the fertile valley to a sense of spiritual desolation. The villagers of Hayslope form that body of opinion which it is Dinah's apparently hopeless mission to sway: 'for there was not one of them that would not have disclaimed the imputation of having come out to hear the "preacherwoman"—they had only come out to see "what war a-goin' on, like"' (20). In their declared suspicion of anything unfamiliar to their mental and spiritual habits, they embody that comfortable, and therefore intensely conservative community which so many of Eliot's protagonists confront so unsuccessfully. Dinah will be preaching largely to the converted few, the Methodists come from Treddleston for the occasion, and the objects of some curiosity, with their 'Quaker-like costume and odd deportment' (21).

In the middle of this group portrait, or in a strong position off-centre, is the vividly individual Chad's Bess, who, highly amused at the doleful regard of the Methodists, attracts their sorrowful disapprobation:

Chad's Bess was the object of peculiar compassion, because her hair, being turned back under a cap which was set at the top of her head, exposed to view an ornament of which she was much prouder than of her red cheeks, namely, a pair of large round ear-rings with false garnets in them, ornaments contemned not only by the Methodists, but by her own cousin and namesake, Timothy's Bess, who, with much cousinly feeling, often wished 'them ear-rings' might come to good. (21)

For all the impartial comedy of the scene, Eliot here deploys some of her major themes. Bess, in her concern for her appearance, is implicitly contrasted also to Dinah, registered for us through the curious but neutral gaze of the anonymous traveller and his 'surprise, not so much at the feminine delicacy of her appearance, as at the total lack of self-consciousness in her demeanour' (23). Dinah and Adam Bede, himself 'unconscious of the admiration he was exciting' in the mind of this same observing stranger (15), thus form a moral grouping set against Chad's Bess and her dedication to her own appearance, the illustrations, as it were, to Dinah's sermon and her denunciation of the ear-rings:

Here Dinah turned to Bessy Cranage, whose bonny youth and evident vanity had touched her with pity. . . .
    'Ah! poor blind child!' Dinah went on, 'think if it should happen to you as it once happened to a servant of God in the days of her vanity. *She* thought of her lace caps, and saved all her money to buy 'em; she thought nothing about how she might get a clean heart and a right spirit, she only wanted to have better lace than other girls. And one day when she put her new cap on and looked in the glass, she saw a bleeding Face crowned with thorns. That face is looking at you now,' here Dinah pointed to a spot close in front of Bessy.—'Ah! tear off those follies! cast them away from you, as if they were stinging adders. They *are* stinging you—they are poisoning your soul—they are dragging you down into a dark bottomless pit, where you will sink for ever, and for ever, and for ever, further away from light and God.'
    Bessy could bear it no longer: a great terror was upon her, and wrenching her ear-rings from her ears, she threw them down before her, sobbing aloud. (32)

Eliot does not shirk the sheer excess of sentiment generated around these poor objects of worldly vanity. If we were to judge Dinah's preaching by this example of its effects, we should hardly see it as greatly enlightening: she is replacing light-mindedness with superstition, and in the process turning her Saviour into a bogyman. Even before being turned upon by Dinah, Bess 'began to feel as if the constable had come to take her up and carry her before the justice for some undefined offence'. Dinah gives shape to that 'undefined' guilt and replaces the constable, through her 'belief in the visible manifestations of Jesus' with the figure of Christ: Bess feels that 'Jesus was close by looking at her, though she could not see him' (30). Clearly we are not being asked to believe that Bess Cranage is spiritually improved by her public renunciation of her ear-rings in response to such intimidation; furthermore, Dinah's influence over Bess is hardly permanent: by the time of the sack-race she has 'taken to her ear-rings again' (266). We know where we stand in relation to the 'conversion' of a simple countrywoman by a hell-fire sermon.

Or we may think we do. But if we reduce Bess's conversion to its components—a vain woman brought through terror and humiliation to repent of her own vanity—we recognize the essentials of the conversion plot as Eliot was to use it in her later fiction, and in this novel in the story of Hetty. Whereas Bess is brought to her terrified repentance through Dinah's exemplum, Eliot's other women are subjugated by the novelist's own plot; and whereas Bess's conversion is subordinated to a master narrative, those other conversions themselves constitute the master narrative. Bess's terror prefigures that dread that so often in Eliot is the prerequisite to redemption, the reminder of a world beyond the visible. Gwendolen Harleth's literary lineage is clearly enough traceable to Rosamond Vincy and Esther Lyon; but their common ancestor is Bess Cranage, their common failing reducible to her pair of large round ear-rings.

Now Bess is not a tragic or even a pathetic character; but she is in many ways a lightly sketched precursor of Hetty Sorrel, united in the first place by their common taste for ear-rings and, incidentally, by their bemused incomprehension of Dinah's cap. Hetty, it must be conceded, is a limited young woman, and George Eliot captures particularly well the unattractive unresponsiveness of the totally self-centred to anything not contributing directly to that self. But however unappealing her essential coldness, her situation is not unlike that of other Eliot protagonists, say Maggie Tulliver, whose surroundings fall short of their imaginations. Maggie has somehow to derive a sense of values from the absurd frippery of the Dodsons; Hetty is under an authority quite as antipathetic to *her* ambitions, the redoubtable and sober Mrs Poyser: 'nothing could be plainer or less noticeable than her cap and gown, for there was no weakness of which she was less tolerant than feminine vanity, and the preference of ornament to utility' (73). Mrs Poyser's ruling passion is clearly more sensible than that of the Dodsons, but in her unswerving dedication to agricultural and domestic values, she offers as little purchase to the young imagination as Maggie's female relatives. Hetty's beauty is her only means of escape from an environment she finds stifling and unfulfilling; almost instinctively, she realizes that it is her only card, her only potential release from butter-making.

But Hetty is by implication enjoined to find the world of the Hall Farm adequate. Her failure to respond to the 'round downy chicks peeping out from under their mother's wing' is registered against her as a manifestation of an all-engrossing vanity: 'that was not the sort of prettiness she cared about, but she did care about the prettiness of the new things she would buy for herself at Treddleston fair with the money they fetched' (151–2). Hetty's indifference to downy beauty is made to seem of a piece with her impatience of little things in general, things requiring her care and tender-ness—like children: 'Hetty would have been glad to hear that she should never see a child again' (151). Now this seems an understandable enough response to the constant presence of little Totty, but Hetty's exasperation is made to establish a connection with the death of her own child: vanity, in terms of the dynamics of the irony, is somehow connected with child-murder.

That irony becomes almost gloating in observing Hetty parading in her room 'in her coloured stays and coloured skirt, and the old black lace scarf round her shoulders, and the great glass ear-rings in her ears' (148). The narrator comments: 'Ah, what a prize the man gets who wins a sweet bride like Hetty! How the men envy him who come to the wedding breakfast, and see her hanging on his arm in her white lace and orange blossoms' (149). And so on, to culminate in the crowning sarcasm of 'How she will dote on her children!' R. T. Jones comments about passages like this that George Eliot 'seems to need Hetty to be, if not positively wicked, at least in some perceptible degree blameworthy, so that the consequences of her relationship with Arthur can be regarded as having been brought on by her'.[16] Certainly Eliot pointedly connects Hetty's terrible journey with the vanity that preceded and, so the implication runs, brought about the present misery: 'And yet, even in her most self-conscious moments, the face was sadly different from that which had smiled at itself in the old speckled glass, or smiled at others when they glanced at it admiringly' (369). The 'Journey in Despair' is movingly described, Eliot's imaginative sympathy almost vanquish-ing her suspicion and dislike of Hetty and her kind; but the formal expressions of sympathy remain self-conscious and moralistic: 'Poor wandering Hetty, with the rounded childish face, and the hard unloving despairing soul looking out of it—with the narrow heart and narrow thoughts, no room in them for any sorrows but her own, and tasting that sorrow with the more intense bitterness! My heart bleeds for her' (374). Narratorial sympathy in Adam Bede tends to be of the same order as Dinah's pity for Bess Cranage, or

---

[16] R. T. Jones, George Eliot (Cambridge, 1970), 17–18.

for that matter as the 'melancholy compassion' of the Methodists; here it is directed less at 'poor wandering Hetty's' suffering than at her spiritual benightedness in not having room in her heart and thoughts 'for any sorrows but her own'—surely under the circumstances an understandable enough preoccupation.

VI

Adam Bede is of course an early work, and not representative of Eliot's most finely balanced moral judgements. But it is precisely because of the relative obtrusiveness of her ethical motive that it provides us with a usefully simplified model of her later procedure. For the immense wealth of *Daniel Deronda*, its finely detailed characterization of Gwendolen, its meticulous if massive construction, even the weight of its scholarship, may blind us to what that novel has in common with its predecessors: the simple parable underlying the realist narrative, and the puritan didacticism animating it. The redemptive pattern of *Daniel Deronda* remains in essence that of the Methodist sermon: the character is instructed in the pitfalls of vanity by a kind of compassionate terrorism ('My heart bleeds for her'), the novelist taking Dinah's place as the inspirer of the terror.

Dorothea Barrett has argued that 'In *Daniel Deronda*, George Eliot can finally sympathize with a heroine who, like herself, is not earnestly and implausibly altruistic but humanly self-seeking and limited' and that 'She accepts human nature as it is, relinquishing the longing apparent in her earlier novels for something better than the simply human.'[17] My reading of Gwendolen is almost exactly the opposite: as an embodiment of 'human nature as it is', she is reduced to a shadow of her previous self, a pathetic exemplar of a hubristic faith in the 'simply human'. If Eliot does indeed 'sympathize' with Gwendolen, it is with the same kind of grim compassion as she extends to Hetty Sorrel. Gwendolen figures as the culmination of a variety of types which Eliot returned to throughout her career. If she may be seen as a more sympathetically treated Rosamond Vincy, she is also a harshly treated Esther Lyon: she shares with these two precursors a belief in the power of her

[17] Dorothea Barrett, *Vocation and Desire: George Eliot's Heroines* (London, 1989), 158, 159.

own femininity. Like Esther and unlike Rosamond, she is brought low before a superior male power. Married, like Dorothea and Romola, to a supreme egoist, she is not granted even Romola's opportunities to be useful or Dorothea's second chance. With something of Tito Melema's faith in the power of her own charm, she lacks his ruthlessness in exploiting it. Brought, like Janet Dempster, to repentance through the influence of a spiritual mentor, she is not rewarded, like Janet, with 'children about her knees, and loving young arms round her neck' (SCL 412). But her primary link remains with that early precursor, Hetty Sorrel, and her precursor, Chad's Bess, and their 'love of finery'.

Daniel Deronda is usually read, with some justification, as an indictment of English 'good' society at Eliot's time;[18] but its founding inspiration is still that puritanical distrust of the world and its objects that animated Adam Bede. Gwendolen may be in the first place a personification of a certain type of young woman of the 1860s; but she is also the type of earthly vanity, more specifically female vanity:

it is too painful to think that she is a woman, with a woman's destiny before her—a woman spinning in young ignorance a light web of folly and vain hopes which may one day close round her and press upon her, a rancorous poisoned garment, changing all at once her fluttering, trivial butterfly sensations into a life of deep human anguish. (AB 242)

That, in fact, is said about Hetty Sorrel, but might have been applied to Gwendolen, and with more justice. Hetty is indeed a butterfly broken upon the wheel of Eliot's plot, a spectacle too pathetic to have the kind of moral significance Eliot claims for it as 'a woman's destiny'. Gwendolen, on the other hand, does have the substance to sustain Eliot's judgement, and to face that challenge confronting all Eliot's major woman characters, the call to create a destiny for herself.[19] The claim that Eliot expected more from her women characters than from her men may find some support in the

[18] For instance, Sally Shuttleworth: 'George Eliot's goal in Daniel Deronda is not to represent a fixed "reality" but to challenge contemporary social values and conceptions. The novel presents a bitter critique of the economic and social practices of English society' (George Eliot and Nineteenth-Century Science: The Make-Believe of a Beginning (Cambridge, 1986), 175).

[19] Pace Henry James's Pulcheria, who maintains that 'Gwendolen is not an interesting girl, and when the author tries to invest her with a deep tragic interest she

slightly odd emphasis in the reflection on Hetty: 'It is too painful to think that she is a woman'—as opposed to a young girl, perhaps, or as opposed to a man? Conceivably both; for if to Dickens women were the ambivalently regarded guardians of the hearth and thereby the custodians of a patriarchal ideology, Eliot, proceeding exactly from an intelligent woman's resentment of that role, imposes upon her women a far more difficult duty, that of achieving equality of fulfilment while accepting inequality in status.[20] In this respect, too, Gwendolen is made to embody the female plight. Lamenting the lot of women in terms that are more applicable to her than she can realize at this stage, she speaks also for all her predecessors :

We women can't go in search of adventure—to find out the North-West passage or the source of the Nile, or to hunt tigers in the East. We must stay where we grow, or where the gardeners like to transplant us. We are brought up like the flowers, to look as pretty as we can, and be dull without complaining. That is my notion about the plants: they are often bored, and that is the reason why some of them have got poisonous. (*DD* 113)

But not all plants are poisonous, and Eliot's fiction lends only partial support to Gwendolen's plea in justification of her own pettiness of ambition. Discontent, for Eliot, is distinguished into a reformist dissatisfaction with the way things are, and a petulant preoccupation with one's own convenience. The presumptuous Felix Holt draws the distinction for Esther Lyon: 'You are discontented with the world because you can't get just the small things that suit your pleasure, not because it's a world where myriads of men and women are ground by wrong and misery, and tainted with pollution' (*FH* 104). Esther is made to feel, apart from some perfectly understandable indignation, 'that she could not

does so at the expense of consistency. She has made her at the outset too light, too flimsy; tragedy has no hold on such a girl' ('Daniel Deronda: A Conversation', *Atlantic Monthly* (1876); rpt. in *Partial Portraits* (Ann Arbor, 1970), 88). This judgement is by implication upheld in Robert Liddell's unenchanted reading of Gwendolen in *The Novels of George Eliot* (London, 1977), *passim*.

[20] As Dorothea Barrett maintains : 'Regardless of what Marian Lewes felt about women, George Eliot's clear bias towards her own sex saturates the canon: books named for male characters are focused on female protagonists; and these female protagonists are subjected to a more rigorous examination of the moral nuances of their behaviour and feelings than are their male equivalents' (*Vocation and Desire*, 23). This is demonstrably true, with the exception of *Romola*, in which the decentring of the eponym works against the woman: Melema is by common consent a more interesting study than Romola.

contradict what Felix said'; but she might have asked exactly how she could have manifested such a reformist discontent. Even the most visionary and determined of Eliot's male heroes find their discontent difficult to translate into action; how much more difficult for a woman to translate the wrong and misery of myriads of men and women into a programme of practical action. Eliot herself could do so in her capacity as novelist, of course; but through an anomaly that has earned her some critical displeasure, she denied her woman characters the opportunities she herself enjoyed.[21]

The impotence of Eliot's women lends itself readily to a feminist analysis; but Eliot's own treatment seems to imply, by and large, that power should be meted out to women only very cautiously, if at all. Felix Holt, who voices some of Eliot's less enlightened thinking on the subject, postulates a second-order sort of power for women in 'the force there would be in one beautiful woman whose mind was as noble as her face was beautiful—who made a man's passion for her rush in one current with all the great aims of his life' (221). This force, though, remains a passive potential until energized by male action; noble mind and beautiful face can only wait to be recruited in the male cause, sublimely unconscious of its own beauty, as in Dinah Morris and Dorothea Brooke. If these women figure as the exemplars of female force, Gwendolen represents the possibly more revealing antithesis, the cautionary example of the beautiful woman who attempts to use her beauty on her own account, as power *over* the man, as one of the 'various orders of beauty, causing men to make fools of themselves in various styles' (*AB* 82). The men are guilty only of folly—and even then, the folly may be the woman's, as is suggested by the curmudgeonly Felix Holt in lambasting 'the foolish women who spoil men's lives' (*FH* 105).

Eliot's women, then, are in a peculiarly strenuous position. In aspiring towards self-realization they must not use such power as their femaleness gives them, except in inspiring male endeavour. In using that power on her own account, the woman incurs

[21] 'Feminist critics are angry with George Eliot because she did not permit Dorothea Brooke in *Middlemarch* to do what George Eliot did in real life: translate, publish articles, edit a periodical, refuse to marry until she was middle-aged, live an independent existence as a spinster, and finally live openly with a man whom she could not marry' (Zelda Austen, 'Why Feminist Critics are Angry with George Eliot', *College English*, 37 (1976), 549).

responsibility for ruining an existence that by implication is more valuable than her own. All she can aspire to is the subordination of her own desires, by definition selfish, to the larger human purpose served by male enterprise. Failing to do so, she is held responsible both for his failure and for her own inability to realize her human potential. However frequently Eliot dramatizes the woman's rebellion against the smallness of her opportunity, she almost as often punishes her for presuming to exercise such power as that small opportunity affords her.

In a famous passage from *Daniel Deronda* women are accorded only a right of veto, combined with light transport duties: 'What in the midst of that mighty drama are girls and their blind visions? They are the Yea and Nay of that good for which men are enduring and fighting. In these delicate vessels is borne onward through the ages the treasure of human affections' (103). The vessel, though, is likely either to drift or to be rowed by a man, Stephen Guest abducting Maggie Tulliver or Deronda rescuing Mirah; or otherwise to be at the mercy of prevailing winds: 'Desire has trimmed the sails, and Circumstance / Brings but the breeze to fill them' (*DD* 251), we are told in the motto to the crucial chapter in which Gwendolen accepts Grandcourt.[22] Even Romola, the most schematically heroic of Eliot's heroines, and the one who breaks away most decisively from male authority (she is emancipated, in turn, from the authority of her father, her brother, her godfather, her husband, and her spiritual mentor, Savonarola), literally drifts, asleep in a fishing boat, to a limited and temporary secular sainthood in a plague-stricken community, to which she is summoned by the crying of a baby.

Now Eliot obviously saw much to criticize in the position granted to women in her society: she had more opportunities than most women to discover the limits of the tolerance of her contemporaries and peers. Clearly some of this experience feeds into her novels, in such creations as Mrs Transome in *Felix Holt*, condemned to

[22] Hetty Sorrel's vessel, unweighted by human affection, is hardly seaworthy: 'Yes, the actions of a little trivial soul like Hetty's, struggling amidst the serious, sad destinies of a human being *are* strange. So are the motions of a vessel without ballast tossed about on a stormy sea. How pretty it looked with its parti-coloured sail in the sunlight, moored in the quiet bay!' (*AB* 328). Walter Allen comments of this passage and others like it that 'one is outraged not primarily by the authorial intrusion but by something much more serious—the author's plain lack of charity' (*George Eliot* (New York, 1964), 102).

inactivity and impotence by her femaleness. Mrs Glasher, too, expresses something of the bitterness of the woman who has cut herself off from society by falling in love in the wrong place: 'it was as if some ghastly vision had come to [Gwendolen] in a dream and said, "I am a woman's life"' (DD128). And most eloquently of all, the Princess, Deronda's mother, speaks not only for the gifted Jewish woman contending with the conservatism of tradition, but for all women trying to fulfil themselves in the face of at best a condescending incomprehension of their wants.[23] But the feminist note sounded through Mrs Transome, Mrs Glasher, and the Princess is muted by its very source. In their different ways, all three women come to regret their past choices, and though none of them will spell it out, the reader is left to gather that their unhappiness is the consequence of their rejection of the traditional role of wife and mother that was offered to all three. Romola, heeding the crying of the baby, is atypical of the Eliot strong woman: Mrs Transome, the Princess, and Mrs Glasher all repeat at a symbolic level Hetty Sorrel's crime of child-murder, and in all instances by reaching beyond what marriage legitimately offers to the women of Eliot's fiction.[24]

Gwendolen, on the other hand, tries to succeed through the means traditionally at her disposal. Hers is not a revolutionary desire to make an unorthodox marriage, simply an ambition to make a 'good' marriage. She has, in spite of a show of dissidence, passively absorbed her society's platitudes about marriage as an enhancement of freedom and an increase in power, from her mother's 'Marriage is the only happy state for a woman' (22) to her uncle's 'When you are married, it will be different: you may do whatever your husband sanctions' (64). And in Grandcourt's appearance Gwendolen finds no reason to suspect that 'whatever

[23] Even Mirah, who is an unlikely sort of feminist, has a moment of rebellion against the complacency of the adored Mordecai, as he maintains 'rather insistently' that 'women are specially framed for the love which feels possession in renouncing, and is thus a fit image of what I mean'. The occasion of this rare disagreement is the tale of the Jewish maiden who died in the place of the woman loved by the Gentile king the maiden loves; Mirah's interpretation is that 'She wanted the king when she was dead to know what she had done, and feel that she was better than the other' (DD 629).

[24] For a discussion of Eliot's treatment of motherhood, see Pauline Nestor, Female Friendships and Communities: Charlotte Brontë, George Eliot, Elizabeth Gaskell (Oxford, 1985), 177–81.

your husband sanctions' may be a qualification of freedom rather than a large allowance: 'Gwendolen conceived that after marriage she would most probably be able to manage him thoroughly' (115). Gwendolen has no enlightened notions of an equal marriage: she intends to be the stronger partner.

VII

Thus it is that Gwendolen, in spite of and partly because of not aspiring to any exceptional destiny, tells us more about 'a woman's life' than those women more openly rebellious, who lose their freedom by seeking it in unconventional places. As Gillian Beer remarks: 'George Eliot saw that it is the ordinary case that tests the true state of affairs.'[25] Gwendolen believes herself to be exceptional and to be entitled to exceptional treatment, but always within the traditional societal structures:

She rejoiced to feel herself exceptional; but her horizon was that of the genteel romance where the heroine's soul poured out in her journal is full of vague power, originality, and general rebellion, while her life moves strictly in the sphere of fashion; and if she wanders into a swamp, the pathos lies partly, so to speak, in her having on her satin shoes. Here is a restraint which nature and society have provided on the pursuit of striking adventure; so that a soul burning with a sense of what the universe is not, and ready to take all existence as fuel, is nevertheless held captive by the ordinary wirework of social forms and does nothing particular. (43)

The passage, though of course satirical, is perhaps more forgiving of Gwendolen than the dominant tone would seem to suggest. The satire at the expense of the heroine of 'genteel romance' yields to a more neutral view of 'a soul burning with a sense of what the universe is not', passively 'held captive' by 'social forms'. Whereas the first sentence seems to locate the limitation in the heroine herself, in the triviality of her imagination, the second returns to the 'ordinary wirework of social forms' that so often in Eliot binds even the exceptional individual—Lydgate, for instance, who in Middlemarch 'was feeling the hampering threadlike pressure of small social conditions, and their frustrating complexity' (M 148).

[25] Gillian Beer, George Eliot (Brighton, 1986), 201.

Gwendolen, in other words, features in the two sentences as respectively Rosamond Vincy and Dorothea Brooke. There may be a certain presumption underlying the 'sense of what the universe is not'—in Gwendolen less a reformer's discontent than a complaint about an unsatisfactory hotel room—but it is a presumption, as we have seen, that she shares with all Eliot's 'ardent' characters.[26]

Gwendolen, though, has no intention of reforming the universe; rather, like Hetty, she believes that she can escape the limits of her environment by projecting herself as a desirable object. She manipulates, or tries to manipulate, her own status as object in a society whose habits of valuation she thinks she understands:

and this delicate-limbed sylph of twenty meant to lead. For such passions dwell in feminine breasts also. In Gwendolen's, however, they dwelt among strictly feminine furniture, and had no disturbing reference to the advancement of learning or the balance of the constitution; her knowledge being such as with no sort of standing-room or length of lever could have been expected to move the world. She meant to do what was pleasant to herself in a striking manner; or rather, whatever she could do so as to strike others with admiration and get in that reflected way a more ardent sense of living, seemed pleasant to her fancy. (DD 31)

The passage is once again less uniform in implication than appears at first: from the slighting reference to 'strictly feminine furniture', the sarcastic disparagement of her 'knowledge', through the imputed selfishness of 'she meant to do what was pleasant to herself', we arrive at the after all less reprehensible desire for 'a more ardent sense of living'. At this level of generality, Gwendolen's vanity originates in the same hunger as Dorothea's dedication to good works; her determination to lead, when put in those terms, is no more pernicious in itself than Deronda's. But if the passage contains one of Eliot's most frequent terms of endorsement—*ardent*—it also employs, twice, one of her most ominous

---

[26] Gillian Beer refers to the 'sense of what the universe is not' as a 'negative vision', and points out that the passage recalls 'the tonic irony of [George Eliot's] early essay "Silly Novels by Lady Novelists"' (*Darwin's Plots: Evolutionary Narrative in Darwin, George Eliot and Nineteenth-Century Fiction* (London, 1985), 231). This is true, but ignores the fact that a 'negative vision' is something Gwendolen has in common with Eliot's most admirable characters. Even Dorothea Brooke is disappointed to find the Lowick cottages not in need of improvement.

words: *pleasant*.[27] Like Tito Melema's 'unconquerable aversion to anything unpleasant' (*R* 161) Gwendolen's avoidance of the unpleasant is seen as a symptom of a light-mindedness in need of correction, that correction then being the business of the plot.

It is thus appropriate that Gwendolen, when first seen by Deronda as by us, is in what passes for a place of pleasure, the gambling resort. Deronda is discovered, famously, pondering Gwendolen's beauty: 'Was she beautiful or not beautiful?' His scrutiny is, in the first place, aesthetic, but almost immediately modulates into the moral: 'Was the good or evil genius dominant in those beams?' Gwendolen is being assessed rather like the emerald bracelet that so perplexed Dorothea Brooke; beauty itself exerts a 'coercion' which is to be resisted.[28]

Gwendolen's pleasure, her appearance, her pleasure in her appearance, are scrutinized, in an attempt to interpret her moral meaning. She becomes, we might say, the personification of the realist conundrum, the spiritual signification of mortal beauty. She bodies forth the calm confidence of·the material world in its own self-sufficiency, its apparently unconscious enjoyment of being admired. But at her most 'ardent', in being most consciously the object of observation, she is confronted with a gaze which implicitly questions the grounds of her ardour and pleasure:

and instead of averting [her eyes] as she would have desired to do, she was unpleasantly conscious that they were arrested—how long? The darting sense that he was measuring her and looking down on her as an inferior, that he was of a different quality from the human dross around her, that he felt himself in a region outside and above her, and was examining her as a

[27] For instance, in *Daniel Deronda*: 'Could there be a slenderer, more insignificant thread in human history than this consciousness of a girl, busy with her small inferences of the way in which she could make her life pleasant?' (102–3); 'He wished his niece parks, carriages, a title—everything that would make this world a pleasant abode' (120). In *Adam Bede* we have had Bess Cranage's 'puzzling speculation as to what pleasure and satisfaction there could be in life to a young woman who wore a cap like Dinah's' (30); and the little downy chicks which 'never touched Hetty with any pleasure' (151). Less damningly, Dinah describes Mr Irwine's face as 'as pleasant as the morning sunshine' (93)—but even this, given Dinah's preference for Snowfield, may not be an altogether unmixed commendation.

[28] Jacqueline Rose proposes an interesting feminist reading of this opening in *Sexuality in the Field of Vision* (London, 1986), 105–22. For an earlier discussion of many of the details noticed by Rose, see Adrian Poole's '"Hidden Affinities" in *Daniel Deronda*', *Essays in Criticism*, 33 (1983), 294–311.

specimen of a lower order, roused a tingling resentment which stretched the moment with conflict. (*DD* 5–6)

Given the questionable status of the pleasant in Eliot's novels, it is fitting that Deronda's first effect upon Gwendolen should be 'unpleasant'. Deronda disturbs those 'habits of mind' of hers in which 'it had been taken for granted that she knew what was admirable and that she herself was admired' (7). It is part of this habit to assume the right to judge 'the human dross around her'; hence the moral shock of finding herself judged, the object not of admiration, but of critical assessment.

The opening of the novel, then, dramatizes Gwendolen's awakening to the possibility of being judged by a measure that she herself does not understand. But, paradoxically, Gwendolen's loss of confidence in her own power to control the impression she makes coincides with her assumption of narrative command: the narration unobtrusively but decisively shifts from the outward estimate and interpretation of her ('she looked around her') to her own consciousness ('she was unpleasantly conscious'). Initially projected as a function of Deronda's wondering gaze, Gwendolen assumes the burden of her own definition, which is to say responsibility for her own destiny. An amalgam of 'pictorial' realist presentation and psychological notation, she is the central object of observation, but also the central consciousness.

That double identity as subject and as object complicates another early description of Gwendolen; having spent the night packing after receiving her mother's news, Gwendolen waits for the dawn, and gazes at her own reflection:

She had a *naïve* delight in her fortunate self, which any but the harshest saintliness will have some indulgence for in a girl who had every day seen a pleasant reflection of that self in her friends' flattery as well as in the looking-glass. And even in this beginning of troubles, while for lack of anything else to do she sat gazing at her image in the growing light, her face gathered a complacency gradual as the cheerfulness of the morning. Her beautiful lips curled into a more and more decided smile, till at last she took off her hat, leaned forward and kissed the cold glass which had looked so warm. (12–13)

Subject and object fuse in the image of the woman kissing the cold reflection of herself, a self-adoration recalling Hetty Sorrel's simpler devotions, 'bent on her peculiar form of worship' in front of the mirror in her bedroom.[29] Gwendolen's kissing of her own reflection is both an act of vanity and a natural expression of joy in her own health and beauty, an instinctive delight in what she has retained despite misfortune. Hetty, under the far worse circumstances of her 'Journey in Despair', cherishes her own body, not in vanity, but in the sheer instinctive buoyancy of a young creature: 'The very consciousness of her own limbs was a delight to her; she turned up her sleeves, and kissed her arms with the passionate love of life' (*AB* 371). Compared with the dramatic irony brooding over the description of Hetty, Gwendolen's narrator would seem to be more sympathetic, more understanding of her '*naïve* delight in her fortunate self', professing even 'some indulgence' for a self-admiration so natural. At such moments Eliot seems to recognize as natural the desire to live and to be healthy and beautiful. But in the event harsh saintliness carries the day. Gwendolen is being watched, as coldly as Hetty, by the sardonic eye of a moralistic *eiron*. Both Hetty and Gwendolen are 'cured' of the vanity of valuing their own mere flesh. Hetty is seen 'clinging to life only as the hunted wounded brute clings to it' (*AB* 374) before she is brought to bay and to justice; Gwendolen is to recall, in her sadness, for her own and our edification, this moment of young vanity: 'This beautiful, healthy young creature . . . no longer felt inclined to kiss her fortunate image in the glass; she looked at it with wonder that she could be so miserable' (*DD* 363).

Gwendolen's fate, of course, is considerably less desperate than Hetty's; but her history has in common with Hetty's the determination with which she is hunted down by her author. Hetty goes from favoured position, courted by the most eligible

---

[29] *AB* 146. George Levine puts forward an analogy between Hetty's mirror and the mirror as image of realist representation: 'The mirror that threatens clarity and fidelity recurs opaquely by the candlelight in Hetty's bedroom, but transforms into a window in Dinah's. The dangers of reflection are averted by the powers of imagination to project itself through the glass. And if Hetty suffers from the fatal flaw of realism, the imaginative projection of self on an intransigent reality, the novel itself authenticates another kind of imagination, one that succeeds in its guesses at truth because it tries to remove the self as an obstacle' (*The Realistic Imagination: English Fiction from Frankenstein to Lady Chatterley* (Chicago, 1981), 44). In *Daniel Deronda*, of course, that other kind of imagination is granted to Deronda—to say which is to recognize how relatively feeble as fictional subject are these 'guesses at truth', compared with 'the imaginative projection of self on an intransigent reality'.

working man in the area and flirted with by the young Squire-to-be, to outcast and exile; Gwendolen, sought in marriage by the most eligible man in *her* circle, is reduced to helpless dependence on a man who is leaving her behind in order to found a national home for his people. In our first view of Gwendolen she is imperiously dominating the view at an international resort; we leave her as she is emerging from hysteria, being watched over by her mother. So much has been wrought by that 'year's experience which had turned the brilliant, self-confident Gwendolen Harleth of the Archery Meeting into the crushed penitent impelled to confess her unworthiness where it would have been her happiness to be held worthy' (603).

Gwendolen's history consists in a series of lessons in her own powerlessness to manipulate the admiration of others. In 'real' time as opposed to narrative sequence, Gwendolen's first setback occurs at the 'sort of general introduction for her to the society of the neighbourhood' (34), the dinner at the Arrowpoints. The scene sets the pattern of several later episodes: triumphal entry checked by some unforeseen mishap. She enters the gathering 'visible at first as a slim figure floating along in white drapery, approach[ing] through one wide doorway after another into fuller illumination and definiteness' (34). But she exceeds the terms of her own pictorial charm in naïvely consenting to sing: 'used to unmingled applause' (38), she is ill-prepared for the uncompromising judgement of Herr Klesmer on both her performance ('you produce your notes badly') and her choice of music ('the passion and thought of people without any breadth of horizon. . . . It makes men small as they listen to it'). For the second time in the novel Gwendolen is made to feel that a criterion she does not understand is being applied to her, and diminishing her—'with a sinking of heart at the sudden width of horizon opened round her small musical performance' (39). Gwendolen depends on admiration and applause for validation of her performance or actions, even her identity; her subjectivity, we might say, is realized only through her objectification. Klesmer's criticism, like Deronda's regard, has the effect of isolating her from that reassuringly admiring or at any rate uncritical social estimate which normally guarantees her sense of herself and her power: she is left helpless in an alien landscape.

On a later occasion, Gwendolen's dramatic disruption of the tableau gives prophetic shape to her spiritual dread, reminding her, in the midst of her vanity, of her susceptibility to an order of experience excluded from her day-to-day existence. Once again, she is the centre of attention when her confidence fails her: she 'stood without change of attitude, but with a change of expression that was terrifying in its terror. She looked like a statue into which a soul of Fear had entered: her pallid lips were parted; her eyes, usually narrowed under their long lashes, were dilated and fixed' (49). Again Gwendolen loses control of her own presentation: she is not seen as she had intended herself to be seen—although this time Klesmer pretends, out of kindness (music not being in danger of being betrayed by such charitable hypocrisy), to ascribe it to her admirable *plastik*.

The incident recalls that other bit of unintended *plastik*, Tito Melema's response to the sudden appearance of Baldassarre, and the painting based upon the incident by Piero di Cosimo: '[Tito] saw himself with his right hand uplifted, holding a winecup, in the attitude of triumphant joy, but with his face turned away from the cup with an expression of such intense fear in his dilated eyes and pallid lips, that he felt a cold stream through his veins, as if he were being thrown into sympathy with his imaged self' (R 247). As with the painting behind the panel in *Daniel Deronda*, the frame, as it were, fails to contain the latent content of the painting: both pictures escape their purely pictorial reference and speak peremptorily to the living. Melema's 'dilated eyes and pallid lips' may be merely conventionalized signs of fear, but the correspondence does suggest a connection between his dread and Gwendolen's. Tito, of course, has reason for his fear: he is fleeing a dead face, or a face that he conveniently assumed to be dead until Baldassarre clutched his arm. Gwendolen, on the other hand, is at this point fleeing nothing but her own dread, unfocused as yet on any particular object or person, deriving from no transgression. Eliot's iconography suggests that she imagines Gwendolen as even at this early stage being pursued by a Nemesis akin to Melema's: she is conceived in sin, as it were, guilty of that 'aversion to anything unpleasant' that is her weakness as much as his.

Gwendolen's next public appearance would seem to constitute a complete triumph, even over the hitherto intractable Klesmer: at last she is making that impression which she thought herself destined to make upon the neigbourhood. At the Archery Meeting, she distinguishes herself by her appearance and her performance alike:

and she at last raised a delightful storm of clapping and applause by three hits running in the gold—a feat which among the Brackenshaw archers had not the vulgar reward of a shilling poll-tax, but that of a special gold star to be worn on the breast. That moment was not only a happy one to herself—it was just what her mamma and her uncle would have chosen for her. There was a general falling into ranks to give her space that she might advance conspicuously to receive the gold star from the hands of Lady Brackenshaw; and the perfect movement of her fine form was certainly a pleasant thing to behold in the clear afternoon light when the shadows were long and still. She was the central object of that pretty picture, and every one present must gaze at her. That was enough; she herself was determined to see nobody in particular, or turn her eyes any way except towards Lady Brackenshaw, but her thoughts undeniably turned in other ways. It entered a little into her pleasure that Herr Klesmer must be observing her at a moment when music was out of the question ... and the unconquered Klesmer threw a trace of his malign power even across her pleasant consciousness that Mr Grandcourt was seeing her to the utmost advantage, and was probably giving her an admiration unmixed with criticism. (89–90)

The description places Gwendolen at the centre, not only of 'that pretty picture', but of Eliot's realist aesthetic as it has developed by the time of her last novel. We recall the celebration, in *Adam Bede*, of the painting of the old woman 'bending over her flower-pot, or eating her solitary dinner, while the noonday light, softened perhaps by a screen of leaves, falls on her mob-cap': Eliot's own art clearly has gone beyond this, both in subject-matter and treatment. The scene presents itself still as a 'pretty picture', in 'the clear afternoon light', with Gwendolen as 'the central object' of the composition. But the pictorial analogy is unobtrusively faded out, first, in our sense that the scene is being described from inside the frame, by an observer capable of appreciating 'the perfect movement of her fine form', and secondly, under the free indirect rendering of Gwendolen's own consciousness, as the objective placing shades into the more indeterminately angled opinion (Gwendolen's? the narrator's?) that 'every one present must gaze at her'—finally to settle firmly on Gwendolen's decisive 'That was enough'. The 'pretty picture', in other words, is charged with non-pictorial meaning derived from the tension between Gwendolen-as-object and Gwendolen-as-subject, observation of Gwendolen blending with Gwendolen's consciousness of herself as being observed.

Not having access to Grandcourt's thoughts as we did to Deronda's, we cannot judge the accuracy of Gwendolen's pleasant speculations; but we do note that while she is revelling in her power and pre-eminence, the description subverts her triumphant subjectivity. She is 'the central *object* of that pretty picture', 'a pleasant *thing* to behold': Gwendolen's power to charm is dependent upon her assent to her own objectification. The scene pictorially enacts the dictum that 'to desire to conquer is itself a sort of subjection' (89); and the subjection is in part a willingness to present oneself to the observation and judgement of the other. Tito Melema's Nemesis is the vindictive Baldassarre whom he does everything in his power to avoid; Gwendolen's Nemesis is the man she does everything in her power to impress.

VIII

Gwendolen's 'pleasant consciousness' of being admired, and the ironic resonances of that consciousness, recall another such 'pretty picture' centred upon an attractive woman, Hetty Sorrel in Mrs Poyser's dairy, as observed by Arthur Donnithorne:

Hetty blushed a deep rose-colour when Captain Donnithorne entered the dairy and spoke to her; but it was not at all a distressed blush, for it was inwreathed with smiles and dimples, and with sparkles from under long curled dark eyelashes; and while her aunt was discoursing to him . . . Hetty tossed and patted her pound of butter with quite a self-possessed, coquettish air, slily conscious that no turn of her head was lost. (*AB* 82)

Here the governing perspective is that of the male spectator: we are invited to look with Arthur, to share his charmed gaze. But the centre of consciousness, as in the passage from *Daniel Deronda*, shifts from observer to observed. Hetty's 'self-possessed, coquettish air, slily conscious' makes of her a conscious and willing object of observation, delighting in her power to charm even while she is unconsciously demonstrating her own enthralment to the need to charm. Arthur, admitting to Mr Irwine that he had gone 'to look at the pretty butter-maker', adds 'if I were an artist, I would paint her' (100); but he is not an artist and his interest in Hetty is not artistic. In life pretty pictures have consequences for subject and observer alike. Gwendolen and Hetty might have been admired even if they had been perfectly unaware of it; but of course they *are* aware of it, and in consenting to it, are set up for their author's dramatic irony.

Gwendolen's humbler precursors in *Adam Bede* may not tell us very much about that aspect of her that usually receives most attention, the psychological complexity of this vain, confident, and yet dread-ridden heroine; what they do reveal are the simpler lines of the moral fable upon which Gwendolen's history, like theirs, is constructed. Thus Gwendolen's victory at archery recalls another outdoor gathering, another sporting meeting, another prize-giving, another triumphant young woman, ultimately another disappointment: Chad's Bess, coming forward to claim her prize for sack-racing:

Bessy, I am sorry to say, had taken to her ear-rings again since Dinah's departure, and was otherwise decked out in such small finery as she could muster. Any one who could have looked into poor Bessy's heart would have seen a striking resemblance between her little hopes and anxieties and Hetty's. . . .

Bessy had been tempted to run the arduous race, partly from mere hoidenish gaiety, partly because of the prize. Some one had said there were to be cloaks and other nice clothes for prizes, and she approached the marquee, fanning herself with her handkerchief, but with exultation sparkling in her round eyes. (*AB* 266)

Bess's sack-race is about as different from the dignified archery meeting as two outdoor gatherings involving the use of the limbs could be, and Gwendolen's cool beauty presents a corresponding contrast to Bess's 'large red cheeks and blowsy person' (266). Bess's round eyes are not formed to conceal that exultation which Gwendolen is so careful to keep 'inward': she is simply, naïvely glad at having won. Whereas 'among the Brackenshaw archers the prizes were all of the nobler symbolic kind: not property to be carried off in a parcel, degrading honour into gain' (*DD* 84), 'Poor Bessy' is awarded just such a parcel, and for the second time in the novel is reduced to tears: instead of a scarlet cloak she receives 'an excellent grogram gown and a piece of flannel' (*AB* 266) bought by Miss Lydia (herself resplendent in lace), in keeping with her precept of providing as prizes 'nothing but what is useful and substantial' because 'I should not think of encouraging a love of finery in young women of that class' (267). Bess, who 'throwing down the odious bundle under a tree, began to cry' (267), would seem to be getting her second lesson in the vanity of human wishes; but, given the hint in the somewhat obtrusive comparison 'between her little hopes and anxieties and Hetty's', we are presumably meant to see here, as in the earlier humiliation of Bess, a prefiguring of Hetty's much sadder fate, also the consequence of her 'love of finery', the bundle she leaves under a tree in her despair. 'Poor Bessy' is pitied at her moment of 'exultation', not because she herself finds as yet anything pitiable in her situation, rather because Eliot is adopting something of Dinah's pity at her 'bonny youth and evident vanity'; we might say that she is pitied for the fate that Eliot is planning for Hetty.

Gwendolen, like Bess, is participating in the contest at least 'partly because of the prize'. Gwendolen's prize, being of 'the nobler symbolic kind' would seem not to be tainted by the mere human motive of greed; but in the event what it symbolizes is Grandcourt, whose attention Gwendolen wins in addition to the gold star. The prize is spoilt, of course, by Mrs Glasher's revelation, but ultimately, as the title of Book IV tells us, 'Gwendolen gets her choice'. It is true that Gwendolen 'chooses' Grandcourt in that she finds him preferable to penury or Mrs Mompert, but on any other interpretation, it is Grandcourt who gets *his* choice. In Eliot's moral universe, however, this is not available to Gwendolen as extenuating circumstance: her decision remains a free choice freely taken, as the shift from Gwendolen's free indirect thought to stern narratorial comment makes clear: 'She seemed to herself to be, after all, only drifted towards the tremendous decision:—but drifting depends on something besides the currents, when the sails have been set beforehand' (257). 'The sails have been set': the impersonal construction leaves open the question as to how and by whom, but the chapter motto has told us: 'Desire has trimmed the sails' (251). Strictly speaking, of course, desire has had very little to do with Gwendolen's 'choice': at her most passionate, what she feels is 'a momentary phantasmal love for this man who chose his words so well, and who was a mere incarnation of delicate homage' (256). Grandcourt presents himself to Gwendolen as an opportunity to avoid that unpleasance to which she, like Tito Melema, has an unconquerable aversion:

'here in this man's homage to her lay the rescue from helpless subjection to an oppressive lot' (256).[30]

Gwendolen's gravest offence, in George Eliot's moral system, is the attempt to avoid that 'oppressive lot' and to buy for herself a life of ease. Marrying Grandcourt, she gets not only her choice, but Hetty Sorrel's as well, fulfilling the dairymaid's pathetic fantasy: 'she feels the bracelets on her arms, and treads on a soft carpet in front of a tall mirror' (AB 243). Gwendolen's entry into married life promises an abundance of material ease: 'Gwendolen felt herself being led by Grandcourt along a subtly-scented corridor, then into an ante-room where she saw an open doorway sending out a rich glow of light and colour' (DD 302). Even this ostensibly private moment is registered, like so many of the scenes that have led up to this one, as a public performance: Gwendolen feels herself to be 'the heroine of an admired play without the pains of art' (301). Into this setting Mrs Glasher's diamonds are introduced, the artificial serpent in a false Eden:

Within all the sealed paper coverings was a box, but within the box there *was* a jewel-case; and now she felt no doubt that she had the diamonds. But on opening the case, in the same instant that she saw their gleam she saw a letter lying above them. She knew the handwriting of the address. It was as if an adder had lain on them. . . .

Truly here were poisoned gems, and the poison had entered into this poor young creature.

After that long while, there was a tap at the door and Grandcourt entered, dressed for dinner. The sight of him brought a new nervous shock, and Gwendolen screamed again and again with hysterical violence. He had expected to see her dressed and smiling, ready to be led down. He saw her pallid, shrieking as it seemed with terror, the jewels scattered around her on the floor. (302–3)

Adrian Poole has traced allusions in this scene to, amongst others, the Euripidean *Medea*, and he draws attention to the 'quick shift of mythic reference' that enables Eliot to refer to the Furies immediately after this description.[31] The mythic parallels do extend

---

[30] I agree with Joseph Allen Boone that 'the relentless logic of these events [leading to Gwendolen's acceptance of Grandcourt] renders any illusion of free choice in the matter a moot point' (*Tradition Counter Tradition: Love and the Form of Fiction* (Chicago, 1987), 181). Unlike Boone, however, I believe that Eliot nevertheless judges it as a free choice.

[31] Poole, 'Hidden Affinities', 305.

the local moral reference, Gwendolen's broken promise to Mrs Glasher, to older and larger notions of justice and vengeance; but the scene simultaneously re-enacts another episode, in its own way as charged with atavistic significance as the Medea myth. Gwendolen's hysteria at receiving the 'poisoned jewels' recalls Bess Cranage's hysterical scattering of *her* jewels, in her 'terror' at Dinah's preaching ('they are poisoning your soul') and her exemplum of the bleeding face of Christ. The 'stinging adders' to which Dinah likens 'those follies' are here provided, packaged, and delivered by the novelist's metaphorical turn, and the pity that Dinah expresses for Bess ('poor blind child') is now professed by Gwendolen's narrator ('this poor young creature'). In both instances, then, the pity proceeds from the same source as the terror. The parallels between the two scenes suggest that, possibly unconsciously, Eliot is rewriting her Methodist exemplum as a central incident in her great realist novel; and whereas the presence of Dinah made possible a distancing irony that controlled our perception of the preaching on the Green, Gwendolen's devastation is described by the agent of that devastation and allows of no irony.

IX

Creating Gwendolen as a representative of her society and then according her the duty to aspire beyond that society, Eliot in effect asks of her to reach beyond the limits of her own definition. It is a problem Conrad was to address in *Lord Jim*, and in the next chapter I discuss his attempted solution, in making of Jim an inhabitant both of the realist novel and of the romance, and founding his major theme on the separation between the two worlds and their mutual incomprehension. But in George Eliot the split can not yet articulate itself as subject; it incapacitates the realistic mode of the novel and invalidates its ethos. As George Levine has it:

By the time of *Daniel Deronda*, George Eliot had in effect renounced the limits of realism by renouncing the possibility of satisfactory life within society, the sanction of meaning conferred by a community organically coherent. The ultimate realistic project in George Eliot becomes the projection of community into fictions from which her realist's integrity has banished it. Daniel is sent off, in fact, to create a community, outside the reaches of the society and of the novel whose language can no longer evoke one. The language of realism becomes fit only for that experience of loss and absence that is Gwendolen Harleth's at the end. Meaningful truth must be projected into the distance.[32]

Of course, Eliot's most ardent protagonists have always had to revise their notions of 'satisfactory life within society' in order to survive. Dorothea Brooke and Lydgate, Felix Holt, Dinah Morris, even Romola: the social wirework has always been there as a confinement to be adjusted to or compromised with.[33] But given the kind of fictional community that *Daniel Deronda* creates, the complacent Philistinism of the English upper classes, the narrative community is necessarily elsewhere—an elsewhere, possibly, that Eliot herself can imagine only in the vaguest terms. Gwendolen, then, conceived in the realist mode, is, as it were by definition, excluded from the kind of visionary future which Eliot tries to imagine for her most ardent protagonists.

Eliot, as is well known, resented the tendency of her first readers to concentrate on Gwendolen, in that she 'meant everything in the book to be related to everything else there'.[34] That intention speaks clearly enough from the neatness with which certain patterns repeat and modify themselves in the novel, usually, so to speak, at Gwendolen's expense: she is used to define the need for the larger vision, as Deronda is used to measure the smallness of Gwendolen's horizon. But reading partly against that intention, we might choose to use him rather as the measure of her smallness of *opportunity*.

Deronda's heroic aptitude consists mainly in his passionate readiness for some vaguely defined destiny: 'what he most longed for was some external event, or some inward light, that would urge him into a definite line of action, and compress his wandering energy' (308). Apart from that, he is distinguished from Gwendolen largely by a matter of that luck called variously destiny and election. 'External event' does in fact intervene, in Deronda's discovery of

[32] Levine, *The Realistic Imagination*, 46.

[33] Gilbert and Gubar say about Dorothea Brooke's marriage to Ladislaw: 'If she still does not escape the confining maze of social duties and definitions, this is because no such transcendence seems possible or even necessarily desirable in Eliot's world' (*The Madwoman in the Attic*, 530).

[34] *The Letters of George Eliot*, ed. Gordon Haight, vi (New Haven, Conn., 1954), 290 (2 Oct. 1876), quoted, amongst many others, by Graham Handley, Introduction to *DD*, p. xiv.

Mirah and his consequent meeting with Mordecai. Both Deronda and Gwendolen are chosen: Deronda as the fulfilment of the spiritual ambition of Mordecai, Gwendolen as meeting the requirements of the imagination of Grandcourt. They are both in a sense coerced into their destiny, but Gwendolen is allowed, as we have seen, the pleasant illusion that she is exercising a free choice. By contrast, Deronda is twice summoned to his Jewish identity: first in the synagogue in Frankfurt when he 'felt a hand on his arm, and turning with the rather unpleasant sensation which this abrupt sort of claim is apt to bring, he saw close to him the white-bearded face' (311) that he is to get to know as that of Joseph Kalonymos; and later, in Mr Ram's shop, when he 'felt a thin hand pressing his arm tightly' as Mordecai asks him 'You are perhaps of our race?' (327), a question which Deronda, 'not liking the grasp', curtly dismisses. Thereafter, he and Mordecai conduct a kind of courtship, proceeding, like Gwendolen and Grandcourt's, from 'an exchange of fascinated, half-furtive glances' (336). At the Cohens' evening meal (less elegant than the Archery Meeting, but no less ceremonious) Mordecai, disappointed in his hope that Daniel might know Hebrew, 'cast down his eyelids, looking at his hands, which lay crossed before him' (338)—not unlike Gwendolen, 'upright, with downcast eyelids' (254), as Grandcourt makes his proposal. And in this courtship, Mordecai is no less determined and masterful than Grandcourt. The significant meeting, in other words, the one which doubles Gwendolen's fateful decision, is that between Mordecai and Daniel, rather than Daniel's rescue of Mirah.[35] Daniel is determined by the designs of Mordecai rather than by his own desire.

The two different destinies which Daniel and Gwendolen are chosen by are clearly not in themselves 'unfair': in literature as in

---

[35] Mirah is thus for a second time an object of a bartering transaction between men: her father wanted to sell her for money; her brother wants her to marry Daniel into the family. Eliot softens the implications of the parallel by making Mirah properly in love with Daniel, but this only partially masks the nature of the transaction, which is what Eve Kosofsky Sedgwick calls, in relation to Charley Hexam and his offer of Lizzie to Bradley Headstone, 'the male traffic in women' (*Between Men: English Literature and Male Homosocial Desire* (New York, 1985), 167). A related instance is Romola's marriage to Tito Melema, encouraged by her father Bardo because it provides him with an amanuensis better qualified than he thinks Romola to be. Tito's infidelity to Romola is carefully doubled by his betrayal of Bardo's trust in selling his library.

life some people are born to found nations, while others are born to
marry blackguards. But there is something oddly Calvinist about an
election that is then taken to confer salvation (or worse, a non-
election that is taken to confer guilt). If finding a higher duty is a
matter of being called to it, can anybody be held culpable for not
finding such a duty?[36] Gwendolen's destiny, when related to
Deronda's, shows the novel to have been preconceived towards
her defeat and humiliation. Barbara Hardy, in discussing the series
of spatial images shared by Gwendolen and Deronda, the 'broad
view' delighted in by Deronda as against Gwendolen's self-enclosed
fear of open spaces, stresses their 'inevitability'.[37] She does not
elaborate on this, but taking the hint, we may say that the dwarfing
of Gwendolen by Deronda's 'wide-stretching purposes' has been
predetermined by the novel's metaphorical landscape: Deronda is
elected as much by the image pattern as by destiny.

Thus the limits of Gwendolen's musical horizon are plotted, as we
have seen, with merciless precision by Klesmer (39), and the
narrator characterizes her horizon in general as 'that of the genteel
romance' (43). That metaphor opens up into the literal horizons
Deronda encounters in his outings on the river, with 'a great
breadth of water before him reflecting the glory of the sky' (160);
the prospect distinguishes him from Gwendolen and her contracted
horizon, and aligns him with Mordecai, whose 'thought went on in
wide spaces' and who frequented Blackfriars Bridge for 'the breadth
and calm of the river' (406) where Deronda duly appears as the
'prefigured friend . . . from the golden background' (422).

But the metaphor that creates opportunity for Deronda imposes
restriction and culpability upon Gwendolen. In the most literal of
senses, Deronda's horizon is larger than Gwendolen's because he is
a man: she simply cannot go rowing on the Thames on her own. As
we have seen, Eliot's women are in any case more likely to be
passengers than to row themselves. She remains trapped in the
circumscribed world of the genteel romance, whereas he has access

[36] A useful summary of the history of vocation and its connection with the Puritan
teaching of predestination is to be found in Alan Mintz, *George Eliot and the Novel
of Vocation* (Cambridge, Mass., 1978), 8–13. My question rather bluntly sums up an
abiding Puritan concern: 'The doctrinal impossibility of achieving one's own
salvation, together with the practical impossibility of knowing definitely who has
been saved, became a source of immense anxiety to the Puritan saint' (10).

[37] Barbara Hardy, *The Novels of George Eliot: A Study in Form* (1953; rpt.
London, 1963), 230–1.

to the sphere of adventure and opportunity. Gwendolen's horizon is never of her own choosing: marrying partly in order to be free of the kind of county constraint that prevents her from joining the hunt ('When you are married, it will be different: you may do whatever your husband sanctions' (64)), Gwendolen earns the hellish privilege of an extended voyage on Grandcourt's yacht, with 'the glory of sea and sky' (574) patrolled, as it were, by the hateful step and regard of her husband. When she goes rowing with that husband, ostensibly steering, 'she sat guiding the tiller under her husband's eyes, doing just what he told her' (583)—free, indeed, to do whatever her husband sanctioned.[38] The opportunity for heroic action that she is offered—saving Grandcourt from drowning—seems almost like a bitter joke: Deronda had rescued the appealing Mirah; Gwendolen must rescue a worthless and disagreeable man in order to spend the rest of her life with him. Whatever our view of the morality of such an obligation, we must see that opportunity presents Daniel and Gwendolen with an unequal sort of test.

X

If, then, Gwendolen's horizon remains that of the genteel romance, that may be because the horizon of Eliot's realist novel does not provide her, as woman, with much scope for heroic action. Her inability to understand Deronda's project for the future, though clearly intended to reflect unfavourably on her horizon of comprehension, may offer a damaging comment on the reality of that project. She asks, rather pathetically, 'Can I understand the ideas, or am I too ignorant?' (688); and her sense of her own insignificance against 'the bewildering vision of these wide-

[38] I have commented on the fact that even Romola gets to her destination by falling asleep in a boat. Maggie Tulliver, having literally drifted into disgrace in Stephen Guest's company, effects a reconciliation with her brother by rowing to his rescue; it is entirely characteristic of him that he should say 'Give me the oars, Maggie' (MF 520), and equally characteristic of Eliot that she should allow Maggie to do so. Gillian Beer comments that 'The difference between drifting and rowing has frequently come to represent within her books the difference between half-conscious acquiescence in unconscious forces and the activity of the will resisting and attempting to govern such energies' (Darwin's Plots, 232). More simply, the difference between drifting and rowing is usually the difference between being female and being male.

stretching purposes in which she felt herself reduced to a mere speck' may be intended to suggest that she is indeed too ignorant, capable only of awe-stricken and uncomprehending apprehension of 'something spiritual and vaguely tremendous' (689). But those wide-stretching purposes matter to us mainly for their effect on the mere speck we call Gwendolen; the 'vaguely tremendous', we feel, may just be tremendously vague, also to George Eliot. In other words, our measure of the reality of Deronda's vision remains that much more limited understanding, which cannot encompass the alternative to itself. Cowed as she is by circumstances, Gwendolen takes Deronda's word for it all, but it remains a huge unreality to her, comprehensible, if at all, only in the largest of terms: 'she was for the first time feeling the pressure of a vast mysterious movement, for the first time being dislodged from her supremacy in her own world, and getting a sense that her horizon was but a dipping onward of an existence with which her own was revolving' (689). The cosmic imagery seems to suggest that the moment constitutes a personal Copernican revolution for Gwendolen, but the whole sentence depends for its effect on our not interrogating the details too closely.[39] The grandiose metaphor obscures what is in essence a familiar recognition in Eliot; Maggie Tulliver, for instance, feels quite early in life what it takes Gwendolen much longer to learn:

It flashed through her like the suddenly apprehended solution of a problem, that all the miseries of her young life had come from fixing her heart on her own pleasure, as if that were the central necessity of the universe; and for the first time she saw the possibility of shifting the position from which she looked at the gratification of her own desires—of taking her stand out of herself, and looking at her own life as an insignificant part of a divinely-guided whole. (MF 290)

An equivalent moment in *Middlemarch* dramatizes Dorothea's 'release' from the narrow prison of self in her looking out of her window and recognizing that 'she was a part of that involuntary, palpitating life' (M 644). Both visions are clear enough to focus such generalizations as are based upon them; Deronda's experience,

---

[39] Sally Shuttleworth renders the rough sense of the image as 'Deronda has played the role of Copernicus, displacing Gwendolen's Ptolemaic sense of cosmology' (*George Eliot and Nineteenth-Century Science*, 198).

on the other hand, remains unintelligible to Gwendolen and reader alike.

For Gwendolen has been consistently our guarantee of Deronda's existence; it is no coincidence that the novel introduces him to us as a consciousness of her ('Was she beautiful . . .?'). As intelligible denizen of her own novel, she vouches for him in surroundings alien to his disengaged goodwill. Without Gwendolen, Deronda could have gone about his heroic business of saving Mirah and Hans, and he could have met Mordecai—but without her embodiment of what they are the alternative *to*, his commitment would have lacked even such reality as it has. Gwendolen defines Mirah physically and Deronda morally: they are both most real as not-Gwendolen, rather as Fanny Price is most real as not-Mary. If it is true that the character of Daniel was inspired by Titian's wonderful *Young Man with a Glove*, then Eliot has not succeeded in animating the portrait: Daniel seems always to have his gaze fixed slightly to the right and over the heads of the rest of us, with no interest in our boots or ponies. Grandcourt's sneer 'Do you take off your hat to the horses?' (361) is not without its point: taking off his hat to horses and feeding women sugar lumps, Deronda does seem an awkward citizen of the realist novel.[40] He owes his moral authority, that is to say his influence over

[40] He is, indeed, almost the epic and tragic hero as described by Bakhtin: 'Outside his destiny, the epic and tragic hero is nothing; he is, therefore, a function of the plot fate assigns him; he cannot become the hero of another destiny or another plot' ('Epic and Novel: Toward a Methodology for the Study of the Novel', *The Dialogic Imagination: Four Essays* (1975); ed. Michael Holquist, trans. Caryl Emerson and Michael Holquist (Austin, Tex., 1981), 36). Bakhtin's description of 'The individual in the high distanced genres' bears some similarity to Deronda as we come to know him: 'he is a fully finished and completed being. This has been accomplished on a lofty heroic level, but what is complete is also something hopelessly ready-made; he is all there, from beginning to end he coincides with himself, he is absolutely equal to himself. He is, furthermore, completely externalized. There is not the slightest gap between his authentic essence and its external manifestations' (34). As put here, this may be too absolute to do justice to Eliot's conscientious attempts to provide Deronda with a sense of a discrepancy between his 'authentic essence and its external manifestations'; but Deronda's uncertainties do seem little more than the throat-clearings of destiny.

[41] Joseph Allen Boone makes a similar point, to somewhat different effect: 'Gwendolen's story unfolds in a highly "realistic" mode befitting its deterministic logic of cause and effect, whereas Daniel's career gradually assumes the trajectory of a romantic quest, in which prophecy and vision subsume realistic truths' (*Tradition Counter Tradition*, 178). Boone sees in the discrepancy an implicit subversion of the dominant ideology reflected in the novel; to me, it signals Eliot's inability to imagine in realist terms the mission she nevertheless would have Gwendolen discover for herself.

Gwendolen, largely to that immunity to her attractions derived from his inhabiting a different order of fictional creation.[41]

He has to intersect with that other order, though, and Gwendolen is the point of intersection: his intervention in her life is also his point of entry into the novel. His most interesting identity in the novel is as Gwendolen's spiritual adviser, and the most thorough-going test of his credentials is Gwendolen's demand: 'You must tell me then what to think and what to do' (382). Given the difficulty of supplying advice on demand, Daniel is decently articulate; his admonitions are deficient only in not suggesting any very clear line of action: 'Try to care for what is best in thought and action—something that is good apart from the accidents of your own lot' (383). This is about as specific as advice can be under the circumstances; but Daniel is called upon to provide spiritual guidance in a spiritual desert. Where is Gwendolen to find 'the best in thought and action'? Her spiritual mentor in Deronda's absence is her uncle the Rector, who urged marriage to Grandcourt as 'a duty here both to yourself and your family' (119). All Deronda can do for her is to teach her what she should want: the good of others, some course of action that will liberate her from the narrow concerns of self. He has woken her to a need that he cannot satisfy; and Eliot has posited a redemption she cannot imagine. Gwendolen's conviction that 'it will be better with me' remains a touching unreality.

Gwendolen is left at the end of her novel where Dorothea is at the beginning of hers, with a vaguely formulated sense of a mission, and nothing to expend this sense on. She is provided at best with some sound masculine advice; as Pauline Nestor says, the 'peculiarly feminine instability' Eliot ascribes to women needs to be countered by 'the stability of an external, masculine world' and 'Consequently women are dependent on men in a most fundamental way'.[42] This is true of several of Eliot's women but particularly so of Gwendolen Harleth: whereas some, like Romola and Maggie Tulliver, are shown justifiably to resent the undervaluing of their 'feminine' capacities, Gwendolen is brought to understand and implicitly acknowledge her own inferiority in terms of power and intellect to both Grandcourt and Deronda, and to submit to the stern ministrations of Deronda:

[42] Nestor, *Female Friendships*, 167.

This sorrow, which has cut down to the root, has come to you while you are so young—try to think of it, not as a spoiling of your life, but as a preparation for it. Let it be a preparation . . . See! you have been saved from the worst evils that might have come from your marriage, which you feel was wrong. You have had a vision of injurious, selfish action—a vision of possible degradation; think that a severe angel, seeing you along the road of error, grasped you by the wrist, and showed you the horror of the life you must avoid. And it has come to you in your spring-time. Think of it as a preparation. You can, you will, be amongst the best of women, such as make others glad that they were born. (658)

Within the dramatic situation Deronda's words are intended as consolatory, and they do manage to be reasonably gentle without sentimental concessions to Gwendolen's distress. But he is also propounding his author's moral purpose, who is herself the severe angel who has taken Gwendolen by the wrist; that is, whereas Deronda is pronouncing upon an unhappiness he has become a witness to, Eliot is generalizing about the didactic function of the suffering she has created in her novel. And as generalization the statement is more dubious altogether: pain seems as likely to harden the sufferer as make her more responsive to the pain of others. It is unfortunate, too, that Deronda's consolation should come so close to echoing Mr Gascoigne's words, intended at the time to reconcile Gwendolen to subordinating herself to Mrs Mompert's moral and social superiority: 'This trouble has come on you young, but that makes it in some respects easier, and there is benefit in all chastisement if we adjust our minds to it' (245).

Daniel's choice of metaphor, the idea of suffering as the grasp of 'a severe angel', is again an understandable attempt at making an unpleasant fate seem morally coherent; but within the broader context of Eliot's fiction the metaphor acquires a more ambiguous resonance, signifying a kind of spiritual arrest, a combination of Nemesis and vocation. In the early 'Janet's Repentance' the image occurs unambiguously as the clutch of Nemesis upon the arm of the richly deserving Mr Dempster: 'Nemesis is lame, but she is of colossal stature, like the gods; and sometimes, while her sword is not yet unsheathed, she stretches out her huge left arm and grasps her victim. The mighty hand is invisible, but the victim totters under the dire clutch' (SCL 336). In Daniel Deronda that clutch is an admonition rather than a punishment: we have noted how Deronda's own destiny is announced to him by the initially resented grasp on his arm, first of Joseph Kalonymos, then of Mordecai. In *Romola* the gesture is, as we would expect, more strongly punitive: Tito Melema, upon being touched upon the shoulder by Macchiavelli, starts so violently that his friend asks him 'Why, Melema, what evil dream did you have last night, that you took my light grasp for that of a *sbirro* [policeman] or something worse?' (221). Eventually that 'something worse' is realized in the 'tightening grip of [Baldassarre's] soiled worn hands on [Melema's] velvet-clad arm' (283): Melema is grasped by the hand that he dreads, that of the foster-father he has betrayed. So Gwendolen is the last in a series of characters to feel that grasp or clutch, the summons to seriousness, retribution, correction, suffering, or redemption—a calling to account. The policeman, Nemesis, the stern angel: the figures of retribution and vocation merge, suggesting that to Eliot there is a fundamental connection between calling and punishment, between duty and the unpleasant.

We have seen that to Dickens, too, the figure of the angel was equivocal; and Eliot's ambivalence, although morally rather than sexually based, no less testifies to an identity she does not examine too closely, that between redemption and punishment, compassion and cruelty. 'There is no kind of conscious obedience', declares the narrator of *Romola*, speaking of the excesses of the young Piagnoni, 'that is not an advance on lawlessness' (R 500); and whereas every one of Eliot's *obiter dicta* is probably not to be universalized, her narratives do seem to be shaped so as to enforce obedience as a value in itself: transgression of a moral law, followed by retribution, is central to her plot design. Tito Melema, Hetty Sorrel, and Gwendolen Harleth are all persecuted in the name of a moral law that has no sponsor. Intended as exemplars of the need for human sympathy, they paradoxically end up as victims of what Girard has called naïve persecution:

I call those persecutors naïve who are still convinced that they are right and who are not so mistrustful as to cover up or censor the fundamental characteristics of their persecution. . . . Naïve persecutors *are unaware of what they are doing.* Their conscience is too good to deceive their readers systematically, and they present things as they see them.[43]

[43] René Girard, *The Scapegoat* (1982); trans. Yvonne Freccero (London, 1986), 8.

To call George Eliot a persecutor at all is perhaps to give an unduly lurid cast to the punitive aspect of her plots. And yet we have seen that her protagonists are almost literally persecuted by the machinery of plot. What Baldassarre is to Tito Melema, the author's moralized narrative is to Hetty Sorrel and Gwendolen Harleth, with this difference that Baldassarre is self-confessedly motivated by the desire for revenge, whereas the plot claims to be propelled by sympathy, like Dinah Morris denouncing Chad's Bess out of pity. The naïvety may lie exactly in the sincerity of the belief underlying the persecution, and persecution may be motivated by a vision of the greater good of humankind. The practice of presenting things 'as they see them' is not peculiar to persecutors: it is also the aim of the most humane of writers. But such representation becomes persecution when the writer is convinced that she is depicting a reality independent of the registering vision. Believing that she is rendering a 'faithful account of men and things as they have mirrored themselves in my mind' (*AB* 171) George Eliot elevates to the status of external reality her own intensely moralized perceptions. But that 'truthfulness' that she admires so much in the Dutch painters is in her own practice more than an attentive observation of objects: it is the interpretation of objects in the light, not of heaven, but of the novelist's purpose. Henry James expressed something of this after her death: 'We feel in her, always, that she proceeds from the abstract to the concrete; that her figures and her situations are evolved, as the phrase is, from her moral consciousness, and are only indirectly the products of observation.'[44] Now moral consciousness and observation are perhaps a more mixed affair than James allows for in this formulation, and yet it is true, as much of this chapter has attempted to demonstrate, that Eliot seldom observes with an eye only for pictorial effect: she knows, as it were, what it is that she is looking for. Thus, we know what James means when he says that 'the novel, . . . for her, was not primarily a picture of life, capable of deriving a high value from its form, but a moralized fable, the last word of a philosophy endeavouring to teach by example' (50). If moralized fable and picture of life are not to be as cleanly separated as this, we may yet say that for Eliot, the

---

[44] Henry James, 'The Life of George Eliot', *Atlantic Monthly* (1885); rpt. in *Partial Portraits* (Ann Arbor, Mich.,1970), 51.

picture of life was necessarily a moralized fable, directed at showing the spiritual consequences of guimp.

Realism as deployed by Eliot remains caught within its own fictions because it believes that it is rendering a sovereign truth distinct from its own processes, whereas its very form imposes the ethical sanctions of older traditions on to its material. Shaping Eliot's 'picture of life' is the moralized form of the parable, the retributive patterns of classical tragedy: thus Nemesis, the Furies, and the severe angel, emerging from their different traditions to meet in Eliot's fiction as agents of correction. In Bakhtinian terms, we might say that Eliot reverts, through Deronda, to the 'world of the epic', with its suppression of dialogue in the interests of an absolute language.[45] That 'hidden structural principle' that Girard traces in all scapegoating texts is here driving Eliot's realist narrative in the tracks of the moral fable; like Girard's example, 'This text is controlled by the effect of a scapegoat it does not acknowledge' (119). But realism that recognizes the 'truth' that it renders as partly of its own making, liberates itself from unconscious thraldom to its own processes. The temptations of narrative, its tendency to create a truth after its own desires or convictions, and the conflict of those temptations with the exigencies of everyday reality, are embodied in Conrad's Lord Jim: a scapegoat who, through being recognized as such, frees the novel from the constraints of its own means of representation.

---

[45] 'The world of the epic is the national heroic past: it is a world of "beginnings" and "peak times" in the national history, a world of fathers and of founders of families, a world of "firsts" and "bests"' (Bakhtin, 'Epic and Novel', 13).

Chapter 4

The Solidarity of the Craft and the Fellowship of Illusion: *Lord Jim*

The birthplace of the novel is the solitary individual, who is no longer able to express himself by giving examples of his most important concerns, is himself uncounseled, and cannot counsel others. . . .

A man listening to a story is in the company of the storyteller; even a man reading one shares this companionship. The reader of the novel, however, is isolated, more so than any other reader.[1]

why should the memory of these beings, seen in their obscure sun-bathed existence, demand to express itself in the shape of a novel, except on the ground of that mysterious fellowship which unites in a community of hopes and fears all the dwellers on this earth?[2]

I

On the one hand, a solitude speaking to solitude; on the other, the expression of a universal fellowship: this is a radical divergence, even as relating to a form on which it is notoriously difficult to agree. But Benjamin's theory and Conrad's recollections are cited here not as opposed debating positions, rather for their common preoccupation with human solitude, a concern which distinguishes both from even that qualified faith in community which George Eliot's fiction professes. Conrad, to be sure, would seem to be speaking here of the converse of solitude; but his 'mysterious fellowship' is asserted against a vision of isolation which makes the 'community of hopes and fears' seem almost abstract, compared with the fictional communities created by Eliot.

[1] Walter Benjamin, 'The Storyteller: Reflections on the Works of Nikolai Leskov', *Illuminations* (1950); trans. Harry Zohn (London, 1970), 87, 100.
[2] Joseph Conrad, *A Personal Record* (1912); ed. Zdzisław Najder (Oxford, 1988), 9.

For whereas Eliot can imagine solitude, as for instance in the ostracization of Silas Marner, it is recognized as that exactly because it entails exclusion from the human companionship that does exist in Raveloe, and to which Silas eventually gains access through the humanizing influence of Eppie. As Silas Marner and Dolly Winthrop accompany Aaron Winthrop and his bride, Eppie, to the house Silas is to share with the young couple, Eliot closes on a vision of domestic bliss:

The garden was fenced with stones on two sides, but in front there was an open fence, through which the flowers shone with answering gladness, as the four united people came within sight of them.

'O father,' said Eppie, 'what a pretty home ours is! I think nobody could be happier than we are.'[3]

Eliot's resolution, though more in keeping with the fairy-tale aspect of the tale than with her usual mode, is not at odds with the belief animating and structuring her fiction in general and this tale in particular, the conviction that the natural human state is with others of one's kind. In the Conrad universe, on the other hand, 'four united people' are more likely to constitute, say, the domestic unity of Mr Verloc, his wife, mother-in-law, and brother-in-law, precariously held together by the indolent good nature of Verloc and the dire need of the other three. Even where human community is represented more hopefully than in *The Secret Agent*, it tends to consist in that professional bond that is posited upon the homelessness of the participants. As the Accountant, the Captain, the Director, and the first narrator of 'Heart of Darkness', between whom there is the 'bond of the sea',[4] resign themselves to hearing Marlow's tale, clearly nobody has to get home to dinner. The hearth simply does not feature very often in Conrad; and when it does, it may well be the focus of human loneliness rather than of companionship, as, for instance, the little living-room in 'Amy Foster': 'There was a wicker cradle on the floor, a kettle spouting steam on the hob, and some child's linen lay drying on the fender.'[5]

[3] George Eliot, *Silas Marner The Weaver of Raveloe* (1861); ed. Q. D. Leavis (Harmondsworth, 1967), 244.

[4] Joseph Conrad, *Youth, Heart of Darkness, The End of the Tether* (1902); ed. Robert Kimbrough (Oxford, 1984), 45.

[5] Joseph Conrad, 'Amy Foster' (1901); in *Typhoon and Other Tales*, ed. Cedric Watts (Oxford, 1986), 236.

If the scene has any obvious precursor, it is in the profoundly ironical opening to *Dombey and Son*—with the important difference that Dickens's opening prefigures its own resolution in Dombey's reconciliation with his daughter, whereas Conrad's scene has as its main point the terrible loneliness of the stranger Yanko in his own home, alienated from his wife by the son of whom he is so proud. The apparently cosy scene anticipates Yanko's despairing death, deserted by his terrified wife: 'The lamp smoked, the fire was out, the chill of the stormy night oozed from the cheerless yellow paper on the wall. "Amy!" I called aloud and my voice seemed to lose itself in the emptiness of this tiny house as if I had cried in a desert' ('Amy' 238). The narrator's cry echoes that of the delirious Yanko, whose voice is also lost in his own house as if in a desert.

If Dickens's scene, as I have argued, is informed no less than Conrad's by the fear of solitude, that fear is subordinated to the plot movement which expels the threat to the hearth and unites the chosen few. In Conrad's tale there is not even that pretence: Yanko dies in loneliness, betrayed like so many of Conrad's figures—like, for instance, that other foreigner on British soil, in all other respects the diametric opposite of the lithe and energetic Yanko: Mr Verloc, the indolent Secret Agent of foreign embassies and of the British police, the model husband, son-in-law, and brother-in-law. For if Yanko's deserted hearth becomes a sadly ironic comment on his lost domestic unity, there is hardly less irony, though of a less tragic cast, in the depiction of Mr Verloc's hearth, 'the house in which Mr. Verloc carried on his business of a seller of shady wares, exercised his vocation of a protector of society, and cultivated his domestic virtues': 'He found at home the ease of his body and the peace of his conscience, together with Mrs. Verloc's wifely attentions and Mrs. Verloc's mother's deferential regard.'[6] It is symptomatic of the sardonic irony of this novel that it is indeed in this home and next to his fireside that Mr Verloc should find ultimately 'the ease of his body and the peace of his conscience' as a result of 'Mrs. Verloc's wifely attentions', leaving him 'in the fullness of his domestic ease reposing on a sofa' (*SA* 285), with the carving knife she provided for his supper in his chest. But this is more than a ghastly irony: it is a complex demonstration of what Jacques Berthoud has called 'the

[6] Joseph Conrad, *The Secret Agent* (1907); ed. Roger Tennant (Oxford, 1984), 5–6.

appalling fact that "normality", far from shielding us from
"disaster", may in fact drive us straight into it'.[7] Conrad at last
admits the lurking Other to the fireside, and it proves to be the
Angel in the House with a knife in her hand.

To Conrad, then, the great moral imperatives are those which are
conceived to sustain a solidarity maintained only fitfully, or which,
the nightmare runs, may be only illusory. In his own much-quoted
words: 'Those who read me know my conviction that the world, the
temporal world, rests on a very few simple ideas; so simple that they
must be as old as the hills. It rests notably, among others, on the
idea of Fidelity' (*PR*, p. xix). This idea, indeed, is at the centre of
Conrad's fiction, certainly at the centre of *Lord Jim*, the focus of this
chapter. But those who read Conrad know also that the world must
rest upon the idea of Fidelity because its contrary, the threat of
betrayal, is so prevalent and so real. Nostromo, the ironically
named Captain Fidanza, dies '"betrayed—betrayed by—" But he
did not say by whom or by what he was dying betrayed.'[8] Our Man
rather than One of Us, Nostromo struggles to articulate the insight
which comes to so many of Conrad's characters, though usually too
late. Mr Verloc, for instance, also, though much less reassuringly,
'our man', 'a servant of law and order, faithful, trusted, accurate,
admirable, with perhaps one single amiable weakness: the idealistic
belief in being loved for himself' (*SA* 288), dies knowing nothing
except that he was not, after all, loved for himself. Verloc's sole
revenge is to bequeath the belief in being loved for oneself to his
widow and murderess, who in turn dies betrayed by Comrade
Ossipon. And in all these instances, the terrible poignancy of
betrayal is intensified by the victim's *knowledge* of that betrayal:
Winnie Verloc's murderous blow is 'leisurely enough' for her
husband 'to take in the full meaning of the portent' (262); Haldin,
in *Under Western Eyes*, is informed before his execution that it was
'the man well known to you, in whose rooms you remained for
several hours on Monday . . . on whose information you have been
arrested'.[9] Fidelity in Conrad, in short, is more often known by its
absence than by its presence: community and solitude do not
preclude each other.

[7] Jacques Berthoud, *Joseph Conrad: The Major Phase* (Cambridge, 1978), 146.

[8] Joseph Conrad, *Nostromo* (1904); ed. Keith Carabine (Oxford, 1984), 559.

[9] Joseph Conrad, *Under Western Eyes* (1910); ed. Jeremy Hawthorn (Oxford,
1983), 93.

II

In *Lord Jim* Conrad most consciously and profoundly extends his concern with human loneliness and solidarity, with fidelity and betrayal, to his practice of the novelist's craft, and to the social function of narrative, ultimately the communal value of art and the imagination. On the face of it, the whole of the novel presents a refutation of Benjamin's assertion that the novel reveals the individual's inability 'to express himself by giving examples of his most important concerns': *Lord Jim* seems so demonstrably an anxious pondering of Marlow's—and Conrad's—most important concerns, dramatized exactly, for the most part, as a communal narrative. But if we follow that pondering through all its assertions and retractions, its certainties and its tentativenesses, we may find that it issues in a rueful abstention from counsel, leaving Marlow affirming, paradoxically, 'I affirm nothing. Perhaps you may pronounce—after you've read.'[10]

Marlow does not affirm, because he is the vehicle of Conrad's doubt rather than the exponent of his beliefs. The relation in which he stands to his material is as much part of Conrad's subject as the content of his narration: in parallel to Marlow's enquiry, Conrad enacts his own investigation into the relationship between story-teller and audience, between novelist and reader—finally between individual aspiration and communal effort. Edward Said has with admirable clarity traced Marlow's lineage as part of 'the novel's consolidation of authority':

There is first the authority of the author—someone writing out the processes of society in an acceptable institutionalized manner, observing conventions, following patterns, and so forth. Then there is the authority of the narrator, whose discourse anchors the narrative in recognizable, and hence existentially referential, circumstances. Last, there is what might be called the authority of the community, whose representative most often is the family but also is the nation, the specific locality, and the concrete historical moment. Together these functioned most energetically, most noticeably, during the early nineteenth century as the novel opened up to history in an unprecedented way. Conrad's Marlow inherits all this directly.[11]

[10] Joseph Conrad, *Lord Jim* (1900); ed. John Batchelor (Oxford, 1983), 339.
[11] Edward Said, *Culture and Imperialism* (London, 1993), 92.

Exactly—and Conrad knows it very well, which is what prevents his novel from being the 'self-validating' (92) structure that Said, like Jameson before him, seems to want Lord Jim to be. Marlow is in fact called into being to question exactly the three kinds of authority Said identifies so cogently.

To start with only one aspect of 'the novel's consolidation of authority': that concept of a community of readers so essential to George Eliot's own sense of her novelistic calling is in Conrad undermined by scepticism, not only in the face of a mysterious and possibly hostile reality, but also as regards the social, moral, ultimately linguistic processes whereby a community attempts to establish and maintain itself. 'Words, as is well known, are the great foes of reality', says the narrator of Under Western Eyes, to explain his lack of faith in his own narration (3); a far cry from the confident flourish with which George Eliot's narrator introduces himself to the readers of Adam Bede: 'With a single drop of ink for a mirror, the Egyptian sorcerer undertakes to reveal to any chance comer far-reaching visions of the past. This is what I undertake to do for you, reader.'[12]

The novel—Conrad's novel, that is—has lost that faith in its own power to mediate between the reader and a represented reality. What it gains through its sacrifice of certainty is self-awareness: awareness of itself as creating structure and as created by structure; and by analogy, awareness of human beings as creators and creations of social structure. Characters in novels, like characters outside novels, may create their own fictions and yet be structured by larger narrative purposes than their own. Jim's 'vocation for the sea had declared itself' after a 'course of light holiday literature' (LJ 5); Kurtz's high-minded intentions had been similarly shaped by the fictions of the colonial enterprise, represented to the gullible and the idealistic as 'weaning those ignorant millions from their horrid ways' (HD 59). 'All Europe', Marlow tells us, 'contributed to the making of Kurtz' (117); Jim, though less cosmopolitan in origin, is no less made by his participation in the fictions of his society, and he

---

[12] George Eliot, Adam Bede (1858); (London, 1960), 7. George Levine makes a similar point, though using different extracts from both authors: 'Conrad speaks without the confidence we have heard in the passage from Adam Bede, where the narrator knows she is talking to somebody, that she and her readers form a community and are talking about a community' (The Realistic Imagination: English Fiction from Frankenstein to Lady Chatterley (Chicago, 1981), 48).

creates his own fictions accordingly. The Patusan sections of *Lord Jim*, which have not in general received much critical favour, may become more intelligible if seen *as* a fiction, the creation not so much of Conrad's ethical intention as of his imaginative identification with Jim.

In what follows, then, I shall attempt to assess the status and effect of Jim's romance through the intricate oppositions set up by a complex system of narrative.[13] Placing the various levels of narration in *Lord Jim* with precision can be a niggling and not necessarily rewarding business:[14] even Genette, whose taxonomy of narrative would seem to provide for every eventuality, confesses that in this novel 'the entanglement [of narrations] reaches the bounds of general intelligibility'.[15] Still, it is possible to identify three major narrational blocks, entailing two shifts in narrative mode: from anonymous narration to Marlow's spoken recitation, and from that to his written account. Each such block addresses a different implied audience, that is, a different narrative community, which in turn has to be seen in relation to the narrative as a whole and to that romance which is filtered through Marlow's narration.[16] It is the argument of this chapter that those shifting relations are crucial to the meaning of the novel, in reproducing

[13] For the argument that Jim's romance is only one of *three* romances in the novel, see Tracy Seeley, 'Conrad's Modernist Romance: *Lord Jim*', *ELH* 59 (1992), 495–511: 'the opposing impulses of dream and disillusion shape three romance narratives: Jim's, Marlow's and Conrad's' (497). Seeley's hospitable definition of 'romance' seems to me unnecessarily to blur a distinction that it then has to redraw in order to differentiate between the three narrations.

[14] This is not meant to reflect on Jacob Lothe's meticulous analysis in *Conrad's Narrative Method* (Oxford, 1989), which I had not read at the time of writing this chapter. Lothe consistently relates narrative effect to thematic function, thus avoiding the soulless taxonomizing that narratology is capable of.

[15] Gérard Genette, *Narrative Discourse: An Essay in Method* (1972); trans. Jane E. Lewin (Oxford, 1980), 232. For the record, the first narration in *Lord Jim* would seem to be extradiegetic-heterodiegetic, whereas Marlow's is intradiegetic-heterodiegetic, absorbing into it Jim's intradiegetic-homodiegetic narration. I am not sure, though, that this is what Genette means by general intelligibility.

[16] I have throughout used Genette's distinction between *récit*, *histoire*, and *narration*. These are translated as *narrative*, *story*, and *narrating* by Jane E. Lewin, the last as a gerundal equivalent of the French noun. I have accepted her translation for the first two terms, but have preferred *narration* to her *narrating*, as designating, I think, more naturally both the act of narrating and its product. Thus the *narrative* is *Lord Jim*; within it is contained the *story* of Jim himself, a story that exists nowhere as such, but is constituted of the various *narrations* belonging to different narrators.

different narrative communities, which is to say different bodies of value.

But to talk of *meaning* is to suggest a unified abstraction recoverable from the intricacies of the novel, an assumption which would be more damaging to *Lord Jim* than to most other novels: *meaning* in this novel inheres so much in the process of the search, in the always-deferred problem of closure, the quest for the final pronouncement that will close the account. That this was true at the most literal level we know from Conrad's well-documented dismay and delight at the growth under his hand of what was originally projected to be a short story;[17] in that sense Marlow's quest for meaning becomes the equivalent of Conrad's own quest for that Finis which *Blackwood's Magazine* was no less anxious than Marlow himself to hear spoken. The novel is self-conscious also in this sense, in its troubled search for a resolution: after the first four chapters, at any rate, it is not moving towards a predefined goal as much as cumulatively defining that goal.

III

The fact that Marlow's voice commences its marathon narration only in chapter 5 may well derive from Conrad's change of intention regarding the treatment of his material; but if we consider the effect of the peculiarity rather than its cause, we note that it does more than simply 'introduce' Marlow. In its way, the first narration is as much as Marlow's a performance structured by certain presuppositions:

He was an inch, perhaps two, under six feet, powerfully built, and he advanced straight at you with a slight stoop of the shoulders, head forward, and a fixed from-under stare which made you think of a charging bull. His

---

[17] Conrad's correspondence with his editor and publisher, stretching from 4 June 1898 ('I rather think it ought to be worked out in no less than 20–25 thousand words') to 12 Nov. 1900, is usefully reproduced in the Norton Critical Edition of *Lord Jim*, ed. Thomas C. Moser (New York, 1968), 291–305; the correspondence is taken mainly from *Joseph Conrad: Letters to William Blackwood and David S. Meldrum*, ed. William Blackburn (Durham, NC, 1958). From the correspondence it is clear that whereas Conrad at any given moment felt confident that the end was in sight, or at any rate deemed it advisable to tell his publisher that it was, that end kept receding as Conrad approached it. As late as 3 Apr. 1900 he writes to his editor, 'now I start to write the last chap.'—which eventually gets written in a 23-hour stint on 14 July.

voice was deep, loud, and his manner displayed a kind of dogged self-assertion that had nothing aggressive in it. It seemed a necessity, and it was directed apparently as much at himself as at anybody else. He was spotlessly neat, apparelled in immaculate white from shoes to hat, and in the various Eastern ports where he got his living as ship-chandler's water-clerk he was very popular. (*LJ* 3)

This blandly informative narration ostensibly aims for the illusion of transparency favoured by the realist narrative: it is possible to believe that we are simply being told about Jim. But though the narration is anonymous, it has its own voice, an implied persona: well-informed, discursive, but not premissed upon its own omniscience. Omniscience does not have to hover between 'an inch' and 'perhaps two', or speculate about what 'seemed' to be or was 'apparently' the case: it would know these things. The narrator's conversational register, involving his audience in the pronominal hospitality of 'straight at you' and 'made you think', assumes that speaker and audience potentially share the perception.

In short, the first narrator is also 'one of us'. But reinforcing this narrative bonding between story-teller and audience is another convention: the tacit reliance of literary narrative on the informed receptivity of the reader to ironic resonance. The ironic force, for instance, of Jim's 'immaculate white' clothing, his 'spotlessly neat' apparel, is made accessible only through the variation from *immaculate* to its synonym *spotless*, to produce the common term *spot*: 'the soft spot, the place of decay, the determination to lounge safely through existence' (13)—the spot which Jim, it would seem, is not as free of as his apparel would suggest. Even so simple an irony depends on that collusion between reader and author that we have seen Jane Austen exploiting, and that in turn depends on the reader's access to a larger context than the narrative instant, either through a prior reading or as part of a generic expectation. Narrator and reader are united in the fellowship of irony.

From this fellowship Jim is excluded. The companionable tone of the narration invites us to share its own perspective, whereby Jim's experience on the *Patna* is explicable as one of 'those events of the sea that show in the light of day the inner worth of a man, the edge of his temper, and the fibre of his stuff; that reveal the quality of his resistance and the secret truth of his pretences, not only to others but also to himself' (10). The generalizing strain postulates a simple presence or absence of worth, temper, stuff, resistance—near-synonyms for that 'truth' which the narration assumes is demonstrable and knowable. By this doctrine, Jim's failure on the *Patna* merely releases the ironies that have been potentialized by the earlier narration: Jim's romantic notions have incapacitated him for true heroism; he is 'really' a coward. If the tone of the opening chapters is never snide, there is yet the condescension of omniscience to delusion that characterizes dramatic irony, the 'had he but known' that is at the root of tragedy and of comedy, the plight of Oedipus and of Malvolio. The ironies in the first four chapters, based on the relatively simple contrast between Jim's early conception of himself—'always an example of devotion to duty, and as unflinching as a hero in a book' (6)—and his behaviour in the crisis on the *Patna*, terminate in the court-room.[18]

If, then, the first narrator is also 'one of us', he is united with us in our slightly sardonic distance from the *alazon* and our tolerance of a weakness that does not threaten our own security. And if Jim's tale had ended there in court, it would have been no more than a not-unsympathetic account of hubris meeting its conventional reward, a wry ironic fable on the wishes of human vanity, a symbolic expulsion in the cancelling of his certificate. By the conventions of this narrative, the court trying to arrive at the facts is the community's appointed judiciary: its jurisdiction quite properly constituted, consisting of a magistrate and two nautical assessors, it is capable of reaching a verdict and entitled to pass judgement. It is in a special sense the narrative community: it listens and judges.

But here, by the first of those inversions that are to complicate our reading of this novel, Jim figures both as subject of the narration and as narrator, and in his halting attempts at reaching the 'facts' required by the court, he introduces a narration that questions, albeit very tentatively, the certainties of the narration enclosing him: 'They wanted facts. Facts! They demanded facts from him, as if facts could explain anything!' (29). And as Jim's narration culminates in a sense of its own pointlessness, his eyes fall on Marlow, and the novel's centre of gravity shifts, averting the

---

[18] Ian Watt speculates, partly on the evidence of the Harvard manuscript of 'Lord Jim: A Sketch', that in the original conception 'Jim would probably have ended up, like Almayer and Willems, as a contemptible outcast in a Malay village' (*Conrad in the Nineteenth Century* (London, 1980), 264). If so, these ironies would have been simpler and more central.

imminent closure: 'The sound of his own truthful statements confirmed his deliberate opinion that speech was of no use to him any longer. That man there seemed to be aware of his hopeless difficulty. Jim looked at him, then turned away resolutely, as after a final parting' (33).

The text mimics closure in the spurious resolution of Jim's turning away: in the event the final parting is to be deferred by several years. The first narration is truncated without ever achieving that recognition that marks the classic resolution of irony. And the scapegoat of the narrative, at the moment of submitting to the ceremony of expulsion, becomes conscious *to* the narrative, as the burden of words is passed on to Marlow. By an effect of overlapping narration, the case is reopened, to question exactly that which the first narration has taken for granted: 'the sovereign power enthroned in a fixed standard of conduct' (50). The effect is something as if, say, Tiresias were to question the justice of Oedipus' fate at the moment of *anagnorisis*: breaking the pattern of resolution, it calls for a completely new narrative structure. Sophocles produced that new structure much later in *Oedipus at Colonus*; Conrad, in one of his bolder transitions, cuts immediately from the court-room to the 'verandah draped in motionless foliage and crowned with flowers' (33) which is to constitute the locus of the new narration.

IV

Marlow's narration is suited to its languid setting, the style and rhythms adapted to the entertainment of 'a lot of men too indolent for whist' (94). Confronted with, or rather flanked by, an audience whose lives would seem to be in every respect congruent with his own, Marlow could be seen as the archetypal story-teller, recounting a tale reflecting and reinforcing the certainties of his community; indeed, he has a good deal in common with the story-teller as characterized by Benjamin.[19] But in the event his narration owes much of its force to the disappointment of expectation, that is,

---

[19] For instance, 'the trading seaman' is the 'archaic representative' of the first of the two main groups of story-tellers, those who travel and those who stay at home (Benjamin, 'The Storyteller', *Illuminations*, 85); and 'The storyteller takes what he tells from experience—his own or that reported by others. And he in turn makes it the experience of those who are listening to his tale' (ibid. 87).

to the contrast between the socially-binding and the disruptive narrative.[20] Although constructed with a wonderful instinct for the giving and withholding of information, the delicate game of keeping an audience's attention without exasperating it, the narration turns out to be, in effect, aimless: it achieves no conclusion, no resolution, despite Marlow's groping for some pronouncement which will clarify also to himself the significance of Jim's history.

One way of registering the indirection subverting Marlow's narration is through the absence of that dramatic irony lending pungency to the first narration. Whereas the first narrator can prepare his ironies and spring his traps with the Olympian austerity of the omniscient ironist, Marlow's doubt undermines his irony. Of course, his tone is habitually ironic, but it is no longer the stable irony of the first narrator, resting upon certainty about both the outcome and the significance of the story.[21] Since there is no revelation to follow, and more significantly, since Marlow's narration questions the stability of the beliefs supporting such irony, Jim no longer figures as the deluded actor, the scapegoat of the narrative. The ceremony of expulsion having been performed, the structures validating that ceremony are themselves examined.

In examining what is in essence the system of beliefs of his listeners, Marlow is made to pick his way carefully between the opposed dangers of alienating his audience and soothing them to sleep. His strategy is to introduce Jim not as an egregious aberrancy, but as 'one of us', indeed as a representative of the solider elements of social cohesion:

[20] Fredric Jameson comments that 'The representational fiction of a storytelling situation organized around Marlow marks the vain attempt to conjure back the older unity of the literary institution, to return to that older concrete social situation of which narrative transmission was but a part, and of which public and bard or storyteller are intrinsic . . . components' (*The Political Unconscious: Narrative as a Socially Symbolic Act* (London, 1981), 219–20). I think Conrad does not so much make a 'vain attempt' as recognize the vanity of attempting to recover 'that older concrete social situation' of which he questions the foundation.

[21] I am using the term *stable irony* in Wayne C. Booth's sense of that irony which 'does not mock our efforts by making general claims about the ironic universe, or the universe of human discourse. . . . it delimits a world of discourse in which we can say with great security certain things that are violated by the overt words of the discourse' (*A Rhetoric of Irony* (London, 1974), 6). Anthony Winner maintains that 'Jim's leap, his trial, and his banishment from trust all involve familiar standards; they can be judged against a set of values that provides a firm tenor for a stable moral irony' (*Culture and Irony: Studies in Joseph Conrad's Major Novels* (Charlottesville, Va., 1988), 35).

He stood there for all the parentage of his kind, for men and women by no means clever or amusing, but whose very existence is based upon honest faith, and upon the instinct of courage. I don't mean military courage, or civil courage, or any special kind of courage. I mean just that inborn ability to look temptations straight in the face—a readiness unintellectual enough, goodness knows, but without pose—a power of resistance, don't you see, ungracious if you like, but priceless—an unthinking and blessed stiffness before the outward and inward terrors, before the might of nature, and the seductive corruption of men—backed by a faith invulnerable to the strength of facts, to the contagion of example, to the solicitation of ideas. (43)

To the casual listener, Marlow's digression on the stolid predict-ability of unimaginative courage will have the ring of a eulogy on some stock Conradian virtues. In fact, Jim's representative, even symbolic, significance casts doubt on 'that inborn ability': it may after all fail us, may in fact not be inborn at all. What Jim stands for is, it seems, not a reality but an ideal, perhaps even a fiction. It is his anxiety to retain belief in that ideal that initially engages Marlow's interest in Jim:

Why I longed to go grubbing into the deplorable details of an occurrence which, after all, concerned me no more than as a member of an obscure body of men held together by a community of inglorious toil and by fidelity to a certain standard of conduct, I can't explain. . . . I see well enough now that I hoped for the impossible—for the laying of what is the most obstinate ghost of man's creation, of the uneasy doubt uprising like a mist, secret and gnawing like a worm, and more chilling than the certitude of death—the doubt of the sovereign power enthroned in a fixed standard of conduct. (50)

Marlow finds in Jim a test case, and what is at issue is not Jim's innocence or guilt: on that score the court's verdict is in accordance with the 'facts' and, as far as it goes, perfectly accurate. As Jacques Berthoud says, 'The problem is not that the verdict against Jim is wrong, but that it is *right*.'[22] But the code of conduct that restricts itself to facts may itself be deficient just in that restriction; the court may not have jurisdiction over the larger issue, the efficacy and the moral authority of 'a fixed standard of conduct'. This doubt, however, asserts itself without producing an alternative measure to

[22] Berthoud, *The Major Phase*, 68.

help Marlow to exculpate Jim. So if he can 'now see' that he was hoping 'for the impossible', this does not prevent his narration from re-creating exactly that impossible quest, the laying of the ghost of doubt.

It is his membership of 'an obscure body of men held together by a community of inglorious toil' that denies Marlow the distance required for a sustained ironic view of Jim. He is at least as capable as the first narrator of noting ironic discrepancies, but he cannot contemplate them dispassionately: he is involved with them, appalled at them, at times angry at Jim's own blindness to them, as when Jim comments on the death of the donkey-man:

> 'Why don't you laugh?' he said. 'A joke hatched in hell. Weak heart! . . . I wish sometimes mine had been.'
> This irritated me. 'Do you?' I exclaimed with deep-rooted irony. 'Yes! Can't *you* understand?' he cried. 'I don't know what more you could wish for,' I said angrily.

Marlow's anger stems from an identification with the victim of his irony that no *eiron* can afford. In this, it is similar to Brierly's exasperation with Jim, with this difference that Marlow's irritation is of a piece with his sympathy, and is easily baffled by the helplessness of its object:

> He gave me an utterly uncomprehending glance. This shaft had also gone wide of the mark, and he was not the man to bother about stray arrows. Upon my word, he was too unsuspecting; he was not fair game. I was pleased that my missile had been thrown away,—that he had not even heard the twang of the bow. (108)

Being 'unsuspecting' is of course exactly what makes one 'fair game' for irony as deployed in the first narration. Marlow's relief at missing his mark derives from his seeing Jim as 'one of us' also in the wider sense of a fellow human being, whereby we feel for others as for ourselves: 'If he had not enlisted my sympathies he had done better for himself—he had gone to the very fount and origin of that sentiment, he had reached the secret sensibility of my egoism' (152).

And yet it would probably not do to take too exalted a view, at this point, of Marlow's compassion; the other sense of 'one of us', that is, one of that select group of British seamen and gentlemen who subscribe to a particular code, remains operative and precludes sympathy for outsiders like the chief engineer, who, after all, has his own Furies, not the less harrowing for being pink and batrachian. If these people are beneath the irony of the first narrator, they are also beyond the anger and compassion of Marlow: 'I had no solicitude for him; I was not furious with him and sorry for him: his experience was of no importance, his redemption would have had no point for me. He had grown old in minor iniquities, and could no longer inspire aversion or pity'(51). Rather like Jim himself, Marlow seems to believe that 'The quality of these men did not matter' (24): he saves his fury and his pity for a member of his own class and background, whose failure he can measure so much more precisely against their common standards. If the first narration moves towards extinction of the difference between Jim and his fellow crew members, Marlow's narration credits Jim, as it were, with that difference and then tests the reality and implications of this distinction—a distinction he draws even before he has spoken to Jim : 'And note, I did not care a rap about the behaviour of the other two' (41):

There he stood, clean-limbed, clean-faced, firm on his feet, as promising a boy as the sun ever shone on; and, looking at him, knowing all he knew and a little more too, I was as angry as though I had detected him trying to get something out of me by false pretences. He had no business to look so sound. I thought to myself—well, if this sort can go wrong like that ... (40)

Marlow's first response, then, is that of the first narrator: to assume that Jim's 'promising' appearance is a matter of 'false pretences', in other words, that there is a 'real' Jim that is somehow masquerading as 'one of us'. Significantly, this belief allows him one flicker of dramatic irony, which is to say a moment of certainty, in his reflection that he knew 'all he knew and a little more'—for a last instant Jim is seen as deluded, knowing less, factually speaking, than his narrator: in this case, the fact that the *Patna* did not sink. If Marlow could have persisted in this, seeing the true and the false as distinct, the demonstrable difference between a 'genuine sovereign' and the 'infernal alloy' (45), his faith would not have been much shaken except in his own ability to tell a bad penny from a good; it's the suspicion that the whole currency is unsound that horrifies him. But in spite of this suspicion and for all his detachment from the proceedings of the court of inquiry, he retains a concept of value derived from community; otherwise his narration could have adopted the free-floating, devastating irony of *The Secret Agent*.

V

Thus Marlow's account is a search for the certainty of closure, for that 'sense of blessed finality' that ends narratives as well as lives: 'End! Finis! the potent word that exorcises from the house of life the haunting shadow of fate' (176). One way of closing the account would have been to adopt Brierly's proposed 'solution' of sending Jim out of sight, thus sparing society the embarrassment of publicly examining the failure of its own codes: in a classic scapegoating procedure, Jim would have been taking upon himself the communal failure: 'The fellow's a gentleman if he ain't fit to be touched—he will understand' (67), as Brierly so inimitably says.

But Jim, inconveniently, 'was eager to go through the ceremony of execution' (153); he is quite as aware of his gentlemanly duty as Brierly could wish him, but he interprets that propriety differently: whereas to Brierly it is a matter of saving communal face, a closing of the ranks, to Jim it is a matter of salvaging individual self-respect: '"I couldn't clear out," Jim began. "The skipper did—that's all very well for him. I couldn't, and I wouldn't. They all got out of it in one way or another, but it wouldn't do for me"' (79). Jim's 'it wouldn't do for me' is not unlike Brierly's 'I can't do it myself—but you . . .' (68) that understandably offends Marlow. Jim's version of this moral fastidiousness is a kind of *noblesse oblige*: it's 'all very well' for the skipper to clear off, not possessing the exalted standards which somehow Jim still believes himself to have: 'He was not one of them; he was altogether of another sort' (80). So if classically, the resolution of irony coincides with the victim's achievement of self-knowledge, this is not a terminus reached by the first narration, or available to Marlow's narration. Jim, as much as Marlow, regards himself as 'one of us'; indeed, he shows a certain fastidiousness in his choice of confidant: 'Of course I wouldn't have talked to you about all this if you had not been a gentleman' (131).

Thus Jim, unlike Marlow, never questions the 'sovereign power' of the code in whose name judgement is passed on him: in this, if not in all respects, he is the opposite of Chester, to whom the cancelled certificate is 'A bit of ass's skin' (161). Though he has no very high opinion of the proceedings themselves—'Apparently he shared Brierly's contemptuous opinion of these proceedings ordained by law' (80)—he accepts the judgement: not as establishing his guilt, but as a manifestation of his disgrace, which may perhaps be exorcized by the ceremony. If Marlow is looking for the substance of the code, its underlying moral reality, Jim is concerned with its shadow, its public face, whether of praise or blame—to assume for the moment a distinction between underlying reality and public face that the novel questions. The distinction is drawn by Marlow, in his uneasy confession that 'still the idea obtrudes itself that he made so much of his disgrace while it is the guilt alone that matters' (177). But matters to whom? To Brierly, whose idea of 'professional decency' slips unguardedly into 'the name for that kind of decency' (68)? To the French lieutenant, who refuses to consider whether honour might not 'reduce itself to not being found out' (149)?

Jim, at any rate, finds some kind of validation in the very public aspect of his trial: disgrace moves on the same public stage as heroism; guilt can be an extremely private matter. Marlow, by contrast, recognizes the meaning of the crime but deplores the ceremony of punishment: 'The real significance of crime is in its being a breach of faith with the community of mankind, and from that point of view he was no mean traitor, but his execution was a hole-and-corner affair' (157). Punishment is perhaps of all forms of closure most dependent for its moral efficacy on consensus as to its significance and appropriateness: the expulsion of Oedipus can cleanse Thebes and end the play only if the community and Oedipus are in accord on its significance and justice. Thus what prolongs the narrative is Marlow's questioning of the decorum of communal retribution: 'These proceedings had all the cold vengefulness of a death-sentence, had all the cruelty of a sentence of exile' (158). Marlow confronts without resolving the dilemma of community: premissed upon the solidarity of its members, it cannot enforce that solidarity except by expulsion of those who do not conform, which confirms the breach in the act of reaffirming the community.

If Jim has broken faith with 'the community of mankind', he nevertheless appeals to Marlow in the name of a solidarity for which 'one of us' comes more and more to seem a question-begging imprecision. For there are other loyalties and kinships than the bonds of class and profession:

he was a youngster of the sort you like to see about you; of the sort you like
to imagine yourself to have been; of the sort whose appearance claims the
fellowship of these illusions you had thought gone out, extinct, cold, and
which, as if rekindled at the approach of another flame, give a flutter deep,
deep down somewhere, give a flutter of light . . . of heat! (128)

Against or apart from 'the solidarity of the craft' (131), then, we
have the fellowship of illusions: 'besides the fellowship of the craft
there is felt the strength of a wider feeling—the feeling that binds a
man to a child' (129). If this is the feeling that binds Marlow to the
boyish Jim, whom 'people, perfect strangers, took to . . . as one
takes to a nice child' (198), it is also Wordsworth's natural piety
that binds the man to his own childhood, and, in this case, Marlow
to the illusions of his own youth. It is the fellowship affirmed, at the
end of 'Youth', by 'the man of finance, the man of accounts, the
man of law', not only with each other and with Marlow, but with
their own youth: 'we all nodded at him . . . our weary eyes looking
still, looking always, looking anxiously for something out of life,
that while it is expected is already gone—has passed unseen, in a
sigh, in a flash—together with the youth, with the strength, with the
romance of illusions' (Y 42).

Marlow's bond with Jim even at times anticipates that between
the narrator-captain in 'The Secret Sharer' and his uninvited
'sharer', the fugitive Leggatt: 'my Jim, for the most part, skulked
down below as if he had been a stowaway' (*LJ* 201). And like the
Captain's instant accord with Leggatt, based upon nothing more
substantial than the fact that he is also 'a *Conway* boy', Marlow's
identification with Jim contains an element that unites them both
against the fellowship of the craft, in so far as that fellowship
requires the expulsion of Jim. The Captain defies proper maritime
authority in sheltering Leggatt and abetting his escape, and
endangers his craft and his crew in facilitating that escape. There
is then a fellowship that may transcend or take priority over even
the solidarity of the craft, a less communally based, more
individualized solidarity with a single other human being, and it
is that fellowship to which Marlow more and more responds. But,
for the time being, the fellowship of illusion generates no narrative
of its own, establishes no coherent structure to contain Jim's case.
Marlow's narration continues to test for a mode that will disperse
the cloud obscuring Jim.

VI

The three interpolated cases of Brierly, the French lieutenant, and little Bob Stanton can thus be seen also as narrative controls, essays in narrational mode. All three figures contribute to a complex perspective on Jim, but not as a simple measure of his failure. It may be true, as Guerard maintains, that 'The natural unreflective heroism of the French lieutenant and Stanton thus help us to put Jim's reveries of heroism, and his actual failures and excuses, into a clearer perspective',[23] but that is hardly a new perspective: the novel has from the first chapter enforced this ironic view of Jim's reveries. From a professional and ethical point of view these histories merely confirm what we know already; and since the narrative is searching exactly for a mode that can accommodate that aspect of Jim's story *not* contained by the sentence of the court, these three wonderfully managed narrative digressions can contribute only by indirection.

Of the three, Bob Stanton seems to have been closest in temperament and situation to Jim. Indeed, his story is introduced parenthetically to Jim's, as part of a comment on the unromantic quality of the life of a water-clerk: 'You can't imagine a mode of life more barren of consolation, less capable of being invested with a spark of glamour' (149). And yet Bob risks—and loses—his life in an attempt to save a lady's maid. On the face of it, saving a lone woman from a sinking ship is just such stuff as Jim's heroic dreams are made on. But Bob also has that in him which 'made us laugh till we cried' (150), and it is his fate to die as he lived, provoking laughter—or tears only as an excess of mirth. The awkward logistics of real life, the mere necessity to house the heroic spirit in a body of a certain shape and size, provide such an ill-matched cast for the heroic deed—'poor Bob was the shortest chief mate in the merchant service, and the woman stood five feet ten in her shoes and was as strong as a horse'—that Bob's courageous determination comes to seem like a comic tussle, 'for all the world, sir, like a naughty youngster fighting with his mother' (150). The wry comedy of the seaman's anecdote (the teller 'hiding a smile at the recollection'), culminating in the ship going down 'plop', irresistibly determines our response to the event: however much we may admire Bob's courage, it's somehow not the point of the

[23] Albert J. Guerard, *Conrad the Novelist* (Cambridge, Mass., 1958), 159.

story. The quality of an action, narratively speaking, consists not merely in its moral components but also in its physical trappings. Poor Stevie in *The Secret Agent* dies for a better social order as much as Victor Haldin in *Under Western Eyes*, but, though one feels a brute for saying so, his death occurs in a different register. Thus, given the decidedly comic perspective on Bob's death, it's difficult to agree with Tony Tanner that he 'died like the hero Jim could only dream of being'.[24] To us, Bob's death may seem heroic, but only if we abstract it from its telling; and it would have fallen pitifully short of Jim's dreams. Jim needs a larger stage, or at any rate less recalcitrant props—which is to say a different narrative mode.

The laconic account of Bob's unequal struggle follows directly upon Marlow's meeting with the French lieutenant, who also, in one sense, succeeds where Jim fails—in this instance much more pointedly, as it were, in that he stays on the *Patna* for thirty hours, and lives to tell the tale. But if he displays exactly the kind of stoic obedience to duty that the Service requires—'"It was judged proper," he said, lifting his eyebrows dispassionately, "that one of the officers should remain to keep an eye open'" (141)—his formulation speaks of the impersonal agency of the hierarchy in which 'it was judged', and in which he acts merely as 'one of the officers'. It is not a system which is designed to appeal to the individual romantic imagination. Of course, this may, and does, argue against the romantic imagination as an aid to seamanship; but again we have the double-edged comparison, whereby the lieutenant falls short of Jim's ideal quite as much as Jim falls short of his. The unreflecting courage that can come to terms with the origins of fear in 'a simple head-ache or a fit of indigestion' (147) situates the spirit in the bowels. There is much to be said for this practical view of impractical emotions, and Conrad was to say it memorably through MacWhirr in 'Typhoon'; but in *Lord Jim* it is no more than a blocked perspective. Although the lieutenant seems leniently disposed towards Jim in his recognition that 'Given a certain combination of circumstances, fear is sure to come' (146), his verdict is absolute and unimaginative: 'I can offer no opinion—because—monsieur—I know nothing of it' (148). The lieutenant's courage is 'a faith invulnerable to . . . the solicitation of ideas', his one abstraction—honour—a concept that he cannot bring himself to question with any acuteness; in him the 'blessed stiffness before the outward and inner terrors' seems to be part of a physical inertia rather than a 'power of resistance'. It is true, as Tony Tanner says, that the lieutenant 'speaks as the worthiest possible representative of the world of "facts"': he embodies the kind of behaviour that would be commended by a court of inquiry. So if indeed 'effectively he passes the most adverse judgment on [Jim]' (36), that judgement is merely a confirmation of the court's judgement, which is not in dispute as much as beside the point. The lieutenant's own 'few simple notions' make of him 'one of those steady, reliable men who are the raw material of great reputations, one of those uncounted lives that are buried without drums and trumpets under the foundations of monumental successes' (143–4). It is not a denial of the value of steadiness and reliability to note that they minister mainly to the more grandiose ambitions of others, but it *is* a recognition of their limited romantic appeal.[25] Indeed, the lieutenant's testimony is no more and no less damning and no more conclusive than that of the Malay helmsman who 'had a knowledge of some evil thing befalling the ship, but there had been no order; he could not remember an order; why should he leave the helm?' (98). And there is even a sense in which the testimony of the other helmsman becomes also a wry comment on the lieutenant's unthinking courage: 'He says he thought nothing' (98).[26]

Brierly, of course, takes the coward's way out, as the tradition to which he subscribes would have it. And yet he belongs here, in a consideration of possible heroic alternatives to Jim, because in his

[25] Dorothy Van Ghent advances 'the fairly inescapable impression that the only character in the book in whom we can read the stamp of the author's own practical "approval" is the French lieutenant' as evidence for her contention that 'our notion of what constitutes a "hero" is thus surely divided: if the French lieutenant's heroism is the true heroism, Jim's is not, and conversely' (*The English Novel: Form and Function* (1953; rpt. New York, 1961), 231–2). As my argument suggests, I don't think the point lies in a distinction between true and sham heroism, rather in the implication that heroism is not necessarily a matter of practical approval.

[26] Suresh Raval also links the French lieutenant's dedication to duty with that of the helmsman, and argues that 'the French Lieutenant's conduct does not necessarily undermine Jim's. . . . If . . . the helmsman and the French Lieutenant seem heroically to mock Jim, Jim seems to mock them by a heroic gesture of self-assertion. Neither response by itself is adequate, and each requires the other to comprehend *Lord Jim*' ('Narrative and Authority in *Lord Jim*: Conrad's Art of Failure', *ELH* 48 (1981), 393–4).

early career he seems to have achieved citizenship, if not command, of Jim's world of heroic achievement:

He had saved lives at sea, had rescued ships in distress, had a gold chronometer presented him by the underwriters, and a pair of binoculars with a suitable inscription from some foreign Government, in commemoration of these services. He was acutely aware of his merits and of his rewards. (57)

But Brierly has not conquered the dream as much as domesticated it. His bravery is a matter of 'merits' and 'rewards', in other words, institutionalized achievement; his exploits are contained within the commercial and political structures that benefit by his impeccability. He is an exemplary citizen and meritorious sailor rather than a hero: the gold chronometer, the inscribed binoculars, are the solid marks of corporate and governmental appreciation, not the emblems of romance, like Stein's gold ring. Brierly fights, in short, in the ranks, is indeed a much-decorated veteran of that fight; and he deserts, having lost faith either in himself or in the code guaranteeing the value of his chronometer and his binoculars.

His suicide remains inexplicable, if what we are searching for is a single explanation. Whether Brierly was indeed guilty of a matter 'of the gravest import, one of those trifles that awaken ideas' (59) or was, like Marlow, led by Jim's case to doubt the validity of everything he had believed in: the pertinent fact is that, unlike Jim, he has no alternative to the 'sovereign power', in that he has no illusion to sustain him in his failure, actual or potential.[27] For Brierly inhabits that world that believes it can distinguish between 'reality' and 'sham' (68), that recognizes a single reality and mercilessly records deviations from that reality. His achievement has been as tangible as his chronometer and his binoculars; failure must present itself to him just as substantially. Jim's 'achievements', having been entirely imaginary, are not subject to the same unequivocal proof of failure.

It is appropriate that Brierly should die in accordance with that code to which he has devoted his life. In his preparations for his own death, he remains scrupulous in the performance of his duty, as

[27] The majority opinion would seem to be that his failure was only potential; see, for instance, Guerard, *Conrad the Novelist*, 148–9; Berthoud, *The Major Phase*, 75; Tanner, *Lord Jim*, 25; and Watt, *Conrad in the Nineteenth Century*, 279.

embodied in the Company, his first mate, his dog. But in the event old Jones is deprived of the position Brierly thought he was securing for him (and the dog is left desolate). Brierly's story, at any rate in Jones's narration, achieves closure, in that the Finis is written, and the pronouncement made: 'Ay, ay! neither you nor I, sir, had ever thought so much of ourselves' (65). And for all his rectitude, Brierly's suicide reduces his end to an ignominious failure: 'the squalor of that fly-blown cuddy which was the only shrine of his memory, threw a veil of inexpressibly mean pathos over Brierly's remembered figure, the posthumous revenge of fate for that belief in his own splendour which had almost cheated his life of its legitimate terrors' (64).

This anticipates, in one of those intersections whereby Marlow becomes the unconscious vehicle of the larger narrative, Jim's own death; but it prefigures that more ambiguous end only as Brierly's achievements reflect Jim's: as a 'realistic' rendering of the 'romantic' version, not so much inadequate as inappropriate. If its very inappropriateness is a comment also on those dreams, it yet does not provide us with a way of understanding them; rather like the French lieutenant, it pleads *nolo contendere*: 'This, monsieur, is too fine for me—much above me—I don't think about it' (149). Realism, too, declines to think about Jim in his own terms.

VII

Unlike Brierly, whose achievements are all too public and whose failures are private, Jim's initial failure is public, his achievements private—as private, indeed, as all imaginary achievements are. Jim measures himself in terms of an as yet unrealized potential rather than in terms of the failure proved against him. Oddly, perhaps, his romanticism proves more resilient than Brierly's rectitude: having submitted to his 'ceremony of execution' he can believe naïvely that punishment obliterates the crime, can cherish the illusion of starting with 'a clean slate' (185). He is proved wrong, of course; but so is Marlow, who believes that in providing for Jim's physical welfare, he is leaving his 'wounded spirit' to 'hop and flutter into some hole to die quietly of inanition there' (184–5). Marlow re-creates in his narration a yearning for closure, a less brutal version of Brierly's 'let him creep twenty feet underground and stay there!' (66). For a moment, the narrative energy flags, and confesses to the seductions of expulsion, a narrational death-wish: 'To bury him would have been such an easy kindness!' (174).

The temptation quite literally takes the shape of Chester, appearing 'on the blank page, under the very point of the pen' (174)—the page and the pen with which Marlow is copiously writing letters. The apparition fuses Conrad's own business of writing with Marlow's hallucination: in both cases a matter of finding a resolution to Jim's story.[28] Marlow's resistance to this particular resolution as 'too phantasmal and extravagant to enter into any one's fate', in other words his search for an acceptably 'normal' mode of accommodation, forms a paradoxical and temporary alliance with Jim's romantic resilience, to force the narration onwards, to seek some other resolution.

An alternative outcome unexpectedly presents itself through Jim's remarkable success with Denver, Marlow's misanthropic bachelor acquaintance, who comes to feel, through Jim, 'more in touch with mankind than I had been for years'. The happy ending looms, a less plangent Finis: 'I laid on Jim's behalf the first stone of a castle in Spain' (188). Jim may yet turn out to be, if not the long-lost son, then the new-found heir, who restores the recluse to the fellowship of men: the closure of comedy rather than of tragedy, the affirmation of community rather than the reckoning of its cost.

But this is not to be. The court's sentence of exile is perpetuated by Jim himself in his series of retreats, his attempts 'to lay the ghost of a fact' (197), 'the nature of his burden as well known to everybody as though he had gone about all that time carrying it on his shoulders' (199). This self-scapegoating narrative, an impulsion rather than an expulsion, can have no closure, because the communal judgement has become internalized and exaggerated in Jim's own perception of his disgrace (one of the first things we are told about him is that he was 'very popular'). The two different quests, Marlow's 'impossible' endeavour to lay 'the most obstinate ghost of man's creation', and Jim's doomed resolve to 'lay the ghost

[28] Jeremy Hawthorn, in *Joseph Conrad: Language and Fictional Self-Consciousness* (Lincoln, Nebr., 1979) suggests tentatively that 'The passage [about Chester and Robinson] has the appearance of being a sort of meta-commentary by Conrad on the process of writing a novel. Should the two characters be given fictional existence?' (54). Given the latitude of my own interpretation, this suggestion does not seem nearly as 'far-fetched' as Hawthorn fears it may be.

of a fact', combine to demand a medium in which these spectres will lose their potency.

VIII

The ghosts haunting Marlow's narration are visitants from a realm of value that renders the *Patna* incident if not insignificant then inconclusive. To that realm Marlow has only intermittent access, glimpses which can, on occasion, issue in rash and defiant pronouncements on Jim:

My last words about Jim shall be few. I affirm he had achieved greatness; but the thing would be dwarfed in the telling, or rather in the hearing. Frankly, it is not my words that I mistrust but your minds. I could be eloquent were I not afraid you fellows had starved your imaginations to feed your bodies. I do not mean to be offensive; it is respectable to have no illusions—and safe—and profitable—and dull. (225)

These are not Marlow's last words on Jim (which, in the event, are not few); but they express a loss of narrative confidence, a lack of faith in his listeners. Marlow's narrative, that is his search, can not reach closure because he cannot agree with his audience on a common basis of belief for the transaction. Nor can he really enter fully into that faith in his own words that he proclaims here; for in doing so, he would be severing the ties that make him, too, 'one of us', a member of that community that after all values respectability and safety and even profitability, at whatever price in dullness. For all his confident affirmation of Jim's greatness, the rest of his narration is inhibited not only by lack of faith in his audience but also by lack of certainty in his own mind. His words but imperfectly approach the world of imagination and illusion in which Jim has part of his being. Two narrative strains contend for dominance: Marlow's attempt to comprehend Jim in 'our' terms, and Jim's romantic quest. In co-ordinating these two strains, Conrad solves the realist quandary which splits, as we saw in the previous chapter, *Daniel Deronda* into two imperfectly assimilated parts: the problem of embodying the vision that transcends the quotidian reality in a novel that remains true to that reality.

Jim's case demands, in addition to the various perspectives Marlow gives us so conscientiously, the perspective of romance, a perspective which does not come instinctively to Marlow, and which is not suited to the ethical bias of his earlier narration. He does, in his earlier conversations with Jim, have intimations of a 'mystery', glimpses of 'the impossible world of romantic achievements' (83), but that world remains largely unamenable to his perception and analysis, to the terms of his enquiry:

These were issues beyond the competency of a court of inquiry: it was a subtle and momentous quarrel as to the true essence of life, and did not want a judge. . . . I was made to look at the convention that lurks in all truth and on the essential sincerity of falsehood. . . . the mystery of his attitude got hold of me as though he had been an individual in the forefront of his kind, as if the obscure truth involved were momentous enough to affect mankind's conception of itself . . .93)

The obscure truth that Marlow is straining towards here seems to be the insight which he can express more succinctly much later on: 'of all mankind Jim had no dealings but with himself' (339). The issue in this 'subtle and momentous quarrel as to the true essence of life' is thus whether life is a matter of fighting in the ranks or the pursuit of individual achievement—whether Jim is 'one of us' or 'an individual in the forefront of his kind'. But it is not really a quarrel about Jim at all: it is an enquiry into the basis of what we call truth and falsehood, the structures, whether conventional or imaginative, that produce value.

In interpreting Jim as 'a straggler yearning inconsolably for his humble place in the ranks' (224–5), Marlow comes as close as he ever does to being totally wrong: for whereas Jim may feel keenly his exclusion from the ranks, a humble place would not satisfy him. The imagination does not feed on humble yearnings: it demands a place 'in the forefront of his kind'. Jim has from the start been set apart, or set himself apart, from the ranks: his station in the foretop establishes a solitary position which, metaphorically, he never surrenders, even when literally surrounded by his fellows: 'On the lower deck in the babel of two hundred voices he would forget himself, and beforehand live in his mind the sea-life of light literature' (6). That kind of forgetting himself, which is in effect a finding of an alternative and more appealing self ('He saw himself saving people from sinking ships') is of course disastrous when the attendance of the everyday self is required for the saving of people from sinking ships. In the humdrum world registered merely as 'the babel of two hundred voices', heroism, if it exists at all, is not solitary: the rescue that Jim fails to be part of is carried out by 'a mob of boys' urged on by their instructor: 'Keep stroke, you young whelps, if you want to save anybody! Keep stroke!' (8). Not for Jim that kind of team heroism, the humble task of keeping stroke: 'The gale had ministered to a heroism as spurious as its own pretence of terror' (9). Whereas Jim's disdain here clearly savours of sour grapes, it is also genuine in that heroism of the communal kind means little to him. Jim is the hero of his own narration; Marlow's narration, incapable of accommodating a hero in its collective reference, strives unsuccessfully to contain Jim as 'one of us', unexceptional, representative, yearning for a humble place. The romance is needed as much to free Marlow's blocked narrative as to give Jim his opportunity.

In order to embody the reality of Jim's heroic dreams, Conrad has to transcend, as it were, Marlow's narrational range, and create the conditions in which Jim's imagination can fulfil itself, and his story can achieve closure. Marlow needs Stein as interpreter, to furnish him with the simple but paradoxical key to Jim: '"He is romantic—romantic," he repeated. "And that is very bad—very bad. . . . Very good, too," he added' (216). If Stein is literally the link between the practical realities of Marlow's world and the dream-like world of Patusan, he is also the transitional figure between two sets of narrative terms, we might say two ontologies, that of literary realism and that of the romance. Of Jim's romantic imagination the romance is the natural emanation, as a self-valorizing fiction with its own semantic conventions—to which the 'very bad. . . . very good too' paradox is an appropriate introduction. And if Stein's injunction to 'follow the dream, and again to follow the dream—and so—*ewig—usque ad finem*' (215) has its primary if cryptic application to Jim's case, it also forms, in narrative terms, the equivalent of Marlow's endeavour 'to lay the ghost of a doubt': in both cases a search *usque ad finem*, a searching for the *finality*, the endedness, of Finis. The romance may provide Conrad with the resolution that Marlow's narration has merely succeeded in postponing.

Marlow's visit to Stein dramatizes the modulation from one mode to the other, in Marlow's uneasy sense of the elusiveness of Stein's identity, of Stein's capacity to move between two inverse mediums:

taking up the case in both hands he bore it religiously away to its place, passing out of the bright circle of the lamp into the ring of fainter light—into shapeless dusk at last. It had an odd effect—as if these few steps had carried him out of this concrete and perplexed world. His tall form, as though robbed of its substance, hovered noiselessly over invisible things with stooping and indefinite movements . . . (213)

If much of the account of Marlow's visit to Stein seems itself to hover breathlessly over some rather insubstantial abstractions, that may be an effect of an uneasy meeting of modes, which is in fact meticulously plotted as a kind of ontological tension. Marlow is more at ease in his own 'concrete and perplexed world' than in the potentially treacherous 'charming and deceptive light, throwing the impalpable poesy of its dimness over pitfalls—over graves' (215). Stein, his form 'robbed of substance', hovering over 'invisible things', is much more in his element than Marlow: he has an affinity with the many ghosts that haunt the novel, and it is as 'shadow prowling amongst the graves of butterflies' that he pronounces with most assurance: 'His voice leaped up extraordinarily strong.' Conversely, as he returns to 'the bright circle of the lamp', his certainty fails him: 'The light had destroyed the assurance which had inspired him in the distant shadows' (214).

Stein's pronouncements on Jim and the human dilemma belong to this shadowy world, have little force in the world of bright light. Nevertheless, partly under the charm of the surroundings, partly under the spell of Stein's vatic utterances, Marlow's own concept of reality expands to accommodate that mode in which nothing is but what is not, in which, according to Stein, Jim's reality is a function of his romanticism:

At that moment it was difficult to believe in Jim's existence—starting from a country parsonage, blurred by crowds of men as by clouds of dust, silenced by the clashing claims of life and death in a material world—but his imperishable reality came to me with a convincing, with an irresistible force! I saw it vividly, as though in our progress through the lofty silent rooms amongst fleeting gleams of light and the sudden revelations of human figures stealing with flickering flames within unfathomable and pellucid depths, we had approached nearer to absolute Truth, which, like Beauty itself, floats elusive, obscure, half submerged, in the silent still waters of mystery. (216)

With this release of Marlow's customary restraint and his surrender to the romantic element, his perception of 'reality' is liberated from his understanding of 'existence', as derived from his own concrete world. Jim no longer exists in terms of 'a material world', but acquires a compensatory 'imperishable reality' in the romantic medium. The surface truth of the material world yields for a moment to absolute Truth, that Truth which is here, in the 'flickering flames', connected with Marlow's apprehension in Jim of 'the fellowship of these illusions you had thought gone out, extinct, cold, and which, as if rekindled at the approach of another flame, give a flutter deep, deep down somewhere, give a flutter of light . . . of heat!' Truth and illusion become interchangeable, a scenic rendering of Marlow's shrugging off of the novel's major binary opposition as 'some such truth or some such illusion—I don't care how you call it, there is so little difference, and the difference means so little' (222).

Surrendering, for the moment, to the power of illusion, Marlow sees Stein not as the public figure, 'the head of the firm, the welcome guest at afternoon receptions, the correspondent of learned societies, the entertainer of stray naturalists', but interprets 'the reality of his destiny' as 'rich in generous enthusiasms, in friendship, love, war—in all the exalted elements of romance' (217). Existence, like reality, like truth, is, to the socialized human being, a function of our place in the ranks—in that sense intended by Marlow elsewhere in less romantic mood: 'Woe to the stragglers! We exist only in so far as we hang together' (223). But the world of the imagination, filled 'with all the exalted elements of romance', affirms an equally valid and perhaps more vivid existence—indeed, claims primacy for its own mode, relegating the world of facts to insubstantiality. Since each world treats the other as spurious, transactions between the two would seem to be impossible, as Jim's failures on the training ship and the *Patna* demonstrate. The exception to this is Stein, who has, apart from anything else, become extremely wealthy on such transactions. His commerce with the world of Patusan has a literal enough financial basis, but his history has given him also a kind of presence and reality there, as his ring symbolizes: it is the one token from the world out there that is recognized by the denizens of Patusan.

IX

Jim's voyage to Patusan is thus more than a change of setting; it is a transposition to a different mode of existence:

I only meant you to understand that had Stein arranged to send him into a star of the fifth magnitude the change could not have been greater. He left his earthly failings behind him and that sort of reputation he had, and there was a totally new set of conditions for his imaginative faculty to work upon. (218)

Patusan, as the fulfilment of Jim's romantic dreams, is the realm of romance, which provides for Conrad, too, 'a totally new set of conditions for his imaginative faculty to work upon'. The Patusan sequence, though its intrinsic plot appeal tends to pall for most readers,[29] is not a yarn tacked on to Marlow's narration, but the realization of a centre of value that has been from the first chapter of the novel a potential alternative to those values based on 'a fixed standard of conduct'. In material terms, Patusan is unreal: its reality is that of the romantic imagination. Jim, in entering it, leaves that existence that is a function of 'hanging together': 'Once he got in, it would be for the outside world as though he had never existed. . . . "Never existed—that's it, by Jove!" he murmured to himself' (232). Patusan is, as the skipper's malapropism has it, 'situated internally' (240): its geographic location becomes a metaphor for its ontological status. Jim's confident sense that 'nothing can touch him', his indifference to Cornelius, 'the irony of his good fortune that he, who had been too careful of it once, seemed to bear a charmed life' (285), the apparent ease with which he conquers his enemies: Patusan has the strange dream-like susceptibility of imaginary creations to the wishes of their creators. If, as Marlow says, 'He had regulated so many things in Patusan—things that would have appeared as much beyond his control as the motions of the moon and the stars' (221), that is entirely in keeping with a

[29] Guerard finds chs. 25-7 'the weakest of all', in not justifying by their matter the pondering Marlow expends on them: 'They deal with nothing more ambiguous than practical matters' (*Conrad the Novelist*, 168, 169). I would exempt ch. 25 on the grounds that the account of Jim's escape from the stockade does consolidate some of the links between the earlier and the later sections of the novel; but in defence of chs. 26 and 27 one can note only that they dramatize Jim's capacity for heroic action and that they are short.

moon-and-starlit world which seems to be created by as much as for Jim—and which bears the marks of his essentially naïve imagination.

In that Patusan becomes the ideal extension of Jim's imagination, Jim is, as it were, the author of his own text. As Jacques Berthoud has demonstrated in some detail, Jim's 'conquest of his ideal self is accomplished through a step-by-step re-enactment of his original failure', enabling a 'rewriting [of] his past as a success story'.[30] Given the obliging correspondence of dream to desire, Patusan appears to Jim as an opportunity to 'slam the door' (235) on his past; but every act of his whereby he seeks to efface that past, every detail as it were, of this revised text, has its full significance only in relation to that past, the narrative as a whole. The end-directed, apparently stable irony of the opening narration is now reversed; if we read irony in Jim's present situation, it is not because of a foreseen end, but because of an already-seen past which charges the present with greater significance than the protagonist is aware of.[31] As Jim puts thirty miles of forest between himself and his past, that past re-enacts itself in his actions. His very solitude (his three rowers disregarded, like the crew members of the *Patna* on the lifeboat), at one level a perfectly plausible condition of his mission, is at another level determined by his dream of individual heroism, which has survived its own failure aboard the training ship and the *Patna*. He comes to Patusan alone, untroubled by, if also unaided by, those to the right and left of him; and for all the risks involved, his solitary arrival, paddled upstream in a dug-out, seems not so much a dangerous exploit of which the issue is in doubt as a taking possession through heroic trial of 'the land he was destined to fill with the fame of his virtues' (243). In the opening narration, our knowledge, shared with the narrator, of the disastrous issue of Jim's heroic visions was ironically poised against those visions; here our

---

[30] Berthoud, *The Major Phase*, 90. I differ from Berthoud in his contention that 'Patusan is not essentially different from the great world: it is merely cut off from it'. Patusan's essential difference seems to me to consist exactly in its enabling medium, its hospitality to the fictionalizing of Jim's earlier failures.

[31] Jacques Berthoud complains that in the Patusan section 'the novel is turning parasitic on itself' ('Narrative and Ideology: A Critique of Fredric Jameson's *The Political Unconscious*', in Jeremy Hawthorn (ed.). *Narrative: From Mallory to Motion Pictures* (London, 1985), 111). That is one way of putting it, certainly, but as I try to show, what we have is a creative rewriting, an accumulation of significance, rather than a process of attrition, as Berthoud's metaphor would seem to suggest.

knowledge of the future reinforces Jim's own confidence. We are being charmed into accepting the romantic premisses of his dream.

Whatever uncertainty Jim faces here 'with precaution' (243), it is not a moral uncertainty; he is eminently ready for what awaits him, the unloaded revolver being a sign not so much of unpreparedness as of indifference to such unheroic trappings. In the lifeboat 'there was not the thickness of a sheet of paper between the right and wrong of this affair' (130); here right and wrong are distinct, the bad chaps easily told from the good. The rowers have decided to turn him over to the Rajah, who is bad, whereas Jim has to get to Doramin, who is good (or a 'jolly old beggar' in Jim's characteristic locution (234)), and identified as such by a talisman: 'The ring was a sort of credential—("It's like something you read of in books," he threw in appreciatively)' (233–4).

Patusan is indeed like something you read of in books—or something that Jim would have read of in the books of his youth. As Jim says 'triumphantly' of the people of Patusan: 'They are like people in a book, aren't they?' (260). And Jim, 'one of us' though he be, can enter that fictional reality and become part of it, whereas it remains a foreign element to Marlow :

There is something haunting in the light of the moon; it has all the dispassionateness of a disembodied soul, and something of its inconceivable mystery. It is to our sunshine, which—say what you like—is all we have to live by, what the echo is to the sound; misleading and confusing whether the note be mocking or sad. It robs all forms of matter—which, after all, is our domain—of their substance, and gives a sinister reality to shadows alone. (246)

Marlow feels himself, as it were, to be in the wrong book, deprived of that element which 'is all we have to live by'—'we' as opposed to 'they', the denizens of a Patusan seen so often by starlight or moonlight, and who themselves seem insubstantial—as when Jewel, while she is talking to Marlow, seems to disappear 'like the intangible form of a wistful and perverse spirit' (313–14).

Jim is the one element of Patusan that retains its substance, its everyday reality, for Marlow—'Jim by my side looked very stalwart, as though nothing—not even the occult power of moonlight—could rob him of his reality in my eyes' (246). Nevertheless, Jim's ability to enter into the Patusan mode makes him part also of that other reality so alien to Marlow. His love for Jewel is the token of his emotional commitment to the terms of the romance: it is utterly conventional, declared under the light of the stars, with all the stereotyped ingredients of the love-story: 'Strong arms, a tender voice, a stalwart shoulder to rest her poor lonely little head upon' (311). To Jewel, too, Jim seems 'stalwart', possessed of a reassuring reality in her own terms; he has a reality in the romantic world that is inaccessible to Marlow, except as a creation of 'fancy':

But next morning, at the first bend of the river shutting off the houses of Patusan, all this dropped out of my sight bodily, with its colour, its design, and its meaning, like a picture created by fancy on a canvas, upon which, after long contemplation, you turn your back for the last time. It remains in the memory motionless, unfaded, with its life arrested, in an unchanging light. (330)

The static quality of Patusan is not merely a trick of Marlow's memory: it is the visual equivalent of the narrative principle animating it—or suspending its animation—the perpetuated ever-after of happy endings. On Marlow's last visit to Patusan, then, the romance for which it is the setting and the occasion has reached its terminus, is no longer narratable; all that is possible in its own terms is a perpetuation of Jim's dominance, which is also to say his captivity: 'all his conquests, the trust, the fame, the friendships, the love—all these things that made him master had made him a captive, too' (247).

Yet this closed system in which Jim is a captive, by virtue of the imaginative reality which grants him heroic being only in this world of his own creation, does not fully contain him. Patusan, though ostensibly self-contained, derives its full meaning for Jim from a code unintelligible to Patusan itself. For all the reality of his achievement in Patusan, it cannot supersede that other measure of truth that he has brought with him: 'If you ask them who is brave—who is true—who is just—who is it they would trust with their lives?—they would say, Tuan Jim. And yet they can never know the real, real truth' (305). So we have involutions of contradictory truths: 'the deep hidden truthfulness, of works of art' (282) characterizing Patusan, and Jim's truth to the inhabitants, are yet distinguished from the 'real, real truth' (305)—which from yet another perspective is one of the 'haggard utilitarian lies of our civilisation' (282). The measure of truth derived from his allegiance to 'the ranks' remains to test his achievements in the world of the imagination:

'I must stick to their belief in me to feel safe and to—to' . . . He cast about for a word, seemed to look for it on the sea . . . 'to keep in touch with' . . . His voice sank suddenly to a murmur . . . 'with those whom, perhaps, I shall never see any more. With—with—you, for instance.' (334)

So Jim, paradoxically, can keep in touch with the outside world only by remaining in Patusan. Jim's romance, complete in all other ways, seeks verification of its reality in the ordinary world of work and duty. Thus the apparently closed romance of Jim's conquest of Patusan retains this fissure, Jim's reading of his present in terms of a past that he thought he was putting behind him. That past constitutes a point of narratability which makes the romance vulnerable to, even hospitable to, the irruption of another narration, that of Gentleman Brown.

X

The story of Gentleman Brown remains enclosed if not contained within Marlow's own narration, in the written account he sends, more than two years later, to the 'privileged man' who alone had expressed an interest in Jim. The omniscient narrator returns to stage-manage the reading process, and the after-dinner narrative community, that euphoric, uncritical fellowship, is replaced by the solitary space of the individual reader, remote from a busy world:

His rooms were in the highest flat of a lofty building, and his glance could travel afar beyond the clear panes of glass, as though he were looking out of the lantern of a light-house. The slopes of the roofs glistened, the dark broken ridges succeeded each other without end like sombre, uncrested waves, and from the depths of the town under his feet ascended a confused and unceasing mutter. The spires of churches, numerous, scattered haphazard, uprose like beacons on a maze of shoals without a channel . . .
    The light of his shaded reading-lamp slept like a sheltered pool, his footfalls made no sound on the carpet, his wandering days were over. . . . The hour was striking! No more! No more! (337–8)

Given our ignorance of the character involved, the melancholy of this would seem merely gratuitous, were it not instrumental in establishing yet another narrative relationship: the lone writer speaking to the lone reader. The solitude of the reader seems intensified by the inhospitable cityscape outside, contrasted with the exotic, companionable verandah which was the setting for Marlow's spoken narration. Furthermore, the setting recalls the earlier description of Jim in the foretop, looking down on 'the peaceful multitude of roofs cut in two by the brown tide of the stream'. The privileged man is also elevated above his surroundings, but whereas Jim had before him, literally and figuratively, 'the hazy splendour of the sea in the distance, and the hope of a stirring life in the world of adventure', here the metaphorical recollections of the sea, the lighthouse, the waves, the depths, the shoals, merely reinforce the sombre refrain 'No more!' Jim had also, on the lower deck, 'the babel of two hundred voices' (6): a youthful, major-key version of the 'confused and unceasing mutter'. So the 'sheltered pool' of the reading-lamp is also a retreat from that 'world of adventure' of Jim's romance, of which the final episode is contained in the pages in the man's hand. As Marlow says elsewhere, 'words also belong to the sheltering conception of light and order which is our refuge' (313), and the lone reader inhabits, as it were, that sheltering conception. This man's surroundings, then, provide their own implicit comment on the romantic tale which he is to read, and are in turn commented upon: neither tale nor setting finally contains the other. If Jim's story is reduced to 'a thick packet', then conversely 'the opened packet under the lamp brought back the sounds, the visions, the very savour of the past' (338).

The reader's ideological bent is defined with some explicitness: he is untroubled by suspicions of the relativity of truth and illusion: 'You had said you knew so well "that kind of thing", its illusory satisfaction, its unavoidable deception' (338–9). Illusion to him is akin to deception, and fellowship is exclusively the solidarity of the craft, the group, the race: a kind of ontological community, that produces 'the truth of ideas racially our own, in whose name are established the order, the morality of an ethical progress'. The reader is the most uncompromising exponent of a view Marlow has with some anxiety held in abeyance throughout his narration: 'In other words, you maintained that we must fight in the ranks or our lives don't count' (339).

In this transitional section, the separate lonelinesses of reader, writer, and protagonist create a tenuous community unsure of a common ideological basis. The tale that is told repeats that uncertainty in its construction: the brisk heroic action of the earlier Patusan sequences yields to inactivity, hesitation, moral perplexity. Whereas the earlier narration was directed towards its own previously announced successful conclusion, this one moves towards the event reported, as a prelude to Marlow's final narration, in Jim's own inarticulate, undated, unfinished attempt at communicating his distress: 'An awful thing has happened' (340). The present perfect tense completes the event we are yet to be told of.

The account of that 'awful thing' comes, ironically, not from Jim, but largely from Gentleman Brown—and the story is presented as beginning anew with him: 'It all begins with a remarkable exploit of a man called Brown' (344). Earlier villains, the Rajah, the Sherif, were seen from Jim's perspective, as so many negligible but necessary negative terms in the structure of his romance. Brown's narration removes the encounter with Jim from the charmed, self-contained, and self-validating circle of the romance—or rewrites it in terms of Brown's equally self-validating anti-romance. If Brown's sheer malevolence, insistently opposed to Jim's moral uprightness, would seem at first to belong to the melodramatic oppositions congenial to the moral simplicities of the romance, he is also the hero of his own story, a story based on an inversion of the Western code which Jim has brought with him. It intersects with the romance through Jim, the factor common to both Brown's narration and the romance.

If Brown had indeed been purely the villain of romance, Jim could have dealt with him in the brutally direct methods of romance, as Dain Warris wants to do. But Brown derives his reality and thus his potency from another sphere altogether: he and his crew are 'White men from "out there" where he did not think himself good enough to live' (385). Brown is a link with Jim's past and with that code that Jim once betrayed. He also speaks to Jim as 'one of us', and derives his understanding of Jim from the code they share in opposition, as, in *The Secret Agent*, burglar and policeman 'recognize the same conventions', being 'products of the same machine' (*SA* 92): 'And there was something in the very neatness of Jim's clothes, from the white helmet to the canvas leggings and the pipe-clayed shoes, which in Brown's sombre irritated eyes seemed to belong to things he had in the very shaping of his life contemned and flouted' (*LJ* 380). Jim is not an insoluble mystery to Brown, as he is to the people of Patusan. Brown misjudges him, of course, in ascribing to him his own motives of exploitation, but that is simply a misreading of a shared system of signification, not the incomprehension of an alien system.

And as Brown interprets Jim in the cynical light of his own experience, so Jim reads Brown in terms of *his* own experience of that world where there is not the thickness of a sheet of paper between the right and wrong of an affair: 'Men act badly sometimes without being much worse than others' (394). Jim's mistake is the counterpart of Brown's: in both instances, a failure of moral imagination, an inability to imagine its own opposite, and yet an instinctive understanding deriving exactly from that definition by opposition. They are 'on the opposite poles of that conception of life which includes all mankind' (381)—defining each other as a negative pole is defined by the positive and vice versa. Where the simpler moral oppositions of the romance assume that good and evil have independent existence, Brown's intrusion questions that separation. The *Patna* incident is, in Brown's narration, once again rewritten, not as a romance *manqué*, a chance missed, but as the 'real, real truth' underlying Jim's presence in Patusan. The point is not that Jim is revealed as 'really' bad through his handling of Brown; as Watt argues, 'the weight of the evidence is far from supporting the view that Jim acted as he did out of guilt, whether conscious or unconscious, or that any other decision was possible'.[32] At a conscious level, Jim is brought to see in Brown's situation a parallel to his own, and resolves to give him the 'second chance' he himself had: this is perfectly in keeping with the notions of 'fair play' on which Jim has been brought up. But at a subtler level than Jim can understand, the text enacts the linguistic and moral axiom that our very notion of good derives its identity from its necessary and intimate reliance on its opposite: in order to be good we must be capable of being evil. Brown's appeal to Jim, at the level of plot, serves merely as an uncanny reminder of Jim's own failure; at another level it establishes the dialectic inherent in all narrative, the interdependence of opposites: 'And there ran through

[32] Watt, *Conrad in the Nineteenth Century*, 342.

the rough talk a vein of subtle reference to their common blood, an assumption of common experience; a sickening suggestion of common guilt, of secret knowledge that was like a bond of their minds and of their hearts' (387). There is then, also this fellowship, this bond of evil, which draws Jim into its ambit by its connection with the solidarity of the code to which the two men in their different ways owe allegiance. Brown's remarkable exploits lack the high-minded heroism of Jim's, but are as single-mindedly based upon an ideal concept of existence: he has not been pursuing his own ends as much as demonstrating the 'immensity of scorn and revolt at the bottom of his misdeeds' (383). And both men are haunted, exiles from the community that created them: as Jim owes his presence in Patusan to the attempt 'to lay the ghost of a fact' so Brown is also fleeing a ghost: he 'was running away from the spectre of a Spanish prison' (356).

The essential connectedness of the two poles of the fellowship is reflected in the double-stranded narrative, whereby Jim's story and Brown's move in parallel towards their respective resolutions. Both stories achieve closure, in that both are validated, in the eyes of their respective protagonists, by a coherent system of belief; and each man sees the other as the antagonist, the opposite term that has to be expelled or eradicated. Brown, indeed, 'clawing the air with skinny fingers . . . bowed and hairy . . . like some man-beast of folk-lore' (372) is, in Marlow's horrified and fascinated account, near-explicitly represented as the dreadful Other that haunts the racial memory and has to be ritually expelled. Whereas, in the opening narration, Jim was subjected to that unconscious scapegoating effect that, I have been arguing, is endemic to ethical structure, here Conrad dramatizes, through Jim, civilized man's recognition of the repressions on which his social structures are posited, the fellowship that has to be denied through expulsion. As the first narration was energized by the aberration of Jim, this one needs Brown, the opposite term to Jim, to bring it to closure, to define Jim for us.[33] But what sets this narration apart, and Conrad's novel apart from its tradition, is the nature of the recognition that takes place: the

---

[33] Conrad seems at an early stage of composition to have envisaged 'a happy termination of Jim's troubles' (Letter to Meldrum, 10 Aug. 1898, rpt. in *Lord Jim*, Norton Edition, 292). Gentleman Brown was thus almost as much of an 'unforeseen partnership' for Conrad as for Jim, suggesting that he also was not 'satisfied—quite' with a resolution purely in romance terms.

acknowledgement of the kinship between Gentleman Brown and Lord Jim. The novel has, in a sense, as Jameson says 'to conjure up the mythic feeling of the villain—so archaic and historically ugly a feeling, which has its genealogy deep in immemorial lynchings and pogroms, in the expulsion of the scapegoat and the ritual curse'; but this creation is not the act of unconscious magic that Jameson's conjuring metaphor suggests; nor does the novel aim to contain the monstrous creation of Brown through Marlow's 'powerful rhetoric'[34]—although Marlow, here desperately trying to preserve his own 'sheltering conception', does try to master his own horror through his account. Brown, if an unforeseen development of Conrad's design, is nevertheless a product of his conscious art, as appears from the way in which he is deployed in the resolution which he precipitates. And if Jim has his victory, so does Brown—not only practically, in his gratuitous revenge, but also in his own imagination, in the consciousness which lends exultance to his dying breath as 'The corpse of his mad self-love uprose from rags and destitution as from the dark horrors of a tomb' (383). In 'this almost posthumous illusion of having trampled all the earth under his feet' (384) there is a horrible parody of Jim's vision of his own victory, as 'with the growing loneliness of his obstinacy his spirit seemed to rise above the ruins of his existence' (410). Brown, too, 'gave up his arrogant ghost' (344) in the belief that he had triumphed over the Powers of Light that he had so assiduously fought all his life. Marlow's own earlier reflections on the reality of illusion return to haunt him, to suggest that also Brown's 'illusion' has the force of 'some such truth'. Ultimately and horribly, Lord Jim and Gentleman Brown are united also in the fellowship of illusion.

Jim, granting Brown his scapegoat's request to be 'kicked out to go free and starve in my own way' (383), attempts to rid the community of the embodiment of the evil upon which, in a sense, that community has been built: Jim's Patusan has come into being as a reaction to the *Patna*. Brown, in the 'almost inconceivable egotism' (394) of his resentment, the counterpart of Jim's 'superb egoism' (413), attempts to destroy the community to which he was denied access, the scapegoat turned scourge:

---

[34] Jameson, *The Political Unconscious*, 269.

Thus Brown balanced his account with the evil fortune. Notice that even in this awful outbreak there is a superiority as of a man who carries right—the abstract thing—within the envelope of his common desires. It was not a vulgar and treacherous massacre; it was a lesson, a retribution—a demonstration of some obscure and awful attribute of our natures which, I am afraid, is not so very far under the surface as we like to think. (404)

Marlow thus ascribes a kind of moral intention to Brown: a 'lesson' from some 'awful attribute of our natures' that we try to deny in 'the sunny . . . arrangement of small conveniences' which we have brought about 'thanks to our unwearied efforts'. Through Brown that 'vast and dismal aspect of disorder' which it is our unceasing endeavour to banish from the 'sheltering conception of light and order which is our refuge' (313) asserts itself, in an action that instantly disrupts the painfully won social order. Society could, by expelling Jim, preserve, in Brierly's words, 'the name for that kind of decency' that Jim failed in; Brown does not so readily accept his expulsion. Behind his act is the 'retribution' of a whole rogue's gallery of literary villains and outcasts.

XI

But if Brown disrupts the community, Jim's giving himself over to Doramin to be shot may be said to confirm that disruption; and indeed, his act is often interpreted as a desertion equivalent to his desertion of the *Patna*. Jim, by this reading, 'destroys his city' through what is in effect an act of suicide.[35] Now it is true that Jim's sensitivity to his own failure on the *Patna* makes him vulnerable to Brown's insinuations: an impeccable man would have been impervious to the dark appeal of his corruption. An impeccable man, indeed, would not have been in Patusan in the first place: the community has been constructed upon fallibility, and Brown lays bare that foundation. Thus Jim commits the error of judgement that devastates the community; and having 'taken it upon his own head' (415) to guarantee its safety, he pays with his life. Having once put his own life above the safety of the community entrusted to him, he now forfeits his life in terms of his contract.

---

[35] Van Ghent, *Form and Function*, 232.

That, at any rate, is how Jim would have seen it. For him, to have fought for his life against the community that he had undertaken to protect, as Jewel and Tamb' Itam urge him to do, would have been a repetition of his jump from the *Patna*—a cowardly act of self-preservation.[36] But from the point of view of the survivors, nobody is served by his death; in that sense his act is thoroughly uncommunal. As Guerard says: 'Jim's "truth" and "constancy" . . . turn out to be a truth and constancy to the exalted egoism rather than to Marlow's own strong sense of community obligation.'[37] If his act does affirm his solidarity with that world which has never lost its hold over him, it has no effect in the community to which it refers for its immediate meaning: Patusan does not share with him the beliefs which animate his action, and in whose name it is destroyed. That loneliness which has always been behind his prominence in Patusan, the loneliness which is the price of his solitary heroism, now asserts itself without the distractions of fame and success: 'Loneliness was closing on him. People had trusted him with their lives—only for that; and yet they could never, as he had said, never be made to understand him' (409). The community of his own imaginative creation is not served by his death; it is a tribute to the world out there that has forgotten about him. The 'talisman that had opened for him the door of fame, love, and success' is returned to him, and he leaves Patusan as he entered it, 'ready and unarmed' (415)—and alone:

They say that the white man sent right and left at all those faces a proud and unflinching glance. Then with his hand over his lips he fell forward, dead.

And that's the end. (416)

---

[36] Not, surely, as H. M. Daleski suggests, the equivalent of 'hanging on'. In maintaining that Jim 'never considers fighting either, never entertains the possibility of refusing, as a man with a steeled soul would do, to give way' (*Joseph Conrad: The Way of Dispossession* (London, 1977), 102), Daleski does not seem to consider what Jim would have had to steel his soul *to*: taking up arms against his community in order to save his own life. Tanner, in calling his death 'a suicide . . . an easy way out' (*Lord Jim*, 55), similarly seems to suggest that Jim should have stuck to his guns—which, since all the powder in Patusan was in the fort, would have been easy but murderous.

[37] Guerard, *Conrad the Novelist*, 141.

In terms of Jim's own dream his death is the Finis that closes his account: in that 'proud and unflinching glance' is signalled Jim's own interpretation of his death as a triumph, the grasping of the opportunity to prove himself true, 'to go out decently in the end . . . and with dashed little help to expect from those we touch elbows with right and left' (35). In death as in life, 'of all men Jim had dealings only with himself', even at this moment when the self is extinguished in the name of a communal code of conduct. Jim's death is his sacrifice to 'that faithfulness which made him in his own eyes the equal of the impeccable men who never fall out of the ranks' (393).

It is not only Brown's narration that restricts the closural force of Jim's romance to its own terms; even Marlow has to accommodate the evidence—which he does not shirk—that if Jim, by his lights, was true to those standards which he once betrayed, he was false, by Jewel's standards, to those vows he once made to her. One truth lacks reality in the domain of the other; for Marlow's sense that Jim owes allegiance to another order of being, that at times he 'passes from my eyes like a disembodied spirit astray amongst the passions of this earth, ready to surrender himself faithfully to the claim of his own world of shades' (416), is paralleled by Jewel's exactly inverse perception of Marlow and Jim as the shades, herself as the mortal: 'Thus a poor mortal seduced by the charm of an apparition might have tried to wring from another ghost the tremendous secret of the claim the other world holds over a disembodied soul astray amongst the passions of this earth' (315). Fidelity to the one world is infidelity to the other; for Marlow the reality of Jim's existence is a function of his fidelity to 'this world', and is inaccessible in so far as he has reality also in 'his own world of shades'; to Jewel 'this earth' is the romantic world of Patusan, haunted inexplicably by 'the charm of an apparition'. To ask whether Jim was true or false is really only to ask which version of the truth we prefer. He remained faithful to the truth that he had been pursuing all along, the truth that the dream had been based on and which reduces Patusan to an illusion; by the same token he was unfaithful to Jewel, who could see his reality only in terms of her own world, and unfaithful to that community which he had created.

The conflict between the community and the dream is one that Conrad, in *A Personal Record*, traces back to 'that exalted and dangerous figure', Don Quixote: 'After reading so many romances he desired naïvely to escape with his very body from the intolerable reality of things. . . . He rides forth, his head encircled by a halo—the patron saint of all lives spoiled or saved by the irresistible grace of imagination. But he was not a good citizen' (*PR* 36-7). Jim has a cloud rather than a halo—but what is a halo but a Quixotic interpretation of a cloud? Jim, like Don Quixote, is not a good citizen; and the contradiction whereby his last act combines the fellowship of illusion with the solidarity of the craft produces no ideal synthesis: paradoxically, his dying in the ranks is also his loneliest moment.

For at the heart of the rival ontologies of the novel is the vision of a reality that is never to be captured in any mode, the essence of another human being:

It is when we try to grapple with another man's intimate need that we perceive how incomprehensible, wavering, and misty are the beings that share with us the sight of the stars and the warmth of the sun. It is as if loneliness were a hard and absolute condition of existence; the envelope of flesh and blood on which our eyes are fixed melts before the outstretched hand, and there remains only the capricious, unconsolable, and elusive spirit that no eye can follow, no hand can grasp. (*LJ* 179-80)

Unlike Stein's butterflies, which with skill and luck and readiness can be captured, the elusive human spirit flees the outstretched hand, cannot be contained even in the imagination, cannot be preserved in death-defying beauty. This 'hard and absolute condition of existence' may be the only absolute we are offered in this novel, the bedrock of all truth and illusion: the perspective from which all creatures (and here the largest fellowship of all is posited, in that the opposition between starlight and sunlight, elsewhere seen as mutually exclusive mediums, is collapsed) are insubstantial and ungraspable by another human being.[38] Stein's preparation 'to leave all this', 'while he waves his hand sadly at his butterflies' (417)

---

[38] Daniel R. Schwarz concludes his study of the novel on the strong note that 'Marlow, like his creator, suggests the possibility of creating a community of understanding which he believes is the only possible replacement for a community based on moral standards' (*Conrad: Almayer's Folly to Under Western Eyes* (London, 1980), 94). The ending of the novel seems to me not to support such a possibility. Stein expresses, somewhat desperately, some such hope in saying of Jewel 'Some day she *shall* understand'—to which Marlow, 'looking hard at him', replies 'Will *you* explain?' (350).

seems an admission of the failure of even the romantic spirit to overcome that loneliness, to grasp that human spirit. 'That mysterious fellowship which unites in a community of hopes and fears all the dwellers on this earth', the fellowship which according to Conrad gives rise to the novel, and to which the lone reader in his 'sheltered pool' is admitted through his reading, may be, paradoxically, the fellowship of the illusion that we can know another human being, the solidarity based on our knowledge of our aloneness—finally, the Sophoclean sense in which the humiliated Ajax is one of us in being most alien to his kind, as his enemy Odysseus can recognize:

> I think of him, yet also of myself;
> For I see the true state of all of us that live—
> We are dim shapes, no more, and weightless shadow.[39]

Conrad's characteristic mode, as the Sophoclean parallel implies, is a tragic one: the transience of human existence is fatally at odds with that importance we need to ascribe to our own activity and achievement. But that discrepancy between our destiny and our sense of our own significance, the fact that the human, in Stein's words, 'sees himself as a very fine fellow—so fine as he can never be' (213), has, too, its comical side—'Very funny this terrible thing is' (214). To turn from Conrad to his contemporary Henry James is to find that ambiguity exploited by a clear-eyed ironic intelligence taking into its ambit a whole range of its predecessors' achievements. The comic realism of Jane Austen, the dark imaginings of Dickens, the moral intensity of George Eliot, the tragic elevation and the mordant irony of Conrad: in the works of Henry James these elements combine in the service of a complex vision informing a supremely conscious artistry.

[39] Sophocles, *Ajax*, trans. John Moore, from *Sophocles II*, ed. David Grene and Richard Lattimore (Chicago, 1957), 124–6.

Chapter 5

A Community of Interest:
The Golden Bowl

'I think there's nothing they're not now capable of—in their so
intense good faith.'
'Good faith?'—he echoed the words, which had in fact
something of an odd ring, critically.
'Their false position. It comes to the same thing.'[1]

I

Fanny Assingham's ingenious equivocations, though unusually
blatant, are not untypical of the linguistic procedures prevailing
in her novel, whereby any particular interpretation of events can be
protected by a redefinition of the terms ostensibly governing the
situation. *The Golden Bowl* owes much of its elusiveness to this
bewildering disorientation of language, consistently subverting that
community of meaning premissed on the fiction of common
meaning. And as Fanny Assingham is merely the most audacious
player of this language game in her novel, so *The Golden Bowl* is
merely the most extreme example in the Jamesian *œuvre* of this
disorientation.

In this respect, James's fiction enacts something similar to
Marlow's searching, ruminative narratives, declining to take for
granted any of its own terms. The novels seem to explore the
possibilities of meaning rather than to deploy a reserve of
predefined terms, in a linguistic strategy closer to Jane Austen's
than to George Eliot's: reminiscent of the teasing demolition of

---

[1] Henry James, *The Golden Bowl* (1905); ed. Virginia Llewellyn Smith (Oxford,
1983), 276. The Oxford text is that of the first English edition of the novel; whereas I
have in general preferred the New York edition of James's novels, this late novel was
much less substantially revised than the others—having, James claimed, 'altogether
better literary manners' than the earlier works (*The Art of the Novel* (New York,
1934), 344). For convenience's sake I have thus kept to the text reprinted in the
World's Classics edition.

cliché in *Northanger Abbey* or the gradual devaluation of Fanny Price's moral vocabulary, rather than of Eliot's semantically static terminology. James's vocabulary, like Austen's, is dynamic, subject to constant redefinition; and in his case that elusiveness serves to deflect the narrative movement that seeks to expel elements hindering its own resolution. Vacated of the standard terms of reference, the process of signification itself becomes contestable. Power, then, in James is often a matter of assuming control of signification in situations that have become linguistically vulnerable; and nowhere more so than in his last completed novel. As in *Mansfield Park*, but more ruthlessly, the fictional community of *The Golden Bowl* protects itself by its control of value-formation, which is to say its control of language. If, as I argued earlier, Mary Crawford is defeated by language, so is Charlotte Stant, who discovers, in another of Fanny's dazzling oxymorons, 'the misfortune of being too, too charming' (*GB* 288). Her very charm serves to simplify the moral position of her antagonist by polarizing the terms of the opposition. It's the service performed by Mary Crawford for Fanny Price, and by Gwendolen Harleth for Mirah Lapidoth. Charlotte gives structure to Maggie's fiction, in ways which the rest of this chapter will explore; and her charm comes to constitute the basis of her expulsion, both its unacknowledged reason and its fulsomely celebrated justification. She is, finally, sent away because she is so beautiful and wonderful and good—unlike Lord Jim, who is 'not good enough'.

The linguistic disorientation at the centre of the novel is prefigured by, in a sense is a function of, the geographical displacement of the subject. *The Golden Bowl* is one of James's 'London' novels, and yet it is also one of his most 'American' novels. Apparently as firmly located in London as any Dickens novel, its absent centre of value is American City. The opening of the novel would seem to be, like so many other fictional openings, an *orientation*: as, say, the openings of *Bleak House* or *Little Dorrit* serve as powerful creators of a particular medium—the fog, the prison—through which to view the rest of the novel. But the opening of *The Golden Bowl* is different from these; and in its difference it is revealingly similar to Conrad's procedure in 'Heart of Darkness', which offers us in more ways than one a convenient perspective on James's novel.

Conrad's London is angled through the perception of the anonymous first narrator who is to be superseded by Marlow. Complacently regarding 'the biggest, and the greatest, town on earth'[2] next to the Thames, 'after ages of good service done to the race that peopled its banks, spread out in the tranquil dignity of a waterway leading to the uttermost ends of the earth', this narrator recalls 'the great spirit of the past':

Hunters for gold or pursuers of fame, they all had gone out on that stream, bearing the sword, and often the torch, messengers of the might within the land, bearers of a spark from the sacred fire. What greatness had not floated on the ebb of that river into the mystery of an unknown earth! . . . The dreams of men, the seed of commonwealth, the germs of empires. (*HD* 46–7)

The whole of 'Heart of Darkness', of course, functions as a corrective to this enthusiastic view of the exploits of Empire, an adjustment of the 'misread' historical significance of the Thames. The celebration of the old explorers as 'bearers of a spark from the sacred fire' has. to contend with Marlow's laconic reduction: 'The conquest of the earth, which mostly means the taking it away from those who have a different complexion or slightly flatter nose than ourselves, is not a pretty thing when you look into it too much' (50–1).

All this may seem remote from the world of *The Golden Bowl*, where irregularities of complexion and of nose shape go no further than the exotics of Fanny Assingham. But James's novel, like Conrad's, takes its bearings, or rather its point of departure, from an appreciation of London as a centre of Empire:

The Prince had always liked his London, when it had come to him; he was one of the modern Romans who find by the Thames a more convincing image of the truth of the ancient state than any they have left by the Tiber. Brought up on the legend of the City to which the world paid tribute, he recognised in the present London much more than in contemporary Rome the real dimensions of such a case. If it was a question of an *Imperium*, he said to himself, and if one wished, as a Roman, to recover a little the sense of that, the place to do so was on London Bridge . . . (*GB* 3)

<hr/>

[2] Joseph Conrad, *Youth, Heart of Darkness, The End of the Tether* (1902); ed. Robert Kimbrough (Oxford, 1984), 45.

The Prince on London Bridge (though it is in fact Bond Street to which he betakes himself) presents a potent image of a graceful, indeed almost a grateful, admission of defeat: the least chauvinistic representative of an outdated power admiring its modern equivalent. Like Conrad, James invites the long historical view: the Prince pays tribute to London, the New Rome, supreme in military and economic power. Around him in the shop windows, as he wanders into Bond Street, cluster 'objects massive and lumpish, in silver and gold, in the forms to which precious stones contribute, or in leather, steel, brass . . . as tumbled together as if, in the insolence of Empire, they had been the loot of far-off victories' (3).

But the Prince's pleasant historical reflections are out of date: his is the London of Edward, not Victoria. This is more than a quibble about dates (indeed, strictly speaking we don't know exactly when the events in the novel take place): it is another way of noting that England, in this novel, does not figure as a country at the height of its imperial or even commercial power. The British presence in the novel is reduced to Colonel Bob, his rank like a decoration won in a forgotten war, his role confined to impotent spectatorship. On the sidelines of the action Mr Blint plays duets with Lady Castledean while Lord Castledean, the owner of Matcham, commutes between his ancient seat and his new role in the City. The Matcham so admired by Milly Theale, in part for 'the honoured age of illustrious host and hostess, all at once so distinguished and so plain, so public and so shy',[3] is now presided over by the adulterous and gaudy Lady Castledean, whom Maggie, at any rate, finds far from plain or shy—'Lady Castledean whom she knew she, so oddly, didn't like, in spite of reasons upon reasons, the biggest diamonds on the yellowest hair, the longest lashes on the prettiest, falsest eyes, the oldest lace on the most violet velvet, the rightest manner on the wrongest assumption' (334). The diamonds, lace, and manner, inherited from an older order, sit unconvincingly upon the new generation.

The Prince, however, cannot know that his very presence in London, by courtesy of Mr Verver, signals the passing of an order. His preconceptions and assumptions would have equipped him for

---

[3] Henry James, *The Wings of the Dove* (1902); ed. Peter Brooks (Oxford, 1984), 148.

dealing with the London of *The Wings of the Dove*: he and Mrs Lowder could have reached an understanding. But in *The Golden Bowl* the brash confidence of 'Britannia of the Market Place' has been replaced, as fictional subject, by a different kind of power—'the power of the rich peoples' (14), which is to say the *very* rich people, as exemplified by the enigmatic Adam Verver. Whereas Mrs Lowder almost pathetically aspires to admission to the 'old' society of Matcham, Adam Verver's power makes that society irrelevant: he treats with cavalier indifference the invitations she cherished so anxiously. Even Milly's 'success' at Matcham was frankly acknowledged as a compliment paid by a superior social order to an upstart with an immense amount of money; Adam Verver, 'taking' Fawns for the summer as a matter of course, whimsically considering shipping the little church back to America, is immune to such compliments and such discriminations. The City to which the world, like the Prince, is to pay tribute is not London, but American City, in the process of being embellished with the 'loot' of Adam Verver's victories. American City is the Unreal City of this Waste Land, as the Sepulchral City of Brussels looms at the Heart of Darkness.

But the Prince cannot at this stage see 'the power of the rich peoples' as rendering anachronistic his reading of the signs in the shop windows of Bond Street. As potential consumer of these satisfyingly expensive objects, he takes essentially a shopper's view of 'the loot of far-off victories', without sparing a thought for the far-off defeats that yielded the loot. Nor would we expect this kind of sensitivity to colonial exploitation from the Prince; but, aristocratically innocent as he is of political realities, he is with some ironic relish being set up to discover at first hand 'the insolence of Empire'. 'If it was a question of an *Imperium* . . . and if one wished, as a Roman, to recover a little the sense of that'—well, then there are more direct ways of doing so than window-shopping in Bond Street. The sense of *Imperium* has always been most acutely experienced by those subject to its power—a large and unenviable group to which the Prince has just been admitted by the signing of the marriage contract. For the 'insolence' directing the fortunes of the denizens of *The Golden Bowl* is that of Adam Verver, in his conviction that 'a world was left him to conquer and that he might conquer it if he tried' (104). *The Golden Bowl* is the record of that conquest and an exploration of its methods.

In 'Heart of Darkness' the conquest of the earth, when looked at closely, is, as Marlow says, not a pretty thing:

Six black men advanced in a file, toiling up the path. They walked erect and slow, balancing small baskets full of earth on their heads, and the clink kept time with their footsteps. Black rags were wound round their loins, and the short ends behind waggled to and fro like tails. I could see every rib, the joints of their limbs were like knots in a rope; each had an iron collar on his neck, and all were connected together with a chain whose bights swung between them, rhythmically clinking. . . . They were called criminals, and the outraged law . . . had come to them, an insoluble mystery from the sea. . . . Behind this raw matter one of the reclaimed, the product of the new forces at work, strolled despondently, carrying a rifle by its middle. He had a uniform jacket with one button off, and seeing a white man on the path, hoisted his weapon to his shoulder with alacrity. This was simple prudence, white men being so much alike at a distance that he could not tell who I might be. He was speedily reassured, and with a large, white, rascally grin, and a glance at his charge, seemed to take me into partnership in his exalted trust. After all, I also was a part of the great cause of these high and just proceedings. (*HD* 64)

Not for Mr Verver this crude and unattractive subjection of human beings: under the new *Imperium* the conquest is apparently benevolent, and the conquered, like the Prince, are mainly left in pleased bewilderment at the high price they fetched. But the conquest is also complete, as both the Prince and Charlotte are to discover. Adam Verver's exercise of power, like everything else about him, is marked with the stamp of the connoisseur:

He had ever, of course, had his way of walking about to review his possessions and verify their condition; but this was a pastime to which he now struck [Maggie] as almost extravagantly addicted, and when she passed near him and he turned to give her a smile she caught—or so she fancied—the greater depth of his small, perpetual hum of contemplation. It was as if he were singing to himself, *sotto voce*, as he went—and it was also, on occasion, quite ineffably, as if Charlotte, hovering, watching, listening, on her side too, kept sufficiently within earshot to make it out as song, and yet, for some reason connected with the very manner of it, stood off and didn't dare.
    . . . Charlotte hung behind, with emphasised attention; she stopped when her husband stopped, but at the distance of a case or two, or of whatever succession of objects; and the likeness of their connection would not have

been wrongly figured if he had been thought of as holding in one of his pocketed hands the end of a long silken halter looped round her beautiful neck. He didn't twitch it, yet it was there; he didn't drag her, but she came; and those indications that I have described the Princess as finding extraordinary in him were two or three mute facial intimations which his wife's presence didn't prevent his addressing his daughter—nor prevent his daughter, as she passed, it was doubtless to be added, from flushing a little at the receipt of. They amounted perhaps only to a wordless, wordless smile, but the smile was the soft shake of the twisted silken rope . . . (507–8)

Mutatis mutandis, the silken halter Maggie imagines looped round Charlotte's beautiful neck is as violent an image of subjection as the iron collars round the necks of the hapless 'criminals'; and Marlow's sardonic reference to 'the great cause of these high and just proceedings' differs from James's implication only in the more openly ironic comment Marlow's narrative persona permits. The grin with which the overseer extends 'partnership in his exalted trust' to Marlow is curiously similar to the smile of complicity Adam directs at his daughter; and Maggie's 'flushing a little' at receiving these 'facial intimations' is the equivalent of Marlow's noting of his own part in these proceedings. In terms of human misery, there is of course no comparison between Charlotte's silken-looped subjection and the abject enslavement of the black men; but whereas the exercise of power may vary with the opportunities offered by the social structures sanctioning it, the impulse to power is a common element, underlying, in James's novel as in Conrad's, the 'horror' at its centre. In both cases, too, the 'high and just proceedings' take place in the name of the law: the chained men are 'criminals', Charlotte is an adulteress. The punitive principle which, as I argued in an earlier chapter, is internalized in the plot of a George Eliot novel, is in James, as in Conrad, subjected to the critical irony of the work itself. *Daniel Deronda* requires the humiliation of Gwendolen Harleth as part of its own narrative dynamics; *The Golden Bowl* analyses the social dynamic necessitating the humiliation of Charlotte Stant as part of its own self-preservation.

In *The Golden Bowl*, then, the 'justice' enacted by the plot has nothing to do with an external moral force exacting punishment for a misdeed, like Baldassarre hounding Tito Melema to his death in *Romola*: it is an instrument of the dominant power structure, in this instance 'the power of the rich peoples', to regularize conduct within that structure. That power may manifest itself with less open brutality, but no less absolutely than that colonial system of justice explained to Marlow by one of the faithless pilgrims at the Central Station: 'Transgression—punishment—bang!' (*HD* 80). The power of the rich peoples operates more subtly but then also more insidiously: it prevents, for one, the Prince from realizing that he himself has become subject to it. He does recognize that in signing the contract drawn up by his lawyers and those of the Ververs, he has sold his title and his name for an immense consideration, but he has as yet an imperfect notion of what the contract consists in, believing as he does that Mr Verver's 'easy way with his millions had taxed to such small purpose, in the arrangements, the principle of reciprocity' (*GB* 4). What the Prince learns in the course of the novel is the true nature of the principle of reciprocity. In *The Wings of the Dove*, Lord Mark explained to Milly that 'Nobody here, you know, does anything for nothing' (*WD* 114). In *The Golden Bowl* the seat of power has been relocated, and the social mechanisms have changed accordingly; but we are still very much in the world where, as Kate Croy instructed Milly, 'the working and the worked . . . [are] the parties to every relation' (*WD* 127).

Not that the Prince envisages anything other than being one of the working in *this* relation. His historical sense does not balk at a process that seems to be arranged so much for his convenience: 'What was it but history . . . to have the assurance of the enjoyment of more money than the palace-builder himself could have dreamed of?' (8). To be part of history, though, is by and large a matter of being either one of the (very few) conquerors or one of the (very many) conquered. The Prince, in musing pleasantly on the symbolic value of a crank lowering an iron shutter over a display of 'objects massive and lumpish' in Bond Street, assumes that he belongs to the privileged few: 'There was machinery again, just as the plate glass, all about him, was money, was power, the power of the rich peoples. Well, he was of them now, of the rich peoples; he was on their side—if it wasn't rather the pleasanter way of putting it that they were on his' (14). But he is '*of* them' mainly in the sense of being *theirs*, of belonging to them in the most literal of senses, and they are on his side only in the sense that all people are on the side of their possessions: they protect them with plate glass and iron shutters in the face of illegitimate claims. In this the wishes of the possessions are not consulted: they are emblems not sharers of power; in Conradian terms, the Prince is not so much 'one of us' as 'Our Man'.

The Prince is not even deterred, though he *is* vaguely puzzled, by his dim apprehension of the nature of his value for the Ververs:

He had stood still, at many a moment of the previous month, with the thought, freshly determined or renewed, of the general expectation—to define it roughly—of which he was the subject. What was singular was that it seemed not so much an expectation of anything in particular as a large, bland, blank assumption of merits almost beyond notation, of essential quality and value. It was as if he had been some old embossed coin, of a purity of gold no longer used, stamped with glorious arms, medieval, wonderful, of which the 'worth' in mere modern change, sovereigns and half-crowns, would be great enough, but as to which, since there were finer ways of using it, such taking to pieces was superfluous. That was the image for the security in which it was open to him to rest; he was to constitute a possession, yet was to escape being reduced to his component parts. What would this mean but that, practically, he was never to be tried or tested? (18)

The Prince, as we have seen, is not in the habit of examining his own metaphors,[4] otherwise he might have found something disquieting in 'the image for the security in which it was open to him to rest'. He is not at all discomfited by the potentially disturbing thought that 'he was to constitute a possession', nor by speculation as to the nature of the 'finer ways of using it'; somewhat complacently he concludes that what the Ververs appreciate in him is his 'essential quality and value'. But it is one of the implications of this novel, as of *The Wings of the Dove*, that there is no such thing as 'essential value': value is determined in relation to other things, other values, other interests.

The image of the coin is an extraordinarily rich example of the process of value-formation in the novel. In the first place, it introduces a distinction between intrinsic, conventional, and

---

[4] As Ruth Yeazell points out in her fine chapter on metaphor in late James: 'If James's characters seek to escape themselves through metaphors, they thus risk eventual defeat—for by a Newtonian emotional law, the fears and desires they so energetically suppress emerge with an equal and opposite force through those very same metaphors' (*Language and Knowledge in the Late Novels of Henry James* (Chicago, 1976), 61).

ascribed or perceived value. The pure gold, after being stamped with a fixed 'face' value, has now moved into a realm of altogether less stable values, just as the Prince, whose title has become devalued in the land of his birth, has now been subjected to a different kind of appreciation. Even as legal tender, a coin has an arbitrary value, just as the Prince's title is validated only by the system to which he belongs, but at least the arbitrariness is fixed to the extent that it has been agreed upon by convention; once it loses conventional value, it acquires a more variable, if often far greater, value. The Ververs, who have more 'mere modern change' than they can sensibly spend, attribute value to the Prince's quaint impotence, the decorative ('embossed') and historical function of 'glorious arms' that no longer signify any real power. His own power as a prince of an antique civilization has become, like the rest of his value as a *morceau de musée*, best appreciated in a room in the British Museum, to which his wife pays proprietary visits (the Prince having become over the centuries separated from his certificates of authenticity).

The Ververs, in acquiring the Prince, are merely applying the considerations obtaining in the purchase of any object with rarity value. These have been incisively anatomized by Thorstein Veblen in *The Theory of the Leisure Classes* (1899), a work which makes an instructive companion to *The Golden Bowl*. Here is Veblen on the relative value of two spoons; he might as well be talking about a Prince and a commoner:

The utility of articles valued for their beauty depends closely upon the expensiveness of the articles. . . . A hand-wrought silver spoon, of a commercial value of some ten to twenty dollars, is not ordinarily more serviceable . . . than a machine-made spoon of some 'base' metal, such as aluminum, the value of which may be no more than some ten to twenty cents. . . . It appears (1) that while the different materials of which the two spoons are made each possesses beauty and serviceability for the purpose for which it is used, the material of the hand-wrought spoon is some one hundred times more valuable than the baser metal, without very greatly excelling the latter in intrinsic beauty of grain or color, and without being in any appreciable degree superior in point of mechanical serviceability . . . [5]

[5] Thorstein Veblen, *The Theory of the Leisure Class: An Economic Study of Institutions*, (1899; rpt. London, 1970), 94–5.

Like Veblen's silver spoon, the Prince, without very greatly excelling the baser metal of ordinary mortals (and certainly 'without being in any appreciable degree superior in point of mechanical serviceability'), is at least 'some one hundred times more valuable' to the Ververs. But Adam Verver did not become a millionaire on the strength of his sense of beauty alone, and the Prince also constitutes an investment. And Adam is too astute to hang on to a bad investment, as a later modulation of the coin image suggests. The Prince, having drifted into adultery with Charlotte, finds more of the business man and less of the art lover in the mild gaze of his father-in-law:

This directed regard rested at its ease, but it neither lingered nor penetrated, and was, to the Prince's fancy, much of the same order as any glance directed, for due attention, from the same quarter, to the figure of a cheque received in the course of business and about to be enclosed to a banker. It made sure of the amount—and just so, from time to time, the amount of the Prince was made sure. (238)

Adam Verver is, as it were, biting the coin assessingly; but the substitution of the cheque for the antique coin, with 'value' yielding to the less ambiguous terms 'figure' and 'amount', introduces a more disquieting implication to the assessment: the Prince realizes that Mr Verver, for all his aesthetic fervour, would soon notice if his investment ceased to yield a healthy return. As Veblen goes on to say:

(2) if a close inspection should show that the supposed hand-wrought spoon were in reality only a very clever imitation of hand-wrought goods, but an imitation so cleverly wrought as to give the same impression of line and surface to any but a minute examination by a trained eye, the utility of the article, including the gratification which the user derives from its contemplation as an object of beauty, would immediately decline by some eighty or ninety per cent, or even more. (95)

The Prince, whose own 'trained eye' could easily discount the Golden Bowl as a gilded cracked crystal, uncomfortably faces his own potential devaluation. But his misinterpretation of his own value is merely one example of 'the power of the rich peoples' to control value. If in the first place this is a matter of converting an aesthetic or even ethical value to a financial value, the reverse is perhaps a more fundamental transaction: the money staked on such aesthetic investments has first to be made, and laundered, as it were, by being transferred to the aesthetic, ethical, even religious sector. The financier Holroyd in Conrad's *Nostromo*, with 'the temperament of a Puritan and an insatiable imagination of conquest',[6] is not unlike Adam Verver; but where, in Mrs Gould's words, Holroyd 'looked upon his own God as a sort of influential partner, who gets his own share of profits in the endowment of churches' (71), for Verver it is 'the exemplary passion, the passion for perfection at any price' that represents 'the religion he wished to propagate' (*GB* 107). Holroyd appoints God as an influential partner; Verver dispenses altogether with partners.

II

As literary creation Adam Verver's line can be traced back to such disreputable forebears as Dickens's Merdle and Trollope's Melmotte: whereas their philanthropy, such as it is, founders on the rocks of financial vicissitudes, his survives the perils of his methods of acquisition. But an alternative or complementary genealogy can be traced for Adam in terms of his antecedents in James's own fiction, the recurrent figure of the patron or Prime Mover—Rowland Mallet in *Roderick Hudson*, Olive Chancellor in *The Bostonians*,[7] Mr Touchett in *The Portrait of a Lady*, Mrs Gereth in *The Spoils of Poynton*, various more or less disreputable adults in *What Maisie Knew*, Mr Longdon in *The Awkward Age*, Mrs Lowder in *The Wings of the Dove*: in all these cases, some older and richer person decisively changes the life of another, sometimes with benevolent intention, often with disastrous consequences, and frequently as an exercise in power, calculated to advance the interests of the patron at least as much as those of the protegé(e). The ambiguity of Adam Verver's exercise of financial power is thus only a development of a recurrent interest in the morality of intervention.

[6] Joseph Conrad, *Nostromo* (1904); ed. Keith Corbaine (Oxford, 1984), 76.
[7] Adrian Poole has drawn an interesting comparison between the at first sight unlikely pair of Olive Chancellor and Rowland Mallet, on the grounds of their both competing for possession of their protegé(e) against the claims of 'an orthodox heterosexual passion from which they are excluded' (*Henry James* (Hemel Hempstead, 1991), 85).

In Adam that intervention is so much a matter of total management that the little world of Fawns is easily imagined as his creation. Regulating every detail of the financial well-being of his ménage, Adam becomes also the determinant of its moral meanings, the negotiator of material and non-material value alike. To put it differently, the supreme arbiter of value in Adam's world is Adam: as aesthetic value is converted to price in his bargaining for a set of oriental tiles, so moral value is fixed in terms of their relation to his power. In these transactions, human beings do not have 'essential value' any more than a set of oriental tiles: the value is fixed by Adam Verver in accordance with a taste he has come to regard as infallible. The other characters indulge, of course, their own 'personal' values; but ultimately these values are referred back to Adam, and those which do not accord with his 'idea' are ruthlessly expunged—or rather, more insidiously, redefined into conformity with that idea. By this process the act of aesthetic valuation becomes analogous to that other process of value-discrimination, the semantic play of the text. It is by a manipulation of value, and then in particular of the value of words, by a process which I shall trace in the rest of this chapter, that Adam achieves his 'success'.[8] In this, too, his control is similar to the semantic processes whereby colonialism, in 'Heart of Darkness', validates its exploitation through a constant redefinition of the subjects of its oppression: 'I had no idea of the conditions, he said: these heads were the heads of rebels. I shocked him excessively by laughing. Rebels! What would be the next definition I was to hear? There had been enemies, criminals, workers—and these were rebels' (*HD* 132). If, in Conrad's grisly little scene, language sanctions by strategic redefinition even these disembodied heads on posts, in James's novel language is no less central to the process of control. If the Prince, early in his marriage, finds a 'general explanation' for his difference from the Ververs in the formula 'We haven't the same *values*' (*GB*

[8] The value of words in *The Golden Bowl*, as in *The Wings of the Dove*, anticipates Saussure's distinction between *meaning* and *value*: 'The content of a word is determined in the final analysis not by what it contains but by what exists outside it. As an element in a system, the word has not only a meaning but also—above all—a value' (*Course in General Linguistics*, ed. Charles Bally and Albert Sechehaye, trans. Roy Harris (London, 1983), 114). I discuss this in '"The Language of the House" in *The Wings of the Dove*', *Essays in Criticism*, 34 (1989), 116–36.

102)—well, by the end of the novel that difference has also been defined out of existence.

The power propelling the action of the novel, the power of the rich peoples, is thus also the power over good and evil, the power to shape moral concepts to one's own ends. As applied by Adam to himself, this is a reasonably straightforward process of rationalization, whereby even the most dubious aspects of his career are made to seem providential: 'A wiser hand than he at first knew had kept him hard at acquisition of one sort as a perfect preliminary to acquisition of another, and the preliminary would have been weak and wanting if the good faith of it had been less' (106). It is, in short, clear that in surrounding himself with precious objects, Adam is executing the design of the 'wiser hand'—and thus retroactively justifying the 'preliminary': 'It was the strange scheme of things again: the years of darkness had been needed to render possible the years of light' (106). Except for this backward glance, we are not invited to speculate on the nature of the darkness, the methods Verver must have used to amass a fortune as stupendous as his apparently is: the novel deals exclusively with the years of light, the achievement of which must be assumed to have been the purpose of the strange scheme of things.

The light, we may say, is dark enough, as light comes to be used in *The Golden Bowl*.[9] Thus Adam's illumination as to Charlotte's proper use ('the idea shone upon him'—154) is preceded by an extraordinary hallucination on the terrace of Fawns: 'Light broke for him at last . . . The sharp point to which all his light converged was that the whole call of his future to him, as a father, would be in his so managing that Maggie would less and less appear to herself to have forsaken him' (153–4). The light, then, is intimately associated with the elaborate 'idea' in whose execution Maggie will be deceived and Charlotte will be used; it is, as it were, the medium of Adam's hallucination. Adam is not the only creature of this deceptive light—light permeates the novel—but he is, as it were, at the heart of light, unfathomable, impenetrable, invisible. The aura of 'goodness' that surrounds—and conceals—Adam forms, in the Prince's vision, a 'great white curtain', a 'white mist' which obscures

---

[9] For a diametrically opposed reading of the significance of the imagery of light and dark in the novel, see Greg Zacharias, 'The Language of Light and Dark and James's Moral Argument in *The Golden Bowl*', *Papers on Language and Literature*, 26 (1990), 249–70.

'the state of mind of his new friends'—'that element of the impenetrable which alone slightly qualified his sense of his good fortune'. The Prince, native of a country of darker but more straightforward intrigue, having 'never known curtains but as purple even to blackness—but as producing where they hung a darkness intended and ominous', feels 'his own boat move upon some such mystery' as that confronting the shipwrecked Gordon Pym, a 'dazzling curtain of light, concealing as darkness conceals' (17–18).

The light so insistently associated with Adam figures as an element of concealment, suggesting that Adam's view of his own career as divinely sanctioned manifests itself in a blinding veil of righteousness. In this, he is true to the type to which he belongs; as E. J. Hobsbawm says of the philanthropic enterprises of Carnegie and Rockefeller: 'Philanthropy on this scale, like art collecting, had the incidental advantage that it retrospectively softened the public outlines of men whose workers and business rivals remembered them as merciless predators.'[10] Adam Verver is, then, James's representation, with outlines duly softened, of the American robber-baron-turned-philanthropist-art-collector. This is not to suggest that *The Golden Bowl* is in any narrow sense a satire on the self-exculpations of the robber baron; it is rather to propose that James's material and even his notorious treatment of his material are less remote from the social realities of his time than is commonly conceded. For if Adam derives something of his meaning from intertextual reference to his literary predecessors, the industrialists and financiers of Dickens and Trollope as well as the benefactors–controllers of James's own earlier novels, this does not preclude the more traditional kind of referential meaning. Adam Verver is not a symbolic abstraction: he is a tolerably recognizable instance of a phenomenon of his time. It has been suggested that James simply did not know enough about the type to render it in any detail, or was not interested enough to do so.[11] But the great capitalists of the time were for the most part highly visible, and what James gives us

---

[10] E. J. Hobsbawm, *The Age of Empire: 1875–1914* (London, 1987), 187.

[11] See, for instance, Sallie Sears, *The Negative Imagination: Form and Perspective in the Novels of Henry James* (Ithaca, NY, 1968): 'But James is not interested in giving us a realistic picture of a John D. Rockefeller, the conditions that he created, or the conditions that created him. The figure of the millionaire caught James's imagination . . . because of certain suggestive qualities it symbolized' (161–2).

in Adam Verver is almost paradigmatic of his class. Verver's assumption that all things conspire to the greater prosperity and glory of Adam Verver forms a clear parody of the providential views cultivated by the Protestant work ethic—for all that he is nominally a Catholic. The art collecting, the marriage into an old European noble family,[12] the international opulence, are all features that Adam Verver shares with the prominent financiers of his time. To complain that 'Mr Verver's moral tone is far more like that of a benevolent Swedenborgian than it is like that of either John D. Rockefeller or Jay Gould'[13] is to confuse Quentin Anderson's allegorized version of Verver[14] with Henry James's actual rendering, not as a benevolent Swedenborgian at all, but as a shrewd capitalist whose wealth has enabled him to retire from its more sordid aspects, without losing any of the acuteness and acquisitiveness that created that wealth.[15] Similarly, to see him as 'a visionary figure, eloquent of the difference between the American millionaire as he was and as James would have liked him to be' and then to pronounce him 'improbable'[16] is to miss James's ironic intent and to credit him with an extraordinary taste in millionaires. Adam Verver is all too probable as an ironic depiction of the American millionaire 'as he was'—that is, an unscrupulous manipulator conspicuously returning some part of his gains to the community he gained it from, and thereby earning the obsequious admiration of those benefiting by this generosity.[17] As Caroline Gordon says,

---

[12] In buying a titled foreigner for the family, Adam is following a fashion of the era. Matthew Josephson notes that 'By 1909, Gustavus Myers calculates that more than 500 American women had married titled foreigners, and that the draining away of a surplus of some $220,000,000 became possible as a consequence' (*The Robber Barons: The Great American Capitalists 1861–1901* (1934; rpt. New York, 1962), 340).

[13] F. O. Matthiessen, *Henry James: The Major Phase* (1944; rpt. London, 1946), 90.

[14] Quentin Anderson, *The American Henry James* (London, 1958).

[15] Jonathan Hughes, *The Vital Few: American Progress and its Protagonists* (London, 1973): 'The Andrew Carnegie now [after his death] chiefly remembered was the philanthropist. . . . A man who could cheerfully give away more than $350 million could easily be remembered as the kindest man ever known. After 1901 the "little boss" of Pittsburgh was slowly blotted out of men's memories and replaced by the gentle Laird of Skibo Castle' (265–6) .

[16] John Bayley, *The Characters of Love* (London, 1960), 249.

[17] I don't think that James modelled Adam Verver on any single figure, but John Pierpont Morgan could quite easily have stood in for Adam. He was also, of course, a great art collector, intent upon furnishing his native city with a great museum, only to

though apparently intending it as a compliment to Verver, 'He is the spiritual ancestor of the philanthropists of our day'.[18]

Adam's benevolence of aspect, far from militating against the potency of his influence, is one of the signs of his power; his mildness is an effect of his sublime confidence in his own dominance:[19] 'he looked, at the top of his table, so nearly like a little boy shyly entertaining in virtue of some imposed rank, that he *could* only be one of the powers, the representative of a force—quite as an infant king is the representative of a dynasty' (237). The shyness is deceptive: Mr Verver, having made it 'the business of his future' to 'rifle the golden isles' (104), is well on his way towards establishing his own dynasty, complete with a Prince and a Principino to succeed him. 'Stout Cortez' (104) with the demeanour of an infant king: the ambiguity of a power that can present itself as so benevolent, so innocent, so childlike, and yet can be so absolute in its domination, is, in James's rendering, essential to 'the power of the rich peoples'. From this ambiguity derives much of the elusiveness of the novel; for, beguiled by the apparent benevolence of this power, all the characters pursue their various courses on the blithe assumption of their own freedom of action. And if we absorb their assumptions while we share their points of view, it may take us as long as it takes them to discover the illusory nature of their freedom, the limits of their silken halters.

In the case of Adam, we are armed against the beguilement of the universal admiration he excites by our privileged access to his aspirations and ideals; indeed, in a novel not notable for open narratorial intrusion, the presentation of Adam is at times remarkably direct:

meet with indifference from those he was intent upon enlightening (much of his collection nevertheless made its way into the Metropolitan Museum). His ambitions seem to have been larger than Verver's: where Verver whimsically entertained the notion of transporting the little church at Fawns to America, Morgan would have liked the Sistine Chapel. (He also, incidentally, seems to have spent more time with his daughter and her child than with his wife.)

[18] Caroline Gordon, 'Mr Verver, Our National Hero', *Sewanee Review*, 63 (1955), 35. The title of Gordon's essay is not ironically intended.

[19] For a similar point used to different effect, see Mark Seltzer, *Henry James and the Art of Power* (Ithaca, NY, 1984), 68: 'Adam represents power, but only by appearing powerless.' Seltzer also develops a parallel with Conrad to support his contention that James is addressing the discontents of colonialism.

Representative precious objects, great ancient pictures and other works of art, fine eminent 'pieces' in gold, in silver, in enamel, majolica, ivory, bronze, had for a number of years so multiplied themselves round him and, as a general challenge to acquisition and appreciation, so engaged all the faculties of his mind, that the instinct, the particular sharpened appetite of the collector, had fairly served as a basis for his acceptance of the Prince's suit.

Over and above the signal fact of the impression made on Maggie herself, the aspirant to his daughter's hand showed somehow the great marks and signs, stood before him with the high authenticities, he had learned to look for in pieces of the first order. Adam Verver knew, by this time, knew thoroughly; no man in Europe or in America, he privately believed, was less capable, in such estimates, of vulgar mistakes. (103)

That Adam, like J. P. Morgan in his notorious purchase, at a huge price, of a 'Raphael' that no gallery in Europe would touch,[20] should here be making one of the 'vulgar mistakes' he fancies himself immune to, could have been seen only as an example of that human proneness to error which has propelled narrative at least since the account of the Fall; but Verver's hubristic error, if not unprecedented, is rendered specific to James's purpose by his application of aesthetic criteria to his human associates. Nor are his human collectibles, in being judged 'pieces of the first order', treated as objects of delight or humble admiration, but as 'a general challenge to acquisition and appreciation', presumably in that order. As Browning's Last Duchess is replaced by her more tractable portrait, so the 'representative precious objects' of Adam's collection are to be turned into 'good things'. And we are left in no doubt that 'this application of the same measure of value to such different pieces of property as old Persian carpets, say, and new human acquisitions' leaves no space for distinctions between different orders of possessions: 'As it had served him to satisfy himself, so to speak, both about Amerigo and about the Bernardino Luini he had happened to come to knowledge of at the time of his daughter's betrothal, so it served him at present to satisfy himself about Charlotte Stant and an extraordinary set of oriental tiles of which he had lately got wind' (145). That Adam's proposal to Charlotte should be preceded by her attendance at his purchase of

[20] The incident is referred to with some relish by Josephson, *The Robber Barons*, 344.

the tiles is thus appropriate: the two transactions are more similar than she realizes, based as they both are on 'the idea (followed by appropriation) of plastic beauty, of the thing visibly perfect of its kind' (145–6). Adam miscalculates, as Gilbert Osmond and Browning's Duke also do, in assuming that 'human acquisitions' are as compliant as old Persian carpets. But that miscalculation does not deflect his purpose; indeed, the novel records the process whereby everything is brought back into ostensible accord with Adam's 'measure of value'.

The one experience not sipped from Verver's 'one little glass' is his love for his daughter. This makes him entirely ruthless in dealing with people whom he sees as secondary to his office as father. Mr Verver, 'caring for special vases only less than for precious daughters' (139),[21] can persuade himself that this one non-aesthetic passion of his life justifies any use to which he puts whatever material, human or otherwise, presents itself for his acquisition:

He had seen that Charlotte could contribute—what he hadn't seen was what she could contribute *to*. When it had all cleared up and he had simply settled this service to his daughter well before him as the proper direction of his young friend's leisure, the cool darkness had again closed round him, but his moral lucidity was constituted. . . . To think of it merely for himself would have been, even as he had just lately felt, even doing all justice to that condition—yes, impossible. But there was a grand difference in thinking of it for his child. (154)

The aesthetic in Mr Verver, we note, does not preclude the utilitarian: he saw, as it were, Charlotte's usefulness before he saw her use, her 'plastic beauty' happily combining with her instrumentality, to make her, as Gilbert Osmond foresaw with equal inaccuracy of Isabel Archer, 'as smooth to his general need of her as handled ivory to the palm'.[22] What Adam sees Charlotte as able to 'contribute *to*' is the greater domestic snugness of the

---

[21] To read into this quotation a non-aesthetic basis to Adam's love for Maggie is to give him the benefit of the doubt as to whether he distinguishes between vases and daughters in terms of *kind* or *degree* of preciousness. In the New York Edition James emended 'special vases' to 'precious vases', increasing the ambiguity by the parallelism.

[22] *The Portrait of a Lady* (1881, rev. 1907); ed. Nicola Bradbury (Oxford, 1981), 329.

Ververs. The insolence with which he 'simply settle[s] this service to his daughter . . . as the proper direction of his young friend's leisure' is transformed into an act of selflessness by his 'moral lucidity'—'lucidity' here, as elsewhere in the novel, recalling that light that dawned upon Adam so early in his career and has guided him ever since.[23] The reassuring conclusion that selfishness on his own account would have been '—yes, impossible', is undercut by the strong placing of 'for his child': Maggie consistently figures as an extension of himself, '*his* child' (in the course of the paragraph just quoted, Maggie is referred to twice as 'his child' and once as 'his daughter').[24]

This identification of Maggie's interests with his own is, as acutely analysed by the Prince, more than an excess of family feeling: it is part of a principle of cohesion that extends beyond the family:

Mr Verver then, in a word, took care of his relation to Maggie, as he took care, and apparently always would, of everything else. He relieved him of all anxiety about his married life in the same manner in which he relieved him on the score of his bank account. And as he performed the latter office by communicating with the bankers, so the former sprang as directly from his good understanding with his daughter. This understanding had, wonderfully—*that* was in high evidence—the same deep intimacy as the commercial, the financial association founded, far down, on a community of interest. . . . Those people—and his free synthesis lumped together capitalists and bankers, retired men of business, illustrious collectors, American fathers-in-law, American fathers, little American daughters, little American wives—those people were of the same large lucky group, as one

---

[23] Adam's illumination, his need to etherealize his mundanity, has an amusing counterpart in the career of Andrew Carnegie. In 1872 this agnostic experienced his equivalent of conversion: 'The change that came over the man resembled the religious experience known as a conversion, and like that experience it came as the exaltation of a single moment. A mind that had lived in apparent darkness was illumined by a sudden flash of light. . . . It was the dazzling brilliance of a Bessemer converter that, in the twinkling of an eye, transformed Andrew Carnegie into a new man' (quoted by Josephson, *The Robber Barons*, 107, from Carnegie's 'chief apologist'). If the Bessemer converter follows somewhat bathetically upon that preamble, Adam's 'lucidity' is hardly less disproportionate to its cause.

[24] Merle Williams in her finely gauged account of Verver finds evidence here of 'a touching modesty' (*Henry James and the Philosophical Novel: Being and Seeing* (Cambridge: Cambridge University Press, 1993), 192)—a reading which seems to me to take the free indirect rendering of Adam's rationalizations too much at his own valuation. Williams's fine chapter on *The Golden Bowl* (166–221) is one of the most balanced I know.

might say; they were all, at least, of the same general species and had the same general instincts; they hung together, they passed each other the word, they spoke each other's language, they did each other 'turns'. (214)

The Prince's perceptive analysis of the 'community of interest' shared by his wife and father-in-law distinguishes that community from more traditional concepts, first by the absence of a shared locale: it is not a geographic community. Nor does it contain the various strata, classes, interest groups, none of the neighbourhood aspect of, say, Jane Austen's or George Eliot's communities: for all its apparent openness, its freedom from barriers of nationality, it is a stringently exclusive and homogeneous community, admitting to itself only those who can further the communal interest. Like the members of other communities, they 'spoke each other's language'—but here not in the sense of a national or regional tongue, rather in the sense of a shared frame of reference. It is, in short, a modern community: the near-abstract community of international finance, the community of the 'rich peoples' that in James's time formed the great Trusts and in our own time has become the electronically linked multinational corporation. (The term 'community of interests', indeed, was coined and given wide currency by J. P. Morgan to express what he regarded as the overriding consideration tending towards the co-operation of competitors in the same field.) It is furthermore, for all the impersonality of communication, a community founded on a 'deep intimacy'. It is what, in *Nostromo*, unites people as disparate as Holroyd and Gould, Monygham and Nostromo—the last precisely until he no longer finds his own interests served by the community that has claimed him as 'our man'. But where Conrad dramatizes, in the course of the Gould marriage, the incompatibility of bonds of affection with material interests, James suggests that the community of interest can serve and be served by such bonds in a near-incestuous closing of the ranks.

The severely reduced community of *The Golden Bowl*, then, mirrors the exclusiveness of the great financial families, which can afford to limit intercourse with the inconvenient outside world to carefully regulated invitations: if the Misses Lutch overstep the mark by introducing into the community the egregious Mrs Rance, they are dealt with in the manner of inconvenient courtiers at the court of the Borgias—in this instance by the use of Charlotte,

recruited for the purpose. The sparseness of the human landscape of
the novel represents not so much a narrowing of James's vision as
the self-sufficiency of the collector whose world finally is reduced to
his own collection of precious objects, while yet retaining intimate
bonds with the structures from which he derives his power.[25]

Like any other community, the community of interest has its
criteria of acceptability and exclusion. To be 'one of us' in Verver's
world is to be privileged indeed—but it is also more difficult than
the Prince initially assumes, in his cheerful sense of being '*of* them
now, of the rich peoples'. The Prince and Charlotte, carefully
authenticated as they have been, are never really admitted to that
community: they are acquired by it. The distinction becomes
apparent only once they no longer conform to their function as
acquisitions; before that, they assume that their interest can also be
served by that of Adam and Maggie, that in fact it is a common
interest. As we have seen, the Prince is only too willing to form part
of Verver's collection, sees indeed a new freedom in subjection on
such easy terms. Charlotte takes a no less sanguine view of the
possibilities opening up to her in being admitted to Mr Verver's
millions, with the added pleasures of attending splendid receptions
accompanied by her former and future lover:

She was herself in truth crowned, and it all hung together, melted together,
in light and colour and sound: the unsurpassed diamonds that her head so
happily carried, the other perfections of aspect and arrangement that made
her personal scheme a success, the *proved* private theory that materials to
work with had been all she required and that there were none too precious
for her to understand and use—to which might be added lastly, as the
strong-scented flower of the total sweetness, an easy command, a high
enjoyment, of her crisis. (180)

Charlotte's illusion of independence is even more complete than the
Prince's. Her sense that 'she was herself in truth crowned' fails to
plumb the implications of the passive voice, stops short of ascribing
an agent to the process. Rather like Gwendolen Harleth at her

---

[25] Again J. P. Morgan provides a precedent: 'His royal manner of living and of
traveling insulated him from the great mass of men and women; and though he might
by an impulsive act of kindness make connection with them, most of the time they
were to him creatures apart' (Frederick Lewis Allen, *The Great Pierpont Morgan*
(London, 1949), 206).

moment of triumph at the Archery Meeting, Charlotte assumes that because she commands attention she also controls the process whereby she is perceived. In truth, 'her personal scheme', her 'private theory' merely happen to coincide, at this stage, with Adam's personal scheme, or his 'idea' as he calls it ('Isn't a man's idea usually what he does marry for?'—165). The 'materials to work with' granted to her, precious as they are, are decorations embellishing the human materials Mr Verver works with—of which there are truly none too precious for him to understand and use. She is wearing, as Veblen would say, Mr Verver's insignia; and as 'representative precious object', she is subject ultimately to Verver's control and use, the diamonds to be replaced with the silken loops of Maggie's vision.[26]

But if Verver's power owes part of its insidiousness to the willing compliance of its subjects, a related and perhaps more potent reason for this paralysing efficacy lies in the shining robes of righteousness in which it clothes itself, in the control it exerts over others' perception not just of the dominant power but also of themselves. Adam's and Maggie's belief that their devotion to each other is an absolute value sanctioning anything done in its name contaminates everyone drawn into its sphere of influence. The Prince and Charlotte, for reasons of their own, find that the arrangement beautifully suits them, not only in the opportunities it affords, but also in the amiable light it sheds on their adultery:

'Tender as I am for her too,' she went on, 'I think I'm still more so for my husband. *He's* in truth of a sweet simplicity—!'
   The Prince turned over a while the sweet simplicity of Mr Verver. 'Well, I don't know that I can choose. At night all cats are grey. I only see how, for so many reasons, we ought to stand toward them—and how, to do ourselves justice, we do. It represents for us a conscious care—'

---

[26] Veblen sees 'vicarious consumption' as based on the desire of the possessor to display his own power: 'Throughout this graduated scheme of vicarious leisure and vicarious consumption the rule holds that these offices must be performed in some such manner, or under some such circumstance or insignia, as shall point plainly to the master to whom therefore the resulting increment of good repute of right inures' (*Theory of the Leisure Class*, 66). Veblen also traces the process whereby the insignia can become a livery, a mark of servitude: 'Something of a honorific character always attached to the livery of the armed retainer, but this honorific character disappears when the livery becomes the exclusive badge of the menial. The livery becomes obnoxious' (67).

'Of every hour, literally,' said Charlotte. She could rise to the highest measure of the facts. 'And for which we must trust each other—!'

'Oh, as we trust the saints in glory. Fortunately,' the Prince hastened to add, 'we can.' With which, as for the full assurance and the pledge it involved, their hands instinctively found their hands. 'It's all too wonderful.'

Firmly and gravely she kept his hand. 'It's too beautiful.'

And so for a minute they stood together, as strongly held and as closely confronted as any hour of their easier past even had seen them. They were silent at first, only facing and faced, only grasping and grasped, only meeting and met. 'It's sacred,' he said at last. (228)

The Prince and Charlotte are all too evidently parading their contempt for the 'sweet simplicity' of the Ververs as 'sacred' solicitude; and in so far as the 'pledge' which they seal so passionately constitutes anything beyond the occasion for an embrace, it amounts to an agreement not to let the Ververs find out the lengths to which they have taken their conjugal duties. The ingenious exculpation is all their own, and we cannot hold the Ververs responsible for the sins about to be committed in their name. But the Prince and Charlotte are really only learning the rules of the language game in operation. 'Wonderful' and 'beautiful', we remember, are the epithets bestowed by Charlotte on Adam's 'idea' at the time of his proposal: the devotion of father and daughter provides an impeccable absolute for others whereby to justify their actions. The comic discrepancy between the Prince and Charlotte's dialogue and their actions is merely an extreme form of the prevalent manipulation of language, whereby bedizened description does duty for moral definition.

By a trick of perspective, everybody in the novel is made to seem blameless—an exoneration that Fanny Assingham, for one, performs valiantly in the face of her husband's sceptical catechism:

'The state of things existing hasn't grown, like a field of mushrooms, in a night. Whatever they, all round, may be in for now is at least the consequence of what they've *done*. Are they mere helpless victims of fate?'

Well, Fanny at last had the courage of it. 'Yes—they are. To be so abjectly innocent—that *is* to be victims of fate.'

'And Charlotte and the Prince are abjectly innocent—?'

It took her another minute, but she rose to the full height. 'Yes. That is they *were*—as much so in their way as the others. There were beautiful intentions all round. The Prince's and Charlotte's were beautiful—of *that* I had my faith. They *were*—I'd go to the stake. Otherwise,' she added, 'I should have been a wretch. And I've not been a wretch. I've only been a double-dyed donkey.'

'Ah then,' he asked, 'what does our muddle make *them* to have been?'

'Well, too much taken up with considering each other. You may call such a mistake as that by whatever name you please; it at any rate means, all round, their case. It illustrates the misfortune,' said Mrs Assingham gravely, 'of being too, too charming.' (287–8)

The high comedy of this, as indeed of much of the novel, should not blind us to the nature of the transaction taking place, whereby Fanny, in order to avoid judging herself a wretch, has to find abject innocence in adultery and see the adulterers as victims of fate. But her semantic juggling is more than that: her presentation of the forms that 'have succeeded in setting themselves up as the right ones' (287) acutely prefigures the uneasy accommodation of content to form that concludes the novel. Her exonerations make explicit the language game ruling relations in the novel, the game required by a power founded on the assumption of righteousness.

III

No character is more adept at this game than Maggie herself. She of course has privileged access to the community of interest; but she is nevertheless subject to that power that relies on the willing submission, even the eager participation, of those it rules. If the God–Christ analogy favoured by some critics for the Adam–Maggie nexus has any force, it is in Maggie's correspondence to a Christ who is part of and yet subordinate to a power that can exact absolute obedience in the name of love. As in the subjugation of the Prince and Charlotte, this power operates through controlling Maggie's perception of her own value. She is, like several Jamesian women before her, an heiress; no less than Catherine Sloper or Milly Theale, she derives her desirability, her 'value' in one important sense of the word, from the money she is to inherit. It is almost impossible to imagine Maggie without her money—as is said of Milly Theale, 'that was what it was to be really rich. It had to be *the* thing you were' (*WD* 87). But where poor Milly discovers only at the end of her life that her value to others is supremely simple—her money—Maggie accepts the power of her wealth, and then strives to transfigure her own value, to claim a validity other than that derived from her father's money. She is innocent of 'the years of darkness' required to amass the millions on which those values rest: as evinced by the high moral tone of Woollett in *The Ambassadors*, philanthropic capitalism can afford admirable laundry facilities. And yet, as Verver's daughter, Maggie is close enough to the maker of the money to experience, without fully understanding, the kind of power behind such accumulation of wealth. Her half of the novel dramatizes her growing understanding of that power, and her successful suppression of that understanding, even as she uses it to her own ends.

This emphasis on Adam as the source of Maggie's power seems necessary as a counterweight to the many critical accounts that take, as it were, Maggie's word for her own efficacy. Nicola Bradbury, for instance, maintains that 'Maggie, at least, we must trust, if we are to follow the novel at all', and sees Maggie's authority as 'based upon this: that the process is analogous for heroine and reader'.[27] But to trust Maggie is to share her self-imposed blindness: the process becomes analogous for heroine and reader also in avoiding a full apprehension of Adam Verver's sustained power. No single character, not even Maggie, has access to the total system whereby value is created in the novel. In one sense she does 'rewrite' the novel: she reshapes the forms observed by everybody so as to maintain certain fictions. But this does not prevent her own version of events from being a fiction amongst other fictions, and, more important, a fiction within that fiction that we call the novel. But Maggie undertakes to actualize her fictions, that is, she acts in accordance with them, and gets others to do likewise.

Her most urgent fiction is her conviction 'that she must never intermit for a solitary second her so highly undertaking to prove [to Adam] that there was nothing the matter with her' (356). But in fact, every practical decision in the novel (except, for a significantly short period, those of the Prince and Charlotte) is taken by her supposedly ignorant father: *he* decides that he and Maggie will not go on their European trip; *he* decides that nor will he and the Prince do so; he takes the whole family to Fawns, and, having established

[27] Nicola Bradbury, *Henry James: The Later Novels* (Oxford, 1979), 194.

his mastery over Charlotte, takes her into exile in American City. All Maggie can do is to protect, ever more desperately, her cherished image of her 'divine' father by preventing an open confrontation from taking place. Faced with the prospective ruin of her small world, she places her faith in her father:

He was strong—that was the great thing. He was sure—sure for himself, always, whatever his idea; the expression of that in him had somehow never appeared more identical with his proved taste for the rare and the true. . . . The sense that he wasn't a failure, and could never be, purged their predicament of every meanness . . . Wasn't it because now, also, on his side, he was thinking of her as his daughter, was *trying* her, during these mute seconds, as the child of his blood? . . . she wasn't in that case a failure either—hadn't been, but the contrary; his strength was her strength, her pride was his, and they were decent and competent together. This was all in the answer she finally made him.

'I believe in you more than anyone.' (498–9)

This ends on another one of those embraces with which various pacts, most of them deceitful, are sealed in this novel. In this case, the embrace marks Maggie's undertaking never to allow herself to cease to believe in her father—that is, never allow herself to fathom his motives. Her reflections make clear why her idealization of her father is so necessary to her self-esteem: 'his strength was her strength', which implies also the moral validation of her actions: 'they were decent and competent together.' In him is contained their whole value system, based as it is on his 'proved taste for the rare and the true'. To question that, to admit that in this case his 'proved taste' has let him down badly, would be to question the moral validity of their power over the Prince and Charlotte.

This dependence on her belief in her father explains why she makes so little, practically speaking, of her insight into her father's motives. The most famous instance of her ability to see through his eyes and reconstruct his thought processes is the chilling vision, shortly after her declaration of faith in her father, of Charlotte's being led by 'a long silken halter looped round her beautiful neck' (508), which brings Maggie as close as she ever gets to perceiving the nature of the power that has been delegated to her in her dealings with the Prince ('his strength was her strength'). The corollary of this vision is the imaginative sympathy which enables her to interpret Charlotte's 'high coerced quaver' (514) as 'the shriek of a soul in pain' (512). In this novel about moral blindness, this perception of Maggie's is an important achievement; and yet, in spite of her 'flushing a little at the receipt' of his 'wordless smile' (508) she never wavers in her complicity with that power of her father's that is slowly revealing its true ruthlessness.

Maggie's resistance to her own newly awakened perceptions is most powerfully dramatized for us in her vigil outside the smoking-room at Fawns, where the others are involved in a game of bridge. In her conviction of her own benevolent power, she sees them as completely within her control, capable at best of executing with practised grace the lines she dictates:

They might have been—really charming as they showed in the beautiful room, and Charlotte certainly, as always, magnificently handsome and supremely distinguished—they might have been figures rehearsing some play of which she herself was the author; they might even, for the happy appearance they continued to present, have been such figures as would, by the strong note of character in each, fill any author with the certitude of success, especially of their own histrionic. (470)

It is true that Maggie could shatter the harmony by confronting the company with the uncomfortable truths everybody is conspiring to suppress. What prevents it is that she sees 'why it was she had been able to give herself so little, from the first, to the vulgar heat of her wrong' (470). But Maggie's wrong, like all moral terms in this novel, is a matter of interpretation, and that interpretation is kept rigidly within the limits of the fiction she has constructed for herself. This applies also to her famous vision, her 'horror of finding evil seated, all at its ease, where she had only dreamed of good; the horror of the thing hideously *behind*, behind so much trusted, so much pretended, nobleness, cleverness, tenderness' (471). Maggie's horror, like Kurtz's in 'Heart of Darkness', could be seen as a 'summing-up', a judgement on the whole charming and beautiful civilization portrayed in the novel; indeed, in its application to Adam's little universe, the perception easily transcends Maggie's application of it. But it is Maggie's reading of it that we are given at this point, and that reading is cautiously incomplete, taking refuge in generalized injustices, 'innocence outraged and generosity betrayed' (471). But shortly after this Charlotte joins Maggie outside and together they look at the same scene:

Side by side, for three minutes, they fixed this picture of quiet harmonies, the positive charm of it and, as might have been said, the full significance—which, as was now brought home to Maggie, could be no more, after all, than a matter of interpretation, differing always for a different interpreter. As she herself had hovered in sight of it a quarter of an hour before, it would have been a thing for her to show Charlotte—to show in righteous irony, in reproach too stern for anything but silence. But now it was she who was being shown it, and shown it by Charlotte, and she saw quickly enough that, as Charlotte showed it, so she must at present submissively seem to take it. (476)

Again, then, Maggie arrives at an important insight—in this instance, indeed, at a crucial one: that she is not the author of the play, merely a spectator, that 'the full significance . . . could be no more, after all, than a matter of interpretation'. Charlotte may have her own interpretation of the scene: for her, too, evil may be seated all at its ease where she had dreamed only of good. Maggie's realization of this could have redeemed her from the incompleteness of vision that is such an important aspect of the human condition for James; but again the curious check operates whereby Maggie merely registers her insight without acting on it. Her view of Charlotte's potential interpretation gives no real weight to the possible legitimacy of Charlotte's reproach, reduces itself to pretending to submit to the demonstration: 'as Charlotte showed it, so she must at present submissively *seem* to take it.'

The rest of the scene, in fact, seems to confirm Charlotte's implied grievance. For Charlotte is 'showing' Maggie the whole room; it is Maggie who fixes on Adam as the focus of Charlotte's indignation: 'Not yet, since his marriage, had Maggie so sharply and so formidably known her old possession of him as a thing divided and contested' (476). Thus, rather oddly, Maggie, having felt aggrieved at Charlotte's bid for possession of the Prince, 'knows' her own possession of *Charlotte*'s husband to be 'a thing divided and contested'. She does not see what Charlotte is showing her: if her husband has been taken away from her, so has Charlotte's; if her 'old possession' of her father is being 'contested', so is Charlotte's of the Prince. Of course, any indignation on Charlotte's part would be a refinement of hypocrisy; but the point is exactly that she may have just as flattering a view of her own situation as Maggie has of hers. And instead of recognizing that Charlotte's case may be the counterpart of her own, Maggie assumes the scapegoat's role: 'Straighter than ever, thus, the Princess again felt it all put upon her' (477). What she feels put upon her, presumably, is the responsibility for restoring Adam to Charlotte and the Prince to herself. The rest of the novel shows us Maggie toiling to achieve this end, drawing on her sense of 'all the possibilities she controlled' (470), without attending to the part her supposedly ignorant and innocent father plays in the resolution she imagines she has brought about.

Maggie's sense of her own blameless efficacy is exposed in a sharp little interchange with Fanny Assingham. The latter momentarily liberates herself sufficiently from her social thraldom to the Ververs to be fairly honest with Maggie, and to take up Maggie's claim that she is 'letting' her father go: 'You let him, but you don't make him.'

'I take it from him,' she answered.
'But what else can you do?'
'I take it from him,' the Princess repeated. 'I do what I knew from the first I *should* do. I get off by giving him up.'
'But if he gives you?' Mrs Assingham presumed to object. 'Doesn't it moreover then,' she asked, 'complete the very purpose with which he married—that of making you and leaving you more free?'
Maggie looked at her long. 'Yes—I help him to do that.'
Mrs Assingham hesitated, but at last her bravery flared. 'Why not call it then frankly his complete success?'
'Well,' said Maggie, 'that's all that's left me to do.'
'It's a success,' her friend ingeniously developed, 'with which you've simply not interfered.' (541–2)

Fanny's catechism, forcing Maggie, almost comically, to change the grounds of her self-congratulation several times, systematically deprives Maggie of her illusion that she 'has done all', even of her illusion that submission to Adam's action constitutes a choice on her part. Her sacrifice of Adam may amount to no more than Adam's sacrifice of her; and for all her claim of planned and independent action ('I do what I knew from the first I *should* do'), all that is 'left [her] to do' is to admit that she has 'simply not interfered' with Adam's grand design. Maggie's independence of action proves to be as illusory as that of the Prince and Charlotte; she too, whose happiness Adam was trying to ensure, has been the puppet of 'the very purpose with which he married'. Paradoxically, the more 'free' she feels, the more closely she conforms to that purpose.

The rest of Maggie's conversation with Fanny is no less revealing of her motives and illusions. She yet again denies that she knows what her father knows; but the more important denial this time concerns the Prince. Having 'with tears in her eyes' agreed that Charlotte is 'held' in a 'torment' by her ignorance of what Adam knows, and having stated that the Prince shares this ignorance, she is confronted with Fanny's last and perhaps most uncomfortable question:

> 'But the Prince then—?'
> 'How is *he* held?' Maggie asked.
> 'How is *he* held?'
> 'Oh, I can't tell you that!' And the Princess again broke off. (543)

Maggie is understandably reluctant to ascribe her hold over her husband to her father's power, to the Prince's terror at how much Adam knows. On this, the reader is better informed than Maggie, having witnessed the Prince's uncomfortable sense of being made sure of by Adam Verver:

> The net result of all of which, moreover, was that the young man had no wish to see his value diminish. He himself, after all, had not fixed it—the 'figure' was a conception all of Mr Verver's own. Certainly, however, everything must be kept up to it; never so much as to-night had the Prince felt this. (238)

Though at this point, confident in his assumption of the Ververs' obtuseness, he does not foresee it, keeping up 'everything' to Mr Verver's assessment will involve the sacrifice of Charlotte: she is the one luxury he cannot afford. Our knowledge, then, of how the Prince is held reinforces the implication of the conversation between Maggie and Fanny, that all Maggie's efforts have been but splashings on the surface of her father's 'unfathomable' power. It is also consistent with her earlier perception that 'his strength was her strength', although in a less elevated sense than she imagined at the time: her hold on the Prince is dependent on Adam's money. Given the Prince's resolve to live up to his value as perceived by Mr Verver, Maggie's master-stroke in this guessing game is her reply to her husband's anxious question: '"Then does any one else know?"—"Find out for yourself!"' (448). From the moment that the Prince sees she suspects something, he toes the line meticulously, making up to Maggie in the only way he knows: by making love to her, by persuading her by word and deed that he loves only her—'The Prince's notion of a recompense to women', we remember from the opening reaches of the novel, 'was more or less to make love to them' (17). His denial of Charlotte is as suspect as it is heartless: '"She's stupid," he abruptly opined' (552). Thus Charlotte's prophecy at Matcham is fulfilled: 'Ah, for things I mayn't want to know, I promise you shall find me stupid' (266). Whether or not the Prince makes the connection (the fact that his abrupt little betrayal makes him 'quickly change colour', as well it might, suggests that he does) and realizes that Charlotte may have been keeping up her own act; whether or not, even, he believes what he says: we know that for the Prince, as for Maggie herself, the most important fact about Maggie is that she is Adam's daughter.

Still, if it is success to get what one wants, then Maggie has succeeded. But the last part of the novel questions even that circumscribed success. The Prince's newly awakened appreciation of his wife (and it is perfectly plausible that he comes to find her more interesting as she proves less gullible and more self-assertive) seems to contain a strong element of cowed submission to her show of strength. Maggie, at any rate, feels secure enough in Charlotte's imminent departure and her own power over the Prince to praise her husband's ex-mistress to him: 'But shan't you then so much as miss her a little? She's wonderful and beautiful' (550). The scapegoat is being festooned with garlands before being sent off into the desert. By this stage the flowers are decidedly wilted, though: the 'wonderful and beautiful' formula has been flourished on so many occasions that even if we had not been told that it is intended as a 'challenge' to the Prince, we should have doubted its sincerity. It is in fact a fairly direct echo, not only of the Prince and Charlotte's sanctification of their own adultery, but also of the 'conscious perjury' of Maggie's reassurance to Charlotte, preceding their public embrace: 'You must take it from me that I've never

thought of you but as beautiful, wonderful and good' (481)
—which Maggie originally derived from Fanny Assingham in an
equally deceitful interchange also culminating in an embrace.[28]
Here, as increasingly towards the end of the novel, Maggie coerces
the value of a term that has, like an antique coin, only the value
'fixed' for it in a highly specialized market.

In this context, even the Prince's famous statement, 'Everything's
terrible, *cara*—in the heart of man' (553), is suspect: it is too facile
to convey any very specific insight, and as a reply to Maggie's 'I see
it's *always* terrible for women', it merely expresses his bland
responsiveness to everything Maggie says at this stage. It also
conveniently relegates his treatment of Charlotte to the metaphy-
sical sphere of Man's Fallen State. Given a situation fraught with
such unexpressed tensions and uncertainties, it remains for them to
establish a basis on which to spend their lives together. The Prince
offers something conveniently intangible and irrefutable:

'If ever a man, since the beginning of time, acted in good faith—!' But he
dropped it offering it simply for that.
For that then, when it had had time somewhat to settle, like some
handful of gold dust thrown into the air—for that then Maggie showed
herself, as deeply and strangely taking it. 'I see.' And she even wished this
form to be as complete as she could make it. 'I see.' (553)

What Maggie sees, presumably, is that her husband's 'good faith'
will have to be another of the fictions sustained in order to preserve
the forms. We, at least, have seen the exact extent of the Prince's
good faith, culminating in his 'beautiful' pact with Charlotte to
commit adultery for the Ververs' sake. The comparison here of the
Prince's assurance to 'some handful of gold dust' is, in a novel
whose central symbol suggests the deceptive quality of gold, not
reassuring; and as for dust, it is mainly known as a medium to be
thrown into the eyes of those we wish to blind. In this context, the
compound image also sounds a disturbing echo of Maggie's
'translation' of Charlotte's 'tap against the glass': 'why was I
myself dealt with all for deception? Why condemned after a couple
of short years to find the golden flame—oh, the golden flame!—a

---

[28] 'You've never affected me, from the first hour I beheld you, as anything but—in
a way all your own—absolutely good and sweet and beautiful' (380).

mere handful of black ashes?' (538). Maggie, at least, has gold dust
rather than black ashes—perhaps a substitute for the 'silver mist'
that, earlier in the novel, she saw as no longer adequately hiding the
general deception: 'They would then have been, all successfully,
throwing dust in each other's eyes; and it would be at last as if they
must turn away their faces, since the silver mist that protected them
had begun to grow sensibly thin' (333).

Such images of blindness give a certain edge to Maggie's repeated
'I see'. Seeing becomes more and more a matter of pretending *not* to
see, of taking the form for the content. This preservation of forms is
most triumphantly demonstrated in the famous closing scenes of the
novel. Again James permits himself an unusual explicitness in the
sardonic rendering of the Ververs inspecting their 'things':

She had passed her arm into his, and the other objects in the room, the
other pictures, the sofas, the chairs, the tables, the cabinets, the 'important'
pieces, supreme in their way, stood out, round them, consciously, for
recognition and applause. Their eyes moved together from piece to piece,
taking in the whole nobleness—quite as if for him to measure the wisdom
of old ideas. The two noble persons seated, in conversation, at tea, fell thus
into the splendid effect and the general harmony: Mrs Verver and the Prince
fairly 'placed' themselves, however unwittingly, as high expressions of the
kind of human furniture required, aesthetically, by such a scene. The fusion
of their presence with the decorative elements, their contribution to the
triumph of selection, was complete and admirable; though, to a lingering
view, a view more penetrating than the occasion really demanded, they also
might have figured as concrete attestations of a rare power of purchase.
There was much indeed in the tone in which Adam Verver spoke again, and
who shall say where his thought stopped? '*Le compte y est*. You've got
some good things.'

Maggie met it afresh—'Ah, don't they look well?' (560–1)

Le compte y est: triumph of selection and rare power of purchase at
last harmonize to fulfil the aesthetic requirements of the Ververs,
and as long as they 'look well' it doesn't really matter what the
Prince and Charlotte can possibly find to say to each other on such
an occasion. The general harmony is in fact the head-on collision of
two hitherto supplementary discourses, the aesthetic and the
ethical: in Adam's 'You've got some good things', *good* is finally
pulverized as a moral term, in being applied to *things*; the Prince
and Charlotte, like the good things they will hereafter be, are at last

submissively taking their places with 'the other objects in the room'. We recall the Prince's bemused appreciation of the 'objects massive and lumpish' in the Bond Street shop window; here he and Charlotte embark on a life on the wrong side of the iron shutter.

IV

Whatever credit we give Maggie for her efforts on behalf of the others, the last scenes of the novel reassert the true focus of her allegiance, the 'wisdom of old ideas' as reinterpreted by the new American connoisseurs. The ultimate irony of the novel is that for all Adam's much-vaunted 'instinct for authenticity', it really wouldn't have mattered that the golden bowl was a cracked crystal—looking well is his only criterion: 'He cared that a work of art of price should "look like" the master to whom it might perhaps be deceitfully attributed' (108). This presumably means that Adam believes he can tell the difference by looking; but that is one of his illusions that the novel has dispelled. Having erred in his selection of a wife, his remedy is to ship her back to American City, where perhaps nobody will notice that she is not authentic.

As Adam talks of 'shipping' back to American City with Charlotte, Maggie has another of her imaginative insights. Like the others, it comes to nought, but it does serve to point, as it were, the moral of Adam's own vision on the terrace at Fawns when 'Light broke for him' and 'the idea shone upon him' that Charlotte could 'contribute' by 'putting his child at peace' (154); *now* Maggie's peace demands that Charlotte be taken away: '*There* was his idea, the clearness of which for an instant almost dazzled her. It was a blur of light, in the midst of which she saw Charlotte like some object marked, by contrast, in blackness, saw her waver in the field of vision, saw her removed, transported, doomed' (496). The idea is a considerable revision of the earlier one that he 'marries for', but here, as there, light is the medium of Verver's inscrutable intentions; and if here it marks 'in blackness' the expulsion of the person whose 'use' originally constituted his illumination, Maggie refrains from articulating the implications of her own vision. Instead, in the general tidying-up of human furniture, she wraps up the 'object marked . . . in blackness' for transportation:

'Father, father—Charlotte's great!'

It was not till after he had begun to smoke that he looked at her. 'Charlotte's great.'

They could close upon it—such a basis as they might immediately feel it make; and so they stood together over it, quite gratefully, each recording to the other's eyes that it was firm under their feet. They had even thus a renewed wait, as for proof of it; much as if he were letting her see, while the minutes lapsed for their concealed companions, that this was finally just why—but just *why*! 'You see,' he presently added, 'how right I was. Right, I mean, to do it for you.' (563–4)

Right—another term snaps shut. The slight discomfort betrayed in Mr Verver's delay in meeting Maggie's eyes is soon dissipated as they get used to their new 'basis'—the fiction that is to sustain them in—'gratefully'—ignoring the fact that he is deporting his wife to get her away from his son-in-law. As usual in this novel, the moment of wilful blindness is celebrated with declarations of clear-sightedness all round:

> 'Well *now*,' he smoked, 'we see.'
> 'We see.'
> 'I know her better.'
> 'You know her best.' (564)

And what Adam's profound knowledge of his wife issues in is the ultimate collector's accolade: 'She's beautiful, beautiful!' Quite in what sense Charlotte is to be regarded as beautiful is not really important: the word is proffered as adequate and accepted as such—by Maggie, at any rate: 'It was all she might have wished, for it was, with a kind of speaking competence, the note of possession and control; and yet it conveyed to her as nothing till now had done the reality of their parting. They were parting, in the light of it, absolutely on Charlotte's *value*' (564).

Charlotte's *value*, as measured by the criterion of 'possession and control', is yet again that of a prized 'piece'; having proved to be so much more inconvenient an acquisition than the oriental tiles, she has at last been relegated to her proper place in the catalogue. Maggie's pleased appreciation of her father's 'possession and control' sits oddly with her earlier recognition of what exactly that possession and control entails, but is at least consistent with her general suppression of uncomfortable perceptions. So another term—*value*—is appropriated to communal use, as Maggie, looking for 'some last conclusive comfortable category to place him in for dismissal', finds it in 'his ability to rest upon high values' (564). This enables her to find an equally comfortable—for herself–category for Charlotte's dismissal: 'Great for the world that was before her—*that* he proposed she should be; she was not to be wasted in the application of his plan. Maggie held to this then—that she wasn't to be wasted' (565). Being wasted is, we remember, what the Ververs decided long ago Charlotte should be saved from; now that the use then found for her has palled upon everybody, she will be employed 'in the application of his plan'—his new one, that is. In American City Charlotte's 'high coerced quaver' will not be audible to Maggie, nor will the silken loop around her neck be visible. Maggie's last murmur of conscience subsides under the conviction that showing off Adam's treasures to the unenthusiastic inhabitants of a country she hates is just what Charlotte was made for.

Of course, Charlotte's fate is no more than she accepted the possibility of when she married Adam Verver: we cannot really feel that deportation to America is in itself an injustice done to her. The real cruelty of her fate lies in her being made to bear the guilt of the other three:

They thus tacitly put it upon her to be disposed of, the whole complexity of their peril, and she promptly saw why: because she was there, and there just *as* she was, to lift it off them and take it; to charge herself with it as the scapegoat of old, of whom she had once seen a terrible picture, had been charged with the sins of the people and had gone forth into the desert to sink under his burden and die. (469)

That fantasy is of course Maggie's vision of herself, not of Charlotte; she cannot allow herself to see how much more accurately the role applies to Charlotte. If anyone is sent into the desert, Charlotte is—if not quite to die, then to an oblivion that approximates death: 'I feel somehow as if she were dying. Not really, not physically . . . But dying for us—for you and me', says Maggie (550). 'Dying for us' presumably means (as a reminder to the Prince?) no more than 'dying as far as you and I are concerned', but the ambiguity allows us to see Charlotte's 'death' as a sacrifice 'for' the others. She is not a willing victim, of course, but then, nor was the scapegoat of old. At the separation of the couples Charlotte is used as a moral justification: as long as they can all pretend to love and admire her, no uncomfortable qualms need arise. She simplifies, as the scapegoat always does, and disposes of 'the whole complexity of their peril'. Where Mary Crawford was expelled from the community by a vocabulary of righteousness that excluded her, Charlotte is expelled through a vocabulary of aesthetic appreciation enclosing her in a value system that renders her powerless.

Maggie's last words to her father can thus emphatically reassert her 'sense that he wasn't a failure' and that 'she wasn't in that case a failure either'—a sense we have seen to be essential to her self-respect: '"It's success, father." "It's success"' (565). Maggie's pronouncement represents one of the culminating ironies of the novel, as the last of a series of redefinitions of 'success', always in James a problematic concept. At this point we may think of Fanny Assingham's trenchant rejoinder: 'It's a success . . . with which you've simply not interfered.' But we also think, as Maggie cannot, of the Prince's reflections on what he thought was his accession to 'the power of the rich peoples': 'Capture had crowned the pursuit—or success, as he would otherwise have put it, had rewarded virtue' (4). Now, the Prince's interpretation of his own undertaking in marrying Maggie has acquired a sharper application to himself: virtue has been rewarded in his pursuit and capture. Maggie's success draws a straight line from his pleased sense that 'he was *of* them now, of the rich peoples' to this moment of pleasure in her father's 'note of possession and control'. The rich people have reclaimed their own.

V

Upon this note of wrongs covered up in the name of success, of uncomfortable recognitions stared out of countenance, Adam and Charlotte depart, the beautiful fiction of their beautiful lives re-established to everybody's satisfaction—except perhaps Charlotte's. Their departure does at least simplify the 'forms' that have to be observed. As Maggie takes stock of 'her reason for what she had done': 'She knew at last really why—and how she had been inspired and guided, how she had been persistently able, how, to her soul, all the while, it had been for the sake of this end. Here it was, then, the moment, the golden fruit that had shone from afar' (566). 'This' is 'their freedom to be together there always'. Freedom so described may strike the sceptical as not unlike captivity, especially for the Prince, who has, after all, no choice in the matter. It is possible, though, that with Maggie's undivided attention he may be less bored than he was before. Like Charlotte, he settles down to the terms of his contract: 'So far as seeing that she was "paid" went, he might have been holding out the money-bag for her to come and take it' (566). We remember the Prince's rather lame response to the sight of the shattered bowl: 'But shall you at least get your money back?' (444). He should have known that the Ververs always get their money back: that is the true principle of reciprocity.

But the forms have been established, at any rate, on a more workable basis than before. Maggie can now surrender to her husband's sexual power, which she has hitherto so tenaciously resisted as a threat to her freedom of action. Undistracted by the claims of her father and of Charlotte, unconfused by the moral intricacies of trying to justify herself in terms of a cause other than herself, she can indulge her 'selfish' passion for her husband. The 'golden fruit' that looms as her 'reward' is, like all things golden in the novel, ominous; but if there is a flaw in it, Maggie has learnt not to notice. Their final embrace, like all the others in the novel, takes place over abysses of deception, of suppressions, of betrayals; but Maggie's passion, at least, and the Prince's desire to please her, are genuine:

'Isn't she too splendid?' she simply said, offering it to explain and to finish.

'Oh, splendid!' With which he came over to her.

'That's our help, you see,' she added—to point further her moral.

It kept him before her therefore, taking in—or trying to—what she so wonderfully gave. He tried, too clearly, to please her—to meet her in her own way; but with the result only that, close to her, her face kept before him, his hands holding her shoulders, his whole act enclosing her, he presently echoed: '"See"? I see nothing but *you*.' And the truth of it had, with this force, after a moment, so strangely lighted his eyes that, as for pity and dread of them, she buried her own in his breast. (567)

What she 'so wonderfully' gives, as the last of the many wonderful things in the novel, is a basis for their relationship, yet another of her categories for dismissal: Charlotte is 'splendid' and can therefore be disregarded. Maggie will not make her into an occasion for reproach: this will have to do 'to explain and to finish'. Maggie, having pointed her moral, writes Finis at the end of her own fiction. The Prince, though trying 'too clearly, to please her' seems less apt than Adam to recognize the proffered basis. In short, he seems not to know what she means, in spite of his attempt 'to meet her in her own way'—so he meets her in his own inimitable way, by taking her in his arms. His 'I see nothing but *you*' is almost the last act of wilful blindness in the novel: he pledges himself to ignore whatever may distract his attention from the wife he is to serve with his body till death them do part. As Marianna Torgovnick says: 'In the final scene, his actions and words merely mimic those of his wife: as Maggie reluctantly realizes, they do not signal the transformation of the Prince or his insight into moral phenomena.'[29]

The 'truth' that Maggie reads in his eyes is thus not only his devotion to her, but his submission to her power—a truth that for the last time in the novel Maggie evades, in a gesture that combines her love for him with an avoidance of facing the cost of it: 'as for pity and dread of [his eyes] she buried her own in his breast.' If Maggie has grown from naïvety to a full knowledge of evil, she has had to acquiesce to the perpetuation of that evil under the forms of harmony and decency. Maggie's gesture in the darkening room is in effect very much like Marlow's lie in 'Heart of Darkness', in negating the insights she has achieved in the course of the work. The difference is that Marlow's lie consciously preserves something which is beautiful in itself, albeit based on delusion: the Intended's belief in the nobility of Kurtz is nobly selfless, however grotesquely mistaken. Without the Intended's illusion, Marlow feels, 'It would have been too dark' (*HD* 162). In *The Golden Bowl* the darkness comes almost as a relief after the blinding light of delusion.[30]

---

[29] Marianna Torgovnick, *Closure in the Novel* (Princeton, 1981), 154.

[30] Gabriel Pearson's comparison of these two works argues for an essential difference between the two novelists: 'For Conrad, bourgeois civilization is sustained by power and protected by lies. To the initiate into its underlying realities, it is a hollow cheat, one which it is, however deviously, the main impulse of his fiction to confess. The lie in James is sanctified by what it salvages and the disaster it postpones' ('The Novel to End All Novels: *The Golden Bowl*', in John Goode (ed.), *The Air of Reality: New Essays on Henry James* (London, 1972), 302). This is to equate, wrongly I believe, James's perspective with Maggie's. It is in fact symptomatic of the society presented by James that it contains no protagonist with the insight and authority to pronounce upon it. The view that lying in *The Golden Bowl* is somehow redemptive occurs widely; see, for instance, Manfred Mackenzie, *Communities of Honor and Love in Henry James* (Cambridge, Mass., 1976): 'By virtue of their [the Ververs'] honorable, civilized lie, all is amazingly true again' (180).

The invocation of the tragic emotions at this point is as ambiguous as everything else in the novel: instead of the pity and dread based, as in Sophocles, on a recognition of 'the true state of all us that live', we are given a deliberate self-blinding. The embrace of the Prince and Maggie embodies, no less than that of Densher and Kate Croy, 'the need to bury in the dark blindness of each other's arms the knowledge of each other that they couldn't undo' (*WD* 499). The embrace, that time-honoured signal of closure, is here yet another avoidance of *anagnorisis*, yet another of the novel's negotiated agreements between partners in deception.[31]

Maggie's fiction sustains the forms that James's fiction has systematically revealed as empty. The distinction between Maggie's fiction and James's own must modify, I think, the critical view that the novel in general is incapable of escaping from its own methods of representation. As applied to this novel, that view depends on an equation of James's project with Maggie's:

> This mechanism of equilibrium centers the novel: on one level, it is Maggie Verver who perfects a method of supervised freedom, at once producing in her subjects the 'sense of highly choosing' and exercising control by invoking the regulative power of the norm; on another, it is the Jamesian imperative of organic form that underwrites and ratifies this system of supervision.[32]

But as I have tried to show, 'the Jamesian imperative of organic form', though in a trite sense it does of course 'regulate' Maggie, as any fictional work subordinates the designs of its characters to its own design, can detach itself from Maggie's 'system of supervision', as it can, more importantly, detach itself from the forms that are enforced in the fictional community.[33] The contradiction between love and power is not resolved by the novel; it is only in Maggie's deliberate evasion of the contradiction that it can be contained. As

---

[31] For an extended analysis of the last chapter of the novel, see Kenneth Graham, *Indirections of the Novel: James, Conrad, and Forster* (Cambridge, 1988), 74–92. I find myself in almost total agreement with Graham except—crucially—in his contention that James 'draws attention to the profound crack in the bowl by a device of narrative and of commentary *that simultaneously gilds over that crack*—just as his protagonists at their tea-table, for all their individual awareness, are also engaged, *with James's sympathy*, in a gilding operation' (84, my italics).

[32] Seltzer, *The Art of Power*, 61.

[33] The failure to distinguish between the closure of Maggie's fiction and the open-endedness of James's novel gives rise to such readings as that of Mimi Kairschner, who claims that 'Not only does James's narrative closure—by stabilizing these two

Ruth Yeazell comments: 'what we really witness here is less a closed fiction than a character struggling to will such a fiction.'[34] Maggie's fiction, then, is not unlike Lord Jim's romance, in achieving closure in its own terms alone; but where his 'proud and unflinching glance' (*LJ* 416) signalled his own belief in the validity of his act, Maggie, at the last moment of her novel, has to hide her eyes from the truth—perhaps as clear a recognition of truth as any in this paradoxical novel.

I have argued, then, that the scapegoat of the text, what René Girard calls 'the hidden structural principle', comes to be recognized as also the scapegoat in the text, 'the clearly visible theme'. Charlotte is the scapegoat of Maggie's text, in that Maggie's fiction is 'controlled by the effect of a scapegoat it does not acknowledge'; but *The Golden Bowl* 'acknowledges the scapegoat effect which does not control it'. The conclusion of *The Golden Bowl* refuses to validate Maggie's rewriting of the novel, which has determined its structure; instead it suspends sceptically the meanings that traditionally close narratives, the moral vocabulary whereby society seeks to justify its actions. Like Fanny Price's success, Maggie's consists in the imposition of an inadequate vocabulary; but unlike Fanny, Maggie by the end of her novel has come almost avowedly to cling to language as a refuge from things as they are, 'to explain and to finish'. Offering her formula she simplifies, like many a novelist, in order to conclude. But as for James's fiction—in Girard's terms:

Not only is this text no longer a persecution text, but it even reveals the truth of the persecution.[35]

marriages—ultimately serve to valorize the system of capitalist patriarchy, but by allowing his characters to remain *silent* in the end, the unspoken hierarchical relations of both class and gender are reinforced for the audience as well, by virtue of the fact that these structural relations are already shared at an unconscious level by the members of the culture' ('The Traces of Capitalistic Patriarchy in the Silences of *The Golden Bowl*', *The Henry James Review*, 5 (1984), 192).

[34] Yeazell, *Language and Knowledge*, 125. For a reading of the novel drawing and building on this insight of Yeazell's, see Joseph Allen Boone, *Tradition Counter Tradition: Love and the Form of Fiction* (Chicago, 1987), 187-201. Boone's method and argument seem to me happier with this novel than with *Daniel Deronda*, which he also presents as an example of a 'subversive' fiction.

[35] René Girard, *The Scapegoat* (1982); trans. Yvonne Freccero (London, 1986), 119.

Conclusion: To Be Continued . . .

> The novel comes into contact with the spontaneity of the inconclusive present; this is what keeps the genre from congealing. The novelist is drawn to everything that is not yet completed.[1]

> the moral involved . . . is not that the particular production before us exhausts the interesting questions it raises, but that the Novel remains still, under the right persuasion, the most independent, most elastic, most prodigious of literary forms.[2]

We know that by 'the right persuasion' James meant his own handling of *The Ambassadors*, and in prefacing my conclusion with the concluding sentence of his Preface, I do not mean to imply that it is the Jamesian model of independence and elasticity that this study has been pursuing. If James's acute artistic self-consciousness enabled him to escape the dangers of his own methods of representation, *through* those methods, he was helped by his creative absorption in the works of his predecessors and contemporaries. If the late James novels are early masterpieces of modernism, they are also descendants of Jane Austen's novels, in ways that I hope have appeared from this study; for if my method originally committed me to a relatively discrete examination of certain central texts, it has led to a strong sense of the continuity of the methods and themes of fictional representation.

The question that has animated this book—can the realist novel escape complicity with the ideological structures of which it is at least partly a product?—has turned out, unsurprisingly, to have no simple and single answer. The novel shares with all forms of narrative the potential to structure our desires as well as to reflect a

---

[1] Mikhail Bakhtin, 'Epic and Novel: Toward a Methodology for the Study of the Novel', *The Dialogic Imagination: Four Essays*, ed. Michael Holquist, trans. Caryl Emerson and Michael Holquist (Austin, Tex., 1981), 27.

[2] Henry James, Preface to *The Ambassadors*, repr. in *The Art of the Novel* (New York, 1934), 326.

reality assumed to be independent of those desires, and the relative contributions of these two components will vary from narrative to narrative and novel to novel. The novelist deals, amongst other pressures, with the need to turn situations into plots, which in itself is a falsification,' in that in life a situation does not necessarily arrange itself narratively; narrative is a product not only of our experience but also of our need to control that experience. As Hayden White has said: 'If we view narration and narrativity as the instruments by which the conflicting claims of the imaginary and the real are mediated, arbitrated, or resolved in a discourse, we begin to comprehend both the appeal of narrative and the grounds for refusing it.'[3] White is speaking of historiography rather than the novel, and the need to refuse narrative may be less pressing in fiction than in history, which makes a different kind of truth claim. But the difference is not absolute: fiction itself claims also to depict its own kind of truth—whether the simpler aspiration of George Eliot to the 'rare, precious quality of truthfulness' that she finds in the Dutch realist painters, or the more paradoxical 'deep hidden truthfulness of works of art' which in Conrad may belong to 'pure exercises of the imagination'.

It is not surprising, then, that archetypal plot does tend towards resolution, towards a satisfactory arrangement of those aspects of experience which by their very nature defy arrangement. Narrative, from this point of view, derives not from our need to be entertained as much as from our need to be reassured. And in this respect, those theorists who accuse narrative of conspiring with the most conservative tendencies of the imagination must be right.

But the imagination, and more particularly its fictional deployment, has also other tendencies and capabilities. The novel is capable of developing awareness of its own processes, and of the origins of those processes; thus it can teach us not only about experience, but about our own ways of dealing with that experience. The realist text, in short, is a more versatile creature than is allowed for in the suspicions of some modern critics. D. A. Miller's contention, for instance, on which I opened this study, that 'Whenever the novel censures policing power, it has

---

[3] Hayden White, 'The Value of Narrativity in the Representation of Reality', in W. J. T. Mitchell (ed.), *On Narrative* (Chicago, 1981), 4–5.

already reinvented it, in *the very practice of novelistic representation*,[4] now seems to assume too readily that 'the practice of novelistic representation' is a single thing with readily identifiable characteristics and tendencies. Similarly, Mark Seltzer's charge that 'the novel enforces a certain legality in its very forms and techniques of representation'[5] does not make any allowance for *different* forms and techniques. In claiming that 'The novelist is drawn to everything that is not yet completed', Bakhtin may be positing an equally one-sided version of the novel's characteristic business, but he does usefully direct our attention to the novel's history as a questioning medium, of representation, in other words, as an engagement rather than as a passive recording.

Robert Scholes looks towards 'post-modernist anti-narratives' to 'force us to draw our attention away from the construction of a diegesis according to our habitual interpretive processes. By frustrating this sort of closure, they bring the codes themselves to the foreground of our critical attention, requiring us to see them as codes rather than as aspects of human nature or the world. The function of anti-narrative is to problematize the entire process of narration and interpretation for us.'[6] The fact that he restricts such a consciousness of narrative to what he calls anti-narrative makes him see the only possible—but implausible—escape from the constraint of 'narrative structuration' as an abolition of narrative. The realist novel, I have argued, has shown itself to be in fact independent and elastic enough also to 'problematize the entire process of narration and interpretation for us' without abolishing itself. Scholes's distinction between 'codes' and 'aspects of human nature or the world' seems not to consider that it may be one of the qualities of human nature to devise and rely on codes. The novel's medium is words, verbal codes; and words, whatever their dangers and disadvantages, survive to lament their own inadequacies, to make a reality out of their inability to render reality, to represent the impossibility of representing anything but their own processes, to escape the prisons of their own making. In short, as Bakhtin has

---

[4] D. A. Miller, *The Novel and the Police* (Berkeley, Calif.,1988), 20.
[5] Mark Seltzer, *Henry James and the Art of Power* (Ithaca, NY, 1984), 17–18.
[6] Robert Scholes, 'Afterthoughts on Narrative II: Language, Narrative, and Anti-Narrative', in Mitchell (ed.), *On Narrative*, 207.

affirmed, 'Language in the novel not only represents, but itself serves as the object of representation'.[7]

It is through this capacity that the novel may help us to liberate ourselves from our own narratives. Scholes's anti-narrative may in fact be a component of narrative, to the extent that any narrative contains within itself a more or less implicit questioning of its own drift. The scapegoat, by one reading the victim of the narrative, is by another the protagonist of the anti-narrative. The narrative confesses its embarrassment by silencing the scapegoat. Unsurprisingly, Conrad and James are most conscious of this: Conrad in giving the 'remarkable exploits of a man named Brown' a status challenging that of Jim's wish-fulfilling romance; James by hinting at Charlotte's construction of events, even while subordinating it to Maggie's.

But if Conrad and James consciously construct or imply such an alternative narrative, such self-consciousness is not the only medium whereby narrative escapes from ideological coercion. There is also that quality of fiction which we may call its reciprocity of meaning, dependent on a more flexible definition of 'the novel'. 'Novelistic representation' can only on a very narrow definition be discussed as if it were a quality of a single novel; there is also that sense in which both form (*the novel*) and technique (*representation*) are dynamic concepts, taking their meaning from a whole body of works. We have seen this in operation within the novels of a single novelist, for instance by the process whereby a visual trope accretes meaning with each addition to the series of which it forms part. Mrs Dombey and Florence, imaged as clasped together at the bottom of a clear depth, mean something different after *Our Mutual Friend*: we can now see that early metaphor as anticipating the later actual drowning, as part of the meaning of both scenes. Bradley Headstone sitting by his fire in bleak exhaustion, 'as if it were a charmed flame that was turning him old',[8] recalls, and in so doing revises, the picture of Mr Dombey in front of *his* fire. Headstone's desolation emerges as a potential reality underlying the Dombey domestic scene; just as Headstone's solitude is measured as exclusion from the companionship Dombey

---

[7] Mikhail Bakhtin, 'From the Prehistory of Novelistic Discourse', *The Dialogic Imagination*, 49.

[8] Charles Dickens, *Our Mutual Friend* (1864–5); ed. Michael Cotsell (Oxford, 1989), 800.

is to find in his old age—and as both desolation and companionship are related to Pip and Joe at their fireplace.

But even novels not related to one another through a common author reflect upon one another, sometimes deliberately, more often through belonging to the same tradition; and in doing so they reopen narratives previously declared closed. Perhaps those meanings famously *always already* there in fiction have to be supplemented by the meanings *not yet* articulated, the *not yet* inscribed, the potential meaning which awaits incarnation. Mary Crawford alters our reading of Elizabeth Bennet, but we cannot help invoking Elizabeth in our defence of Mary. And ultimately Mary's meaning is extended by Gwendolen, whose significance is in turn enriched if not completed by Charlotte Stant—who herself has something to say to and of Mary Crawford. Fanny may settle at Mansfield Park secure in the knowledge that she has banished Mary Crawford from its precincts; but Mansfield Park is not the House of Fiction, and that larger house remains open to later meanings, remains haunted by Mary, who returns even in the guise of Gwendolen Harleth, that other intrepid horsewoman, to scare another timid little sister, Anna Gascoigne, with her boldness. She is once again defeated, of course; but her significance lies in her return.

The narrative community, like any other community, needs a scapegoat. As Girard comments: 'The community must effectively be emptied of its poisons. It must feel liberated and reconciled within itself. This is implied in the conclusion of most myths. We see the actual return to the order that was compromised by the crisis'.[9] The five chapters of this book have traced different ways in which this scapegoating pressure towards the restoration of order can be embodied in realist narrative, as much as in myth; but it has led also to a redefinition of that narrative community which each novel strives to create around it, and attempts to empty of its poisons, to include denizens of other novels, other systems. In this respect, too, Conrad's creation of Patusan is a reflection on the nature of imaginative creation: its ostensible self-sufficiency remains open to challenge from outside its own community of value. Uriah Heep may be vilified and expelled from the happy ever after of David Copperfield and Agnes, but he will return to haunt the redemptive

---

[9] René Girard, *The Scapegoat* (1982); trans. Yvonne Freccero (London, 1986), 42.

fiction of Lizzie Hexam; indeed, he may even hold the key to the mystery of Edwin Drood. Charlotte Stant may be banished to American City, but in going she commemorates, as it were, and revises the expulsion of all her predecessors. As imaged in Maggie's extraordinary vision of Adam's 'idea', Charlotte's transportation may stand as the type of that expulsive movement that this study has examined in various manifestations: 'It was a blur of light, in the midst of which she saw Charlotte like some object marked, by contrast, in blackness, saw her waver in the field of vision, saw her removed, transported, doomed.'[10] The blur of light, the object marked in blackness, the contrast, the extinction: James's metaphor dramatizes, and thus makes conscious, the dialectic of scapegoating that animates realist narrative; and it is through realist narrative that it does so. If Charlotte's fate is one of the exigencies of realist narrative, Maggie's vision is one of its possibilities.

Perhaps we may escape the straitjacket of tautology that interpretation has been taken to be,[11] by conceiving of interpretation as a series of readings in conversation with one another—about a series of texts similarly engaged. This book, then, has offered a sequence of not yet complete readings, as contributions to that conversation.

[10] Henry James, *The Golden Bowl* (1905); ed. Virginia Llewellyn Smith (Oxford, 1983), 496.

[11] The point has been made in many ways; one uncompromising statement of it is Jonathan Culler's: 'There are many tasks that confront criticism, many things we need to advance our understanding of literature, but one thing we do not need is more interpretations of literary works' (*The Pursuit of Signs: Semiotics, Literature, Deconstruction* (London, 1981), 6).

Bibliography of Works Cited

PRIMARY TEXTS

JANE AUSTEN

Pride and Prejudice (1813); ed. James Kinsley, The World's Classics (Oxford, 1980).

Mansfield Park, ed. R. W. Chapman (London, 1923, 1934).

Mansfield Park (1814); ed. James Kinsley, The World's Classics (Oxford, 1980, 1990).

Mansfield Park (1814); ed. Tony Tanner (Harmondsworth, 1966).

Emma (1816); ed. David Lodge, The World's Classics (Oxford, 1980).

Persuasion (1818); ed. John Davie, The World's Classics (Oxford, 1980).

Northanger Abbey, (1818); ed. John Davie, with *Lady Susan, The Watsons* and *Sanditon*, The World's Classics (Oxford, 1980).

JOSEPH CONRAD

Lord Jim (1900); ed. John Batchelor, The World's Classics (Oxford, 1983).

Lord Jim, ed. Thomas C. Moser (New York, 1968).

'Amy Foster' (1901); in *Typhoon and Other Tales*, ed. Cedric Watts, The World's Classics (Oxford, 1986), 201–40.

Youth, Heart of Darkness, The End of the Tether (1902); ed. Robert Kimbrough, The World's Classics (Oxford, 1984).

Nostromo (1904); ed. Keith Carabine, The World's Classics (Oxford, 1984).

The Secret Agent (1907); ed. Roger Tennant, The World's Classics (Oxford, 1984).

Under Western Eyes (1910); ed. Jeremy Hawthorn, The World's Classics (Oxford, 1983).

A Personal Record (1912); ed. Zdzisław Najder, with *The Mirror of the Sea*, The World's Classics (Oxford, 1988).

CHARLES DICKENS

Martin Chuzzlewit (1843–4); ed. Margaret Cardwell, The World's Classics (Oxford, 1984).

Dombey and Son (1846–8); ed. Alan Horsman, The World's Classics (Oxford, 1982).

The Haunted Man (1847); in *Christmas Books* (1852); (London, 1954).

David Copperfield (1849–50); ed. Nina Burgis, The World's Classics (Oxford, 1983).

Bleak House (1852–3); ed. Norman Page (Harmondsworth, 1971).

Hard Times (1854); ed. George Ford and Sylvère Monod, Norton Critical Edition (New York, 1966).

Little Dorrit (1855–7); ed. Harvey Peter Sucksmith, The World's Classics (Oxford, 1982).

Great Expectations (1860–1); ed. Angus Calder (Oxford, 1953).

Our Mutual Friend (1864–5); ed. Michael Cotsell, The World's Classics (Oxford, 1989).

The Mystery of Edwin Drood (1870); ed. Margaret Cardwell, The World's Classics (Oxford, 1982).

GEORGE ELIOT

Scenes of Clerical Life (1858); ed. David Lodge (Harmondsworth, 1973).

Adam Bede (1858); (London, 1960).

The Mill on the Floss (1860); ed. Gordon S. Haight, The World's Classics (Oxford, 1981).

Silas Marner The Weaver of Raveloe (1861); ed. Q. D. Leavis (Harmondsworth, 1967).

Romola (1863); ed. Andrew Sanders (Harmondsworth, 1980).

Felix Holt, the Radical (1866); ed. Fred C. Thomson, The World's Classics (Oxford, 1988).

Middlemarch (1871–2); ed. David Carroll, The World's Classics (Oxford, 1988).

Daniel Deronda (1876); ed. Graham Handley, The World's Classics (Oxford, 1988).

Essays of George Eliot, ed. Thomas Pinney (London, 1968).

'The Natural History of German Life', *Westminster Review*, 66 (1850), rpt. in *Essays of George Eliot*, ed. Thomas Pinney, 271–2.

HENRY JAMES

The Portrait of a Lady (1881; rev. 1907); ed. Nicola Bradbury, The World's Classics (Oxford, 1981).

The Wings of the Dove (1902; rev. 1909); ed. Peter Brooks, The World's Classics (Oxford, 1984).

The Golden Bowl (1905); ed. Virginia Llewellyn Smith, The World's Classics (Oxford, 1983).

The Art of the Novel (New York, 1934).

SOPHOCLES

Ajax, trans. John Moore, from *Sophocles II*, ed. David Grene and Richard Lattimore (Chicago, 1957).

SECONDARY TEXTS AND BACKGROUND STUDIES

ALLEN, FREDERICK LEWIS, *The Great Pierpont Morgan* (London, 1949).

ALLEN, WALTER, *George Eliot* (New York, 1964).

AMIS, KINGSLEY, 'What Became of Jane Austen?', *The Spectator*, 4 Oct. 1957, rpt. in Ian Watt (ed.), *Jane Austen: A Collection of Critical Essays* (Englewood Cliffs, NJ, 1963).

ANDERSON, QUENTIN, *The American Henry James* (London, 1958).

AUERBACH, NINA, *Communities of Women: An Idea in Fiction* (Cambridge, Mass., 1978).

—— *Romantic Imprisonment: Women and Other Glorified Outcasts* (New York, 1986).

AUSTEN, ZELDA, 'Why Feminist Critics are Angry with George Eliot', *College English*, 37 (1976), 549–61.

BABB, HOWARD S., *Jane Austen's Novels: The Fabric of Dialogue* (Columbus, Ohio, 1962).

BAKHTIN, MIKHAIL MIKHAILOVICH, *The Dialogic Imagination: Four Essays*, ed. Michael Holquist, trans. Caryl Emerson and Michael Holquist (Austin, Tex., 1981).

BARRETT, DOROTHEA, *Vocation and Desire: George Eliot's Heroines* (London, 1989).

BAYLEY, JOHN, *The Characters of Love* (London, 1960).

BEER, GILLIAN, *Darwin's Plots: Evolutionary Narrative in Darwin, George Eliot and Nineteenth-Century Fiction* (London, 1985).

—— *George Eliot* (Brighton, 1986).

BELL, MICHAEL (ed.), *The Context of English Literature: 1900–1930* (London, 1980).

—— 'Introduction: Modern Movements in Literature', in Michael Bell (ed.), *The Context of English Literature: 1900–1930*, 1–91.

BELSEY, CATHERINE, *Critical Practice* (London and New York, 1980).

—— 'Re-reading the Great Tradition', in Peter Widdowson (ed.), *Re-Reading English*, 121–35.

BENJAMIN, WALTER, *Illuminations* (1950); trans. Harry Zohn (London, 1970).

BERSANI, LEO, *A Future for Astyanax: Character and Desire in Literature* (New York, 1984).

BERTHOUD, JACQUES, *Joseph Conrad: The Major Phase* (Cambridge, 1978).

—— 'Narrative and Ideology: a Critique of Fredric Jameson's *The Political Unconscious*', in Jeremy Hawthorn (ed.), *Narrative: From Mallory to Motion Pictures*, 100–15.

BLOOMFIELD, MORTON W. (ed.), *The Interpretation of Narrative: Theory and Practice* (Cambridge, Mass., 1970).

BOONE, JOSEPH ALLEN, *Tradition Counter Tradition: Love and the Form of Fiction* (Chicago, 1987).

BOOTH, WAYNE C., *A Rhetoric of Irony* (London, 1974).

BRADBROOK, MURIEL, 'A Note on Fanny Price', *Essays in Criticism*, 5 (1955), 289.

BRADBURY, NICOLA, *Henry James: The Later Novels* (Oxford, 1979).

BUTLER, MARILYN, *Jane Austen and the War of Ideas* (Oxford, 1975; 2nd edn., 1987).

——Introduction to Jane Austen's *Mansfield Park*, The World's Classics (Oxford, 1990), pp. vii–viii.

CARPENTER, MARY WILSON, '"A Bit of Her Flesh": Circumcision and "The Signification of the Phallus" in *Daniel Deronda*', *Genders*, 1 (1988), 1–23.

CASERIO, ROBERT L., *Plot, Story, and the Novel* (Princeton, NJ, 1979).

——'Supreme Court Discourse vs. Homosexual Fiction', *The South Atlantic Quarterly*, 88 (1989), 268–99.

CHASE, CYNTHIA, 'The Decomposition of the Elephants: Double-Reading *Daniel Deronda*', *PMLA* 93 (1978), 215–27.

CHATMAN, SEYMOUR, 'What Novels Can Do That Films Can't (and Vice Versa)', in W. J. T. Mitchell (ed.), *On Narrative*, 117–36.

COHEN, PAULA MARANTZ, 'Stabilizing the Family System at Mansfield Park', *ELH* 54 (1987), 669–93.

CREWS, FREDERICK C., *The Tragedy of Manners: Moral Drama in the Later Novels of Henry James* (1957; rpt. Hamden, Conn., 1971).

CULLER, JONATHAN, *The Pursuit of Signs: Semiotics, Literature, Deconstruction* (London, 1981).

——*Framing the Sign: Criticism and its Institutions* (Oxford, 1988).

DALESKI, H. M., *Dickens and the Art of Analogy* (London, 1970).

——*Joseph Conrad: The Way of Dispossession* (London, 1977).

DEVLIN, D. D., *Jane Austen and Education* (Basingstoke, 1975).

DOWLING W. C., *Jameson, Althusser, Marx* (London, 1984).

DUCKWORTH, ALISTAIR M., *The Improvement of the Estate: A Study of Jane Austen's Novels* (Baltimore, Md., 1971).

——'Jane Austen and the Conflict of Interpretations', in Janet Todd (ed.), *Jane Austen: New Perspectives*, 39–52.

DUFFY, JOSEPH M., Jr., 'Moral Integrity and Moral Anarchy in *Mansfield Park*', *ELH* 23 (1956), 71-91.

EAGLETON, TERRY, *Criticism and Ideology* (1976; rpt. London, 1978).

——'Critical Commentary', Charles Dickens, *Hard Times* (London: Methuen, 1987).

——*The Significance of Theory*, The Bucknell Lectures in Literary Theory, ed. Michael Payne and Harold Schweizer (Oxford, 1990).

EDEL, LEON, *Henry James: The Master 1901–1916* (London, 1972).

FERGUSSON, FRANCIS, '*The Golden Bowl* Revisited', *Sewanee Review*, 64 (1955), 13–28.

FIREBAUGH, JOSEPH, 'The Ververs', *Essays in Criticism*, 4 (1954), 400–10.

FLEISHMAN, AVROM, *A Reading of 'Mansfield Park': An Essay in Critical Synthesis* (Minneapolis, 1967).

FLINT, KATE, *Dickens* (Brighton, 1986).

FORD, BORIS (ed.), *The Modern Age* (Harmondsworth, 1963).

FORD, GEORGE H., and Lane, Lauriat Jr. (eds.), *The Dickens Critics* (Ithaca, NY, 1961).

FORSTER E. M., *Aspects of the Novel* (1927; rpt. Harmondsworth, 1962).

GARIS, ROBERT, 'Learning Experience and Change', in B. C. Southam (ed.), *Critical Essays on Jane Austen*, 60–82.

GENETTE, GÉRARD, *Narrative Discourse: An Essay in Method* (1972); trans. Jane E. Lewin (Oxford, 1980).

GILBERT, SANDRA M., and GUBAR, SUSAN, *The Madwoman in the Attic: The Woman Writer and the Nineteenth-Century Literary Imagination* (New Haven, Conn., 1979).

GIRARD, RENÉ, *Deceit, Desire, and the Novel: Self and Other in Literary Structure* (1965); trans. Yvonne Freccero (Baltimore, Md., 1984).

—— *The Scapegoat* (1932); trans. Yvonne Freccero (London, 1986).

GOODE, JOHN, 'The Pervasive Mystery of Style', in John Goode (ed.), *The Air of Reality*, 244–300.

—— (ed.), *The Air of Reality: New Essays on Henry James* (London, 1972).

GORDON, CAROLINE, 'Mr Verver, Our National Hero', *Sewanee Review*, 63 (1955), 13–47.

GRAHAM, KENNETH, *The Drama of Fulfilment* (Oxford, 1975).

—— *Indirections of the Novel: James, Conrad, and Forster* (Cambridge, 1988).

GRAVER, SUZANNE, *George Eliot and Community: A Study in Social Theory and Fictional Form* (Berkeley, Calif., 1984).

GROSS, JOHN, and PEARSON, GABRIEL, (eds.), *Dickens and the Twentieth Century* (London, 1962).

GUERARD, ALBERT J., *Conrad the Novelist* (Cambridge, Mass., 1958).

HAIGHT, GORDON S. (ed.), *A Century of George Eliot Criticism* (London, 1966).

HALPERIN, JOHN (ed.), *Jane Austen: Bicentenary Essays* (Cambridge, 1975).

HARDING, D. W., 'Regulated Hatred: An Aspect of the Work of Jane Austen', *Scrutiny*, 8 (1940), 346–62.

HARDY, BARBARA, *The Novels of George Eliot: A Study in Form* (1953; rpt. London, 1963).

—— *The Moral Art of Dickens* (London, 1970).

HAWTHORN, JEREMY, *Joseph Conrad: Language and Fictional Self-Consciousness* (Lincoln, Nebr., 1979).

HAWTHORN, JEREMY, (ed.), *Narrative: From Mallory to Motion Pictures* (London, 1985).

HEYNS, MICHIEL, ' "The Language of the House" in *The Wings of the Dove*', *Essays in Criticism*, 34 (1989), 116–36.

HIRSCH, E. D., Jr., *The Aims of Interpretation* (Chicago, 1976).

HOBSBAWM, E. J., *The Age of Capital: 1848–1875* (1975; rpt. London, 1988).

—— *The Age of Empire: 1875–1914* (London, 1987).

HOLLAND, LAURENCE BEDWELL, *The Expense of Vision: Essays on the Craft of Henry James* (Princeton, NJ, 1964).

HOLLOWAY, JOHN, 'The Literary Scene', in Boris Ford (ed.), *The Modern Age*, 51–100.

HONAN, PARK, *Jane Austen: Her Life* (London, 1987).

HUGHES, JONATHAN, *The Vital Few: American Progress and its Protagonists* (New York, 1973).

IRWIN, MICHAEL, *Picturing: Description and Illusion in the Nineteenth-Century Novel* (London, 1979).

JAMES, HENRY, review of *Our Mutual Friend*, *The Nation*, (1865); rpt. as 'The Limitations of Dickens', in *Views and Reviews* (Boston, Mass., 1908), and in George H. Ford and Lauriat Lane, Jr. (eds.), *The Dickens Critics*, 48–54.

—— 'Daniel Deronda: A Conversation', *Atlantic Monthly* (1876); rpt. in *Partial Portraits*, 63–93.

—— 'The Life of George Eliot', *Atlantic Monthly* (1885); rpt. in *Partial Portraits*, 37–62.

—— *Partial Portraits* (1887; rpt. Ann Arbor, Mich., 1970).

JAMESON, FREDRIC, *The Political Unconscious: Narrative as a Socially Symbolic Act* (London, 1981).

JOHNSON, EDGAR, *Charles Dickens: His Tragedy and Triumph* (Boston Mass., 1952).

JONES, R. T., *George Eliot* (Cambridge, 1970).

JOSEPHSON, MATTHEW, *The Robber Barons: The Great American Capitalists 1861–1901* (1934; rpt. New York, 1962).

KAIRSCHNER, MIMI, 'The Traces of Capitalistic Patriarchy in the Silences of *The Golden Bowl*', *The Henry James Review*, 5 (1984), 187–92.

KAPLAN, E. ANN, 'Is the Gaze Male?', in Anne Snitow, Christine Stansell, Sharon Thompson (eds.), *Powers of Desire: The Politics of Sexuality*, 309–27.

KAPPELER, SUSANNE, *Writing and Reading in Henry James* (London, 1980).

KIRKHAM, MARGARET, 'Feminist Irony and the Priceless Heroine of *Mansfield Park*', in Janet Todd (ed.), *Jane Austen: New Perspectives*, 231–47.

KNOEPFLMACHER U. C., *George Eliot's Early Novels: The Limits of Realism* (Berkeley, Calif., 1968).

KROOK, DOROTHEA, *The Ordeal of Consciousness in Henry James* (Cambridge, 1962).

LANGLAND, ELIZABETH, 'Nobody's Angels: Domestic Ideology and Middle-Class Women in the Victorian Novel', *PMLA* 107 (1992), 290–304.

LASCELLES, MARY, *Jane Austen and her Art* (Oxford, 1939).

LAWRENCE, D. H., 'John Galsworthy' (1928); rpt. in *Phoenix* (London, 1961), 539–50.

LEAVIS, F. R., *The Great Tradition* (1948; rpt. Harmondsworth, 1962).

LEAVIS, Q. D., 'How We Must Read *Great Expectations*', *Dickens the Novelist* (with F.R. Leavis) (1970; rpt. Harmondsworth, 1972).

LEECH, GEOFFREY N., and SHORT, MICHAEL A., *Style in Fiction: A Linguistic Introduction to English Fictional Prose* (London, 1981).

LESSER, WENDY, *His Other Half: Men Looking at Women Through Art* (Cambridge, Mass., 1991).

LEVINE, GEORGE, *The Realistic Imagination: English Fiction from Frankenstein to Lady Chatterley* (Chicago, 1981).

LIDDELL, ROBERT, *The Novels of George Eliot* (London, 1977).

LODGE, DAVID, *Language of Fiction: Essays in Criticism and Verbal Analysis of the English Novel* (London, 1966).

—— *After Bakhtin: Essays on Fiction and Criticism* (London, 1990).

LOTHE, JACOB, *Conrad's Narrative Method* (Oxford, 1989).

LUCAS, JOHN, Introduction to Jane Austen's *Mansfield Park*, The World's Classics (Oxford, 1980).

MACHEREY, PIERRE, *A Theory of Literary Production* (1966); trans. Geoffrey Wall (London, 1978).

MACKENZIE, MANFRED, *Communities of Honor and Love in Henry James* (Cambridge, Mass., 1976).

MARCUS, STEVEN, *Representations: Essays on Literature and Society* (New York, 1975).

MATTHIESSEN, F. O., *Henry James: The Major Phase* (1944; rpt. London, 1946).

MILLER, D. A., *Narrative and its Discontents: Problems of Closure in the Traditional Novel* (Princeton, NJ, 1981).

—— *The Novel and the Police* (Berkeley, Calif., 1988).

MILLER, J. HILLIS, 'The Interpretation of *Lord Jim*', in Morton W. Bloomfield (ed.), *The Interpretation of Narrative: Theory and Practice*, 211–28.

MINTZ, ALAN, *George Eliot and the Novel of Vocation* (Cambridge, Mass., 1978).

MITCHELL, W. J. T. (ed.), *On Narrative* (Chicago, 1981).

MOLER, KENNETH L., 'The Two Voices of Fanny Price', in John Halperin (ed.), *Jane Austen: Bicentenary Essays*, 172–79.

—— *Jane Austen's Art of Allusion* (1968; rpt. Lincoln, Nebr., 1977).

MORGAN, SUSAN, *In the Meantime* (Chicago, 1980).

MOYNAHAN, JULIAN, 'The Hero's Guilt: The Case of *Great Expectations*', *Essays in Criticism*, 10 (1960), 60–79, rpt. in Norman Page (ed.), *Hard Times, Great Expectations and Our Mutual Friend: A Casebook*, 103–18.

MOYNAHAN, JULIAN, 'Dealings with the Firm of Dombey and Son: Firmness vs. Wetness', in John Gross and Gabriel Pearson (eds.), *Dickens and the Twentieth Century*, 121–31.

MUSSELWHITE, DAVID E., *Partings Welded Together: Politics and Desire in the Nineteenth-Century English Novel* (London, 1987).

NESTOR, PAULINE, *Female Friendships and Communities: Charlotte Brontë, George Eliot, Elizabeth Gaskell* (Oxford, 1985).

NEWTON, K. M., '*Daniel Deronda* and Circumcision', *Essays in Criticism*, 31 (1981), 313–27.

PAGE, NORMAN, *The Language of Jane Austen* (Oxford, 1972).

——(ed.), *Hard Times, Great Expectations and Our Mutual Friend: A Casebook* (London, 1979).

PEARSON, GABRIEL, 'The Novel to End All Novels: *The Golden Bowl*', in John Goode (ed.), *The Air of Reality: New Essays on Henry James* (London, 1972).

POOLE, ADRIAN, '"Hidden Affinities" in *Daniel Deronda*', *Essays in Criticism*, 33 (1983), 294–311.

——*Henry James* (Hemel Hempstead, 1991).

POOVEY, MARY, *The Proper Lady and the Woman Writer: Ideology as Style in the Works of Mary Wollstonecraft, Mary Shelley, and Jane Austen* (Chicago, 1984).

PRAZ, MARIO, *The Hero in Eclipse in Victorian Fiction*, trans. Angus Davidson (London, 1956).

RAVAL, SURESH, 'Narrative and Authority in *Lord Jim*: Conrad's Art of Failure', *ELH* 48 (1981), 387–410.

ROSE, JACQUELINE, *Sexuality in the Field of Vision* (London, 1986).

RUSKIN, JOHN, 'Of Queens' Gardens' (1864), *Sesame and Lilies* (London, 1907).

SAID, EDWARD, *Culture and Imperialism* (London, 1993).

SAUSSURE, FERDINAND DE, *Course in General Linguistics*, ed. Charles Bally and Albert Sechehaye (1915); trans. Roy Harris (London, 1983).

SCHOLES, ROBERT, 'Afterthoughts on Narrative II: Language, Narrative, and Anti-Narrative', in W. J. T. Mitchell (ed.), *On Narrative*, 200–8.

SCHWARZ, DANIEL R., *Conrad: Almayer's Folly to Under Western Eyes* (London, 1980).

SEARS, SALLIE, *The Negative Imagination: Form and Perspective in the Novels of Henry James* (Ithaca, NY, 1968).

SEDGWICK, EVE KOSOFSKY, *Between Men: English Literature and Male Homosocial Desire* (New York, 1985).

SEELEY, TRACY, 'Conrad's Modernist Romance: *Lord Jim*', *ELH* 59 (1992), 495–511.

SELTZER, MARK, *Henry James and the Art of Power* (Ithaca, NY, 1984).

SHAW, GEORGE BERNARD, *Introduction to Hard Times* (1912; rpt. in Charles Dickens, *Hard Times*, Norton Critical Edition (New York, 1966), 332–9.

SHOWALTER, ELAINE, 'The Greening of Sister George', *Nineteenth-Century Fiction*, 35 (1980), 292–311.

—— *A Literature of Their Own: British Women Novelists from Brontë to Lessing* (1977; rev. London, 1982).

SHUTTLEWORTH, SALLY, *George Eliot and Nineteenth-Century Science: The Make-Believe of a Beginning* (Cambridge, 1986).

SNITOW, ANNE, CHRISTINE STANSELL, SHARON THOMPSON (eds.), *Powers of Desire: The Politics of Sexuality* (New York, 1983).

SOUTHAM, B. C. (ed.), *Critical Essays on Jane Austen* (London, 1968).

SPACKS, PATRICIA, *The Female Imagination* (New York, 1976).

SPEAIGHT, ROBERT (ed.), *Essays by Divers Hands*, being the Transactions of the Royal Society of Literature, 17 (London, 1972).

SPRING, DAVID, 'Interpreters of Jane Austen's Social World: Literary Critics and Historians', in Janet Todd (ed.), *Jane Austen: New Perspectives*, 53–72.

SPRINKER, MICHAEL, 'Historicizing Henry James', *The Henry James Review*, 5 (1984), 203–7.

STEELE, MEILI, 'The Drama of Reference in James's *The Golden Bowl*', *Novel*, 21 (1987), 73–88.

STEPHEN, LESLIE, 'George Eliot', *Cornhill Magazine*, 43 (1881), 152–68, rpt. in Gordon S. Haight (ed.), *A Century of George Eliot Criticism* (London, 1966), 136–49.

SUMMERS, ANNE, 'The Mysterious Demise of Sarah Gamp: The Domiciliary Nurse and her Detractors, c.1830–1860', *Victorian Studies*, 32 (1989), 365–86.

SUTHERLAND, KATHRYN, '*Jane Eyre*'s Literary History: The Case for *Mansfield Park*', *ELH* 59 (1992), 409–40.

TALLIS, RAYMOND, *Not Saussure: A Critique of Post-Saussurean Literary Theory* (Basingstoke, 1988).

—— *In Defence of Realism* (London, 1988).

TANNER, TONY, *Conrad: Lord Jim* (London, 1963).

—— *Jane Austen* (Basingstoke, 1986).

TAYLOR, GORDON RATTRAY, *The Angel Makers: A Study in the Psychological Origins of Historical Change 1750–1850* (London, 1958).

TODD, JANET (ed.), *Be Good, Sweet Maid: An Anthology of Women and Literature* (New York, 1981).

—— (ed.), *Jane Austen: New Perspectives*, (New York, 1983).

TOMALIN, CLAIRE, *The Invisible Woman: The Story of Nelly Ternan and Charles Dickens* (1990; rpt. Harmondsworth, 1991).

TORGOVNICK, MARIANNA, *Closure in the Novel* (Princeton, NJ, 1981).

TRILLING, LIONEL, *The Opposing Self* (London, 1955).

TRUDGILL, ERIC, *Madonnas and Magdalens: The Origins and Development of Victorian Sexual Attitudes* (London, 1976).

UFFEN, ELLEN SERLEN, 'The Art of *Mansfield Park*', in Janet Todd (ed.) *Be Good, Sweet Maid: An Anthology of Women and Literature*, 21–30.

VAN GHENT, DOROTHY, *The English Novel: Form and Function* (1953; repr. New York, 1961).

VEBLEN, THORSTEIN, *The Theory of the Leisure Class: An Economic Study of Institutions* (1899; rpt. London, 1970).

WATT, IAN (ed.), *Jane Austen: A Collection of Critical Essays* (Englewood Cliffs, NJ, 1963).

—— *Conrad in the Nineteenth Century* (London, 1980).

WEBB, IGOR, *From Custom to Capital: The English Novel and the Industrial Revolution* (Ithaca, NY, 1981).

WHITE, HAYDEN, 'The Value of Narrativity in the Representation of Reality', in W. J. T. Mitchell (ed.), *On Narrative*, 1–23.

WIDDOWSON, PETER (ed.), *Re-Reading English* (London, 1982).

WILLIAMS, MERLE, *Henry James and the Philosophical Novel: Being and Seeing* (Cambridge, 1993).

WILLIAMS, MICHAEL, *Jane Austen: Six Novels and their Methods* (London, 1986).

WILLIAMS, RAYMOND, *The English Novel from Dickens to Lawrence* (1970; rpt. St Albans, 1974).

WILSON, ANGUS, 'The Heroes and Heroines of Dickens', in John Gross and Gabriel Pearson (eds.), *Dickens and the Twentieth Century*, 3–11.

WINNER, ANTHONY, *Culture and Irony: Studies in Joseph Conrad's Major Novels* (Charlottesville, Va., 1988).

WRIGHT, ANDREW, 'The Novel as a Conspiracy', in Robert Speaight (ed.), *Essays by Divers Hands*, 124–31.

YEAZELL, RUTH BERNARD, *Language and Knowledge in the Late Novels of Henry James* (Chicago, 1976).

ZACHARIAS, GREG, 'The Language of Light and Dark and James's Moral Argument in *The Golden Bowl*', *Papers on Language and Literature*, 26 (1990), 249–70.

INDEX

To facilitate cross-reference between chapters, entries are normally placed under a subject heading, subdivided into author names, rather than under the main entry for each author. Extended discussions are indicated in **bold type**.

adultery:
  in Austen 78–80
  in James 233, 249–50, 251, 259
aestheticism 43
  in James 244–5, 260
affective criticism, *see* critical
  approaches
Ajax (Sophocles) 226
Allen, Frederick Lewis 248 n.
Allen, Walter 30, 38, 157 n.
Amis, Kingsley 55 n.
anachronistic criticism, *see* critical
  approaches
Anderson, Quentin 46, 242
angel, angelic:
  in Dickens 25, 104–5, 134–5, 180
  in Eliot 179–80, 182
  in the house 81 n., 88, 90 n., 103, 186
anti-jacobin novel 15–16, 71
anti-narrative 271–2
Auerbach, Nina 9, 16 n., 55, 56 n.,
  101 n.
Austen, Jane 6–18, 50–89, 269, 273
  compared with Dickens 18
  compared with Eliot 137, 138
  compared with James 227–8, 268
  critical approaches to 6–18
  works: *Emma* 10, 18, 53–9 *passim*,
  75, 83; *Mansfield Park* 6–18, 51–
  89, 112, 147, 177, 264, 268, 273;
  Northanger Abbey 50–1, 54–60
  passim, 82, 84, 228;
  Persuasion 54–5, 56; *Pride and
  Prejudice* 53, 54, 57, 78, 273;
  Sense and Sensibility 54, 56
Austen, Zelda 156 n.
authorial intention, *see* intention
authority 187–8
  in Austen 10

Babb, Howard S. 56 n., 60

Bakhtin, Mikhail 14, 49, 177 n., 182,
  269, 271–2
banishment, *see* expulsion
Barrett, Dorothea 30–1, 32 n., 33, 153,
  155 n.
Bayley, John 242 n.
Beadnell, Maria 26
beauty:
  in Conrad 210
  in Eliot 135, 142–3, 151–2, 156, 161
  in James 228, 254, 259, 262
Beer, Gillian 32 n., 33, 159, 160 n.,
  175 n.
Bell, Michael 43
Belsey, Catherine 21 n., 34–5
Benjamin, Walter 183, 187, 193
Bentham, Jeremy 3
Bersani, Leo 86
Berthoud, Jacques 40 n., 185–6, 195,
  204 n., 213
betrayal:
  in Conrad 186, 218, 224
  in Dickens 103, 132
  in Eliot 180
  in James 254–5, 258
biographical criticism, *see* critical
  approaches
Blackwood's Magazine 190
blindess:
  in Austen 69
  in James 262, 266–7
Boone, Joseph Allen 2 n., 170 n.,
  177 n., 268 n.
Booth, Wayne C. 194 n.
Bradbrook, Muriel 84 n.
Bradbury, Nichola 252
Browning, Robert 244
Burney, Fanny 59 n.
Butler, Marilyn 9, 10, 15, 52, 55 n.,
  58 n., 61, 64 n., 69 n., 71 n., 76 n.,
  83

Carnegie, Andrew 241, 242 n., 246 n.
Carpenter, Mary Wilson 36–7
Caserio, Robert 3 n., 22, 111 n.
Chapman, R. W. 8 n., 74 n.
charm, charming:
    in Conrad 210, 224
    in Eliot 30, 135, 154, 167
    in James 228, 254, 255
Chase, Cynthia 35–6, 39
Chatman, Seymour 35 n.
choice:
    in Austen 70
    in Eliot 169, 170 n., 173, 175
    in James 256, 267
Christian criticism, see critical
    approaches
circumcision:
    in *Daniel Deronda* 35–7
Cixous, Hélène 36
closure 4, 5, 271
    in Austen 14, 84 n., 85, 87
    in Conrad 39–40, 190, 193, 198,
        205, 207, 209, 224
    in Dickens 22, 95
    and ideology 14, 16, 19–21, 41, 49,
        82, 87
    in James 48, 267–8
    and scapegoating 52, 94
codes 15, 271
Cohen, Paula Marantz 9 n., 87 n.
collaboration, see complicity
colonialism, see imperialism
comedy, comic 192
    in Austen 15, 52, 56–8, 62–3, 78, 79–
        83, 226
    in Conrad 201–2, 206, 226
    in Dickens 27, 91, 92, 102, 116, 119,
        120
    in Eliot 149
    in James 226, 250–1, 256
commonplace, see ordinariness
community 273
    in Austen 52–3, 247
    in Conrad 183–4, 186, 187, 195–6,
        198, 199, 206, 209, 217–18, 221–4
    in Dickens 23
    in Eliot 172, 183–4, 247
    in James 246–8, 251
    of readers 38, 188
community, fictional 6
    in Austen 6–7, 52–3, 55
    in Dickens 22–3
    in Eliot 172, 183–4

    in James 228, 267
community, narrative 4, 273
    in Austen 6–7, 17, 18, 50–7
    in Conrad 189–90, 192, 216
    in Dickens 18, 22–3, 104–5, 112
    in Eliot 139, 172
    in James 47
    and language 47
    see also scapegoat; scapegoating
compassion:
    in Austen 67
    in Conrad 196–7
    in Eliot 147–8, 152–3, 169, 171, 180,
        181
    in James 253–4, 266–7
complicity 2–3, 18–19, 48–9, 233, 254
Conrad, Joseph 39–42, 183–226, 270,
        272
    compared with Eliot 39
    compared with James 227–35, 266,
        268
    critical approaches to 39–42
    works: 'Amy Foster' 184–5; 'Heart of
        Darkness' 43, 184, 188, 228–34,
        239, 254, 266; *Lord Jim* 5, 39–42,
        171, 182, 186, 187–226, 228, 268,
        272, 273; *Nostromo* 186, 238,
        247; *A Personal Record* 183, 224–
        5; *The Secret Agent* 184, 185–6,
        198, 202, 218; 'The Secret
        Sharer' 200; 'Typhoon' 202;
        Under Western Eyes 186, 188,
        202; 'Youth' 200
consciousness, centre of:
    in Austen 10, 17
    in Eliot 162, 166, 167, 177
conservatism:
    in Austen 6, 15, 18, 56
    in Dickens 29
    in Eliot 29, 31, 34
conversion:
    in Eliot 139, 148, 150
    see also plot, conversion
Copernicus 176
Crews, Frederick C. 46
critical approaches 1–49
    affective criticism 38–9
    anachronistic criticism 7, 9, 11–12
    biographical criticism 26–8
    Christian criticism 46
    deconstruction 35–7, 39
    feminist criticism 16–17, 156 n.
    historical criticism 7–15

mimetic criticism 45
structuralism 40–1
Culler, Jonathan 3, 36, 46, 174 n.

Daleski, H. M. 24, 101 n., 223 n.
death:
in Dickens 118, 124, 130, 134–5
deconstruction, *see* critical approaches
desire 88, 269–70
in Austen 59, 73
in Conrad 213
in Dickens 128
see also triangular desire
detective plot, *see* plot, mystery
Devlin, D. D. 58 n., 62 n., 71 n.
Dickens, Charles 18–29, 90–135
compared with Austen 88
compared with Conrad 185
compared with Eliot 29, 137, 138,
155, 180
critical approaches to 18–29
works: *Bleak House* 19–21, 24–5,
90, 91, 95, 102, 111–12, 133, 228;
Christmas Books 97–8 n.; *David
Copperfield* 91, 92, 95, 106–10,
115–16, 123, 124, 131, 133, 273;
Dombey and Son 87, 90, 91, 94,
95, 97–101, 103–7 *passim*, 112,
185, 272; *Great Expectations* 27,
91, 102–4, 109 n., 115–17, 123,
128 n., 132–3, 273; *Hard
Times* 24, 25–7, 91, 124; *The
Haunted Man* 97–8 n.; *Little
Dorrit* 19, 89, 91–5 *passim*, 112–
16, 123, 124, 130, 133, 228;
Martin Chuzzlewit 24, 90, 91, 131;
The Mystery of Edwin Drood 91,
109 n., 124 n., 128 n., 133–4, 274;
Oliver Twist 123; *Our Mutual
Friend* 19, 21, 28–9, 89, 91, 99–
100, 117–35, 173 n., 272, 274
domesticity 88
in Austen 11, 76–7
in Conrad 184–6
in Dickens 22, 26, 27–8, 29 n., 95–7,
103, 185, 272–3
in Eliot 184
Don Quixote 224–5
Dowling, W. C. 40 n.
dream:
in Conrad 204, 209, 213–4, 224
in Eliot 145
see also romance

Duckworth, Alistair 8–9, 60–1 n.,
71 n., 72–3 n.
Duffy, Joseph 56, 72, 87

Eagleton, Terry 1 n., 25, 26–7, 109 n.
Edel, Leon 48 n.
education 58
novel of 15, 58
Eliot, George 29–39, 136–82, 270
compared with Conrad 183–4, 188
compared with James 227–8
critical approaches to 29–39, 156 n.
as moralist 33, 136, 181–2
works: *Adam Bede* 31–4 *passim*,
140–5 *passim*, 147, 148–53, 154,
156, 157 n., 161 n., 162–4, 167–71
passim, 180, 188; 'Amos
Barton' 146–7, 148; *Daniel
Deronda* 30, 34–9, 87, 138, 139,
141, 146, 147, 148, 151, 153–82,
207, 228, 233, 248–9, 273; *Felix
Holt* 141, 147, 148, 151–8 *passim*;
'Janet's Repentance' 148, 154, 179;
Middlemarch 1, 136–8 *passim*,
141, 142, 146, 147, 151–60
passim, 176; *The Mill on the
Floss* 138, 144–5, 151, 157,
175 n., 176, 178; 'Mr Gilfil's Love-
Story' 147–8; 'The Natural History
of German Life' 143–4;
Romola 30, 136, 139, 146, 147,
148, 154, 161, 165, 167, 169,
173 n., 175 n., 178, 180–1, 233;
Scenes of Clerical Life 136, 146;
Silas Marner 184
embrace:
in Dickens 98–9, 101, 103, 113, 122,
132–3, 134
in James 253, 258–9, 265–7
empire, *see* imperialism
envy, *see* jealousy
epic 182
Evangelicalism:
in Austen 11, 12
in Eliot 148
exclusion 23, 28
in Austen 62, 264
in Conrad 191, 208
in Dickens 23, 94, 98–100, 112, 118,
272
in Eliot 184
in James 248
see also expulsion; isolation

expulsion 199, 274
  in Austen 52, 54–5, 82, 86–7, 264
  in Conrad 194, 200, 220
  in Dickens 22, 25, 104, 105, 108,
    114, 185, 273–4
  in Eliot 34
  in James 228, 261, 264, 274
  see also scapegoat

fellowship:
  in Conrad 183–4, 217, 220
  in Dickens 123
  of illusion 200, 221, 225–6
  of irony 191
  see also community; solidarity
femininity/femaleness 34–5, 87–8
  in Eliot 34, 153–5, 157–60, 178
feminism:
  in Eliot 30–7, 156–9
feminist criticism, see critical approaches
Fergusson, Francis 46
fictions, characters' own 47–8, 188–9,
    209, 213, 228, 252, 254, 259, 264,
    267
fidelity:
  in Conrad 186, 224
Firebaugh, Joseph 45 n.
Fleishman, Avrom 8 n., 11, 12 n.,
    65 n., 84 n.
Flint, Kate 20 n., 95 n.
folktale:
  and novel 40 n.
Forster, E. M. 43
Foucault, Michel 3 n., 19
Frankenstein monster 28 n.
  Fanny Price's similarity to 55
free indirect style:
  in Austen 60, 63, 69, 78
  in Eliot 166, 169

Garis, Robert 82
Gaskell, Elizabeth (Wives and
    Daughters) 88
Genette, Gérard 189
Gilbert, Sandra M. 16 n., 147 n.,
    172 n.
Girard, René 4, 29, 109 n., 122–3,
    128 n., 180, 182, 268, 273
Goode, John 43
Gordimer, Nadine 3
Gordon, Caroline 242–3
Gould, Jay 242
Graham, Kenneth 44 n., 267 n.

Graver, Suzanne 38
Gubar, Susan 16 n., 147 n., 172 n.
Guerard, Albert J. 201, 204 n., 212 n.,
    223

Harding, D. W. 54
Hardy, Barbara 23, 174
Hardy, Thomas 30
hatred:
  in Austen ('regulated hatred') 54
  in Dickens 103, 107, 108, 109 n.,
    115, 126–8
Hawthorn, Jeremy 206 n.
heroines 59 n., 83, 87–8
  in Austen 16, 53–4, 88
  in Dickens 25–6, 90–2, 94–5, 134
  in Eliot 155–7, 159
  in James 251
heroism:
  in Austen 65, 72, 87
  in Conrad 42, 192, 201–4, 209, 213,
    218
  in Eliot 172–5, 177, 182 n.
Heyns, Michiel 239 n.
Hirsch, E. D. 7 n.
historical criticism, see critical
    approaches
history 270
  in Austen 11
  in Conrad 229
  in James 230–1, 234
Hobsbawm, E. J. 96–7, 137–8, 241
Hogarth, Mary 26
Holland, Laurence B. 45
Holloway, John 43
Holquist, Michael 14 n.
home, see domesticity
homosexual fiction 3 n.
homosexuality:
  in Little Dorrit 114
homosocial bonding:
  in Dickens 126–7
  in Eliot 173
Honan, Park 73 n., 78 n.
horror:
  in Austen 74, 78, 79–80, 82
  in Conrad 221, 254
  in Dickens 118
  in Eliot 179
  in James 254
Hughes, Jonathan 242 n.
humour, see comedy

ideology 6
  in Austen 10, 16, 75, 77, 82, 87
  in Conrad 217–18
  and fiction 5, 6, 10, 16, 269, 272
illusion:
  in Conrad 207, 211, 217, 225–6, 266
  in Dickens 97
  in James 248, 257, 261
  see also fellowship of illusion
imagination 42, 273
  in Austen 63–4
  in Conrad 202, 208–16, 219, 270
  in Dickens 132
  in Eliot 151
  in James 253, 261
imperialism:
  in Austen 13, 70 n.
  in Conrad 229, 232, 239
  in James 229–33
Inchbald, Elizabeth 65 n.
intention 3, 9, 31, 37
interpretation 7–18, 40–2, 47, 254–5,
  264, 271, 274
intertexuality 15
irony:
  in Austen 18, 53, 56–8, 75, 191
  in Conrad 185, 191, 192, 194, 196–8
  in Dickens 101, 103
  in Eliot 152, 163, 168, 171
  in James 226, 233, 242, 255, 261
  and narrative community 56–8, 191
Irwin, Michael 76 n., 137 n.
isolation:
  in Dickens 94–5, 102–3
  see also solitude

James, Henry 43–9, 226–68, 269, 272
  compared with Austen 226
  compared with Conrad 226
  compared with Dickens 226
  compared with Eliot 226
  critical approaches to 43–9
  on Dickens 125
  on Eliot 32, 154–5 n., 181
  works: The Art of the Novel 227,
    269; 'Daniel Deronda: A
    Conversation' 154–5 n.; Roderick
    Hudson 238; The
    Ambassadors 252, 269; The
    Awkward Age 238; The
    Bostonians 238; The Golden
    Bowl 45–49, 88, 227–68, 272,
    273, 274; The Portrait of a

Lady 45, 238, 245; The Spoils of
  Poynton 238; Washington
  Square 251; What Maisie
  Knew 238; The Wings of the
  Dove 87, 230, 231, 234, 235, 238,
  251–2, 267
Jameson, Fredric 40–2, 48, 188, 194 n.,
  221
Jane Eyre (Charlotte Brontë) 112,
  147 n.
jealousy:
  in Austen 62, 67–8, 83
  in Dickens 108, 109 n.
  in Eliot 158 n.
Johnson, Edgar 28
Jones, R. T. 152
Josephson, Matthew 242 n., 244 n.,
  246 n.
justice:
  in Conrad 233–4
  in Eliot 171, 233–4
  in James 233–4

Kairschner, Mimi 48 n., 267–8 n.
Kaplan, E. Ann 35 n.
Kappeler, Susanne 40 n.
Kirkham, Margaret 16
Knoepflmacher, U. C. 136 n., 143 n.
knowledge:
  in Austen (self-knowledge) 83
  in Conrad 186, 220
  in Dickens 132
  in Eliot 160
  in James 257–8, 266–7
Kotzebue, August von 65
Krook, Dorthea 46 n.

Lacan, Jacques 36
Langland., Elizabeth 90–1 n.
language 250, 271–2
  and community 47, 48, 188, 217,
    247
  and ideology 6
  and the novel 14
  and power 239, 251, 272
  in Austen 59, 138
  in Eliot 138
  in James 227–8, 250
  see also vocabulary
Lascelles, Mary 81–2
Lawrence, D. H. 38
Leavis, F. R. 5, 34, 43, 44
Leavis, Q. D. 117

Leech, Geoffrey N. 60 n.
Lesser, Wendy 35 n.
Lévi-Strauss, Claude 40–1
Levine, George 2 n., 28 n., 107 n.,
    163 n., 171–2, 188 n.
Liddell, Robert 30, 38, 155 n.
light:
    in Austen 68, 70
    in Conrad 210, 213, 214, 217, 222
    in Eliot 143, 166, 170, 181
    in James 240–1, 246, 261, 266,
        274
Lloyd, Charles 71 n.
Locke, John 58 n.
Lodge, David 79
London 76 n., 69, 228–9, 231
loneliness, see solitude
Lothe, Jacob 189 n.
love:
    in Austen 17–18, 59, 146
    in Conrad 215
    in Dickens 23, 103, 106–8, 113, 127–
        8, 129–31, 133–4, 146
    in Eliot 145–6, 169
    in James 251, 266, 267
Lucas, John 74 n.
lying:
    in Conrad 266
    in James 266 n.
    see also truth; truthfulness

Macherey, Pierre 6 n., 49
Mackenzie, Manfred 266 n.
'male gaze' 34, 161–2, 168
Malvolio (Twelfth Night) 192
Marcus, Steven 35
marriage:
    in Austen 16, 70–2, 92, 94
    n Dickens 92, 94, 99–100
    in Eliot 158–9
    in James 267–8 n.
Matthiessen, F. O. 46 n., 242 n.
Medea (Euripides) 170–1
Melmotte (The Way We Live Now) 238
Merdle (Bleak House) 238
metaphor 2
    in Conrad 217
    in Dickens 98–9, 272
    in Eliot 174, 176, 179
    in James 234–7, 259–60, 274
Miller, D. A. 2, 19–20, 69, 95, 270–1
Miller, J. Hillis 41
mimetic criticism, see critical approaches

Mintz, Alan 174 n.
modernism 39, 44, 269
Moler, Kenneth L. 58 n., 60 n., 68 n.
moralism, morality 48
    in Austen 15, 82
    in Dickens 20–1
    in Eliot 31–3
    in James 48, 240, 253, 254
More, Hannah 58 n., 71 n.
Morgan, John Pierpont 242–3 n., 244,
    247, 248 n.
Morgan, Susan 68 n.
Moynahan, Julian 101 n., 117
murder:
    in Austen 82
    in Conrad 185–6
    in Dickens 113
    in Eliot 158
Muselwhite, David E. 8 n., 40 n., 76–7,
    86 n.
Myers, F. W. H. 31

narration, modes of 42, 191, 201–2
narrative authority 36, 162, 187
narrative movement, see plot, dynamics
    of
narrative, narrativity 4, 36–7, 269–72
    see also plot
narratology 189
Nemesis 165, 167, 179, 182
nepotism 73
Nestor, Pauline 32 n., 33–4, 158 n.,
    178
Newton, K. M. 36
novelization 14 n.
nurses:
    in Dickens 24

Oedipus (Sophocles) 192, 193, 199
ordinariness:
    in Eliot 142–7
organic unity 24–5, 267

Page, Norman 75, 82
painting:
    and fiction 140, 166, 167, 270
Panopticon 3
partnership:
    in Conrad 220 n., 233
    in Dickens 23, 92–5, 99–101, 103,
        114, 118–22, 126, 127, 129, 131,
        133
    in James 238, 267

patriarchy:
in Austen 11, 16 n., 70–1
in James 48
patronage:
in Austen 73 n.
in Dickens 103, 113
in James 238
Pearson, Gabriel 266 n.
persecution text 4, 268
see also scapegoat
phallocentrism 36–7
philanthropy:
in James 241–3
pity, see compassion
plot 270
dynamics of 4; in Conrad 206, 233;
in Dickens 18–19, 22, 23, 29, 91–
3, 104, 105–6, 111, 120, 122, 128–
9, 131, 133; in Eliot 147, 148, 153,
181, 233; in James 228, 233, 268
types: conversion: in Eliot 35, 148,
151; mystery: in Dickens 18–21,
111, 112; punitive: in Conrad 233;
in Dickens 131; in Eliot 30, 148,
180–1, 233; in James 233;
redemptive: in Dickens 122, 128,
131, 133, 273–4; in Eliot 153
point of view:
in Austen 17
in Conrad 193
in Eliot 166, 167
police 180
and the novel 2–3, 19, 270–1
polyglossia 14
Poole, Adrian 161 n., 170, 238 n.
Poovey, Mary 16–17, 59 n., 65–6 n.
post-modernism 271
power 48
in Austen 13, 72
in Conrad 193, 195, 203, 214
in Dickens 25, 90, 90–1 n., 104, 128,
130–1, 132, 134
in Eliot 156–7, 164, 167
in James 228, 230–4, 236, 237–8,
240, 243, 251–4, 257, 258, 266,
267
see also language and power
Praz, Mario 25
punishment 199
in Austen 80, 86
in Conrad 233–4
in Dickens 107, 124, 129, 134
in Eliot 142, 157

in James 233–4
see also plot, punitive
Puritanism:
in Conrad 238
in Eliot 29–30, 153, 174 n.

Raval, Suresh 203 n.
realism 2, 43, 269
in Austen 55 n., 77, 81
and beauty 142–3, 161
in Conrad 182, 205, 207, 209
in Dickens 111
in Eliot 136–45, 171–2, 177, 181,
182
in James 226, 274
and romance 28, 171, 177 n., 205,
207, 209
and scapegoating 39, 274
see also representation, realist
reality 270
in Conrad 181, 210–12, 214–15,
224–5
in Eliot 139, 145, 176–7, 181
see also truth
redemption:
in Dickens 21–2, 91, 101, 117, 121,
130
in Eliot 178, 180, 188
see also plot, redemptive
religion:
in Austen 76
in Conrad 238
in Eliot 145, 148
in James 45–6, 238, 251
representation, realist 3, 5, 39, 48, 138,
141, 162, 163 n., 166, 181, 269–72
see also realism
rescue:
in Dickens 111 n., 117, 122, 130
in Eliot 175
resentment:
in Austen 63
in Conrad 221
in Dickens 27, 105, 108, 111, 112–
15, 116, 122, 126, 133
in James 254–5
resolution 270
in Austen 15
in Conrad 190, 193, 206, 209, 220–1
in Dickens 18–19, 103–4, 110, 122
in James 228, 256
see also closure
Rhys, Jean 112

Rockefeller, John D. 241, 242
romance, romantic 42
  in Austen 16 n.
  in Conrad 189, 202, 205, 207–18, 224, 272
  in Dickens 128 n., 132, 135
  in Eliot 145, 174–5
  see also realism and romance
Rose, Jaqueline 161 n.
Ruskin, John 96

Said, Edward 13–15, 22 n., 70 n., 187–8
Saussure, Ferdinand de 239 n.
scapegoat, scapegoating 4, 112, 272, 273, 274
  in Austen 52
  in Conrad 182, 194, 198, 206, 220–1
  defined 4, 104
  in Dickens 23, 25, 28, 94, 104, 106–7, 115, 116, 123, 133, 135
  in Eliot 34, 39, 135, 182
  in James 256, 258, 263–4, 268
  and narrative 39
  in the text and of the text 4, 6, 122–3, 268
  see also community, narrative; expulsion
Scholes, Robert 271–2
Schwarz, Daniel R. 225 n.
Sears, Sallie 47–8, 241 n.
Sedgwick, Eve Kosofksy 33 n., 128 n., 173 n.
Seeley, Tracy 189 n.
self-conscious fiction 39, 44, 48, 188, 190, 269, 270, 272
Seltzer, Mark 2 n., 44, 243 n., 271
sexuality:
  in Austen 79
  in Dickens 90, 95 n., 104
Shaw, George Bernard 27 n.
Short, Michael A. 60 n.
Showalter, Elaine 32
Shuttleworth, Sally 154 n., 176 n.
social criticism:
  in Dickens 23–4
  in Eliot 154
solidarity:
  in Conrad 186, 187, 199, 200, 217, 223, 225–6
solitude:
  in Austen 67
  in Conrad 183–6, 213, 217, 223, 226

  in Dickens 28–9, 94, 272
  in Eliot 184
  see also isolation
Sophocles 226, 267
  see also Ajax; Oedipus
Spacks, Patricia 34 n.
speech-community, see community, narrative
spirituality:
  and realism 139–41
Spring, David 11
Sprinker, Michael 49
Steele, Meili 47 n.
Stephen, Leslie 29–30
storyteller 183, 187, 193–4
structural principle, see plot, dynamics of
structuralism, see critical approaches
'subversion hypothesis' 2, 31, 49, 268
success:
  in James 239, 254, 256, 258, 264
Summers, Anne 24 n.
surveillance 3, 48
Sutherland, Kathryn 11 n., 77 n., 87–8
sympathy, see compassion

Tallis, Raymond 44 n.
Tanner, Tony 10 n., 55 n., 60 n., 65 n., 69 n., 74 n., 202, 203, 204 n., 223 n.
Taylor, Gordon Rattray 71 n.
Ternan, Ellen 26
Thackeray, William M. (Vanity Fair) 88
theatricals:
  in Mansfield Park 64–7
Tiresias 193
Titian 177
Tomalin, Claire 27–8, 29 n.
Torgovnick, Marianna 266
tragedy 192
  in Conrad 206, 226
  in Eliot 177 n.
  in James 267
'triangular desire' 109 n., 128 n.
Trilling, Lionel 55 n., 68 n.
Trollope, Anthony (The Way We Live Now) 88
Trudgill, Eric 81 n.
truth, truthfulness 270
  in Austen 83
  in Conrad 192, 208, 210–11, 215–16, 221, 223–4, 270
  in Eliot 143, 181, 182, 270

in James 254, 268
see also lying

Uffen, Ellen Serlen 84 n.

value:
in Austen 10–11, 13–14, 58, 70, 75
in Conrad 41, 190, 198, 207, 208
in James 228, 235–7, 239, 251–2, 257, 259, 262–3, 264
and meaning in Saussure 239 n.
Van Ghent, Dorothy 203 n., 222 n.
vanity:
in Eliot 150–3, 154, 163, 169
Vanity Fair (Thackeray) 147
Veblen, Thorstein 236–7, 249
vocabulary:
in Austen 52, 75, 78–82, 227–8, 264, 268
in Eliot 228
in James 227–8, 264, 268
see also language

vocation:
in Eliot 173–4, 179

Watt, Ian 192 n., 204 n., 219
Webb, Igor, 3, 10 n., 11, 12 n., 69 n., 75, 77 n.
White, Hayden 270
Williams, Merle 246 n.
Williams, Michael 84 n.
Williams, Raymond 23, 43, 44
Wilson, Angus 25
Winner, Anthony 194 n.
Wollstonecraft, Mary 65 n.
Wordsworth, William 200
Wright, Andrew 53
Wuthering Heights (Emily Brontë) 147 n.

Yeazell, Ruth 44, 235 n., 268

Zacharias, Greg 45 n.